HUSH LITTLE BABY

ALSO BY R. H. HERRON

Stolen Things

HUSH LITTLE BABY

A Novel

R. H. HERRON

DUTTON

DUTTON

An imprint of Penguin Random House LLC
penguinrandomhouse.com

LIBRARY OF CONGRESS CATALOGING-IN-PUBLICATION DATA

Names: Herron, Rachael, author.
Title: Hush little baby : a novel / R.H. Herron.
Description: [New York] : Dutton, Penguin Random House LLC, [2021] |
Identifiers: LCCN 2020041585 (print) | LCCN 2020041586 (ebook) |
ISBN 9780593183496 (hardcover) | ISBN 9780593183502 (ebook)
Subjects: GSAFD: Suspense fiction.
Classification: LCC PS3608.E7765 H87 2021 (print) |
LCC PS3608.E7765 (ebook) | DDC 813/.6—dc23
LC record available at https://lccn.loc.gov/2020041585
LC ebook record available at https://lccn.loc.gov/2020041586

Printed in the United States of America
1st Printing

BOOK DESIGN BY TIFFANY ESTREICHER

For my favorite New York City cat, Fred

HUSH LITTLE BABY

PROLOGUE

The room I woke up in smelled sweet and rich, like an expensive candle that had burned too long in a small space. The sheet I was lying on was covered with orange California poppies.

But I didn't own poppy sheets.

This wasn't my room. This wasn't my bed.

Through blurry eyes, I saw aggressively yellow walls. A rocking chair sat on an orange rug. A changing table stood on the far side of the room, and a short shelf displayed a line of stuffed animals.

My head pounded, my tongue was thick and fuzzy in my dry mouth, and I was *freezing*. There was no sheet over me, and I was wearing only an oversize red tank top and a black skirt that had risen to rest underneath my massively pregnant belly.

They weren't my clothes.

Sucking in a breath, I pressed my elbows against my sides, my hands cradling my stomach. I tried to remember.

But instead of a memory of the night before, I just had flashes. A terrifying lullaby. A doll. Fear coiled in my torso, too close to the baby. *Something was wrong in my home, really wrong.* They had to finally believe me.

How had I gotten to wherever this was?

I tried to push myself up into a seated position so I could clear my head, but my leg was caught. Tethered, somehow. I tried to shake it loose.

There was a *cuff* around my left ankle.

The shackle was made of leather and attached to a ring of steel. A chain ran from the ring to the foot of the wooden bed frame, where it appeared to be padlocked. The wooden rails of the bed frame were thick, and the padlock was heavy-duty. I tugged on the chain with my arms, but it was real. It held.

I laughed in shocked surprise, although if this was a game, I hated it. "Hello?" My voice caught in the dry terror that coated my throat. What the hell was going on?

Back to last night. *Remember.* I'd been at home—hadn't I? I couldn't quite recall *what* I'd been afraid of. Even though it had been years since I'd had a drink, I felt like I was coming out of a blackout—memory fragments lit up in my brain but didn't want to slide together. A car chase, pausing in front of Whole Foods, then . . . what?

I opened my mouth to call out again, but then closed it. Was it even safe to yell for help?

No. I was shackled to a bed. I was obviously not safe.

And I was so *thirsty.*

I swiveled my head to the right and saw a bottle of water on the nightstand. It was within reach, and I started to lunge for it, but the object sitting next to it froze my hand in place and my heart in my chest.

The doll.

It was the same one I'd found in the box on my doorstep, the one made of rough linen and constructed to look like me, with wavy brown yarn for hair and blue eyes drawn on in pen. But instead of the round stomach that it had also shared with me, the doll's belly had been ripped off, leaving only red batting trailing to her linen knees.

My legs started shaking, and my eyelids slammed shut.

Remember. You have to remember.

ONE

One Month Earlier

"Just five more pushes, Stella." I pressed the blue towel in my left hand against her skin, and my right hand cupped the soft plum dome of the baby's head as she crowned. I caught Lisa's eye over her mask. She had the isolette cart ready—the one that would whisk the new wiggly human to NICU if we needed to start up the lungs or restart the heart the size of a walnut.

I wasn't worried, though. The fetal monitor had been good this whole time. Stella was over six feet tall with a pelvis you could drive a Mack truck through. If we finished this right, she wouldn't even need stitches. Baby was fighting me, a great sign. My neck gave a sharp twinge—my own thirty-six-weeks-pregnant shape had made all my normal movements feel different, and my muscles protested the physicality of my job.

Stella gave the last push with an elongated grunt (but no shouting—she hadn't even sworn once). Then the baby's head was out, and a second later, the rest of her slipped free.

All the parts were in the right place. "Here she is, mama." I gave the infant a quick rubdown and placed her skin to skin on Stella's belly. I continued to dry and stimulate, while Lisa suctioned the baby's mouth and then her nose. The little one gave a startled squall in the pitch of new kitten, my favorite sound in the whole world.

"You hear that?" My voice was low, so only Stella could hear. "That's the sound of your baby saying she loves you for the very first time."

Stella met my eyes for a split second, and in her gaze was that deliciously stunned look that never failed to give me goose bumps. Then I disappeared in her view, as did her husband, a guy named Steve who I couldn't pick out of a lineup of identically bland white men. For a few moments, no one else existed except her new little girl. The rest of us were mere shadows for a few more moments. Soon Stella would refocus from her baby and look up at Steve, and in that moment, he'd become Dad, but not until after Stella had morphed from pregnant to mother.

People always thought the miracle of birth was about what happened between the mother's legs, but honestly, the actual process of giving birth was usually the least of it—the body would do what the body did. Even with modern drugs and birthing pools and hospital tools, the body was the master. If the women didn't need medical intervention, they had their babies in exactly the same way they'd have them laboring alone in a hut on a mountainside. When a woman turned into a mother—that was the real miracle. I watched Stella's face go from red to light pink, watched the tears fill her eyes (I'd almost pegged her as non-crier, something we rarely see).

And then, it happened: The fierceness swamped her. I didn't see it happen in all new mothers. Some were too drugged, and some just didn't have it yet. Some wouldn't get it for months, years, or sometimes ever. But Stella got it. A muscle jumped in her cheek as she bent her head to smell the baby, and I could almost hear her teeth grit with determination to keep this child safe. Steve looked like the kind of guy who would give her a "push" gift, a necklace or a bigger diamond ring. What he should give her was an enemy nation to conquer. The fierceness had turned her into a warrior.

By then, Lisa—one of the best nurse-midwives I worked with—was showing Stella how to tickle the infant's lower lip with her nipple so her mouth would open for a good latch. I gave a small wave and said, "I'll check on you both later," but no one saw me go. That was the way I liked it. Some of my colleagues got possessive of the babies and their mothers. I didn't think of them as mine. I was pit crew, that's all. Okay, yeah, I was really great pit crew but still just a grease monkey. I was the glass you broke in case of emergency.

And I was also an hour past getting off my twenty-four-hour shift. I was exhausted, and being this monumentally pregnant made everything more difficult. I'd have to hurry to make it home, start the Instant Pot, and still get to my meeting on time.

I took a quick shower and changed into my street clothes in the locker room. My Audi slipped me out of the parking garage straight into traffic, which wasn't as bad as it could have been for early evening. I chanced taking Abbot Kinney Boulevard right through the heart of Venice's shopping district. When we'd moved here six years ago, Venice was already upscale, belying its hippie reputation, but it had gotten even more bougie in the last couple of years. Blue Bottle Coffee (six-dollar lattes) vied with Blue Star Donuts (four-dollar mimosa doughnuts) across the street. As usual, there was a line outside of Salt and Straw Ice Cream. Rochelle loved their lavender-bourbon flavor, but I was always going to be more of a Ben and Jerry's Americone Dream kind of person.

I turned up NPR, as if Terry Gross could distract me from thinking about Rochelle's flavor preference. It didn't matter anymore what Rochelle loved. I had to start remembering that at some point.

Five minutes later, I was home. In the driveway, I held up my camera to take a picture. Sunset wasn't for another hour or so, but the sky's color was already fading from bright blue to watercolor slate. I had a million of these shots—the Underwoods' house across the street, that piece of the telephone pole. Of course, I preferred pictures of cloud-streaked sunsets, but since the majority of SoCal days were cloudless, I'd gotten the hang of catching transparent sky colors with my camera. In another life, maybe I'd been a painter. The skies and the myriad colors that floated through them—grays, oranges, even greens some nights—made me ache to catch them somehow, even if my phone was the only way to do it. I couldn't grab my sky picture every night. Life and work got in the way, often, so I hoarded extra pictures for the nights I couldn't actually look up.

I went back through the garage, sending the door rumbling down after me. I unlocked the inner house door, the alarm beeping its warning. I disarmed it and set it back on Stay, congratulating myself for remembering to set it.

It used to be that when I stepped inside, I'd call out for Rochelle. She'd greet me with a kiss, already unpacking takeout and saving all the hoisin sauce packets for me.

But she wasn't here anymore.

TWO

It wasn't that she was *gone* gone. Rochelle wasn't dead, although sometimes when I was swimming around in my self-pity pool I wondered if that might actually be easier to recover from. No, she was just across town, living in Echo Park with her hot girlfriend, the one she'd left me for when I was five months pregnant with *her* biological child. Almost four months later, I was only starting to get used to the idea of living alone.

Funny, it used to be that when Rochelle had late nights out with clients, I'd be overjoyed to have a night to myself. I would have dropped my bag on the kitchen table and gone straight to the kitchen to preheat the oven to cook one of the pepperoni pizzas she didn't like that I always kept in the freezer. On those nights, if I wasn't paged back to work, I cooked the pizza with an extra-crispy crust (Rochelle liked a floppy crust, but I'd loved her anyway) and put on my softest, ugliest clothes. I'd tug on the huge T-shirt that I'd gotten at a novelty store *way* back in the day, even before I'd gotten sober—it was a big man's size, and it was covered with cats shooting lasers out their eyes while fireworks went off all around them. It was the opposite of sexy bedroom wear, but the laser-cat T-shirt was my comfort T-shirt. The way it trapped me in its twisted folds as I slept should have given me nightmares, but instead, it comforted me. It reminded me of the long nightgowns I'd worn growing up. I hadn't been the only girl in Utah who wore a neck-to-toe flannel home-sewn nightgown to bed, and I'd loved the weight of it as I'd gotten into bed. Waking up twisted tightly inside it hadn't felt like being trapped; it had felt like being held. My laser-cat T-shirt comforted me the same way. Only now, my bulging belly actually filled it.

But a night alone wasn't a rare freedom anymore. It wasn't a cause for excitement. It was just my life. The quiet rooms echoed hollowly as I walked through them by myself. I'd always thought of our house as one of those welcoming, cheerful homes. It was empty and cold now.

Tonight it felt *actually* cold. I checked the thermostat—I didn't remember setting the AC to sixty-five. It had been a warm day, and it must have come on automatically even though I tried to remember to turn it off when I went to work. Yet another thing I must have forgotten to do, like picking up cat litter for Fred or paying the car insurance. I reset the thermostat to let the house warm up a bit.

Then I wandered into the kitchen, patting the top of my belly. "No pizza tonight, huh, V?" I was trying hard to keep myself fed with actual food that had recognizable ingredients, not frozen pizzas or Hot Pockets. I threw three frozen chicken breasts into the Instant Pot with a cup of green tomatillo salsa. By the time I got home from the meeting, I'd have shreddable comfort food. This baby was made of tacos loaded with cabbage and crema and cheese and avocado. I figured there were worse things to be made of.

I glanced at the clock on the wall. I had just enough time to write a few lines in the baby journal before I got back in the car. In a clearly inadequate practice run of sharing custody, I was trying to write in it every day when it was my week to have it.

I'd been keeping the book in the nursery, writing in it while sitting in the rocker that I would nurse the baby in.

But the journal wasn't on the shelf.

I stopped, tilting my head a bit. Yesterday, before my shift, I'd written in it, and I had a clear memory of putting it back. The pen I kept with it had rolled off and under the bookshelf, and it had been a feat of ungraceful pregnant yoga to get myself down low enough to grab it.

I started shifting books to look behind the bookcase.

The journaling had been Rochelle's idea, but she'd completely rejected the cute pink birth journals sold at Target. Instead, she'd chosen a black Moleskine, unlined. She'd wanted something classy-looking (maybe to match her new blond girlfriend). We'd been writing to our daughter since the first moment we knew I was pregnant. If the house had caught on fire, I knew that both of us would have run to save the book before any other documents.

Now? It was a challenge not to be passive-aggressive when writing in it. *The house is so gorgeous now that I'm alone. So much room for you to run and play in. I never knew I'd love living by myself so much.* But I didn't feel that way, and I didn't write it. I gave myself one gajillion gold stars for not reading what Rochelle wrote when we exchanged the book every week, even though I almost sprained my eyeballs looking away from her dark, neat handwriting. If I saw that she'd written even one word about Domi I'd have wanted to burn the book. So I didn't look, although I knew it was probably only a matter of time before I cracked. Hopefully, I'd be in a better headspace at the moment I finally gave in, but being abandoned for a hot Swedish model while knocked up didn't leave me in the mood to be all that generous.

Okay, in reality, I knew that Domi was actually from Irvine, was only Swedish by blood, and had never been a model. But she could have been. On bad days, it was all I could do not to hope that Domi had a tragic accident. Not one that would hurt her—I wasn't a monster—but one that would, say, give her total amnesia so that she didn't love my soon-to-be ex-wife anymore. So that Rochelle would come back. I didn't even think I would *take* her back, not now, but tell my hormones that.

I still hadn't found the damn book. I turned in place, hands on my hips. Maybe I'd written in it in my bedroom?

Rochelle had always been the one who would carry the baby, who would deal with the hormone hell, not me. When I called my big orange cat, Fred, my baby, I meant it. I wasn't one of those people who needed a child to prove she was a real woman. I wasn't even one of those OBs who needed to have a child to prove she could help other people have one. Just like every male OB in existence, I'd been fine bringing everyone else's babies into the world. My mom had been a terrible role model, an emotional whiteboard that always stayed blank. Who was to say I wouldn't be the same? Having Fred and an office bulletin board full of photos of perfect children (because they were all perfect, no matter what) had always been enough for me.

But then six IVF cycles failed for Rochelle. Her body rejected every embryo. When we'd first talked about me being the one to get pregnant instead of her, she'd confessed to being worried that I would get selfish about the child. *It'll be yours. Why would you even keep me around?*

I'd held her hands and kissed her face. *We'll use your egg. My body. This baby will be ours. This is what we want.*

She'd wrinkled her nose in that way she did when she was trying not to cry. *It's what I want. Are you sure you want this, too?*

I hadn't been sure, not really.

But I'd said yes because not knowing how I felt was normal for me, and now here I was, with a belly that I couldn't see my feet around and no Rochelle.

In my bedroom, I searched the bedside table and drawer for the baby book. I even checked the one on Rochelle's old side of the bed. I was forgetting a shitload of things lately—the dreaded baby brain had been rolling in, as inescapable as the drift smoke from the wildfires that coated LA every summer. I'd always told my patients that yes, cognitive and executive functioning and memory were often poorer in pregnant women, but the changes would only be noticeable to them and those closest to them. Wasn't that nice? That kept happening to me—things I'd told patients for years that I thought would make them feel better turned out to be stupid when actually applied. How was knowing my memory might get worse supposed to make me feel better when I couldn't find my car keys or the password to our shared Netflix account or, apparently, the baby journal?

It wasn't in the bedroom. Nor was it in the living room or the dining room or the kitchen or either of the bathrooms.

And it wasn't like it was hidden in clutter, either. Rochelle was Marie Kondo's sworn enemy and had liked to pile jackets and Amazon boxes and motorcycle gloves and paperbacks and bags of chips on top of any flat space. Since she'd left, I'd spent any rare bit of extra energy tidying. All the surfaces were clear. There was nowhere for it to hide.

I pulled my cell out of my pocket, wondering how much longer I'd be able to wedge it into the back pocket of my maternity jeans. They were stretchy, yes, but I was learning that nothing was really stretchy enough. I brought up Rochelle's contact, trying to ignore that she'd changed her icon to a picture that I hadn't taken of her.

Can't find baby book. Did you come get it? She still had a key. I kind of hated that she could let herself in anytime after choosing to leave, but it made sense, given the shared custody we had yet to work out.

Dots formed as Rochelle texted back. *I dropped it off three days ago. Remember?*

I wondered if she was with Domi. Were they both home from the office? (Because of course they worked together.)

I know. But I can't find it now. I felt stupid—of course it was here somewhere. Why had I even bothered texting her?

It'll turn up. Give V a pat for me.

We'd agreed that she could choose the baby's first initial, and I'd choose the name itself. Rochelle had chosen *V.* It was killing her that I hadn't decided yet what her full name would be. Before Ro left, she'd spent whole evenings trying to pry the name out of me, but I still wasn't sure yet. *Verity,* she'd say. *Vanna. Valentina. Vava.* I'd always tell her it was just V for now. I had some ideas, but I was in no rush.

And while I hated to admit it, there was something satisfying, especially now, about the fact that she wanted to know the baby's name so much. Once I decided for sure, I'd have to tell her because I was a bad liar. But if I took a long time to decide, then I didn't have to give her the satisfaction of knowing her daughter's name. Who knew I could be so petty?

I glanced at my cell for the time. Damn it. I'd have to find the journal later. Now I had to go.

But for God's sakes, what had I done with it? If Rochelle said she hadn't taken it, then she hadn't. Rochelle didn't lie.

Or, at least, she never used to.

THREE

When I got to the meetinghouse on Pacific, my friend Bree Sydenham was sitting in her silver Bentley Continental. Because this was
Venice, hers wasn't the only Bentley in the lot, but I knew it was hers
by her personalized license plate, CALBREE, which was also her phone
number. It was lucky I loved Bree, or her ostentatiousness would be
plain annoying.

Through the tinted windows, I could see that she'd placed her forehead on the steering wheel.

She didn't look up as I tapped gently on the glass. I tried the handle of the passenger door, which was locked. Startling visibly, she hit
the button to unlock the door.

I slid in as gracefully as I could.

Bree had an official-looking letter in her lap. "Hey," she said, not
meeting my eyes. "I'll come inside in just a minute."

I shook my head. "Could you not think of another place to look dead? I swear this is the same parking space." John H. had died right here the month before. We'd all thought he'd been sleeping in his car, his head back on the headrest, mouth open. He was in his eighties and had diabetes, and he'd slept anywhere he could. He was known for spending long hours in his car sleeping in exactly the same position. But he hadn't been sleeping. I'd been the one to verify that, as the only doctor at that particular meeting. He'd died naturally and hopefully happily, in the parking lot of the AA fellowship he felt was his home.

"Shit," she said. "Sorry. Are you all right?"

"Well, since you're alive, yes."

Small and silver-blond, Bree was dressed in rust-colored athleisure. She managed to make pregnancy look fashionable. Next to her, I always felt rumpled and tired. I recognized her outer layer as the Nagnata cotton sweater I'd lusted over online and hadn't been able to spend four hundred dollars on. "I'd hug you," she said, "but I can't twist that way."

"Girl, same."

She groaned, leaning right as I leaned left so we could exchange cheek kisses.

"What's going on?" I asked. "You okay?"

"Eh." She shrugged and folded the letter back into its envelope, but not before I'd seen the logo, a blue circle with three blue stars and a spiraling blue flame. Struggling to keep my expression neutral, I swallowed the jolt that shot through me. I knew that logo.

Bree had a pallor to her skin that I'd never seen before, and her breath was coming quickly. I pressed my hand against her arm. Hopefully she'd think I was being comforting, instead of what I was actually doing, checking to see if her skin was cold and clammy.

"You can tell me," I said, pretending I didn't already know.

"No. I can't." She sat straighter in her seat and pulled her Louis Vuitton purse from the backseat onto her lap. Tilting the rearview mirror, she applied a quick dusting of powder, a slick of lip gloss. "I'm fine. Anyway. Ripleys at my house this week. It's finally time for my favorite mommies-to-be to see the new house. And you should see the cupcakes I'm ordering. I'll put Maggie and her dumb panda cupcakes to shame."

"First, those pandas were a-freaking-dorable. Second, who's the father, Bree?"

She crumpled the paperwork into the center console and slammed the lid. "Seriously?"

"Do you know how many patients I've seen bring that same envelope into my office over the years? That's the biggest paternity-testing lab in the country."

Bree rested her head on the steering wheel again, no small feat given that her belly was almost the same size mine was. "No one can know," she mumbled. "No one."

Now maybe wasn't the time to trot out my lecture on the ethics of considering the father's rights. "I won't say anything. But are you okay, Bree?" Stupid question. Of course she wasn't. "What can I do to help?"

"There's nothing you can do. I did this to myself. I'm going to lose Hal." Her voice was hollow.

I'd been surprised by the envelope, but this statement pumped shock through my veins. Bree was *not* the kind of woman to worry about losing a man. She'd climbed two of the seven tallest mountains in the world. She hosted an annual charity gala for Children's Hospital that raised more in a night than I'd probably ever make in a lifetime. I once saw her in the Style section in *The New York Times* after she'd led a push for inclusive sizing at Prada (her initiative failed, and at about a size two, she wasn't a good spokesperson, but it was still impressive). And she wasn't just talk—she'd gotten arrested in Tulsa for protesting some fracking thing. She sponsored an annual float at LA Pride for foster kids and families. Hal, her Yale-educated rich-as-fuck husband, was as bland as she was exciting. He was vanilla-flavored *nice*. I liked him—there wasn't anything interesting of him to dislike, honestly. I'd read a little of his blog, which was about his journey to being a father. It was so boring it made my eyes water, but tiny Bree herself was normally larger than life and made up for any dullness on his part. I'd never seen her look this small.

I briskly patted her hand. "Stop that. You've always said that your relationship is idyllic. People work out bigger things than this."

Through gritted teeth, she said, "Not idyllic now. Hal thinks it is, of course. He's so far over the moon he needs a space suit to breathe. Did I tell you he said he's envious of my stretch marks? This is the biggest thing in his life, and I fucked it up."

I congratulated myself for not saying *Literally.* "You want to tell me who the father is?"

"You don't know him."

"Is it an ongoing thing?" I said it lightly but knew it was no small question.

She shook her head, but I couldn't read the side of her face.

"You want me to shut up and give you a hug?"

She nodded hard. "That."

"We're going to have to get out of the car, then."

So we did, and I swear to God, when we were doing the awkward belly-next-to-belly pregnant ladies' hug, I heard her suck back something that sounded like a sob. Bree Sydenham. Crying. That wasn't something I'd seen coming my way tonight.

As we pulled apart, she clutched at my arms. "Don't tell. Not *anyone.*"

"Of course. I said I wouldn't." Surely Bree knew me better than that. We'd been friends for years, and together, we were the founding members of the Ripleys. I pulled away gently. "It's going to be okay."

"I've got to figure something out—Hal can't know." She covered her mouth with her hand. "But he *will* know. The second the baby's born, he'll know. That piece of paper just proved it."

Ah. Skin color was a dead giveaway to paternity, and patients had come to me with similar concerns in the past. Hal was so white that fluorescent bulbs gave him a sunburn, and Bree was almost as pale. If her baby had skin even one shade darker than they did . . .

"Honey, we'll help you."

She shook her head. "You can't. There's no way."

"There has to be." I pointed to my own belly. "Look at me knocked up with . . . my baby."

"So? That's how you planned it."

"Yeah," I said slowly, my heart pounding as I realized what I might be about to tell her. Normally I hated showing anyone my emotionally tender spots, even people in the program. But Bree and the Ripleys had been so there for me when Rochelle left—maybe telling her a secret of mine would make her feel better about her world falling apart. I took a deep breath and tried to hold back the nerves that fluttered in my chest. My sponsor, Nicole, was always telling me to help others. "You know I didn't plan on Rochelle leaving me. Want to know something I haven't told anyone else?"

Bree raised an eyebrow. "Um, yes."

My heart rate ratcheted higher. "I didn't even *want* V when Rochelle left." Hoo-boy—it sounded even worse than I'd thought it would said out loud. My face went hot. "She'd been inside me for five months at that point. You and I had already formed the Ripleys, and I didn't love her yet. When Ro left, I even thought I might just hand the baby over to her when she was born, saying, 'Here's your kid. See ya.'"

Bree narrowed her eyes. "So?"

The word hurt. Couldn't she see a little of what it had cost me to say it out loud? My breath was tight in my chest. "Come on. You don't like my confession?"

"That's not even *close* to the situation I'm in, although, yeah, I kind of think you're a sociopath." Bree frowned. "You would have given her to Rochelle? Just like that?"

I felt a flap of panic behind my ribs. *This* was why I didn't show my underbelly. "No! I mean . . ." Honestly, I couldn't really remember. That first night, after Rochelle had admitted to me about the affair, and so much worse—that she loved the woman—I'd slept alone in our bed for the first time in years. V was Rochelle's biological child, but she was inside my body, not hers. I'd just passed the point of looking like I was carrying an extra spare tire and had moved into definite baby-bump territory. People didn't look nervous anymore when they asked how far along I was. And there I lay, alone in bed, my belly protruding with an alien who wasn't even mine in residence behind my belly button.

I didn't want to be a single mother.

For the first time since we'd boarded the express train to Jillian-Getting-Pregnant, I wasn't sure I wanted to be a mother at all.

I was an ob-gyn. I knew intimately what women went through to have babies. And I—I didn't want this. For a person who had a hard time understanding what she was feeling most of the time, I wasn't confused about what I felt then. I'd thought pregnancy heartburn was bad, but the rage burning behind my broken heart made the heartburn seem like a massage. I tasted betrayal in my mouth every time I rolled over in bed.

Then, eight days after Rochelle left me, I felt V move for the first time inside me.

The quickening wasn't so much a sharp kick but more of a whispered flutter, as if someone had swum past me in the pool. I knew immediately that it was *my* blood inside her veins, *my* body that was busy making hers. At twenty-one weeks, she turned into being all mine.

I fell in love in a way I'd never fallen in love before. The hesitation I'd had before was like a bad mosquito bite—terrible for the time I had it, then forgotten completely. My baby was inside me, and that was all that mattered in the whole world. I was meant to be this girl's mother. It had always been so.

Mine.

Feeling that quickening had been so monumental that it had washed away what the apathy had been like, erasing how deep it had run.

But I didn't want to say all that to Bree in the parking lot, so I simply said, "I felt her move a week later, and then I fell in love."

Bree just shook her blond head. "You can't compare your shit to mine. You just *can't*. You'll be fine. Your daughter will still have two parents. What if my baby only has me?"

I tried to brush aside the pinch of irritation. I actually *could* compare my shit to hers, only in my case, I'd been the one cheated on.

Bree was an amazing woman, a force of nature. And sometimes she was a cactus, her incredible blooms hiding the needles you forgot were there. I honestly didn't mind getting stabbed once in a while, although this needle had gone a little deeper into my skin than normal.

But she was hurting, so I tried my best to shrug it off. "Fair enough." I tucked my arm through hers and we turned to move together toward the door. We waded through the pocket of people smoking—at least it was mostly vapor now instead of cigarette smoke.

"It's going to be okay. Even if it's not okay." It's what my sponsor always said.

Bree sighed. "Bullshit."

She had a point.

FOUR

At home after the meeting, I made my chicken tacos and inhaled three as V backflipped. She liked green salsa as much as I did, which showed she was already a smart girl with her priorities straight. I flicked through the streaming services, settling on a British gardening show on Netflix, only getting two greenhouse choices in before my eyes dropped like lead aprons.

I didn't wake until my cell beeped. My vision blurry, I strained to read the text.

Rochelle. *Did you find the baby book?*

No. It's totally disappeared.

Check one more time.

I could almost hear her saying, *You move too fast and don't look carefully enough. Look again.*

Grudgingly, I sat up. A strange odor filled the air, skunk-like. Kids smoking weed on the street? I rubbed my forehead where a headache was starting as I padded into the nursery.

And holy shit, if that book wasn't right where it hadn't been earlier in the nursery. Smack-dab on top of the picture books, right in plain sight. The pen was carefully clipped to the cover.

Anger burned the tips of my ears as I texted, *That's not right. You know I don't care if you keep the key, but you have to at least let me know if you're coming over. Twice.*

WTF are you talking about?

My headache strengthened. *This isn't a practical joke, it's mean. It freaked me out. All I'm saying is tell me when you're coming over.*

There was a pause. No matter what she said, she wouldn't be able to convince me this was funny. I didn't get why she'd done it. Maybe it wasn't a prank? Maybe she'd thought I'd be out of the house longer; maybe she'd stayed close by to write in it and was planning on dropping it off before I noticed?

Finally, she texted, *I didn't take the book. You just misplaced it, that's all. I didn't.*

But my last text went unread. She was legendary for her ability to ignore texts when she wanted to. It used to drive me crazy. Apparently, it still did.

And the cloying smell hanging in the air was also making me feel insane. Not skunk-like anymore, it was more like an onion. Or maybe old meat.

Or rotten like eggs.

Shit. Gas leak? I raced to the kitchen. All the knobs of the stove were in the correct Off position. And besides, the stove had electronic ignition—when we'd gotten it, I'd made sure of it, having had to struggle with lighting too many pilots in student housing.

The furnace had a pilot light, I knew, but that was under the house. If the smell was this strong in the house and if it was coming from the furnace, then the whole subfloor area might be ready to blow.

Fuck this. I was out. My cell in my hand, my feet still bare, I raced outside and into the front yard. As my head cleared in the night air, I tried to take deep breaths. *We're fine, V. Not poisoned by CO2. Not dead in an explosion.* I patted my belly and started to dial 911.

Next door, Greg came outside carrying a kitchen garbage bag. Greg was one of those great-to-have neighbors, always willing to lend his lawn edger or skilsaw when Rochelle got too ambitious with home repair. The two of them had been close, spending whole weekends in his garage sometimes.

But right now, all I could see when I looked at him was that he worked for Pacific Gas and Electric. I shoved my phone back in my pocket. "Greg!" I called, surprised at how out of breath I sounded.

He dumped his bag of trash into the can and held up a hand in greeting. "How are you doing? Look at how big you are!"

I didn't have time for small talk. "There's a gas leak. In the house. Or under it, I don't know. Should I call 911? Are we too close? What if it explodes?" I was babbling and I couldn't stop.

He smiled lazily, which made me feel instantly better. "Let me grab my detector." He unlocked his truck and reached into the back-seat, coming out with a yellow bag. "It won't explode."

"What about San Bruno?" In 2010, a pipeline had exploded in a Northern California town, destroying thirty-eight homes almost instantly.

He chuckled and shook his head at me as if I were a kid asking about the tooth fairy. "You wait here. I'll be back."

My toes curled into the fog-damp grass. "Don't turn on any lights!" As if I needed to remind a gas man how sparks worked. I heard him laughing as he went in my front door, still standing open from when I'd fled.

He was out three minutes later. "Just the pilot on your hot-water heater. I relit it. You're good to go."

I pressed my knuckles into my chin. "So the furnace is okay. I thought maybe there was gas under the house ready to explode. Is it true static electricity can set it off, too?"

He shook his head. "You're *fine,* mama. No biggie. How's Rochelle doing?"

"So it won't explode."

Greg put his arm around my shoulders and gave a brief squeeze. He smelled of sweat and maybe, lightly, of booze. Gin, I thought, with only the slightest tug of jealousy. "It will not explode, I promise. You're safe."

"Why would a pilot light go out? Will it do it again?"

He secured one of the many zippers on his bag. "Dirty thermo-couple will do it, but yours is good. Sometimes they just blow out. No big deal."

"How, though?" It felt like a big deal. "What if I'd been sleeping? I mean, I was napping, but accidentally. Oh, God, did the gas make me go to sleep?"

"Jillian." He looked at me over his glasses. "We add thiols to it to wake you up. You can't sleep through that stink; it's like smelling salts. Plus, your water heater could leak gas for days, even weeks, without a problem. Big house, lots of air, tiny amount of gas. Not a problem, I swear on Clyde's life." Clyde was his elderly wolfhound, who creaked around his backyard and bayed incessantly on fireworks nights. And honestly, him swearing on his dog's life did calm me down.

Mostly. "It's never blown out before."

"Always a first time."

"It's not windy."

"Could have been as simple as closing a door in another room."

"So it *will* happen again."

"No. But you know where I live. How's Rochelle?" he asked again.

His bestie was fine. "Good. I think. Haven't seen her in a while." It hurt to say. We had an ultrasound coming up soon, and I was emotionally prepping for the encounter, getting ready to see her face. It was hard to see her hair, the long curls I used to wind around my hand while we slept. "You should give her a call." Oh, God. He'd for sure tell her I'd freaked out over a tiny gas leak, and if I asked him not to, that would make it even worse. "Thanks for the help. I wasn't that scared. I was—you know—sleepy. Startled! I was startled by it. Coming out of a nap and all. Just a little startled."

He shot me a thumbs-up and stepped across the grass property divider. "Give a holler if you need me."

Back inside, leaning on the kitchen counter, I only wanted a drink for a moment. I just wanted it for the length of time it took to send a text to Nicole. *Got a craving.*

The feeling was fading the same way it had come, from dark to a flash of brilliant need and back to dark again.

Want to talk?

I'm okay. My text was hurried. I didn't want her to call—then I'd have to answer—

Too late. My phone buzzed.

"You didn't have to call me."

Nicole said, "Yes, I did. That's what sponsors do. And you know what sponsees do?"

I walked down the hall and into the nursery as I recited the words I knew she wanted to hear. "I call you when I have a craving."

"And you didn't. You just texted. I'll yell at you about that later. How are you doing right now?"

"The urge is gone." And it was. Now I only felt a low-grade embarrassment at dragging Nicole away from whatever it was she'd been doing. "What are you up to?"

She didn't bite. "What was the craving about?"

I sank into the nursery rocker, grateful for its wide wooden seat. "Rochelle came by the house and took the baby journal and then I couldn't find it, and when I got back from a meeting, it was put back in the right place."

"Oh, my *God*. Should you call the police? Are you going to be *okay*? You poor thing!"

I rolled my eyes. "Come on. I know. It's just that she lied. Again. Like all the times she was lying about Domi. If she can do that so easily, how are we going to raise a kid together?"

"You misplaced it, maybe?"

"Uh-uh." My throat was tight. Had I simply not seen it? Was that possible? "Also, I just had a gas leak."

She had the grace to have a bit more concern in her voice. "Are you okay?"

"I thought we were going to explode into a billion little pieces. Or pass out, overcome by fumes. Something bad." I could admit it to her—she was the only person I ever got close to talking about my real feelings with. "I was really scared."

"Okay. So what's in your hula-hoop?" She always said I could only control what was in my hula-hoop, and not always that.

"Not much."

"Can you get the leak fixed?"

"Neighbor fixed it. Just a blown-out pilot light."

"Seriously? That's not a legit gas leak. I thought someone hit your gas line!"

Sheepishly, I said, "I know. And he said it probably won't happen again." But *how* had the light gone out? We'd lived in this house for years, and it hadn't happened even once before. Why now? I felt a chill on my arms.

"Check that one off your list. What can you do about it if Rochelle *is* lying?"

"Nothing."

"Sounds about right."

The thought I'd been trying to push away caught up with me. "What if she did it on purpose?"

"What? Lied about borrowing a baby journal? Does that make any sense?"

"No." But I couldn't let go of the weird prickle that was creeping down my spine. "What if she was trying to scare me?"

"How would that even be scary? Suddenly she makes you think you're being targeted by the baby journal thief? Yeah, that guy's got a million warrants out for his arrest, all right. Truly terrifying. What even *is* a baby journal?"

"What if she—"

Nicole's voice was sharp. "Don't even say that you think she might have blown out the pilot light."

I wanted to tell her that wasn't what I'd been going to say, but Nicole could smell a lie on me like onions on a burger. "I know."

"It's *Rochelle*. She may be the bad guy right now, but she's also the mother of your child. She's not trying to kill you."

It did sound stupid when she said it out loud. My grip on the phone eased, and V stopped kicking. She gave what I called a swerve, when she stopped being pointy and moved like a mermaid. A long, wide roll rather than a jab. "You're right. I'm overreacting. I must have—" What? Misplaced the journal? Slammed a door so hard the pilot went out? I was tired. I could just be wrong, all wrong. "Well, now I don't know what to say to Rochelle. If she really didn't borrow the book, she'll think I'm losing my mind."

I heard a *snick* on the other end. The fact that Nicole hadn't been able to quit smoking was the thing that had made me love her at the beginning. She was a titan of sobriety. I wanted what she had—a real peace about not using mind-altering substances. But she was also human, and she still loved her nicotine. I could almost see her—undoubtedly, she was sitting on her back porch on the swing her husband built her, a romance novel parked next to her thigh. In the night air, the cigarette would glow white against her dark skin.

She said, "Does it ever occur to you just to let go of trying to control every damn thing?"

"Only every single time you ever nag me about it."

And I could feel it coming—she always asked me two things: *Did you pray? Did you help someone else?*

Sure enough, Nicole said, "Did you pray about it?"

She knew my version of prayer was simply saying *Help* to whatever the hell was out there. I'd given up on God a long time ago, when I'd left home. I was willing to admit that there was something out there. But I didn't need, nor did I want, it explained to me by anyone. "I texted you. Close enough." Fred came out of nowhere and attempted to sit on my lap, a move that was a lot harder now than it had ever been. I leaned backward to help him, the rocker gliding smoothly with my weight.

"Good job. Did you help someone else?"

At least I had a good answer for that. "I talked to Bree at the meeting. She was having a super-shitty day. I tried to just listen."

"Just listening is all you have to do."

"I don't think I helped, though. What if I listen wrong?" Rochelle had always said I didn't listen hard enough.

Another long sigh. "Have I ever *listened* wrong to you?"

I scratched Fred's chin the way he liked it. "Every time you don't think I'm right."

She laughed. "You have no control over Bree. Your job isn't to help her; it's to hear her. You're watching Bree walk her own path. Her *own*. Not yours."

Now I was the one to sigh. "I just want her to be okay."

"She'll be fine. And be nice to Rochelle. You can't fix everything, no matter how hard you try, so try to meet her where she is, okay? She's not out to get you."

The heat was out of me, and a bone-level weariness was flooding into the spaces where it had been. I nudged Fred to the floor before I stood and moved to the window. Rochelle and I had bickered about whether to put the nursery in the guest room next to our bedroom or in her home office across the hall, but it hadn't been much of an argument. I'd chosen the guest room for it, so that when I nursed the baby in the dropping twilight, I could look west, toward the sunset. "I know."

"Tell me a good thing about her."

"Do I have to?" Nicole kept making me do this. I hated it.

"You do."

"Shit." I looked around the room for inspiration. One day when I'd been stuck on a thirty-hour shift at work, Rochelle had painted all the walls. One bright red one, three white. We'd talked about a nautical theme, and she thought that by adding touches of blue, it would look like a wharf, not knowing I'd only wanted a few boats on the walls. "Remember when I screamed at her about the baby's room walls?"

"Didn't you tell her that the red wall reminded you of blood?"

Arterial blood. I'd been very specific. "I don't know if I told you that I came home from work early a few days later, and she was getting ready to paint over the red, even though it had been her favorite part of the room. She'd already bought boat stencils and everything. She loved that stupid red wall, and she'd just sucked it up and was going to redo it for me without even trying to argue about it." I'd told her she got the points for being willing to repaint but that I'd already gotten used to the color and she didn't have to do it. She'd kissed me, and it had gotten hot, and we'd had sex afterward. Good sex.

But thinking about that reminded me that she'd been having sex with Domi at the same time. My stomach tightened.

"That's nice. Good job," said Nicole. "And remember. Just listen to people. You can't fix anyone."

After we hung up, I puttered a bit, doing dishes and checking work e-mail. I sent a few quick messages, reassuring one of my patients that Braxton-Hicks were normal and, yes, they could be frightening. I told another patient that peppermint tea couldn't hurt her but that goldenseal could.

Then I finally sat in the rocker in the nursery again, and I wrote in the journal. *You want more green salsa than I can possibly give you. You're definitely my girl.* I scratched out the last line, knowing Nicole wouldn't approve if she knew I was being passive-aggressive. The entry right before this one was mine, too, which was another vote for me losing my marbles. These hormones could bite me right in my ever-widening ass.

I moved around the house and shut a window I didn't remember opening. My blood pounded in my ears as my breath whooshed rhythmically. The floorboard in the kitchen creaked right where it always did.

It was so *quiet.* Even when I played music through all the smart-home devices Rochelle had loved, the house still felt empty. I didn't recognize the house's groans anymore, and sometimes when I left a dark room, I fought the urge to turn my head and look behind me.

But I never let myself turn. I refused to become someone who jumped every time the wind made a camellia branch scratch at the window.

Right before I crawled into bed and passed out again, I texted a sunset picture to my mother. There would be no answer—there never was.

FIVE

Friday night I was hot and exhausted. The heat was a normal pregnancy side effect—I had almost fifty percent more blood in my body than a nonpregnant woman. But I hadn't slept in almost thirty-six hours, having gotten paged in early to my shift when one of my patients launched into full-blown labor three weeks early. The lack of sleep made it even harder for my body to regulate its temperature, and in spite of the AC in my car cranked full blast, I wished I could both pass out and take an ice bath. Maybe fall asleep *in* an ice bath. Heaven.

But I also wanted to see the Ripleys. All four women in our group were pregnant and in recovery. We'd named ourselves after the protagonist of the *Alien* movies. We weren't boring mommies-to-be, obsessed with sourcing the most organic cotton for onesies. No, Ripley was the baddest of all mothers. She'd fiercely saved the universe twice. We wanted to emulate her, not mommy bloggers.

I double-checked the GPS and slowed. The group hadn't met at

Bree's house yet, since the whole time we'd been pregnant, she'd been in the process of unpacking. First she'd said the house was too empty for us to come see it, and then she'd claimed it wasn't perfect yet. With traffic, Maggie lived too far away to host, so Camille and I had been trading off holding our meetings. I loved the noise and clatter they made when they were in my now-empty place, but I couldn't wait to see Bree's house.

I had to pull up to the house on the Speedway side, since these houses had no entrances in front of them on Ocean Front Walk. There was just sand. But even from the back, her home looked amazing, all glistening chrome and shining glass. Bree had said she'd leave the garage open and to park inside it if there was a space. The garage was massive, running the whole width underneath the house. Four cars were already parked inside, Bree and Hal's two Bentleys, Maggie's Mercedes, and Camille's Jeep. There was *just* enough room for me to park the Audi between the Jeep and the wall.

I fought back a yawn as I passed the spot. Then I put the Audi in reverse and looked over my shoulder. The car moved smoothly and quickly.

Crunch.

I'd hit the back wall of the garage.

Damn it. I pulled a couple of feet forward and jumped out of the car. I'd had enough room—I knew I'd had.

But nope. I hadn't.

My bumper was toast—had I really been going that fast? Did Audi bumpers just crumple like that? And the plaster on the wall I'd hit was cracked.

The door to the house slammed open. Bree raced down the steps. "Oh, shit, darling! Are you okay?" She strode toward me, bearing her wide, high belly like it was something she could walk around if she moved fast enough. Her blond hair was piled in a pretty mess on top of her head, a look I knew was coiffured to seem casual.

My eyes felt like saucers, so wide the air was cold on my eyeballs.

"I have no idea how that happened. I was just parking. The plaster's crumbling, see—"

"Who cares about that?" Bree's hands fluttered over my forehead and my shoulders. "Are you hurt?" But I saw her trying—and failing—to not look at the wall.

"I'm not hurt. Your *wall* is hurt. Please tell me that's not going to bring down the house." I knew that anything on this block would go for no less than ten million. It was the best location in Venice. I was pretty sure my umbrella insurance wouldn't cover a house I knocked over with my car.

Bree let herself examine the wall. She bit her bottom lip, then said, "It's one hundred percent fine. It'll give Hal something to obsess about other than the baby." She turned back to me with a wide smile. Her makeup was impeccable, her cheekbones contoured, and her perfume rich and jasminey. She wore a T-shirt decorated with black sequins and a perfect black skirt. Her eyes sparkled like her shirt, and she didn't seem to be the same person I'd seen almost cry a few days before.

She clapped her hands. "I'm so glad you're here."

"Me, too." I felt clunky next to her in my Diesel maternity jeans. "I can't wait to see the house."

"Wait till you see what's *not* the garage! Come in. Oh, your poor car! I'm going to wrap you in a blanket and face you toward the ocean. And make you tea! Follow me."

She led the way inside, and even though I was by no means a stranger to LA architecture, I couldn't help gaping. The open floor plan held a vast kitchen to the left decorated with yet more chrome and glass. A long silver island ran next to a twelve-seater table that stood on top of black-and-white cowhides laid over white tile. To the right was an enormous living room full of white furniture. The sofa alone probably cost more than Rochelle and I had spent on all our furnishings put together.

But the most arresting part of the room was the back glass wall. Floor-to-ceiling windows looked out to a covered patio where a fire pit already cheerfully sparked. The sand was mere feet away and the ocean was right *there*. "Wow."

"Thanks." She didn't take the normal ten seconds to preen and look over her domain the way some women did. "And no, we do *not* worry about high tides or tsunamis."

I bet everyone made themselves feel better about not living in this house by saying it, but I would never have wondered it out loud. That was the price you paid for living in paradise. I yawned again. "Bree, I'm so sorry. I can't believe I hit your house."

From upstairs, I heard female voices laughing.

"Stop. Please. I've seen the remodel plans a thousand times, and it's not load bearing. You just got off work, right?" Bree touched my elbow lightly as she put me on the sofa. The white leather beast had screamed elegant discomfort when I'd looked at it, but when I landed on it, I was welcomed, wrapped with all the comfort money could—and did—buy. "Sounds like Hal has the girls on the tour, but you don't need that. Upstairs is simply more of this. With bathtubs. I'll show you later. Now you need some tea and this blanket. Lapsang? Earl Grey? Rooibos?"

"Rooibos, please." Anger at myself rose in my chest—familiar and heated. *Damn it.* I had good car insurance and that's what it was for, I supposed, but it still galled me that I'd misjudged the size and placement of the car I drove every single day. Was this another pregnancy-brain thing? My spatial-relations expertise was wearing off?

But the way Bree touched my cheek before she went to put on the electric kettle made me feel warm inside. I'd been taking care of myself for months. I guess it was getting old.

"You just rest right there till they come down. You poor tired thing. Loose-leaf all right?"

I nodded. I wanted to change the subject to anything but the way I felt. "How's work?"

Bree did something in startup consulting—I'd never really understood what. I did understand two things: First, she didn't seem to *do* very much. She seemed to have plenty of free time to go to AA meetings and to arrange the groups who went out to coffee afterward. I worked odd hours, so I went to a lot of different meetings, and I'd seen her at all times of the day. The second thing I understood was that no matter how much she made, it was a drop in the bucket compared to what Hal had.

"Fine. Never a dull moment. I told you I decided to take a year off for the baby, right?"

No, she hadn't. "Wow, that's—"

She glanced over my shoulder. "Here they come," she said as feet thumped down the staircase behind me.

A thin man with a graying goatee and brown eyes behind thick lenses was the first to appear. "Jillian!"

It was always impossible not to smile back at him. "Hey, Hal," I said.

I opened my mouth to tell him what I'd done to his garage wall, but his gaze went to Bree. "Darling, they loved your bathroom." Bree was pretty far out of his league, and I enjoyed the way he gave the impression that he was both aware of it and grateful for it.

Behind him tumbled Maggie and Camille, both of them laughing. Maggie grabbed me in a tight hug and said, "This bitch has *two* soaking tubs up there, one for sunrise, one for sunset. No lie."

Camille kissed my cheek and patted V's bulge. "Plus the ceiling in their bedroom actually *retracts*. Have you ever heard of that?"

Camille and Maggie couldn't be more dissimilar and I adored them both. We'd actually known each other longer in the fellowship than we'd known Bree, but Bree and I were further along in our pregnancies.

Bree was our blond queen bee, always buzzing, never shy about telling us what we should be doing. She could be confused for Reese Witherspoon (and had been once at La Roche-Posay), if Reese had a rounder chin and a penchant for telling the Bristol Farms bag boys the best way to fill her fair-trade string totes.

If Bree was the bossiest of the group, Maggie was the chicest. Today she'd paired a short black dress with a red leather jacket and a smoky eye. The jacket popped against her skin, which was the blue-white color of milk, and both ears were pierced from top to bottom. Her belly was just starting to round at twenty-four weeks along. I always felt like a big old clodhopper next to her small-boned grace. She was sweet but took no shit. I knew she'd lost her parents young, and they'd left her, like, a huge stack of cash. Unlike other wealthy women I knew, Maggie didn't try to pretend she didn't have it, which was refreshing. She was job-free and didn't complain about how stressful charity work was. She didn't invent an artistic side hustle to make herself look busy. She just liked what she liked—fashion, baking, obscure politicians' biographies, spending a fortune on flowers delivered to her house daily—and never apologized for it. Before I'd gotten so close to Bree and Maggie, I'd thought I made great money. So thank God for Camille, another worker bee like me.

Camille was more down-to-earth than either excitable Bree or stylish Maggie, and she was also the one having the roughest pregnancy so far. Carrying a baby had run her over like a bus. At thirty-one weeks along, the deep circles under her eyes made her look as if she hadn't slept in weeks. It didn't help that she worked insane hours at CrimeWatcher, the all-crime-all-the-time network. Camille was an executive producer and a complete workaholic. Her dark skin didn't hide the clusters of broken veins on her cheeks, probably from high blood pressure (she never allowed me to check it). She was already carrying low. When she smiled, though, her face lit up and you realized that even though she wasn't exactly pretty, Camille was *beautiful*. Her wife was also in recovery, but just like I hadn't invited my wife to this group, she hadn't either. The Ripleys were pregnant ladies only.

Maggie took off her leather jacket and slung it on the back of the couch. "What was that thump?"

I covered my face. "I hit your garage wall, Hal."

His eyebrows rose in alarm. "Oh!"

"It's okay, love," said Bree. "It's just some cracks in the plaster. Her poor car took the brunt of it."

"Are you all right? Anything hurt?" He slid right into seeming to care about me over his home's structural safety, like his wife had, but it sounded a little cooler coming from him.

"I'm fine." Horrifyingly, tears welled in my eyes. "I haven't really slept in about a day and a half. Work stuff."

"Walls can be fixed," Hal said.

"I'm sorry, again. I just really wanted to come." Oh, Jesus, I had to swallow a sob. A *sob*. Like a little girl not getting to go to a birthday party because she was sick.

Hormones. It was all hormones. I trusted myself with emotions about as much as I trusted myself with knowing where I'd left a baby journal. I took a deep breath and sucked it all back in before following Bree and the other women out to the patio.

SIX

We took over the two wide, champagne-colored outdoor couches. I sat next to Maggie, and Camille sat with Bree. The surf pounded loud in our ears, even though it was at least a hundred yards away across the sand. I could smell the particular scent of a beach bonfire—driftwood smoke, salt, and creosote. Venice didn't allow open flames on the sand, so it must have been floating all the way from Dockweiler Beach. The gas fire in Bree's pit snapped cheerfully in the warm air, as if it knew it had no other purpose than to look pretty.

Bree went inside and came out again carrying a platter of cupcakes. Each of them had the bottom half of a mermaid on top, diving into the frosting, which was made to look like waves. We made the appropriate appreciative noises. Maggie took one immediately, biting into the mermaid's tail. "Oh, God, yes," she said around a mouthful.

An inch above the horizon, the sun was drifting down toward the water. My eyelids drifted down with it.

Next, Bree brought out two bowls of chips stacked on top of each other and a platter full of cheese and dips and guacamole. "Health food. I swear it's all organic."

The others had moved to talking about how they'd been doing up their nurseries, and I swore if I heard one more word about cradle bumpers, I'd fall all the way asleep and make them drive me home. I was too tired to give one single damn about the best places to buy baby wipes or bra pads. When Bree and I had put the Ripleys together, we'd agreed we'd talk about jobs and politics and sobriety. Important things. This wasn't just a group of mommies. This was a group of survivors.

We'd all come into the recovery rooms in different ways, of course. Bree had been all expensive wine all the time. Her rehab had cost more than a Tesla S. Maggie had been a vodka-and-opioid girl. Camille's problem had been coke—she said the TV industry ran on it. Alcohol had only been the underpinning. If she drank, she bought an eight ball, guaranteed, but she preferred AA people to NA people.

I'd been more of a Scotch-followed-by-fancy-wine kind of woman, but by the end, I'd moved from Ardbeg and a nice Rombauer Chardonnay to whatever cheap bottles at Trader Joe's were closest at hand as I barreled through the liquor aisle. It didn't matter as long as it got me where I wanted to go.

All four of us had gone through the fire and had arisen like phoenixes. Or maybe more like rather charred but stubborn pigeons. Whatever. What mattered was that we were survivors who had found recovery and made it work. So what had happened to our idea of making this a unique mothers' group in which we talked about the difficult and even the impossible?

Maggie asked, "What did you end up doing with your nursery walls, Jillian?"

Instead of answering, I said, "Look." I pointed at the sun, which was just dropping into the thin line of far-off fog. "Can we get a little closer?"

It worked. We tromped through the sand, Camille breathing harder than any of us. Maggie gave her an arm to lean on, and we all made it to the shoreline right as the orange orb melted, flattening against the horizon.

Something was nagging at me, pulling at me like the waves of exhaustion that battered against the backs of my eyes. I just didn't know what it was. It felt like I'd forgotten something. Like I'd left a candle burning at home, or forgot to pay the water bill.

I tried to shake it off as the waves broke against the shore. Sandpipers darted in and out of the waves as gulls screeched overhead. Maggie held out her other arm to me, so I took it, offering my elbow to Bree. We stood in a single line, all of us linked.

As if we'd agreed on it, we dropped into silence. No one spoke. The sun liquefied more, pouring itself into the sea, a white heart with a yellow rim. I tried to look away to protect my eyes, but I couldn't stop staring. Then, silently, the sun was gone, two stubborn rays streaking up into the red and orange glow.

Bree pulled her arm from mine and clapped. We all followed suit. A jogger looked at us like we were crazy, but he was the crazy one if he didn't appreciate what had just happened in front of him.

Mom would have loved this sunset.

"Someday," said Bree, "we'll bring our babies out here, and we'll show them their first sunset. Together, all four of us. We'll always have that memory. Oh, girls." She spun in a circle and then faced us. "Imagine how lucky these babies will be. Each of them being wanted from the moment they were conceived and loved every single little moment since."

Wait. *Each of them being wanted from the moment they were conceived?*

Was that a barb from one of her cactus-like needles? Or was it simply a nice rah-rah moment? I blinked and stared at her.

She sure as hell wasn't meeting my gaze. Worse, she was looking at Camille and Maggie as if they were in on the joke with her.

No, I was imagining it. She wouldn't have told them that I'd confessed to not wanting V immediately. My imagination was in hyperdrive. That was a normal excited-pregnant-lady thing to say. I wiped my sweaty hands on my jeans. She couldn't mean it like it had sounded. I knew her secret, too. Why on earth would she tell them what I'd shared with her?

But neither Maggie nor Camille met my eyes, either.

I got out my cell and fumbled with it, trying to open the camera app. Turning away from the women, I took a few shots using different angles and exposures of the remaining light playing against the water. My fingers were clumsy.

I heard Bree say into the awkwardness, "You all take your time. I'm going back to whip up a little mocktail I've been planning."

"I'll help," said Camille. "If I can lean on you walking back."

"I'll stay with Jillian." Maggie was kneeling in the sand digging a small hole with a piece of driftwood. "We'll be there soon."

"Just a couple more pictures?" I said to Maggie. "Then I'll be ready." The horizon's glow had turned a pearlescent purple and I didn't want to miss catching it. Plus I needed something to steady my breathing.

"I'm in heaven. No hurry."

I shot for a few more minutes until what I was getting was muddy instead of miraculous.

Maggie stood and brushed her hands off. She pulled back her hair into a ponytail. "Do you know what they call the time after sunset before it's dark?"

We turned and started the short walk back to the patio. "I don't know. Last light or something?"

"Civil twilight."

"Really?"

She nodded. "It lasts until the sun is six degrees below the horizon, or until you can't see well outdoors. It's followed by nautical twilight, you know, that dark blue time when it's really hard to drive. That goes until the sun is twelve degrees below the horizon. That's followed by astronomical twilight, which goes to eighteen degrees below the horizon and is almost totally dark. Then, finally, night."

I stared at her. "How do you know that?"

"I really like sunsets."

"Me, too."

"I know," she said. "I've seen you taking pictures of the sky before the seven o'clock meeting and then again when you come out."

"Sunsets might have been the only thing my mother loved." I swallowed, suddenly embarrassed.

Maggie's eyebrows went up. "You *never* talk about your mom. I just realized that. Is she still alive?"

I shrugged, trying to play it off. No big deal. "I'm not sure."

"Oh, crap. You're not in contact with her? Wait, no, you don't have to talk about it if you don't want to."

But instead of wanting to run away, like I usually did when anyone asked about my mother, somehow I didn't mind as much as I normally did. Maybe my defenses were down because I was so tired, but instead of changing the subject, I actually answered her question. "We're estranged, yeah. No contact." Did sunset texts sent to a number that never responded count? I'd found one of my mother's neighbors (not a church member) on Facebook ten years before, and she'd taken pity on me, giving me Mom's cell phone number.

"When did you leave?"

"When I was seventeen."

"Oof. Why? The gay thing?"

I laughed. As if I'd have been able to tell them that at seventeen. "I got pregnant."

Maggie nodded. "And she flipped out."

"You can still see the mushroom cloud if you look east when the wind is right." *How could you be so stupid, Jillian?* Her voice had been a knife, wielded to sever whatever it touched. *After everything I've worked so hard to teach you.*

Maggie's voice was soft. "Who was the father?"

"A nobody. I just wanted to get my virginity out of the way." I'd thought it might make me straight.

"That must have been hard."

"Eh. The abortion wasn't difficult at all. I went to Planned Parenthood in Salt Lake and used my fake ID, since I didn't have parental consent. This nurse talked me through everything, and she made me look at every side of it." V drove her heel into one of my kidneys. "After the procedure, the doctor held my hand while I cried. She was exponentially more caring to me than I could remember my mother ever being. Mom kicked me out when I got home."

"You had to leave that same day?"

We'd stopped walking, and I nodded, digging my toes into the colder sand below the warm top level. "I packed a bag with some really stupid stuff—I had no idea what I was doing. Looking back now, I was probably in shock. I was a kid who'd just had surgery, in pain, and I was packing for a life I didn't know how to prepare for. I took all my hair bands but forgot my toothbrush. I took three nightgowns because it was nighttime when she put me out, but only one pair of jeans. I didn't bring a single book. I took my most recent diary, but none of the others." That day, I'd lost every trace of the little girl I'd been. I had believed in God and in the church until that point. I thought someday I'd be good enough to make my mother see me and love me.

"That's awful."

"As I left the house, her last words to me were, *You would never have been a good mother anyway.*" The old chill swept over me again simply by saying the words out loud.

The sunlight lit the back of Maggie's dark hair with a gleaming halo. "Did you ever regret it?"

"Nope. Not once. It all got me to where I am now." The abortion itself had been the right choice, and I'd never felt any other way. The whole experience of it had been so overwhelmingly positive that it was the reason I'd gone to med school and into obstetrics. I wanted to help other women do whatever was right for them—I wanted to hold their hands when they cried just like mine had been held, or help them bring a new life into the world, if that was the path they wanted.

"What about your father?"

Ugh, I was starting to regret this flood of emotion, but I wasn't sure how to cap it. I quickened my pace. "He died a few years ago."

"I'm so sorry. How?"

The familiar pain twisted right above my heart. "I don't know. No one told me about it, and I wouldn't have been allowed to attend the funeral anyway. It was his lungs, but I don't know what exactly." *I* was the doctor in the family. What if I'd been able to help him? I should have been allowed to try. God, I had to get Maggie's kind gaze off my pain. So I threw it back to her. "Anyway. I know your parents died when you were young, but I don't know the story. What happened?"

"Plane crash when I was fifteen."

"*Jesus.*"

"You didn't know that? That's why Bree's always ribbing me about flying private. They were on a commercial flight over the Azores."

"Holy shit, that must have been so hard. And no, I've never heard Bree giving you crap about your parents' *deaths.* That's not right."

Was that gratitude I saw flash in her eyes? "No, it's really okay. Even before they died, I swear I saw my parents about a month a year. I had two full-time nannies. It was harder losing them at eighteen when I went to college than it was losing my mother and father. But it was okay. I could afford all the therapy I wanted. They left me money, and the airline paid out big." Her voice was light, but her expression was tight in the sunset's glow. "And I *do* only fly private. Billion Air out of Burbank, in case you're ever in the market for a smooth flight anywhere."

Relieved I could make a comment that wasn't about parents, I said, "It is *not* called that."

"It totally is."

"Wow." *Don't go back to parents.* "So, tell me again, civil, nautical, then astronomical twilight?"

"That's it."

I tucked away the names and the facts, trying to memorize them for my sunset files. I'd text them to Mom later, too. Not that she'd respond. "Is it the same for dawn?"

"Yeah. In reverse. Astronomical, nautical, then civil dawn. Hang on a sec," she said. The rest of us had left our shoes on Bree's patio, but she'd worn her sneakers out to the water's edge. She put her hand on my shoulder and took off a shoe, dumping sand out of it. "Better. Thanks."

"Welcome."

Then she moved her left hand toward my belly. "I patted her earlier, but can I say hi again?"

I smiled. "Always."

Her hand was small and firm, warm through the thin cotton jersey of my shirt. V chose that moment to pirouette, and Maggie gasped, pressing a little harder.

"I felt that!"

"She's a little sea monkey, all right." We were almost at Bree's patio. Camille and Bree were still inside. I dropped my voice. "Hey, did Bree say anything to you and Camille about how much I wanted this baby?" *Or how little?*

Maggie wrinkled her nose. "I was kind of wondering if she was being an asshole back there. Yeah, she texted us the other day, all gossipy-like, that you weren't convinced you wanted to keep the baby, back when Rochelle left. I never answered her."

Anger punched me in the throat. Damn Bree and her spines. "It was for *one* week. Between the time Ro left and I felt V kick. I *told* her that."

"I figured she was exaggerating. Don't sweat it. You know she likes gossip."

True. But still. *Why* would she do that? Knowing I knew what I did about her pregnancy?

I scraped my bare feet on the patio sand mat and then tucked myself up again on the sofa. The warmth of the fire was welcome as the sweat I'd raised on the walk dried, but I still felt out of sorts, unsure if I should be angry with Bree or not. Maybe she'd only shared my terrible week with the other women because she was worried about me?

Maggie thumped herself onto the sofa next to me.

Camille came out and plopped down on the other sofa with a long groan. "I swear I'm dying. Are you both dying?" She reached into her purse and pulled out her iPad.

"No," said Maggie. "Don't you dare."

She made a face that looked as tired as I felt. "Gotta check e-mail. Just one sec."

"Don't do it. You'll start working—you know you will."

But Camille was already in, clicking and making notes on the screen. We'd be lucky to get her back into the conversation at all. I worked hard, yes, but at least I knew how to be off when I was off. Camille didn't, and I worried about what would happen when she had even less time to work after the baby came.

Maggie and I sighed at each other as Bree came out, raising a tray of drinks high in celebration. "You'll *love* this. Pear and passionfruit."

I focused on Bree. When in doubt, go directly to the source. "Bree, did you tell them about that terrible week I told you about?"

Her hand froze lowering my drink to the table. Next to me, Maggie stopped thumping the cushion behind her. Camille, of course, didn't look up from her iPad. I doubted she'd even heard me.

Bree straightened. "I—"

"I was pretty clear that was a secret I hadn't told anyone else."

Bree sent Maggie a tight look.

"Don't blame her," I said. "I asked her outright after that semi-shitty thing you said at the beach."

"Darling, it wasn't meant to be shitty; I *know* your baby has been wanted since the beginning—"

"By Rochelle, sure." I nodded firmly, owning it. "Not by me, not at first."

"Anyway," Bree said brightly. "You sound angry."

"I'm not angry." I was, but I'd be damned if I showed it to her. My negative emotions, as helter-skelter as they were, were mine, and I didn't show them to anyone who—well, I tried not to show them to anyone at all.

Thoughts started to form, a half-built idea. I didn't want to share my negative emotions just like Bree hadn't wanted to show anyone *her* secret. Of all people, she should understand how I felt. I realized I suddenly had a weird power over her, and I hated the weight of having it. What if I—what if I proposed something that would change that? What if I could *make* her share her secret with the other women so that I wasn't carrying it alone, so that she could stop her weird soft-pedaled aggression toward me?

"You know what?" I said. "Yeah. I admit that I only got pregnant because Rochelle couldn't. When she left, and I had her biological child squatting in my womb, I was pissed. I didn't know how I felt about motherhood, but I sure as hell knew I'd never wanted to be a single mother, not for one second of my life. But I'm *sure* you shared with the girls, Bree, how that all changed once I felt V move inside me a week after Rochelle left."

Camille actually looked up from her work, her Apple pencil freezing in midair.

Bree sucked in her expensive-looking lips. I felt a twinge of pleasure. It took a lot to prickle Bree Sydenham.

"If she didn't tell you that, please know that that happened," I said to Camille and Maggie. "Once this little cookie wiggled, she was mine forever."

Bree had the grace to look slightly abashed.

I went on. "Now let's make it even. We'll go around the circle. Confession is good for the soul. Each of you has to tell a secret you've been too scared to share with anyone else." Was it wrong of me to push? Maybe. But I was tired and hormonal, and it was the first thing that had made me feel fully awake in hours.

Camille's eyes widened. "Oh."

"I like it," said Maggie cheerfully. She clinked the ice in her glass. "Who's first?"

Dropping onto the sofa next to Camille, Bree said, "You, since you seem so happy about it."

"Why not? I'm usually an open book. But I do have one thing I've kept from y'all this whole time." She took a piece of ice into her mouth and chewed, obviously waiting for us to ask.

Camille leaned forward. "What?"

Bree's eyes went wide. "What is it?"

"It's a paternity thing, right?" It wasn't my finest moment, poking at Bree in this sideways manner, but it was true that we knew nothing about Maggie's baby's father. She'd only ever told us he'd been an ex enjoying a friends-with-benefits night and that she'd been happy about getting accidentally knocked up.

Maggie looked like she was about to burst into giggles. "I'm having a Tinder baby."

I blinked. "No." I'd heard of using the hookup app as a sperm bank, but not a single patient had ever admitted to me if they'd done it.

Camille said, "You said it was an ex!" Her iPad slipped from her thigh to the sofa, apparently forgotten.

"I said he was *kind of* my ex. We met two times and had sex twice. That's practically a relationship for me. I thought about artificial insemination, but come on. That's no fun. You only get to see the man on paper, and the woman doesn't get an orgasm but he does? What's fair about that? Anyway, you can't trust anyone until you've met them in person, and I trust my gut. I figured a date, even a really short one like getting a single coffee before going back to my apartment, tells you more about the guy than you'd ever learn on a form."

Without thinking, I said, "What about STDs?" That was probably a rude thing to say so far after the deed was done, but I was a doctor.

Bree's and Camille's mouths both fell open, but Maggie didn't seem to mind me asking. "I asked if they were clean. And I didn't get anything. Just a calculated risk."

I'd treated a hell of a lot of women over the years who'd regretted taking that risk. But I didn't say it. That horse hadn't seen the barn for months.

Camille had recovered from her surprise. "I've seen a couple of onesies online. One said, 'My Parents Swiped Right,' and the other said 'Tinder Kinder.' I am *so* getting them for you."

Bree looked impressed. "How did you screen? What were your criteria?"

Maggie held up her hand and counted on her fingers. "Male. Not stupid. Smells good. Is willing to go bareback."

Bree said, "Are you going to tell the father?" She sounded tense. Obviously.

"Nope." Maggie's voice was firm. She shot me a look, and I realized no matter how happy she looked, she was waiting for one of us to say something critical. But I didn't get to judge Maggie. Besides, she probably *had* gotten a better feel (literally) for the guy in person than she would have on paper. Just like with Bree, until Maggie asked me directly what I thought about fathers' rights, I had no official opinions on the matter.

I said, "That's your call."

Maggie blew out a breath. "Yeah. It's my call. If these dudes were careless enough to let me talk them into sex without protection, then they don't really deserve to know. It would be different if I'd given them a sabotaged condom, but I didn't. They were all adults, and they knew the risks. Good sex, everyone comes, I get a baby, win-win all around."

Bree clapped again. "Well! I applaud your bravery!"

Jesus, she clapped a lot.

Maggie said, "Who's next? Camille?"

Camille flipped the cover of her iPad open and then let it shut again. "I don't have secrets."

"Come on," I said.

She raised a hand and massaged her temple. "I do *not* have secrets. Remember when I worked at Your Home TV?"

I reached for my glass. "You used to talk about kitchen tile. A lot." And I'd thought she was a workaholic then, when she'd worked for the 24-7 home improvement channel. It had gotten ten times worse in the last few years she'd been at CrimeWatcher. She'd confessed to me once that she was working with her sponsor on her addiction to work.

"You're right." Camille's nod shook her braids. "I was *obsessed*. I had so many opinions about tile! I literally dreamed about tile, even though I was a producer. I was supposed to be working on budgets and marketing, not what they were laying on the floor on-screen! But I couldn't help it. Ceramic versus porcelain versus stone, glass versus vinyl, although"—she held up a hand—"don't get me started on vinyl. But now that murder is literally my job, I've learned one thing, and I've learned it well. A secret is the first step toward murder. I don't plan on being a murderer *or* being murdered—I seriously do *not* have time— so I try not to keep secrets. From anyone. Ever. I'm over seven hundred e-mails behind right now, and each of them requires a decision from me, and I can barely remember to brush my teeth. A secret requires a good memory, and stress ate my memory long before this child came along to finish the job. No secrets."

Bree said, "Okay, then. No secrets. No murder. I get it."

Camille said, "Honestly, I really miss kitchen tiles. And my Home Depot corporate sponsor discount. No one gives Murder TV a discount on, what, a wood chipper? Duct tape?"

I laughed along with Bree, but Maggie folded her arms. "Nope. I'm not buying it. Everyone has secrets."

Camille shrugged. "Not me."

"You *do* have one," Maggie pressed. "I can see it."

Stretching her legs out in front of her, Camille reached for another cupcake. "Yeah? Tell it to me, then."

Maggie leaned forward, her gaze sharp. "I can tell you have a secret by the way you started moving when I said you had one. I can also tell . . ." She tipped her head sideways. "You didn't tense when you talked about work, so it's about your personal life. And I don't think it's about us. So it's either about your other friends or your wife. You're not the kind of person to waste energy keeping secrets *about* friends, so it's not that. It's Olivia, then. What's the secret you're keeping from Olivia?"

Camille's fingertips tapped at the cupcake paper. "You scare me."

Maggie grinned. "Spill."

"Fine. Goddamn it. I hate you, by the way." Camille took a large bite and then scowled. She put the rest of the cupcake back on the plate, keeping the paper in her fingers. "Olivia doesn't know this."

"Duh," said Maggie.

Camille swallowed her bite. "And it's dumb. It's small. Like the *tiniest* secret ever."

Bree made an impatient go-on-already hand motion.

Camille folded her cupcake paper into smaller and smaller squares. "I forgot to send in the form when we got married. And then . . . I guess I lost the paper entirely."

We all stared.

Maggie threw herself backward. "A paperwork secret? Come *on*."

"No, wait," I said. "So you're not married at all?"

Camille shook her head. "Nope."

"How long have you been *not* married?"

"Six years."

Bree gave a peal of laughter. "What about your taxes?"

"We just file as married, and they believe us. The first year I was terrified they'd catch us, but they apparently don't care."

I pulled out my phone and opened the browser.

"So your baby will be a bastard?" said Maggie.

Bree gave an unladylike snort that would have made me laugh had I not still been irritated with her. I tapped my question into Google.

Camille threw the paper at Maggie, who swatted it out of the air into the fire pit. "Seriously. It's keeping me awake at night. I'm going to have to tell her someday that we've been living in proverbial sin this whole time. She did everything for our wedding, which was *spectacu-*

lar, by the way, and I told her to give me something to do, and she gave me that. And then I dropped the ball. You know me—I do *not* drop balls. When I do, I don't admit to it if I don't have to. So I've been living this lie for six years, and it's killing me." She put the palms of her hands against her forehead. "She'll be so disappointed."

I held up my phone, screen facing out. "You're still married."

Camille dropped her hands and stared at me. "What?"

"In California, the officiant has to file the paperwork within ten days. You should have, too. But even if neither of you did, you're still considered married because you obtained the license first and it was witnessed."

Camille continued to stare, her mouth now dropped open.

"You really never Googled it?"

"I just—I just knew I screwed it up."

I shook my head. "You didn't."

"Jillian. You're sure?"

I waggled the cell at her. "Quick Google, so absolutely not. But this is from LegalZoom, which is pretty reliable, I think."

"You've solved the biggest problem in my life. My one and only deep dark secret." She smiled that smile then, the one that could power all the lights on Venice Beach. "Holy shit. Thank you."

Bree gave me a glance that seemed at once begrudging and approving.

Camille raised her hands above her head. "Ladies, I gotta go. I have a marriage to consummate!" But she made no move to stand.

Maggie said, "Are you going to tell Olivia?"

"*Hell,* no. I would never hear the end of it. So I guess it's still a secret." Camille lowered her head as if she were looking at us all over reading glasses. "We'll never speak of this again, right?"

You ought to check in with Bree on that. But I prudently held my tongue as we raised our glasses. I clinked mine with my sofa-mate, Maggie, and Camille and Bree clinked theirs. None of us were heaving ourselves up and around the fire pit in order to touch glasses.

"I feel a million years younger," said Camille. "So, Bree, that just leaves you, right?"

"Oh," said Bree, flapping her hand. "So many secrets to choose from. Which secret would I share?"

"The worst one," I said flatly.

She didn't meet my gaze. "Okay. Here goes." Tugging at a pillow behind her, she shifted in her seat. She looked over her shoulder at the glass doors behind us. Was she looking for Hal?

"You can do it," said Maggie.

Bree cleared her throat. "This is hard. But I trust y'all. And I've talked this to death with my therapist. I can't bear to tell Hal. He'd be so disappointed in me." She looked over her shoulder again. "I used to struggle with stealing things. Always little things. Mascara from Walgreens, like that. Last year, though, I . . ."

Bree was wussing out.

Maggie leaned forward, her face bright with interest. "You what?"

In a quick rush of words, she said, "I stole a case of champagne from Melinda Gates."

Camille looked impressed. "Really?"

Maggie gave a low whistle. "How?"

I didn't say anything and kept my lips folded tightly.

"I know it's shocking, but it's not like I was going to *drink* it, you know. This was last year, I think. I'd parked in back, with the caterers, because Mel had asked me to bring an enormous flower arrangement that someone had forgotten to pick up. I needed help carrying it in. When I went back out to move my car to the valet, there were six pallets sitting next to my car, each with like fifty cases. I just put one in my car. I didn't even *think*. That's the thing I'm ashamed of—it was like I was fifteen again."

"Did you ever admit the truth to *Mel*?" My voice was icy. Maggie looked at me sharply, but I couldn't help it. Bree had gossiped to them about me, which was something I'd never do. She knew she could trust me to keep an actually important secret, so her stupid humble-brag one raised my hackles.

"Oh, I could never." She put on a look of horror and said, "None of you can mention it to her, either!"

I rolled my eyes.

She went on, "I'd be mortified. I swear, it's the first time I've stolen anything in more than a decade." Her smile grew. "It felt kind of Robin Hoody, you know? Stealing from the rich . . ."

I kept my voice Beverly Hills–catfight polite. "Charming story. But doesn't that phrase usually end in giving to the poor?" I gave a sweep with my hand to encompass our surroundings—the glass and steel of her home, the sand and the broad ribbon of water to the west.

She met me, though, and matched my tone. "Oh, honey. Compared to Melinda, I'm a homeless urchin huddled in a doorway in the freezing rain. Anyway. I donated the case to a fundraiser. It's not like I drank it, *obviously*."

The thing was, I liked Bree. I wanted to help her with whatever she'd need in the difficult times ahead. I assumed that Hal and she had some kind of deal-breaker prenup—it was mostly his money, after all—and I'd bet that giving birth to another man's child was in there somewhere. She'd be out, and I knew she loved him. She'd shared with me her biggest fuckup. (Actually, she hadn't. I'd guessed it from the envelope. She hadn't shared a thing with me, really.) And then she'd blabbed something of mine that felt really private to our friends.

It was a small secret, all things considered. I'd done so much worse before I'd gotten sober, and with my sponsor's help, I'd made amends for most of those things, in whatever ways I could. And I'd wanted to tell Camille and Maggie how I'd felt about the pregnancy early on but I sucked at sharing feelings. This group was supposed to help me get better at it. That had been my hope, anyway. The whole point was to talk about the *real* aspects of motherhood, the hard stuff, the things we couldn't share with other people. We were supposed to be *real*.

But I hadn't shared it with all of them yet. Just with Bree. So I was ticked. She was being cowardly, and I didn't appreciate it.

I could show her how it was done, though. If I could jump off the cliff I suddenly felt myself standing on the edge of, I could show her what bravery looked like.

Once, a long time ago, I'd done something that I'd never made amends for. It was my biggest secret, one that only my sponsor knew.

"You know what, Bree? That secret I told you in the car the other day? The one about not wanting V for a little while? The thing you shared with our friends here? That wasn't a huge secret. I'd tell anyone who asked me that I was shockingly ambivalent about motherhood at first." Would I? Whatever. I could pretend I would. "I was just trying to make you feel better about sharing your secret with me."

She had the sense to look a little alarmed, a tendon standing out in her neck.

But I wasn't going to submarine her. I was going to torpedo myself, instead, and show them the real me. "Here's my biggest secret. The night that got me sober seven years ago, I went to work drunk."

Maggie's eyes widened and Camille set her drink on the table.

"And I almost killed someone."

SEVEN

Seven years before, I'd woken up still drunk from the previous night. I hadn't been out, and I hadn't been partying—I'd simply been drinking the way I liked to drink, which was a lot, and fast, by myself. I was still single—I wouldn't meet Rochelle for another six months. That night, it had been Scotch. Laphroaig, my favorite, all peat smoke and iodine heat. I'd heard someone once say it smelled like a burning hospital, charred iodine-soaked Band-Aids. It was the best scent in the world.

That night, I'd only been planning on having a couple of fingers and then maybe switching to Chardonnay. But I hadn't switched, and I'd eventually passed out when the bottle was almost empty. I'd barely made it to work. I vaguely remembered putting on my scrubs and lab coat and looking in the mirror through bleary eyes. I just looked tired, right? Really, really tired.

I'd rushed to the bathroom to vomit, something that was getting more common in the morning. I didn't understand it. I was *good* at drinking. It got me out of my head, away from thinking about insurance companies that refused to allow my patients to be treated, or the mother who was too strung out to even look at her new child before she started trying to climb off the birthing table. Lately, though, it hadn't been working. I was miserable until I passed out, and when I woke up, I was the same—coated in a low-level depression all day as I waited for the end of the day to roll around so I could try drinking again, so I could try to get the alcohol to work right, like it used to.

I cleaned myself up as best I could in the locker room's bathroom, praying that no one had heard me.

My pager went off. An ER call, not one of my patients. Fine. The staff there knew me a little less than my own staff did on the OB floor. Hopefully they wouldn't notice if my hands were a little shaky, if there was sweat on my brow.

But as I came out of the bathroom, I ran into Loretta Galves, my least favorite nurse. I could admit she was technically good at her job, but she had *no* bedside manner, acting like patients were just problems instead of what they were, people with ailments she was paid to assist.

She looked at me, eagle-eyed as usual. My own eyes weren't as great—for a second I saw two of her.

"I saw you. Changing."

I tried to smile. "Okay, that's weird. But hello to you, too."

"You're drunk."

"*What?*" The word was too loud. Too drunk-sounding.

She held up a Breathalyzer that she must have borrowed from the ER. "Blow, or I go to management."

"Fuck you." My head spun—the vomiting had helped, but now everything smelled metallic and I was shivering with cold. If I blew and the alcohol was still in my bloodstream, I'd lose my license.

And I knew it was still in my bloodstream. I could feel it, and sickeningly, there wasn't *enough* alcohol in me. All I wanted was to get away from her so I could get a drink into my body—that was the only thing that would help me think my way out of this.

"I saw the way you were walking. But if you're not drunk, you shouldn't be scared to blow into this. Are you *scared*, Dr. Marsh?" Her eyes were beady raisins of hatred. I wanted to punch her in the jaw—a visceral urge to physically hurt someone, a feeling I'd never had before.

If I blew, I was fucked. She'd go to management.

If I didn't blow, I was fucked. She'd go to management.

I had to get there first. OB Chief of Staff Walters would protect me if I said I had a problem and needed help. They had to, by law. I couldn't get fired if I admitted addiction.

But I don't need help. I don't have a problem. I just need space. My house. And the bottle of Chardonnay that's chilling in the door of the fridge . . .

My pager beeped again, doubling my heart rate. I glanced at it. "ER, code pink," I said. It was an obstetric emergency in progress. "I'm the only OB on duty."

Her own pager went off, and her face told me it was for something else.

My heart pitched itself into my still-heaving stomach and stayed there, sloshing around in the acid. "I swear to you, I'm okay. I went to a sports bar last night. I'm just hungover as hell."

"You stink."

"I didn't have time to wash my hair."

Galves twitched, glancing at her pager and then at the Breathalyzer in her other hand. Another doctor, Annette Hong, came in and started washing her hands. In the mirror, I saw her look at the Breathalyzer.

"I've got to go." I shook my pager at Galves.

Hong turned, wiping her hands on a paper towel. "What's going on?"

I wanted to insist to both of them that I was fine. But I wasn't. *I was fucked.* "I'll go to Walters."

Galves had the grace to look shocked. "You will? Right now?"

"After I deal with the ER." I knew I wasn't thinking straight—I knew I should go right to Walters—but in the moment of pressure, my pager went off a third time. The ER needed me. I had to uphold my duty. I had to get this right, but what was right? I felt upside-down, my fingertips numb and my throat tight. "I swear to you, I'm okay. I'm okay."

Galves narrowed her eyes even smaller. "Don't operate. You hear me? If you touch a patient, I'll see to it that not even Walters can help you." With as long as she'd been here, she could probably get that done.

I wanted to tell her I hated her, that she was a terrible person, but deep under the lump of poison my soul had curled itself around, I knew she wasn't the one I hated. I didn't hate Hong, either, even though she was already turning to question Galves.

I turned and ran to the ER, pushing down the bile that rose with every painful step.

Luke met me at the desk, shoving an iPad at me with the chart pulled up. "Tori Newbold, supposedly thirty-nine weeks, in labor, zero centimeters dilated."

"Supposedly? Who's her OB?"

"She actually . . ." He paused. "She hasn't seen a doctor." He didn't seem to be registering anything amiss with me, thank God.

I chewed harder on the two pieces of cinnamon gum I'd shoved into my mouth on the run. "Okay, so what's the emergency?" Zero centimeters wasn't a stat to the ER.

"Pseudocyesis, we think."

The headache grew sharper behind my eyes. "Oh, shit." A phantom pregnancy was just that—a woman who carried an invisible, nonexistent child within her sometimes-enlarged womb. Some women had psychosis, but others had never needed so much as a single mental health day. They believed they were pregnant, so their bodies did, too, reinforcing the belief. Their bellies swelled. They lactated. They could feel the kicks, as could others. Their hormone changes often matched those of an actually pregnant woman, and sometimes they went all the way into labor. Only four years before, in North Carolina, an ob-gyn did a C-section on a woman who'd been laboring in the ER for more than twelve hours beforehand. No one in the hospital had done an ultrasound, the only foolproof method of checking whether or not there was a real baby. They hadn't thought to. Then they'd opened her to find nothing inside.

"Ultrasound."

He shook his head. "Ran it. Negative results." His eyes were wide.

"Your first?" I'd had three so far, but two of them had only been a few months along. One had been eight months, or really, "eight months." That one had been harder. I'd never had one go all the way to false labor.

Luke nodded. "It's—holy shit."

Well, at least I couldn't screw this one up. It was a sick thought but something of a relief. My queasiness eased. "Yeah. Buckle up."

The patient knew something was wrong—she was tensed but not in the inward having-a-baby-nothing-else-exists way. "You're the doctor? What's wrong? Is something wrong?"

"Ms. Newbold, I'm Dr. Jillian Marsh. Can I call you Tori?"

She had red, stringy hair pulled back in a sloppy ponytail. Her sheet-white cheeks were covered in fat orange freckles. Her face was puffy, her voice guttural. "They did an ultrasound, and then they said I had to wait for you. What's wrong? Is my baby okay?"

Before I could answer, a contraction hit her, and she doubled as far forward as she could over her extremely-pregnant-looking belly. I stepped forward to take her hand, chewing hard on my gum while praying she had a bad sense of smell. "It's okay. Breathe. Just breathe."

Her grip was clawlike and painful. But I was used to it, and after the contraction finished, I twisted my wrist slightly so that it became her idea to let me go. "Good. Good," I said. My mind was racing—I'd never had to break the news to a woman who thought she was this far along. Pseudocyesis left a woman who came in to have a baby with nothing but a hospital bill.

Tori reached forward to grab my jacket. "*Tell me.*"

I could not vomit again. I told myself sternly that it was impossible. I simply could not. I chomped my gum and swallowed the green feeling and hoped Tori didn't notice the way cold sweat had broken against my brow. My shirt was soaked and my whole body ached. "Tori, this isn't going to be easy to hear, but I don't want to keep you in suspense, so I'll say it quickly and then we'll talk about it. You aren't pregnant. You haven't been pregnant. There's no baby inside you. It's called a phantom pregnancy, and you've been having one." What I didn't say was the other thing it was called: *hysterical pregnancy.* She was about to be exactly that.

Tori only blinked. "No."

To be fair, that was a logical answer to the insane thing I'd just said to her. "One of our nurses has already called for our resident psychiatrist to come talk to you as soon as possible—"

"I'm not crazy."

I held up my hands, keeping my movements slow both for her benefit and to ease my own vertigo. "You're not crazy." For all I knew, she might have major mental illness, but she wasn't presenting it right now if she did. She was simply a woman on the wrong side of very bad luck. "It's kind of like having the flu. It's not your fault. Your body knows how to take care of you when you have flu. Like that, your body knew what to do when it thought it was pregnant. It just . . . got it wrong."

"Bullshit," Tori spat. "Get me another doctor. My husband's on his way. He'll handle this. You go *away.*"

I nodded and ducked outside the curtain, although I wasn't going anywhere till the psych provider got here. From the other side of the fabric, I said to her, "I'm going to send a nurse in with your ultrasound, okay?" I nodded to Luke, who justifiably looked terrified out of his gourd.

But he scuttled in, the printed images from the ultrasound in his hands. If she didn't believe it, we could do another ultrasound to show her in more detail the nothing inside her, but I hoped we wouldn't have to.

There was a brief silence. I expected more denial for a while, but instead, there was a scream that rose like a siren and went on and on and on. It broke for breath and then it started again. It wasn't a wail—it was a horror-movie scream, one that made my ears feel bloody, one that made me wobble on my legs. I pushed back through the curtain.

Luke was standing next to her, one hand firmly on her shoulder. He looked like a statue, his eyes fixed and wide.

Under the air-raid scream, I muttered, "Get the pictures out of here."

He bolted. I took his place at Tori's side. Like we had during her contraction, I held her hand, and she gripped me hard, this time in fury. I'd have welts on my wrist, but that was okay.

The scream stalled, and then she moaned. She bent forward again, in the grip of another contraction. "Why?" She gasped. "Why is this happening?"

"I don't know," I said, and I rubbed the base of her spine while she writhed with the pain. All of this, for literally nothing.

It was fucked.

Just like me. My job. I could lose the one thing that mattered most to me.

But I couldn't stop drinking. So that meant there *was* something that mattered more to me than my job. I'd never admitted it before that moment. I couldn't simply stop. That would be like stopping breathing. Unimaginable. It wasn't like I needed *help*. I didn't *want* to stop.

I kept rubbing her back. What did I want more? I knew I should say that I wanted my job most of all. But not without drinking. I couldn't do this job that was alternately awe-inspiring and completely heartbreaking without knowing I could go home and numb out a little. Or a lot.

Tori started crying as the contraction eased, huge, gulping sobs that sounded painful—she swallowed air and her mouth hung open in a howl.

"I'm sorry," I murmured as I rubbed her arm to give her something to feel, to focus on if she could. "I'm sorry." But I wasn't paying attention to her. I was in my own head, completely.

Luke poked his head in but then retracted like a snail when Tori growled in his direction.

Time slowed to a crawl. I would stay with her until Psych could get there. Then I'd go talk to Walters. Maybe. I should ask for help. But that would mean showing him my broken places. My vulnerable, weak spots.

Your drinking is more than a weak spot.

I'd made a whole career of being smart and chipper and sunny and kind. I'd never once shown my other side, the scared side, the side that couldn't stop buying wine at night even after I swore in the morning that I'd have an evening off for once. I didn't even know how the words would fit in my mouth. Telling Walters that I was sick, that I had a problem, was as impossible as this woman in front of me spontaneously giving birth to an actual infant.

Maybe I'd go home sick and pray Galves wouldn't follow up on her threat. But no, Hong had seen part of it, and who knew how much Galves had told her? I rubbed Tori's shoulders, and I thought about myself, all while repeating nonsense comfort words, words that did no such thing.

She mumbled something I didn't catch while scrubbing the sweat off her face with the blanket.

"Sorry, what?" I said.

"Are you a mother?"

I withdrew my hand. "Nope." My normal answer sounding more chipped than chipper.

"Then you can't know what this is like."

"True."

"You shouldn't have your job if you haven't had a child."

This I'd heard before, too—many times. Usually I just *mmm*'d. People who thought that were simply wrong, and it didn't bother me. This time, though, something tightened inside my chest. I said, "Yeah, fine. Tell that to all my male peers."

She made a snarling noise and said, "I want someone *else*. Not you."

"You've got a psychiatrist coming to help, but I'll stay with you till she gets here." I glanced at the wall clock, which seemed to be stuck. The second hand was moving, but time wasn't.

"I don't need a fucking therapist. I want my husband! I need a real doctor!" Her chest heaved as her voice rose. "I'm still *having contractions*, you're all lying to me, my baby is *stuck* and you won't help me!"

Ooh, that was going to be fun for the other ER patients to hear. I gave a careless giggle that I swallowed as fast as it had arisen.

Shit, I was still drunk. I could feel it in the way my knees were hot and my neck loose. When I was sober, I was rigid as a steel beam. My muscles only ever relaxed when I was a little bit loaded. *Shit*. Where were all the other doctors? Why didn't the ER doc on duty poke her head in to check what was happening? This woman was my case, but I could use some backup.

"She's trying to take my baby away from me!" Tori screamed over my shoulder. "Somebody help me!"

I was drunk and hungover all at once, and I was going to lose the job I'd been born to do. And this woman thought I was trying to steal her baby. The poison—and that's what it felt like—was affecting every part of my body. My knees wouldn't lock into place. My speech was slower than my brain needed it to be.

In a moment I'd regret over and over again, I leaned forward. My words were a sluggish hiss. Pure cruelty came out of my mouth, which still tasted like burning hospital mixed with cinnamon. "You don't have a baby. There never *was* a baby. This is your fault, *not* mine. Just shut your goddamn mouth until the shrink gets here."

It was savage. I regretted it as fast as my slow mind would allow me.

"Go!" Her voice was a shriek. "Get out! Get the fuck out of here!"

My heart thumped wetly in my chest. "I'll get you a sedative." *Hysterical pregnancy*. The woman was hysterical, and I'd made her that way by doing a shit job of managing her. And now I was going to sedate her. It was the nineteenth century all over again up in here and I was suddenly the fucking patriarchy. I pushed through the curtain, my hands shaking. Someone else had to take this case. It couldn't be mine. It couldn't be me. But I was famous for gritting my way through things other people wouldn't. Fourteen-hour surgeries, seventy-two-hour shifts. In my mother's house, if you asked for help, you got mocked, or worse. I did *not* ask for help.

There was a scrabbling noise behind me, but I ignored it. Luke was taking an older man's blood pressure and gave me a quizzical look. "Stay out if you can," I said quietly. "She needs a shot of Ativan and the psych provider, *now*."

I couldn't wait for Luke even though the nurses usually got the meds, so I grabbed a preloaded carpuject syringe from the med room fridge and headed back, reluctantly. The charge nurse said Rasinski was on his way, but he was stuck in traffic, and there was no one else on call. That left me on the hook with her until either the labor deck had a woman actually pushing a baby out of her body, which would take priority over Tori (but please, God, not that, I wasn't sober enough for an actual birth—I knew that now), or until I could sign her over to Psych.

I was the first one to see the blood that ran out from under bed two's curtain in a widening pool.

"Fuck, fuck, *fuck*." I yanked the cloth back. "Code blue!"

Tori was still on the gurney, her face a gray-white under the mass of orange freckles. The rest of her was blood red, including her hands, which rested inside her body. Like, *inside*. She raised them to show me. "There's nothing there," she whispered. "Nothing." Clots of blood dropped to her already blood-soaked thighs.

I couldn't tell at first what she'd used to cut herself open, because I was moving too fast. I dragged on gloves and looked for the weapon. Tori's hands were full of blood and what would turn out to be part of her abdominal wall. She'd lost so much blood she was now almost unconscious; if we didn't get the bleeding stopped, her heart wouldn't have the pressure to pump the blood and would quit. But I'd seen people perform unbelievable feats of strength two seconds before they died, so I was careful as I slid my fingers along her arm and down to her hand—*Please don't be a scalpel. Please don't be a razor. Please don't let her come up swinging.*

A plastic Papermate pencil. That was all it was.

She'd ripped open her belly with a fucking yellow mechanical pencil and no anesthesia, almost silently.

Tori passed out then, a slump that almost slid her off the gurney. All hands were on deck for the next three hours. George Howell, the general surgeon on call, put her body back together. It couldn't be my job. It was a trauma case, not a birth, thank God. But I stood in the room, huffing the foul breath inside my surgical mask, praying. I'd never prayed as an adult, and the words I was coming up with felt stupid. *Please help her. Please help her.* Once I slipped and prayed, *Please help me.*

But I couldn't pray for that. I didn't deserve to. It was all my fault— I'd left her alone after callously telling her a brutal truth she wasn't ready to hear because I was panicked about my own life going up in flames.

As soon as the surgery was done and Tori was resting in Recovery, I got sent home. Dr. Howell didn't even say anything, just pointed. He'd been filled in by someone, I could tell. Probably Galves.

The next day, I wobbled into Walters's office. I almost broke a tooth from grinding my teeth as he waited for me to be able to talk. Finally, he said patiently, "You'll have to say it, Jillian. I can't say it for you."

My skin crawled. By then I hadn't had a drink in more than twenty-four hours, and I was in the beginning of withdrawal, although I hadn't admitted it to myself yet. "I need help." The magic words conjured the forms I needed.

I tried not to think about freckle-faced Tori Newbold, who'd ripped herself open after I'd added to her vast chasm of pain. I dealt with miles of paperwork, and they took me to a place where at first I felt like a prisoner and then I never wanted to leave.

EIGHT

Bree and Maggie and Camille looked at me. Waiting. How long had I been sitting there, remembering? Seconds? A whole minute?

"Okay." My voice sounded stupid in my ears. "I went to work still tanked. The head nurse was onto me and demanded I blow into a Breathalyzer, but before I could, I got paged to the ER, where a woman was having false labor with a phantom pregnancy. I was an inebriated asshole to her. I talked to her like you talk to the bartender after they cut you off. Because of that, she sliced open her own stomach to get the baby out. She almost bled to death."

Bree whispered, "Holy shit."

Maggie said, "Phantom pregnancy? Is that *real*?"

I shrugged. "Yeah. It doesn't happen often, but sometimes the body thinks it's pregnant and just runs with it."

"That's insane," said Camille. She had her arms wrapped tightly around her baby bump. "They think there's a baby in there but there's not?"

"Yeah."

She looked down. "How can you tell . . . What if—"

"Oh, don't worry. If you've seen your baby on an ultrasound, you're for-sure pregnant. It's a super-rare condition."

Camille looked doubtful but then nodded.

Bree said, "Did the woman die?"

"She ended up being okay and didn't sue me for malpractice, which was a miracle. I don't think she knew I was drunk—she was just having her own emergency and I fucked it up." A small, shameful part of myself was enjoying their attention.

Maggie shook her head. "That's a *terrible* story."

Bree held up a hand. "Hey, no judgment."

I was surprised. I thought for sure she'd have an opinion about my actions.

"Oh, I'm not judging." Maggie grinned. "I'm in *awe*. Any rock-bottom story that includes someone almost bleeding out is pretty hard-core."

"Thanks for sharing, Jillian," said Bree, the way we did when someone spoke at a meeting. Camille and Maggie echoed it.

Should I have shared it? I'd done it to get back at Bree for betraying a confidence, to show her that I was brave where she was cowardly, but at some point, my baser desire to bring her down a peg had disappeared.

A dog barked on the beach, a bang of punctuation. The urge I had to take it all back—or to run—went away.

The truth was out there. I'd said it. It became real, right then and there. Other people knew. Not just me and Nicole, who, as my sponsor, had heard everything. I'd never even told Rochelle about that day. And these three women were watching me.

This was what Bree and I had wanted when we'd formed the group.

Real women talking about hard things, knowing we could support one another through them. That had been our goal.

For one long, tired moment, I basked in the feeling of being heard. Then, in a heartbeat, the satisfaction fled.

How did I know they weren't judging me? Honestly, how could they not be? Of course they were. Humans judged. None of us could help it. It helped us keep our communities safe, helped us to protect the insider and throw the outsider into the cold night.

Something shifted in my core, and goose bumps broke out on my arms.

What were they going to say about me behind my back now? The urge to run came back.

Abruptly, I said, "I think I should go." I shouldn't have told them. Stupid. My insides boiled, like I'd poured vinegar and baking soda down my throat at the same time. A horrible sick fizz burned through me. I used the arm of the sofa to push myself to standing.

"Oh, honey, don't run away," said Bree. "You did a good job. Courageous. What bonding we're doing. You've got to love that brave feeling, right?"

She was congratulating *me* on being brave? When she couldn't even . . . A case of wine from Melinda Gates? That was just ridiculous. Maybe she *had* drunk it all. Maybe she hid away everything that didn't look good on her, including a relapse on purloined champagne. I regretted knowing her secret, but I bet she regretted me knowing it even more.

"I have to work a twenty-four tomorrow, and I really need sleep."

They all stood. We exchanged kisses. Bree walked me out, again pushing away my apology for hitting the wall of her house. Her smile seemed genuine.

But as I got to my car, I couldn't help myself. The other women were still in the house. I hadn't seen Hal since I'd gotten there. I leaned against the open car door and said quietly, "Will the baby's skin color be a giveaway? Is that the problem? Or is the guy still in the picture?"

Bree didn't so much as blink. "Sorry. What do you mean?" Her expression remained perfectly friendly.

"What we were talking about the other day. Your paternity test."

"I beg your pardon?"

"In the car. The envelope."

She looked down. "Oh. The genetic testing. Just a carrier screening. CF runs in Hal's family. But our doctor said we should know a little more soon, and I'm trying not to be overly worried. Hal's confident the baby is fine. He says he can feel it, and he's actually very intuitive. I trust him. So you're hosting next, right?"

My mouth opened and then closed. That envelope I'd seen—PaternityUSA did one thing and one thing only. It wasn't a genetic testing lab.

"Right." I gave a short nod. There was no use in climbing a wall when someone was actively adding stones to it from the top. She was firmly outside my hula-hoop. Still, I felt a jab of pain—we were good friends. Or at least I'd thought we were. "Whatever." I slammed my car door shut.

As I drove away, I saw her in my rearview, standing rigidly at attention, her fingers pressed to her lips.

NINE

Most women only had two ultrasounds, one in the first trimester to confirm their due date, and one at four and a half months to confirm the gender of the baby and that everything was okay. A third was only scheduled if the OB was worried about something. *Or* if the pregnant OB had friends in the right places and just wanted to see the shape of her baby again. I craved seeing V stretch lazily in my uterus the same way I craved water and light and peanut butter M&M'S. I didn't consider it risky—2D ultrasounds were the safest radiological modality we could offer to women—but even though there were no known biological effects, insurance companies weren't comfortable with the risk of some negative effect being discovered in the future. My third one wouldn't go through our insurance like everything else did. Instead, it went through LaDawn, the scheduler, and Beatrice, the sonographer, and no one else really needed to know.

Rochelle was late, as usual.

When it came to investing money, Rochelle never dropped her image of perfect LA power lesbian who would work her ass off for her "favorite" clients (she told them all they were her favorite). Rochelle wore her sleek, almost-ironic-but-not-quite pinstripe suits like she wore her jeans on days off—like they were a second skin that felt good. Spending her firm's money with a carefree hand, she never forgot a client's spouse's birthday or any of their children's names. She was never, ever late.

But, in classic *I should have seen it coming*, she'd rarely given me that same courtesy. If we had a date to meet after work for dinner, I could count on her to arrive no less than thirty minutes after I got there. She could never remember which of my friends were from AA and which were from work. She'd greet Camille with a hearty, "Hey, Colleen!"

And she hadn't been on time for anything baby-related even once. Granted, there weren't many appointments to keep, compared to other women. I was mostly monitoring myself. When it came time for the baby to be born, Kelli Clover would be my OB. We'd gone to med school together and I couldn't choose a better person to catch V.

Of course, I couldn't do my own ultrasound, but the nice thing was that they wouldn't have to send the images to anyone. Normally, *I* was the anyone they'd send them to, but while I was on the table, I got the information in real time.

I was already sitting on the table and chatting with Beatrice. She was always up on the latest streaming series, so I listened as she told me about the goriest show she'd seen recently. "Anyway, the way that dude left the knife in all the victims, you just *knew* he was a chef."

I thought of Camille. "I've got a friend who works at Crime-Watcher. She makes all those shows."

Beatrice stood stock-still. "Can she get me in?"

Startled, I said, "To what?"

"I don't know. Backstage, I guess. Or into the writers' room? I'd love to know how much of the story is constructed versus taken from real life, you know, on those docudramas? I wanted to be a TV writer a long time ago."

Oh, Los Angeles. Why would I be surprised my sonographer had wanted to be in the industry? "Sure, I'll ask her."

"*Awesome.* My brother is gonna be *so* jealous. Hey, what about your family? Are they excited about this one coming? Is the little one going to have aunties? Uncles?" She patted my belly with the confidence of a person who touched other bodies all day long.

"Rochelle and I are both onlies." My parents had struggled to have me, although they didn't attempt medical intervention, of course. My mother had told me as much. *I wanted a little girl so I prayed and got you.* I wanted her to keep going, to list all the nice things about me that she was grateful for. Instead, she'd always go on with her wants list. *I wanted a girl who was obedient and who knew her place. A little girl who honored her parents and the Lord in everything she did.* The empty space hung in the air. I was a girl. That was about it. I wasn't anything else she wanted. I always demanded too much, I knew. I was too loud, too fast, too impetuous, too filled with the devil. I wasn't easy—she'd wanted something different when she'd wanted a baby. Instead of being able to simply show me off every once in a while like some kind of godly prop, she had to feed and clothe and bathe me. There'd always been an edge of impatience in everything she did for me.

"That's okay, hon." Beatrice flicked a look at the clock above us. "Family. Right?"

"You're telling me." Rochelle and her late ass could bite me—she could just look at the still images later if she couldn't be bothered to arrive on time. Let her figure them out without my help. She'd be left thinking V had three arms and no legs and a head too small for her body.

But then—of course—the door opened.

"Hey, you." She jerked her head at me in that confident way she had. She was here, and she knew everyone would be glad. And they usually were.

I used to think that confidence was sexy. "You're late."

"So, anyway, I was wondering."

I had this theory that she couldn't even hear the words *You're late.* To her, they were merely white noise. "Mmm?"

"Can Domi be here for this, too?"

Apparently I'd been mid-swallow when she asked, because I was suddenly choking on my own spit. Beatrice patted me on the back as I coughed. Rochelle waited calmly, as if she thought my difficulty to breathe was part of the ultrasound.

I finally had enough air to say, "Are you serious?"

Ro flashed that wide, cheeky grin, the one that had won me. "She's in the hallway. I know it's crazy, but she's *so* excited to meet V, and I thought it would be great if she did that here."

"You realize she hasn't met *me*."

"No time like the present, right? I'll leave it up to you, though. Totally your call."

"You left her in the hallway. How is that leaving it up to me? I'm supposed to just let her chill out there?" The more I thought about it, the more appropriate it seemed. "No, she can wait. You can show her the stills later."

"Oh, *come* on." Her voice made it all my fault. "She's going to be V's coparent. And you can't be bothered to even meet her?"

Beatrice waved a silver package. "I need more HD paper—I'll be right back."

Chicken. But I didn't blame her. I turned my head back to Rochelle. "We were going to talk about all this first. We were going to plan our meeting."

"You know me, I like spontaneity!"

"Bullshit. You plan every single thing." Except staying monogamous.

"I've changed." She caught my hand, and my heart ached with the way our fingers still naturally laced together. "Please, Jilly." She'd been the only one I'd ever let call me that. "Please do it for me. I want her to be part of this. You'll like her, I promise. No, you'll love her. I know you will."

I tugged back my hand. She was wrong—I couldn't possibly dislike a person more than I disliked Domi. How could Rochelle not understand that I was still grieving the loss of what I thought we'd had together? My life partner had become someone I barely recognized. But I wanted us to see our baby. And I knew I'd have to meet Domi at some point. Might as well be when I had backup. *Beatrice, get back here.* "Fine."

She kissed my cheek. "I knew I could count on you."

I thought I could count on you, too.

Rochelle left the room. Thirty seconds later, she returned with both her new girlfriend and my sonographer.

Domi was even worse in person than I'd thought she'd be. So tall, so thin, so blond. There wasn't a tinge of cheap yellow anywhere on her head, just a perfect platinum, a white so clear it almost glowed. Her eyes were huge and blue. Her eyelashes must have been extensions, but there didn't appear to be a lick of makeup on her face besides her lip gloss.

To her credit, Domi didn't rush to greet me. That was good. I didn't know that I could have stopped myself from slapping her if she'd tried to grab my hand or, God forbid, hug me.

Rochelle said, "Domi, this is Jillian." She had the good sense not to put her arm around her. I could still get up off this table if I needed to.

Staying near the wall, Domi gave me a small, short wave. "Hi," she said. "Thank you so much for letting me be here." I'd wanted her voice to be high and squeaky. Instead, it was rich and husky.

I sucked in my lower lip and then said, "Yeah, okay. Beatrice?"

Beatrice looked at Domi warily and then came to my side. "Let's see what baby V wants to show us, huh?" She helped me pull up my dress. For one second, I felt glorious as my body went on display. I compared myself to the stick-like Domi and found her gauntly wanting. I was a fertile goddess. I had full breasts, birthing-wide hips, a fecund belly. I commanded life. I was creation itself.

But then Beatrice tugged down the top of my underwear, and I remembered that I'd worn loose beige cotton panties that were comfortable but kill-me-now ugly. The feeling of divinity left me and instead, I just felt fat and sweaty and gross. I caught a whiff of BO, and I couldn't remember if I'd put on deodorant that morning. I didn't think I had. The smell sure as hell wasn't coming from Domi, whose perfume was both light and dark at the same time. An orchid blooming at midnight. I wanted to barf.

I tried to concentrate on the image. That's what I was here for—to gaze at my perfect child. I ignored the fact that they smiled at each other excitedly as Beatrice pushed the transducer across my belly.

There she was, my little girl, so big the wand could only pick up slices of her. There was her right elbow, her hand curled under her chin. Her heart, jackrabbiting in her chest to match the sound that filled the room.

I could keep everything to myself, I realized. If I inhaled sharply and pasted a look of worry on my face, I could screw with them so hard. Beatrice might even go along with me for a little while.

But that would be cruel.

"Everything looks perfect," I said grudgingly.

Two deep sighs of relief met my words.

Beatrice pointed out landmarks to them as I kept my eyes on the screen. Domi exclaimed over V's beauty, which twisted my heart like a wet rag. Yes, V was beautiful, and she would be even if she weren't perfectly healthy. But Domi didn't get to say it. Not on their first meeting.

Apparently, Domi didn't know when to shut up, either. "Does the ultrasound hurt?"

Beatrice answered for me, thank God. "Nope. It doesn't hurt either of them."

"What does it feel like to be pregnant?"

Raising her eyebrows, Beatrice left that one for me to answer.

I didn't want to give her a real answer. *Terrifying. Uncomfortable. Occasionally really painful. Exhausting. Exhilarating.* "It feels okay."

"Do you love it?"

What kind of a question was that? I looked to Rochelle the way I would have in the past, expecting her to have that inward-eye-roll look on her face. But she had the opposite look. Her expression was one of absolute love. I knew the look well, even though I hadn't seen it in longer than I'd realized. "Um." I didn't want to give Domi much, but I also didn't have the energy to actually lie to her. "Yeah. I do love it."

"But you never planned on having a baby." She glanced at Rochelle nervously, as if she'd realized she might be saying too much. But she continued anyway. "Right?"

Beatrice rescued me. "Nice leg definition here. See those beautiful toes?"

Domi barely glanced at my daughter's right foot. "Are you nervous about going back to work after your time off?"

V jerked as if someone had poked her. "No."

"I mean, I just—it's got to be hard. Knowing you'll be a working mother."

I locked my gaze with hers, winning when she blinked first. "Rochelle will also be one of those."

"But you'll be alone. Single. Whereas Rochelle . . ." Domi sent a shy smile to Rochelle. "I mean, we'll have a two-parent household."

I propped myself up on my elbows, suddenly unwilling to have this conversation while my head lay on paper-covered pillows. "V already has two parents." *She doesn't need three.*

Beatrice turned her back and started the printouts.

Domi held up her hands, palms out. "Oh, I know. I know. I don't ever want you to think I'm intruding. I was just saying—we were talking—"

I arched an eyebrow and looked at Rochelle, daring her to allow Domi to go on rambling. "What?" I said sharply.

Rochelle's voice was blunt. "What if it's too hard for you?"

Beatrice swung back to me. "Do you want me to clean you up?"

I grabbed at the paper towels. "I've got it." I swiped at my stomach, furious that they were looking at me from this angle, at my folded chin, the underside of my gelled belly, my ugly beige panties. I tugged my dress down and struggled to sit up. Rochelle stepped forward to help and I almost hissed. Beatrice gave me her arm and I finally got my head up and my legs swung over the edge.

Then I was ready. I faced Rochelle head-on. "Would you like to ask me that again? Because the way you said it sounded like you thought my being a mother might be too difficult for me to handle alone. I'm *sure* that's not what you meant, so I'm wondering if you'd like to re-phrase that question."

Rochelle nodded calmly. "Of course. Beatrice, would you mind giving us the room for a moment? This is a family conversation."

Family. With *Domi*.

Beatrice, bless her, said, "I'll leave that up to Jillian."

I spoke through gritted teeth. "I'll be okay. But thank you, Bea."

Once Beatrice had shut the door behind her, Rochelle said, "We just want you to know we're here if you need us. For anything. For everything. If you decided it was all too hard, we're here."

Confused, I glanced at Domi before remembering she was the enemy. "What exactly are you saying?"

I saw the muscle in Rochelle's jaw twitch, the one that jumped when she was angry. But she kept her tone smooth. "I know you did this for me."

"Yeah, I did." I put a hand on either side of my belly. "And now I'm doing it for us." I meant for her, and for me, separately. We weren't an *us* anymore. I *had* to have misunderstood. I'd have a laugh about this later with the Ripleys. *I honestly thought my ex wanted to take my baby from me. Can you even imagine?*

Rochelle took one of those deep breaths, the kind that comes up from the bottoms of your shoes, the kind that you take before you do something terrifying. Rochelle wasn't scared of much. "Jillian. If you were okay with it, we'd love to ask you for sole custody of the baby."

I punched the word into the air with all the force in my body. "*No.*"

She didn't back down, but I saw sweat bead at her hairline. "We'll be mediating alimony soon, and between Domi and me, we make a lot more than you and I ever did together. We're prepared to give you an amount that would make you very comfortable. An excessive amount, honestly. Plus, I'm willing to sign over my half of the house to you, free and clear."

It didn't make sense. Nothing made sense. "But . . . V's my baby. My child."

"Not actually yours biologically, though. My egg. Not yours."

Domi stepped closer to Rochelle and put her other hand on top of their interlaced fingers. "Honey, maybe this isn't the right—"

"Jesus, Rochelle!" The base of my neck was suddenly so tense I could barely move my head. *My* body had *made* V. I knew the state of California recognized parental rights based on the intent of conception, so I was protected—wasn't I? What if they actually took it to court? What if they sued for full custody, what if they said I wasn't good enough on my own, what if I turned out to be a bad mother like my own and they could prove it?

Goddamn it.

No, surely I had nothing to worry about. They'd presented a question to me, and the answer was simply no, that was all. I took a deep from-the-soles-of-my-feet breath, too. "I wish I'd asked Beatrice to stay to hear you offer to buy my baby from me. Domi, it's a freaking *miracle* I let you in here at all. Get out."

"Jilly, we're just thinking about you."

"Bullshit. Out."

They both stood, frozen. Rochelle shot a look at Domi, and I couldn't read her expression. I'd always been able to tell what she was thinking before. Or I thought I had.

"*OUT.*"

They garbled things about seeing me soon, and Domi gave some kind of thanks to me again, so grateful to meet me, but I could barely see through the waves of rage that cut black swathes through my range of vision.

Something huge swept over me, a tsunami of fear that threatened to sweep me away.

This was not how it was supposed to be.

Fuck them all the way to Echo Park. What if they *had* been trying to scare me with that whole baby-journal trick? Rochelle was the one who'd told me to look one more time, and there it had been, right where I'd left it, right where it *hadn't* been before.

If she'd been there then, she could have blown out the pilot light. She was a million times handier than I was with house stuff—she probably knew it wouldn't hurt me or the baby but that it would freak me out. She could even probably guess that I'd go next door to Greg for help.

Rochelle knew better than anyone my fear about not being a good mother because of where I came from. What if she was trying to freak me out, trying to make me doubt myself, doubt my mental state?

She wouldn't do that.

Would she?

How the hell would I know? I would have trusted the old Rochelle with my life. This Rochelle was new to me, and I wasn't even sure I could trust her with the house key anymore.

The skin of my arms tingled as a thin sweat broke over me.

But what if—

What if Domi was right? My job, with its hours, and its callbacks, how *would* I do it alone? How would I pick V up from their house after a thirty-six-hour shift and then stay awake for another twenty-four if she had colic? How would that be safe?

What if I couldn't do this? What if I couldn't be a good mother to V?

I curled my hands into fists. How *dare* Rochelle think it was okay to ask for custody?

The thing about marriage is that you always have someone on your side to help you puzzle through things. You have someone to hold you when life is hard. Someone to listen when you shout about life's injustices and to soothe you when you lose your shit. When your partner leaves you, though, the only person who could put you back together is gone, as if she never existed.

Did she know that? Was she capitalizing on it, pushing against my exhaustion and anxiety?

With a click of the heavy door, Beatrice let herself back in and gave me a firm pat on the knee. "Well, that was something else. You okay?"

I nodded, tasting salt in my mouth.

"You'll be fine, mama." She must have said the words a million times before, like I had. They were of absolutely no use. I didn't believe her.

TEN

A week later, the Ripleys were due to descend upon my house. I'd spent the morning schlepping groceries, cursing myself for offering to host when V was two weeks away from making her way into the world.

I went through the house again with my bottle of Mrs. Meyer's geranium-scented cleaner, which always smelled like rose to me, and a clean rag. I dusted shelves that hadn't had a chance to catch a speck of dust since the last time I'd wiped them down. I straightened the guest towels in every bathroom for the fifth time. I rearranged the enormous blue hydrangea blooms from the garden and then wondered if they were too limp. I threw out the old ones and brought in five more and then wondered if they were too ostentatious.

In the nursery, I pulled open the top drawer of V's bureau and ran my fingers over the onesies already stacked inside. Shaking some out,

I marveled at their size. I should have been used to the smallness of newborns, and I was, but there had never been clothes this small in my own home.

Something thumped behind me, followed by a bang and the sound of breaking glass.

I screamed, throwing the onesie I was folding into the air, and then spun, my heart banging against my ribs.

Nothing.

I darted into the hall, my heart hammering triple time. "Hello?"

One of the women must be here early. I must have left the front door unlocked.

But it always locked automatically. I knew that. "Hello?" I called again.

Was the breaking glass the sound of someone climbing in a window? Should I run out through the nearest door, the one in the laundry room?

I grabbed the nearest thing at hand that had any heft to it—a tall votive candle decorated with Dolly Parton's face that stood on the hallway shelf. Rochelle must have let herself in. No—that wouldn't explain the breaking glass.

"Ro! Is that you?"

No one answered me. My hands went to ice, and I almost dropped the candle. I crept farther down the hall toward the kitchen, where the thump had come from. I yelled, "I've already called the police. John, bring the gun!" As if there were a John. Or a gun.

I'd heard no other noise since the thump and breaking glass. The AC was off, the house silent. Too quiet. Something was wrong. My head stayed on its swivel as I moved toward the front of the house. It felt as though someone were creeping up behind me even though every time I looked around the hall was still empty. The atmosphere was chilled and electric, like I was walking behind something spectral that refused to reveal itself to me.

Then—claws. Scrabbling on the hardwood.

Fred flew around the corner and down the hall the way he did in the early mornings after he'd had too much catnip.

One hand on my belly, the other holding the heavy votive, I rounded the same corner, where I could see into the kitchen.

A chair was on its back, and the glass I'd been drinking water out of was shattered on the floor.

Nothing else.

Nothing except that creeping quiet. I couldn't even hear Fred anymore, and I was sure he was hiding under my bed, which was where he went in times of stress. I took a deep breath. It had been him, obviously. I'd been looking at some lab paperwork at the table, and earlier, Fred had gone to sleep on the pages. They were scattered now, as if he'd woken and bolted, knocking over the glass as he went.

Knowing it had been the cat should have calmed me, but it didn't. Sure, Fred zoomed without apparent reason sometimes, but what if something had caused him to?

My rapid heart rate went even higher. Anger at myself, maybe, for getting myself into this ridiculous place. This single-mother-to-be place. It would only get worse when V came, when she was with me in this big, echoing house. Would I be frantic all the time, listening for rustles or footsteps that would signal danger?

But there didn't seem to be a damn thing wrong or out of place except the shards of glass. No sound except the drip of water hitting the tile.

My hand shook as I replaced the candle on its shelf in the hall. *You're okay. There's nothing wrong.* I cleaned up the glass and put away the paperwork I shouldn't have let Fred sleep on anyway. I turned on Spotify to an R and B station, but the Echo device in the kitchen sounded so tinny it made the air around the music sound even more empty. I turned it off.

You're okay. There's nothing wrong. Maybe if I kept repeating it to myself, I'd eventually believe it.

I went out to my car to get the last grocery bag, the one that held the Tostitos, which were V's favorite lately. When I opened the car door, though, instead of grabbing the bag and going back into the house, I dropped into the backseat.

I pulled the door shut. The Saturday afternoon neighborhood noise—lawn mowers and leaf blowers and the whine of a motorized scooter zipping up and down the street—was instantly muffled. God bless German engineering. I wondered if it would be weird if I just lay on the seat for a while and took a nap. It was hot but bearable. And it felt safe here, womb-like.

The house, on the other hand . . .

I was being ridiculous; I knew that. The alarm hadn't tripped. It had been the cat. There was no reason for me to feel so weirded out.

Probably.

I groaned and covered my face with my hands. I'd had anosmia once after a bad cold, and my sense of smell hadn't come back for a month afterward. During that time, I'd felt almost dizzy from missing something I relied on.

Now I felt a similar existential dizziness.

My house was safe. This was true.

My car was also safe. This was also true.

But I knew this—my car *felt* safe. And my home did not.

The rap on my window made me jump even more than the thump inside had. "*Shit!*"

Bree stood next to my car, waving in at me. I opened the door and heaved myself out of the backseat (she tried to help and just made it worse). I gave Bree a belly-bump side hug. She smelled like violet and car-seat leather. I remembered watching her grow small in my rear-view mirror, her fingers on her lips.

"Sugar," she said, pushing me away so she could look at my face. "Are you trying to kill yourself? Because the car's supposed to be in the garage for that. Not in the driveway."

I grimaced. "You're so helpful."

"It's true. I give until it hurts."

Okay, so we were going to gloss over the fact that she'd lied her face off to me in our last conversation. Was I okay with that? On a normal Saturday, no. But this wasn't a normal Saturday. I was exhausted and freaked-out, and the sight of a friend, no matter how awkward the relationship, lifted my heart. She could talk out the truth with me when and if she wanted. For now, I'd simply be grateful she was here. "It's good to see you."

"What were you doing in there? You have a whole house to mope in."

"I guess I was just thinking."

"About?"

Tears rose at the back of my throat. What the hell? I had no interest in crying. But my body did, apparently. "Tired," I gasped. "That's all."

Bree gave me a slightly horrified look, which was quickly masked by one of concern. "There, now! If you cry, I cry. Want to go inside? *Two* pregnant crying ladies are apt to make passersby call an ambulance, and I do *not* feel like flirting with a hot paramedic right now. I mean, who does? They're exhausting, all that savior energy."

As I struggled to smile, Maggie pulled up. She got out of her car carrying a plate of something covered in foil. She wore a bright blue lace cardigan, a white blouse, and skinny jeans that were just starting to pooch in front. I kissed her quickly on the cheek before leading them both inside.

Flapping my hand toward the blue velvet chair Fred had scratched almost to pieces, I said, "Please don't mind the—"

Bree cut me off. "If you say one word about your lovely home, we will slap you. It's always so nice to be here." She handed me the bag she'd been carrying. The smell of a Diptyque Feu de Bois candle rose to my nose, and I peeked inside.

Not one but *three* candles. Two hundred bucks in a paper bag. "Good Lord, Bree, I brought you sparkling water the other day."

She put her hand to her collarbone delicately. "Oh, stop. Accept.

You'll probably be the first of us to pop that puppy out, and we're rewarding you in advance for showing us what not to do."

Maybe burning the candles would banish the thin eeriness from the air, although I didn't feel strangeness in the house now, with them. Only when I was alone.

Maggie pulled the foil off the plate. "Look."

Snickerdoodles, a double-layered pile of them. My absolute favorite, the kind of cookie I couldn't get enough of right now. I was okay at making them, but compared to Maggie's, mine tasted like they came from a box. Hers were somehow so soft they almost melted in your mouth, but they were a little chewy at the same time. They were miracles, and she'd promised me her secret recipe. *After the baby is born,* she'd said. *Let me make them for you until then.* Maggie was so much better at giving gifts than Bree was, but I bet Bree would never realize that.

I grinned. "You shouldn't have. And I mean, you should have. *Thank* you."

"I'm so glad to see you!" Her hug was swift and hard. "How have you gotten so much bigger in just two weeks?"

To my everlasting embarrassment, the tears came back in one big old soggy-tissue lump in my throat.

"I'm so sorry!" Maggie looked mortified, her face turning red. "You look beautiful. The growth is all baby. You look perfect."

I couldn't care less how I looked. I turned to hurry to the kitchen, hoping she hadn't seen my face. "I'm good. Let me get you drinks." My words were strangled.

They followed, asking if I was okay and then telling me it was fine if I wasn't okay.

"You can cry around us, you know," said Bree. "You're *supposed* to cry around friends."

"I brought extra tissues in my bag just for this. I might cry with you," said Maggie. "If it helps you feel less alone."

Not looking over my shoulder, I peered into the fridge as if its contents would surprise me.

I felt, rather than saw, Bree give Maggie a sharp look. "What do *you* have to cry about?"

Maggie's voice stayed even. "Everyone's got something, Bree. Not all of us have a Hal to fix everything."

Ouch. What was with them? "Ice water? LaCroix? Sparkling plain? Iced tea?" I turned to fill the electric kettle with water. "I can make coffee, too, if you want it. I have regular, or if you want decaf, I have Swiss Water Process."

The doorbell rang.

"Can you let Camille in? Both of you?" I pressed my hands against my hot cheeks. "I need to check on something."

There was a silent pause as they looked at each other, and then they left the kitchen. Thank God. I took a deep breath. A hug had almost undone me. This was bullshit. How was I going to make it through a whole afternoon with them?

I slit open two bags of Tostitos while I listened to their laughing voices, which almost immediately fell to a suspiciously quiet level. Twenty seconds passed before Bree and Maggie swept Camille into the kitchen.

By then, I had my work face on. I smiled widely. "Camille. So good to see you."

She put a box of Compartés chocolates on the island and moved in for the kiss. "Hi, you. You're as big as a billboard."

I kept my voice light. "I'll take out advertising! Something to drink?"

She stepped backward and folded her arms awkwardly. "Maggie said she made you cry."

"Nonsense." My mother's word—I'd never heard it come out of my mouth before. "Allergies."

"Oh, yeah? To what?"

"Um." I couldn't think of anything. "Hydrangeas." But even as I protested, the tears rose again.

Camille said gently, "Like the ones you fill your house with, from your front garden? Come on, sweets. You know we want to hear about it, but only if you want to share it with us. We're not going to push you."

Bree said, "Oh, I'll push. But I'll try to do it as gently as I can."

Beside her, Maggie frowned. "So, not that gently."

What was the undercurrent between them? Had they argued? Did Maggie also feel weird about Bree and what she showed us in her life versus what she kept hidden?

"I *have* to get you something to drink." It was of utmost critical importance that I do my job. "And I have sandwiches. Look. So many sandwiches, from my favorite little place down on the water. I'll cut them into pieces."

I reached toward the knife block for my favorite sharp paring knife. Rochelle had always teased me that I enjoyed blunting the edge of it just so she could sharpen it again for me. One of those cute-slash-annoying couple things. I used that knife for everything, from opening Amazon boxes to cutting tomatoes.

The knife wasn't there.

It wasn't in the sink, or in the dishwasher, either. I couldn't actually remember when I'd last used it—yesterday? The day before. It was recently. I'd been in the kitchen . . . slicing an apple; that was it. The knife had to be close by.

But it wasn't.

The women stared at me as I pulled open drawers and slammed them shut. "It's got to be here."

"What, honey?" Bree took a step toward me.

"The knife."

She pointed at the knife block. "One of those?"

"No, *my* knife."

I checked every drawer and rechecked the dishwasher. Sweat broke over me as I yanked open drawers I'd already looked into twice. They stared. The knife had disappeared into thin air.

Then it hit me.

It was my *favorite* knife. And only Rochelle knew that.

ELEVEN

My world slowly turned, and V matched the rotation inside me.

"I can't find my knife." I looked at them and said it again, as if they hadn't understood it the first time. "I think Rochelle took it."

"It's okay, sweetie," Bree said. "It's here somewhere."

"No. There's something wrong."

"Is Rochelle messing with you?" Camille's eyebrows rose. "I'm irritated as hell at work and my mother-in-law's still on our couch, and I'd love to take it out on someone."

Maggie glanced at the other two. "You think Rochelle came in and took your knife?" I could hear a pale tinge of disbelief in her voice.

"I know it sounds—I know, but she's done it before. She took our baby book, and then she put it back. And there was a—" I broke off before I said anything about the gas leak. The words were stupid and empty. And honestly, why would Rochelle take my damn knife? How could I even imagine for a second that she could be out to get me? I was carrying her child, for cripe's sake.

It had to be me. Along with the windows I kept forgetting I'd opened, and the AC blowing colder than I ever remembered setting it. My brain—

"I think I might be going—" I choked on an idiotic sob. The world was officially falling apart, and there were witnesses to me realizing it. The real tears started then, and I was too busy trying to hide my face to do what I really wanted to do, which was run to my bedroom and lock the door, leaving them on the other side.

With a look over my head at Bree, Maggie grabbed three LaCroixs out of the fridge. Bree picked up a sandwich tray and gestured for Camille to grab the other one. "Come on, Jillian. This way."

They put me on the couch in the living room. When it appeared that they really weren't going anywhere, I lay on my side and blindly turned my face into a pillow, willing myself to disappear into it. But that would have required being able to breathe, something I couldn't do while sobbing with my nose buried in the pillow, so I came up for a gasped grab of oxygen and went back down again.

One of them—I wasn't sure which one—sat at my head and stroked my hair. Another one sat behind my knees and put her hand on my hip. I cried for twelve years. Or maybe five minutes. The whole time, they were there. None of the three spoke. They just sat with me until the dam stopped overflowing its banks.

I hiccupped. The pillow I'd cried into was soggy. I rolled over onto my back. It had been Camille's fingers in my hair, and Bree's hand on my hip. Maggie sat on the floor with her fingers on my arm. I brushed them all off and struggled to sit up. None of this was okay. "I *hate* this."

Camille laughed lightly. "We know."

Heat rose in my chest—a good dose of anger that felt way better than the tears had. "I'm serious. I really, really hate crying in front of anyone."

And the women just ignored me.

"Ain't nothing like a good cry." Bree helped me move my feet to the floor. "Don't you *dare* apologize for it, either."

I scowled. "I also hate people telling me what to do. I'm sorry. So there."

She knocked my shoulder lightly with hers. "Fuck off, darling. I'm short, but I can still take you."

A tightness in my chest eased. So what if Bree wanted to keep a secret hidden? It didn't really matter in the long run, did it? All four of us were fighters and screwups who'd landed in recovery. None of us were perfect. My mother had always demanded perfection from me. So did my job, with good reason. Most of all, perhaps, so did I. These women might be the only people who didn't expect perfection from me.

Maggie moved easily into a cross-legged position, still small enough to move gracefully. She squeezed my hand briefly but thankfully didn't hold it. "You want to tell us about it?"

"No." I absolutely did not. They'd already seen enough. They'd seen more than Rochelle had in years. I did not lose it in front of anyone. I didn't lose it, period.

They waited, looking at me expectantly. Bree had her head tilted, ready. Camille nodded encouragingly.

I pushed back my damp hair. "I don't actually *know* what's wrong. It's just—something's off." Facts, not emotions. I could share facts with them. "So Rochelle brought her girlfriend to my sonogram last week."

"Rude," said Maggie. Her face went from sympathetic to annoyed in the space of a second, and I had to admit, I liked it.

"Yeah. It got a lot worse when they asked if they could have my baby. For keeps. Full custody, for more alimony and her half of the house."

While Camille and Maggie gasped, Bree gave a screech of laughter and fell forward over her belly. Coming back up, she exclaimed, "Oh, my God! She literally offered to buy your baby? Did you punch her in the balls? Did you slice off her kneecaps with a rusty saw?"

The temerity of Rochelle's request hit me full force again. How could Rochelle have even *imagined* it would be okay to ask me? "No. I wish I had, though."

"*Fuck* her and her bimbo girlfriend," Maggie said. "You're keeping the house. Obviously."

I looked around at the light green walls. Ro and I had argued over the color and I still thought it was too yellow. Every square inch of this place held a memory. "Do I even want the house, though? It just feels wrong. We built a life here together, and now I'm alone in it. Lately it's . . ." What? Eerie? Ominous? Those were big words for the feeling that had crept into my home.

Bree's voice was all boss. "Stop that. You take that asshole for all she's worth."

My left eye twitched. "That's the thing, though. Rochelle is inconsiderate and always late and obviously cheated on me and left me for another woman, but I've also seen her literally help old ladies across the street. She repainted a stop sign in our neighborhood when someone graffitied it. But now—stuff keeps happening. Things get moved. Doors and windows open and close. The pilot light on the water heater blew out. My knife—I usually wash that knife right away and dry it by hand and put it back because I use it so much, but now it's gone? I keep telling myself it's baby brain, but what if Rochelle's messing with me?"

Bree set her can of LaCroix carefully on a coaster. "Messing with the woman who's carrying her child? She wouldn't dare. She's not that stupid."

Camille reached into her purse—I assumed she'd pull out her phone and check work e-mail, but instead she came out with a lip gloss. This was maybe the longest I'd ever seen her not touch her cell. She said, "Jillian, I hear you, but Olivia keeps catching me doing things that I would swear I didn't do. Yesterday, she watched me put my keys in the refrigerator. Bitch didn't say anything and then later she asked me where I thought my keys were. She laughed for like an hour. I had literally no memory of doing it." She swiped the dark burgundy color over her lips.

"These weren't her keys, though," said Maggie. "A knife is different."

Camille rubbed her lips together and touched the corners with her pinky. "It's still not a threat. Honey, misplacing things is a sign that we're not in control of our own minds right now. No one knows that better than you, right, Jillian? Like, isn't this what you tell your patients?"

All the time. *All* the damn time. "Yeah."

Bree held out her hand and Camille passed her the gloss. It looked different against Bree's pale skin, but still good, more red than the brown it looked against Camille's darker complexion. Camille said, "That's great on you."

Bree looked pleased. "Thanks. Okay, Jillian, I'm with Camille here. I'm betting that there's nothing weird going on. Oh, damn." She stood, one hand on the coffee table, one hand on her lower back. "I have to pee. And by that, I mean I think I'm going to take a *giant* poop, so I'm going to use your bedroom bath, that okay, Jillian?"

Maggie snorted as I nodded and waved my hand.

Camille leaned closer to me. "Have you changed your locks?"

"I only thought of that after the ultrasound. I haven't done it yet because Rochelle *does* come in and out to get our baby journal—"

Camille and Maggie both looked startled.

Maggie said, "Oh, my God! That's got to stop! You're getting divorced!"

I still hated hearing the word. My stomach tensed. "I know."

"So get the locksmith here tomorrow. Tonight! Change everything. From here on out, she can only come in when you're home. When it's a good time for you."

"I *have* been feeling so creeped out . . ."

Maggie nodded. "Changing the locks will solve all that. Promise us you'll do that?"

Maybe it would actually make me feel safe again. I nodded and blinked, trying to pretend the tears that filled my eyes again weren't there. "She's going to get to hold my child while I'm not there." They both knew I wasn't talking about Rochelle. *Domi, holding my baby.* "How did I get here?"

Maggie's brow furrow got a micron deeper. "Totally unacceptable. Rocking your baby and changing her and singing her to sleep on nights Rochelle is out late at work? You can't let that happen."

Camille shifted. "To be fair, she's Rochelle's baby, too. Legally, maybe even more so."

I wanted to snap at her, to tell her to shut up, but she was right. Just the thought of it made me incandescent with rage—a high, bright hum of fury filled me. If Rochelle had walked into the house right then, I would have had to leave out the back door to avoid wanting to hurt her physically.

What was I going to do?

I wanted my cat. I wanted his purr and his fluff and his big head bumping my belly. I stood even more awkwardly than Bree had. "I'm going to go find Fred."

Camille started to rise. "Can I help?"

"No, you stay. I'll be right back."

Where *was* Fred, anyway? I didn't see him anywhere. He was a social sort, and usually he'd be purring around ankles and trying to make friends.

"Fred?"

But he wasn't in the kitchen, nor was he in his usual favorite sunny spot by the back slider. He'd been sneaking into the nursery lately and sleeping on the rocking chair cushion, but the cushion was cold to the touch.

Probably on my bed, then, his second-favorite spot.

When I got to the bedroom, I didn't see my cat. I *did* see Bree bent over on my side of the bed as she rooted through my bedside drawer.

What the hell? "Bree?"

She slammed the drawer shut. "Hey!"

The hair prickled on my arms. This was weird. "Need something?"

She smoothed the two blond waves on either side of her face. "Sorry. Just looking for Tylenol." Pointing to her forehead, she added, "Headache."

No, she wasn't looking for painkillers—you didn't root around in someone's bedroom drawers for that. "Did you think to check the medicine cabinet?" I pointed. "In the bathroom? I'm almost positive there's some in there."

"Oh, good idea. I was trying to get out of there fast." She waved her hand in front of her nose. "Don't go in there. I'm just saying."

I was probably more comfortable with women's poop than most people were. "I'll get some for you." She wasn't telling me the truth again. I didn't like this new habit of hers at all.

But she smiled a brilliant Bree smile at me. "You're a *saint*. Really. What would I do without you?"

Frowning, I led her out of the bedroom. "You'd probably survive. Hey, did you see my cat when you let Camille in?"

"Yeah, I saw him out in the front yard."

I twisted to look at her, my spine protesting the sudden move. "You let him out? He doesn't go outside!"

Bree shook her head. "We didn't let him out! He was sitting next to the hydrangeas when we let Camille in."

I was already racing for the front door. Maggie and Camille stared as I shoved my feet into my Danskos and bolted outside. "Fred!"

Giving a low whistle, I looked under the flower bushes. Then under my car. "Here, kitty, kitty!" When he *had* gotten out in the past (always Rochelle's fault), he'd come to me when I called.

But I didn't hear his chirrup of greeting, and no meow trilled through the front yard. How the hell had he gotten out?

I stared at the street. Which way should I go? Which way would a cat have gone? Left? Right? When Fred was a kitten, I'd let him prowl the backyard under my supervision—something I never should have done because he'd climbed the enormous sycamore once. I'd learned that our fire department doesn't come out for cats in trees. The dispatcher had told me to leave canned cat food at the bottom of the tree, assuring me that she'd never seen a cat skeleton in a tree and that he'd come down on his own. She'd been wrong, and I'd hired an arborist on the third day. Fred was good at going up, not so good at coming down.

I went around the house and through the gate. It was off the latch, as usual. Rochelle had put off fixing it. I couldn't wait on doing that kind of thing anymore. I felt sick to my stomach all over again. Craning my neck, I looked up into the sycamore's leaves. "Fred? Where are you, Fred?"

The three women trailed behind me.

I looked up into all the trees in the backyard. No flash of orange fur.

Maggie said, "Jillian, we'll find him—"

I cut her off. "Can you look under the bushes along the house there? I'll go down to the cottage."

She nodded, and I saw them shoot a look to one another, one I didn't even care to parse.

I went down the path to our mother-in-law unit. The little building was strung with white twinkle lights, lighting it up at night like a fairy cottage. We'd been planning on setting it up as a guest room, but currently it was full of stuff we didn't feel like dealing with: a couch set that we should have gotten rid of when we got the new ones, two tables that I liked but didn't have a place for, an old queen bed that could be used for guests if necessary but never was. The door was unlocked, and I pushed it open, even though I didn't think Fred would have been able to get in—but what if a window was broken or something?

Fred wasn't there.

What *was* there were two beer bottles, Rochelle's favorite brand. One on either side of the rumpled bed. As if there had been two people in that bed, neither of them a recovering alcoholic.

I tumbled out of the cottage and slammed the door shut behind me, trying to distance myself from the images of Rochelle and Domi in my head.

I *needed* Fred. "Freddy! Where are you?" I called, ignoring the tears that rained down my cheeks. "Cat!" It was an order. "Come out, now!"

"Jillian? Can you come here?" Maggie's voice was tentative.

My lungs tightened. "Did you find him?"

"No, but we found how he got out."

She and Bree were holding back the oleander branches at the wall of the house. "Look," said Bree.

The screen to my open bedroom window—the one I'd apparently forgotten to close this morning—was propped against the wall of the house. The shelf below that window was Fred's favorite sunny spot to sleep. Of course he'd popped right out.

"I didn't take that screen off." I looked at Bree. Could she have pushed it out and somehow leaned it against the wall when she was in the bedroom? But why on earth would she do that?

And besides, she'd said Fred was already outside when she'd seen him earlier.

Maggie pointed at the ground. "Are those yours?"

Right under the bedroom window were shoe prints. A lot of the same shoe, it looked like, whorls in a pattern I didn't recognize. There was one that was almost complete. I leaned closer. "What the hell?"

"We didn't want to get too close to them. What room is this?"

"Our—my bedroom." The words chilled me. "What the actual fuck?"

"Did you have workers here recently?" The usually calm and cool Bree looked worried, and I didn't like that at all.

"No. A gutter guy back in March, but not since then."

Camille said, "Your wife's shoe size?"

"She wears a ten. That print's a smaller size. Or maybe a kid's. Right?"

Maggie nodded. "Rochelle's girlfriend? How big is she?"

Rochelle had a girlfriend. Even now, it was still completely unbelievable. "She's tall but really slender. I didn't look at her feet."

Bree pulled out her phone and unlocked it before handing it to me. "Call 911."

The police said they hoped to get someone to me within an hour. Maggie led me inside and made me eat half a sandwich, even though I felt nauseated. Camille grabbed the bag of cat food from the kitchen and went out to look some more for Fred. She came back ten minutes later with him and the bag of food in one arm, feeding him kibble with her other hand. "He was under your front porch playing with what looked like a dead mouse, so maybe you shouldn't let him lick you for a while. What a sweetie he is!" She poured him into my arms, and he set up purring on my lap so loudly he rumbled V and woke her up.

The women stayed with me while I waited for the police to come. Maggie set up shop in the kitchen—it wasn't enough, apparently, that she'd brought snickerdoodles. She said the excitement demanded fresh-baked blueberry muffins, and while I could have sworn I didn't have blueberries, she scrabbled through my freezer and pantry and came up with everything she needed. While she made a companionable clatter next to us, Camille and Bree took turns trying to distract me. Bree gossiped about movie stars she knew from charity work, and Camille kept trying to convince me to retile the kitchen. She only took out her phone to check e-mails once, and she put it away with a rueful shrug when Maggie caught her. The women's conversation shifted and twisted, and I floated along the top of it. They talked about pregnancy Pilates and soy lecithin in cheap chocolate and the best vibrators for pregnancy. What they didn't talk about was the missing knife. The screen. The idea that maybe someone was actually out to get me, and that someone might be my ex. From time to time, they'd look at me with matching faces as one of them said, "This sucks. Don't worry. It's all going to be okay," and then the river of their words would flood the banks of my brain again, and I'd be carried along with it.

It took two hours for the officer to arrive, and half of the blueberry muffins were gone by the time he knocked. Even though we'd been waiting, all of us jumped. Fred flew out of my arms and down the hall.

The officer's name was Jones, and he didn't seem to give one good goddamn crap about the footprints. It had gotten dark while we'd been waiting, so he shined his flashlight on them and just said, "Yep. They're small. You sure you weren't out here cleaning the windows?"

I stared at him. "I was not. And how do you explain the screen being removed?"

"Your cat pushed it off?"

Fred nosed the screens lightly every once in a while. He didn't hurl his body weight at them and then prop them neatly against the house.

Bree said, "I'm dismayed that you're the display of my tax dollars at work. What else can you tell us about the crime scene, Officer?"

He rolled his eyes. "You looked under any of the other windows?"

We had, but cursorily, and it had been twilight. When he got closer with his strong flashlight, we could see pieces of the same tread under three other windows. But they were light and hard to see, unlike the ones under my window.

"And you're sure you don't own no shoes with this pattern on the sole?"

"Yes," I said shortly.

"But have you actually checked? Today? If not, can you go check, please? Easy to forget a tread pattern."

It wasn't as easy to forget standing under a window, but I huffed and went to my bedroom with Maggie. She looked at half of my shoes; I looked at the other half. "This is bullshit," she said.

The words felt good. I wasn't alone.

We trooped back out to where Jones was still in the garden listening to Bree tell him how to do his job. "Just because none of the other windows appear touched doesn't mean there wasn't someone here with ill intent. Look, right there. We missed that earlier. What is that? Is that a *cigarette* butt?"

Jones reached down and picked up the light-colored object. It crackled as he pulled it out of the dirt. It was only a leaf. "Nothin' to worry about," he said.

Bree visibly bristled. "You should have worn gloves to pick that up. You're contaminating the evidence."

"Girls, I'm really thinking this is just some teenage boy trying to get a look at the missus here in her bedroom."

"*Just?*" said Camille. When she puffed up, she looked twice her size. "And if you call us *girls* again, I'm calling your sergeant to file a complaint. You seem to be thinking this is some kind of laughing matter. When you got here, she told you her partner recently moved out. And then this happens: an open window, screen removed, just *waiting* for a prowler to shimmy inside. We already told you about the missing knife, and you didn't seem to care."

"These ain't men's shoes, though."

"Wow," said Camille. "Just. *Wow.*"

He seemed to get it. "I'm sorry. Your partner is . . . female?"

"Yes," I said coldly.

"She got shoes with that tread?"

"No." My voice was ice.

"Her wife and she are separated." Maggie folded her arms. "Jillian, what about her girlfriend? It could be her, right?"

I could almost see the thought pass across the cop's razor-burned face: *angry women pissed off about cheating ex.* "I have no idea what her shoe size is," I said. "Can I get a restraining order against her?"

The cop widened his short, bulldog stance. "Against who? The wife or the girlfriend?"

I wasn't quite sure. "Whatever's necessary."

He took a deep breath. "You can absolutely petition for a restraining order if either of them has assaulted, battered, or stalked you, or if there's a credible threat of real violence. If you haven't been getting that, then no. But I have to tell you that this trespassing would only be a misdemeanor even if we could prove it, which we won't be able to."

"Call out your ID techs," demanded Camille.

"Ma'am." He frowned over his glasses at her as he tapped the fabric badge on his faded shirt. "I'm Los Angeles PD, Pacific Division. If Venice had its own police department? Maybe. But we're a little busy. LAPD isn't going to do ID on a misdemeanor trespass which has literally no suspects."

"There won't be any suspects because you won't do ID!" Camille put her hands on her hips. "What if the person got inside?"

A shiver flashed over my skin. I suppose in the back of my mind, I still hoped I'd just misplaced the knife myself.

He let his head hang in what looked like exhaustion. Then he raised it. "Do you have suspicion that someone got inside the house, ma'am?"

Maggie stepped forward. "She's missing a kitchen knife!"

He pointed, not appearing impressed. "Look at the sill."

We looked. The sill was dirty from smoggy LA air, and the dirt was only disturbed by two perfect cat prints.

"If someone went in or out that window, they flew. And all the other windows are locked with their screens intact." He took off his glasses and wiped them, his radio squawking words and numbers I didn't understand. "I'm sorry this happened to you. I wish I could do more to help," he said to me, replacing the glasses on his face. He didn't sound like he meant it. I honestly could barely blame him. "I have an incident report number for you. And that's all I can do. Look in the dishwasher for the knife, under the rack. That's where my wife always loses them. Put your screen back on, lock the window, and call 911 if anything strange happens, okay?"

TWELVE

After the officer left, the women relaxed, saying he was right, probably just a horny teenage boy. *Trying to catch a look at a hot naked lady. Imagine the poor kid! Your belly probably scarred him for life!*

I tried to believe they were right. The screen, though. That felt like more than a teen in the bushes. Every time I thought about it, my breath caught in my chest. But then again, the size of the shoes meant it really must have been a kid, maybe thinking about breaking in and running out with what—my laptop? I didn't have much in the way of jewelry. I shivered. The thought of anyone being inside my home who wasn't supposed to be there—even a teenage creeper—was terrifying. I wished for a second that Rochelle was still with me in the house. The old Rochelle, that was.

Each woman invited me to stay with her as they left. Bree bribed me with homemade waffles in the morning, made by her chef. Maggie said she'd leave coffee outside the guest-room door and not make me talk. Camille said that she could offer only a couch since her wife's mom was visiting, but three cats and a small dog would sleep on top of me, which did sound pretty nice, even if it would drive Fred crazy when I got home.

I turned them all down as we stood in my driveway, the streetlight casting a yellowish glow on the crowns of my friends' heads. "I have to be at work by six A.M. for a twenty-four. I'm going to go right to sleep. I hope."

Camille said, "What if I stayed with you? Then I'd get a break from Olivia's mom. You could use the company."

I shook my head. "I'll be fine."

Maggie said, "Are you friends with the neighbors?"

I had Greg on one side and the Fitzes on the other. "Yep. I'm good."

Bree narrowed her eyes. "You're still nervous, I can tell. I don't think there's anything to worry about, but what if I send a security guy out to stay in front of the house? Just for tonight."

"You have a security guy you could send? But no Tylenol in your purse?" I marveled at the differences between our lives. "No, thank you."

Bree made a *pfft* noise, then said, "You really are bad at accepting help, aren't you?"

"Nicole says I'm the literal worst."

"You've got to work on that. *Accept our help.*"

I choked on what I thought would be a laugh. "I don't know how to do that." I'd already cried in front of them. I just wanted them to leave so I could go inside and take off my polite face and maybe cry some more. Alone.

Maggie said, "I know an easy ask, a simple thing for you to accept. How well do you know Rochelle's girlfriend?"

"Not at all."

"Do you think she could have left the footprints?"

"I don't know."

Maggie waggled her phone. "Honestly, I'm also of the opinion it was some kid in your backyard. But just in case, you want me to find out about her?"

"I guess I should Google some more." I didn't want to, though.

"But do you have my mad private investigator ability? I got really good at internet research when I was picking out my baby's sperm donor."

I felt a twist of interest. "Okay, then. Yes."

She was already looking into her phone. "I just need her last name."

I closed my eyes. Was I ready? Probably not. But I might not ever be. "Sure. Knock yourself out. Domi Bright. I don't know if she's Dominique or something else."

Maggie put her fingers to her lips. "Not another word. I'm on the case."

Bree clapped, of course, because that's what she did. "Look at you! Letting someone help you! Good job. And I will *not* be outdone! Here's my suggestion: Why don't you go on maternity leave early?"

I frowned. I wasn't expecting that one. "I still have two weeks to go. My whole goal has been to work right up until my water breaks. I want as much time as I can afford with V when she gets here."

"You've got enough stress in your life as it is right now. Everything's upside down, your relationship, your house, your future. Your body's never been more stressed. Why add your crazy shifts on top of that?"

Speaking of stress, I wondered if Bree knew about the new dark circles under her own eyes. "I can't leave my patients in the lurch like that. I have two at almost full term."

Bree pursed her mouth. "They'll be fine. Besides, they've observed your shapely form. They knew the risk. Look at you. You're terrifying. I'd be so worried about you giving birth between my legs that I'd be irritated you were pulling focus away from me. Plus you need *rest*."

"I should—"

Camille, leaning against my mailbox, spoke up. "Screw shoulds. Shoulds are the literal devil. What about the wants? What do you *want*?"

A hollowness rang somewhere inside me. "I don't know."

Maggie nodded along with Camille's words. "She's right. They're right. You deserve time to rest. You're pushing yourself too hard. Take the time off and let the world come to you when it's ready. Stop trying to help everyone except yourself, and just let go, okay?"

Enough was enough. I promised them I'd think about it, then coaxed them into their cars. They called out *I love yous* and I said it back, waving as they drove away into the darkness.

Now I was *really* alone.

After tidying a little, I got ready for bed. I padded around the house three times, looking into the rooms. The baby's room was almost done—I still wanted to paint blue buoys and seagulls above the crib and needed to shop for exactly the perfect mobile. I thought about dragging in a futon and sleeping on the nursery floor, or in the spare room down the hall, but that wasn't where I wanted to be. Even with evidence that someone had been standing outside my bedroom window I still wanted *my* bed with its eight-hundred-thread-count sheets and its fat, lightweight down comforter.

Stubbornly, I wanted to feel in control again. Screw the teenage Peeping Tom, or the roving wannabe burglar who'd taken off my screen, thinking my house would be an easy hit. Whoever it was wouldn't keep me from being comfortable in my own home. I turned out my lights and got in bed, but I couldn't stop glancing at the window.

I was safe. The alarm was on, and I was safe.

I was safe. Maybe if I kept telling myself that I'd eventually feel better.

It wasn't working yet.

I texted my mother a picture of the sunset from the night at Bree's, glad I'd taken extras. This one had a person in it, very small, standing at the edge of the ocean. I'd taken it from Bree's patio. Mom had always said it would scare her to stand on the edge of a continent, but seeing the ocean had been her biggest wish. I had no idea if she'd realized that wish yet, but if I had to guess, I'd lay money on her not having left Utah yet. Ever.

I rolled to my other side clumsily while V kicked in protest. I couldn't smell Rochelle anywhere in the room anymore. The bed smelled like me now, a mix of sleep and my shampoo.

It was after midnight, but I texted Ro anyway. She always left her phone on, which used to drive me crazy. Late-night texts that she said were from her coworkers. (They were, just not in the way I'd thought.) So I have to admit there was a not-so-small part of myself that didn't mind the thought of me waking up her girlfriend with the *ding-dong* of her text tones. Adding to my passive-aggressive shameful pleasure, I sent multiple short texts instead of one long one.

Hi—

Sorry to bother you—

Hope you're not asleep but

There was a trespasser in the backyard.

I waited a beat on that one, rewarded by seeing the dots as she composed a text back.

What!? Are you okay?

I didn't see anything. Lots of footprints outside our—I deleted the last word—*my bedroom window. Took the screen off. Fred got out.*

Shit! Call cops? Fred okay?

Fred's fine. Cop was severely unhelpful. But he said they were small feet, a woman's or a kid's.

No response.

I tapped out, *Does your "girlfriend" have shoes with this on the bottoms?* I attached a picture of the best footprint outside and felt proud of my quote marks. It was the little things.

Are you fn serious?

Does she?

NO.

You know the bottoms of all her shoes? I'm impressed.

A pause. *Can we not. Sleeping.*

Wait, I sent. Then: *I know she knows the layout of the backyard. You left beer bottles in the cottage.*

Nothing.

Are you there? I stared, but it went unread. She'd actually put the phone down. Maybe even turned it off.

I lay in the dark, letting a freezing wave of self-pity wash over me, chased by a second wave of anger that heated my lungs. God, emotions *sucked*. No wonder I used to drink. I lay submerged for a good ninety seconds, willing myself to go to sleep and escape the feelings, but I didn't feel sleepy. I felt exhausted, yes. Every bone and every muscle in my body screamed for rest. But sleep was far away. Benadryl was safe but always gave me a paradoxical reaction, amping me up. Besides warm milk or Sleepytime tea, there wasn't anything I was comfortable taking for insomnia, and I wasn't going to drink a single extra teaspoon of liquid—I had to get up and pee every hour or two as it was. Lying in bed without sleeping had always been agony for me, and it was worse now.

A thud made my eyes fly open. No, it was more like a hollow thump than a thud, and it was *loud*.

I slammed myself out of bed, somehow heaving my body out quickly and efficiently. I was at the window before I even knew I was there. Parting the curtain, I cupped my hands to the glass, willing myself not to scream if I suddenly came face-to-face with an actual person at my window.

I'd left the backyard lights on.

There was nothing there. No one outside.

Fred padded into my bedroom.

Stupid lug. Of course, it had been him. He'd thudded off a piece of furniture out in the main part of the house and that was what I'd heard. I was lucky he hadn't broken a glass again.

I picked him up and set him on the bed. "You stay with me, buddy. You're a guard cat now." I sat next to him, petting him with one hand, rubbing my face with the other one.

I was beyond tired, seasick-exhausted. My leaden bones ached. I unlocked my phone again and left a message for the doctor on call.

"Hi, Sharon, it's me. I'm calling out. Got something coming on, maybe a stomach bug. I'll tell the answering service and send an e-mail to have the schedule revised. Thanks."

Still on my phone, I sent an e-mail to the department that managed our schedules.

In bed, I pulled the covers all the way up to my neck. It had taken less than sixty seconds to get out of going to work in five hours. I was now officially off the hook until my next twenty-four-hour shift on Wednesday.

What if I didn't go back at all till after my maternity leave?

The question echoed in my head.

No. I needed to spend that time off on the other end, with V.

But the women had been right—it was *possible* to go on mat leave now. I had savings that were mine, not connected with Rochelle's or "our" money. I could go on leave without pay for a while if I had to.

Jesus. What would I do with my time? The very thought made me want to get up and clean something. But I could barely move. Never had I had more *drive* to do things, and never had I had less energy. It was a terrible combination, one that made me feel like somehow I didn't deserve this baby I was carrying. I couldn't even do everything I wanted to do in a day. It had been difficult to order the sandwiches for the women. It had been even harder to go pick them up and bring them home. How was I going to take care of a baby by myself? Everyone said that life's busyness quadrupled with a baby, and here I was, almost unable to care for my own solitary life. And I couldn't just *take care* of a baby—it wasn't that simple. I wouldn't be a babysitter. I'd be her mother. I'd have to be perfect, or as goddamn perfect as I could be. How would I do that without regular sleep?

Fred curled into my side and purred with all his might. I stroked his head with one finger. Twenty-five, then fifty times. At seventy-five, he gave a soft snore, and when I stopped petting him, his purr trailed off and the snore picked up.

Me, though. My brain was a battery too fully charged attached to a body that was exhausted *and* twitchy, another god-awful combination. My feet felt electrical, and my legs jerked against my will so much that eventually Fred woke and grumbled his way to Rochelle's old side of the bed.

There had to be some way I could expend some energy while staying in bed. Reminded of my vibrator by the women talking about them earlier, I used it for a mechanical relief. That helped a little, but sleep felt like something other people did. And I had to sleep because—

Hang on, I didn't *have* to sleep at all. I didn't have to work in the morning. I could stay up all night and sleep all day if I wanted to.

This was what the women meant when they told me to take time off. By not having to sleep at any standard time, I could set my own schedule. It was as if someone had handed me a permission slip, one I hadn't known I needed.

I wanted to bake something. Maggie had inspired me earlier, pulling out pantry staples I'd almost forgotten I owned. I'd never be as good a baker as she was, but last year she'd given me her recipe for *pão de queijo,* and I was overwhelmed by my sudden desire for the chewy Brazilian cheese bread. Fast and easy baking: *also* what I needed. I threw the covers back and stuffed my swollen, tired feet into my slippers. I'd bake, and then I'd have cheesy puff bread, and then, come dawn, I could decide whether or not to go on maternity leave.

With one hand on the wall for balance and one hand on my stomach, I felt V do a tilted half roll. "Good girl. Let's get some stuff done."

I almost didn't notice. If I'd walked through the kitchen in the dark, as I usually did when fetching a glass of water, I wouldn't have seen it till morning, but because I was going to bake, I turned on the light.

There, in the doorway of the kitchen, stood the huge potted palm. It was always *next* to the doorway. Not in front of it. It had probably only moved a foot to the left, but I sure as hell knew I hadn't moved it.

My favorite knife was stuck into the soil at the palm's base.

THIRTEEN

I lost my breath as if V had kicked me in the lungs.

A foot-long scrape on the wood showed the heavy pot had been dragged, not picked up and moved. The thud had probably come when it thumped against the wall.

Before I knew I was even moving, I was out of the kitchen and back in my bedroom, slamming the door behind me. Running outside felt too dangerous. Who knew what was out there? Checking the rest of the house—no fucking way. I locked the bedroom door, thankful that Rochelle had wanted a deadbolt on it, and grabbed my cell phone. Nine-one-one answered after the eighth ring, which felt like seven rings too long. I told the dispatcher my address, and when she asked what was wrong, I said, "My plant moved."

A pause. "Pardon me?"

"It's a big palm plant. It moved like a ghost shoved it. But not like a ghost. I mean, I didn't move it, but I just found it in my kitchen doorway, where it doesn't belong. With a knife in it."

I heard a keyboard clicking. "A knife? Where's the knife now, ma'am?"

"Still in the pot. It's my knife that was missing. I couldn't find it earlier, but now it's in the dirt." I sounded like a crazy person. Would they come anyway?

"Mmm." She sounded concerned but I wasn't sure it was in the right way. "And when did this happen?"

I thought back to the thud I'd heard. "Maybe fifteen minutes ago?"

The dispatcher's voice got sharper. "You mean this just happened?"

"I guess." What was *just* to her?

"You believe you possibly had an intruder inside your house less than fifteen minutes ago?"

"Yes." I almost wanted to believe it had been a ghost. A ghost would be less terrifying that an honest-to-God person.

"Who else is home with you, ma'am?"

"No one." An adrenaline rush pulsed through me sickeningly. "I don't think."

"Do you live alone?"

I paused. "Yes. Now I do."

"Where in the house are you?"

"In my bedroom."

Tap-tap-tap. "Upstairs? Downstairs?"

"It's a single level."

"Is your bedroom door locked?"

Her serious voice was freaking me out even more than I already was. "Yes."

"Did you already make sure no one was in your bedroom?"

I froze. "No. I just ran back in here. Should I . . ." The door to the en suite bathroom was closed. Had I closed it? I usually left it open, didn't I? "I don't know."

"Keep your voice real quiet for me, okay? Only talk when you have to. I don't want you to move at all. If you have to drop the phone, leave the line open so I can hear what's happening."

I flattened myself in bed, pulling the covers tighter around me as if they would protect me from anything. I wanted to reach out and turn off the bedroom light so I could better hide, but I couldn't—that would leave me alone in the dark, and that would be worse. I pressed my elbows into my sides and pushed the phone so hard against my ear it hurt.

"You should be able to hear the sirens soon. Don't answer me, only speak if you need to."

In the distance, I heard the wail of a police car. It got louder as it approached. This was a far sight faster a response than I'd gotten earlier in the day for the trespasser's footprints. Apparently someone being inside your house was way more important than someone being outside it. "Should I—do I need to go open—"

"No." Her voice was brisk. "Stay where you are." More tapping, and then, "Is there a key outside?"

"In the frog to the right of the first step."

"Good. Stay right there, and tell me if anything changes."

"I'm pregnant," I whispered. "My wife left me. I had the police here this afternoon for someone standing outside my window."

"Does your wife still have a key?"

"Yeah. But she wouldn't . . ." She wouldn't what? Did I even know Rochelle anymore? And God knew I had no idea what Domi might or might not be willing to do.

"Describe her for me."

As I whispered Rochelle's description, my leg muscles tightened, as if I were getting ready to run.

The dispatcher spoke again. "Do you have any weapons in the house?"

"No. Just kitchen knives, I guess, like the one that was missing and—wait, why? Should I get a weapon?" Did I need to get a gun to live alone? But with the baby coming—a salt-tinged nausea filled my mouth.

I jolted as I heard a door slam and a man's shout. Then again.

"They're clearing rooms. When they knock on yours, I want you to yell really loudly that you're in there, okay? That's how they'll find you."

She was so calm sounding, the polar opposite of me. When I'd gotten to the point in my medical career when I'd started to be allowed to sit between a birthing mother's legs, I'd been so panicked I'd almost hyperventilated. Had this dispatcher felt the same way, the first time she got a call of someone breaking into a house?

Slam. Another shout, this time female, and then I heard feet coming rapidly down the hallway. There was a loud rap at my bedroom door. I dropped my phone to the pillow in abject fear, simply unable to hold it any longer. "I'm in here! It's me! I'm in here!"

The door handle jiggled. "Unlock the door, ma'am!"

Again, moving faster than I'd been able to move in weeks, I launched myself at the door. V wasn't slowing me down at all—it was possible that carrying her made me *faster* than normal.

An officer stepped in and lightly pushed me behind her, up against the wall. "I need you to stay right there." She swept a light under the bed (oh, God, I hadn't even thought to look under there—what if there had been someone lying underneath me, listening to every word?), and then pointed at the closed bathroom door. "Have you looked in there? Is anyone else home?"

I shook my head. "No. No one should be."

She banged a fist against the door as another officer entered my room. "Rest of the house is clear, Sarge."

The sergeant put her hand on the bathroom doorknob, her other hand holding her gun. What if Rochelle really *was* in there? What if she'd moved the plant because she . . . what? Wanted me to call the cops? Wanted me to be scared out of my damn mind so I'd think I couldn't do all this by myself? So I'd give V to her and Domi? My fingernails drove themselves painfully into my palms.

But they swept the room—no one behind the shower curtain—and then the rest of my room, including the big closet that now held only my clothes and no one else's. Their shoes clomped through the house, and I felt stupid in my bare feet and my enormous laser-cat T-shirt, now officially too small around my belly.

Then the lead officer walked me through the house slowly, asking me to identify anything else that might be missing or moved. I felt the need to keep a hand on something at all times—the wall, the dining room table, the island in the kitchen. I couldn't find anything else amiss in the house.

"So, nothing is gone?" She looked at the potted palm. She was the only cop left—the other officers had drifted away like blue-clad smoke when there was nothing exciting to be found.

"I don't think so." When we'd gone through the bedroom again, I'd pulled on a sweatshirt, but it wasn't helping. I rubbed my arms but the goose bumps wouldn't go down. *Someone had been in my house.*

The officer pointed at the planter. "And you're *sure* this wasn't here when you went to bed? Could you have tripped and pushed it and forgotten?"

She'd already asked me twice a variant of this question. Both times I'd been polite, but I was beyond that now. "I told you. You can see the drag mark. Do you think I could have really missed this before? Can you possibly think that is in any way imaginable?"

The officer glanced down at her notebook and flipped a page. "Look. I get it. I have two kids. Being pregnant is weird."

She didn't get it. This had nothing to do with me or anything I'd done. I said aloud the words that kept circling in my mind. "Someone was in my house."

"I'll get ID in to take prints. They'll probably get here in the next two or three hours."

It was just past midnight. I'd have to stay up to let them in. That was fine; it wasn't as if I'd be sleeping. I could bake, my original plan.

"You have a house alarm?"

I nodded. "I *really* thought I'd set it." But I kept doing that—meaning to do things and forgetting to actually do them.

The officer gave me a look like I'd plugged a hair dryer into a loaf of bread. "Use it." She touched her head in some kind of weird salute and passed me a business card with a number written on the back. "That's your report number, in case you need it for your insurance."

"Why would they need it?" Nothing she said made sense.

"In case something does end up missing or if your situation escalates."

A cheerful thought. V gave three wild kicks, as if in protest.

When she was almost out the door, she paused. Turning around to face me, she said, "Look. I know it's hard. My husband left right after my second was born."

"Well, fuck that guy."

She smiled. "Wise words. I wanted to ask before I leave—are you depressed?"

I frowned. "No." It was a knee-jerk answer, but it came easily because it was true.

"Do you ever think about harming yourself? Or another person?"

She had to ask. It was an important part of her job, just like it was mine at the hospital, but I hated it. "*No.*"

She bobbed her head politely. "Good. That's good. But if you did, we could talk about it."

Through gritted teeth and an ER smile, I said, "I appreciate it."

"I know you're an MD." She'd seen my diplomas on the wall of the office and had asked about them when we'd been going through the house. "Obviously you know your job better than I do. But prenatal depression is no joke. Mine moved into postpartum depression, and it was a really hard time in my life. It's what my husband blamed his leaving on, but honestly, he was just an asshole." She pointed at the card I held. "Call me if you need anything."

I shut and deadbolted the front door; then I set the alarm—*really* set it this time—so it would go off if anyone opened a door or window. I wanted to move the plant back into place and sweep up the spilled dirt, but the cop had said not to, to wait until after ID looked at it.

Back in the kitchen, I got out the ingredients for the cheese bread.

I *would* bake it, goddamn it. What was I supposed to do, sit and chew on my fingernails? I had to stay awake anyway.

It wasn't until the milk was almost at a boil that I allowed myself to unlock my phone.

I didn't bother texting. She answered on the third ring, better than the police had done.

"Were you in the house?"

Rochelle's voice was rough with sleep. "Huh? Is the baby okay?"

I faltered. I knew when she was lying. She sounded honestly confused.

Wait, that was the whole point. Domi had been a complete surprise to me because Rochelle had turned out to be such a good liar.

"Were you in this house? Tonight?"

"Shit, Jillian. No." I heard her push herself up to sitting. I assumed Domi was right there, listening. "Why?"

"Someone broke in."

"Are you hurt? What about V?"

Impatiently, I said, "We're fine. Whoever it was moved the palm a foot to the left, and left my favorite knife sticking out of the dirt."

"Jillian." A pause. When she spoke again, her words were slow. Measured. "Are you okay?"

Yeah, I could hear it, too. I sounded insane. But who would know what my favorite knife was besides my estranged wife? The same wife who was obviously deep in sleep and even though I apparently didn't know when she was lying, I did know how she sounded when she was completely clueless about something.

Or did I? Why were my hackles still raised? I didn't trust her, and I hated the feeling of it.

"Never mind."

"No, Jillian, wait."

I didn't. I just hung up.

Someone had been in my house when I was inside it.

My mind flashed to the image of Bree bent over my nightstand.

What had she been looking for, really? I didn't buy the Tylenol excuse, not for a second, but Bree wouldn't have any reason to come into my house and move a plant and a knife.

She knew the missing knife had upset me, though.

I combined the rest of the cheese bread ingredients and poured the batter into the muffin tins. *Think logically. Use your scientific brain.*

But the brain that had gotten me through med school, that kept comorbidities and statistics and dosages in little mental filing cabinets for me to pull out when I needed them—that brain didn't feel okay. I was off my game, rattled and confused. How did someone know— *really* know—if they could trust their own mind?

I put the cheese puffs into the oven. As they baked, I ate one of Maggie's blueberry muffins while scrolling Facebook, but I kept hearing the cop's voice.

Prenatal depression.

I didn't have it. I wasn't depressed. Just to convince myself, I ran through the symptoms in my head. I wasn't crying overly much (except for this afternoon). I didn't have suicidal ideation. I wasn't unable to experience pleasure from usually enjoyable activities (maybe because I wasn't *doing* any enjoyable activities). I didn't have excessive anxiety about the baby's health.

Low self-esteem and feelings of inadequacy at the idea of being a parent? Okay, sure. I had that. Anyone with my mother would have.

Paranoia.

I took a deep breath in through my mouth and exhaled slowly. In some rare cases, prenatal depression could present symptoms of paranoia.

Just once, when I was about eight, I'd asked my father why my mother didn't love me. He'd laughed, but the sound had been dull. *She loves you, Jillybilly. It's the leftover of a little depression she had when she was pregnant. Didn't quite connect with you before you came, the doctors said. Had a hard time after, too. Not your fault, babe. She does the best she can.*

The maternal-fetal attachment concept was something I was familiar with, of course. Healthy psychological well-being, family support, and having an ultrasound were all associated with higher levels. Lower levels of attachment were associated with substance abuse and high anxiety. Obvious ideas, with obvious conclusions.

But—what if I felt paranoid because of prenatal depression? What if I was tumbling down into a hereditary hole that could jeopardize both V and myself?

What if the baby book hadn't been moved—what if I simply hadn't been able to see it?

What if a gust of wind from a slammed door had blown out the pilot light?

What if Fred, who loved to run and run fast, had just run right through the screen? It *could* have bounced against the bushes and landed upright, leaning against the wall.

What if it was all me? My heredity pushing me into something darker? I pushed a memory away, one I wasn't willing to walk through. Not right now. I continued to stare at the oven clock, watching it click the minutes past until my eyes blurred.

No one could tell how their body would change during pregnancy, and changes in sleep patterns were common. Women who'd never had night terrors woke up screaming. Other women who'd never had insomnia a minute of their lives couldn't sleep for six months. Some women started to sleepwalk. What if I'd taken a nap and hadn't woken up from sleepwalking? What if I'd moved the plant myself? Could I have stumbled and knocked it to the side?

How would that explain the knife, though? Maybe I'd used it for something and forgot. Maybe the doorbell had rung with an Amazon delivery and I'd been holding the knife and just poked it down into the dirt because it was handy . . .

I wouldn't do that.

But how could I be sure?

The oven timer beeped, and I rose automatically, almost forgetting to use a potholder to pull the puffs out.

What if I'd inherited the darkness from my mother, and it was only now blooming? I *thought* I felt connected to V, but what if I was wrong? What if I simply felt attached to her because it was keeping me tethered to Rochelle? What if it was jealousy, overgrown and cancerous?

All of it could have been me.

I touched the side of the metal baking pan to feel it heat the tips of my fingers. I wanted to come back into my body. I pulled apart a cheese puff, not minding the way the steam burned my mouth.

The puff was good.

But it wasn't enough. So I made chocolate-chip cookies.

Then banana bread. Not once did I forget to add the baking soda. My measurements were precise. Controlled. It was almost science.

I ate some of everything, my hunger somehow growing bigger with each bite I took. When Fred jumped onto the island behind me, I almost had a heart attack. I checked the house alarm every fifteen minutes, and in between, I baked and ate.

It didn't matter how long it took for the ID technicians to show up. I wasn't sleepy. I might never be sleepy again.

I didn't go to bed until after the techs had left, leaving their black smudges on my walls and doors. By the time I shut the door behind them as they left, the sun was all the way up. I didn't curl under the covers until the world was wide awake. Surely nothing scary could happen when the mailman might arrive at any moment, right?

And nothing did. I fell into a heavy, dreamless sleep. In the early afternoon, I woke, groggily wondering why the light was so strange in the bedroom; then it all rushed back. Someone had *been in my home*. It was a defilement. My home, which hadn't felt safe anyway, was now terrifying. What had the person touched? What had they seen?

It didn't matter. It was what it was. It had happened.

Unless it hadn't.

Prenatal depression. Paranoia.

Lord, I needed a meeting. The relief I felt when I realized it was almost as strong as the comfort I used to feel when I picked up a bottle, even before the glass touched my lips. A meeting would clear up some of this confusion in my mind, would blow out the cobwebs of fear. I glanced at my phone. The three o'clock meeting would be starting in twenty minutes.

I grabbed my purse from the kitchen counter and reached to snag the keys off the hook next to the door.

My hands met air.

No Audi fob. No house key.

"Shit," I whispered as a chill slithered between my shoulder blades.

I walked as calmly as I could to where the car should have been parked in the driveway. "Oh, *come* on."

It wasn't there.

I sat heavily on the front step as I dialed 911 for the third time in less than twenty-four hours.

Then, while I waited for them to arrive, I called the OB chief of staff. While his phone rang, I could almost hear my mother's voice. *A good woman gives. She never takes. You need too much.*

Well, I needed something now.

"Dr. Walters?"

His voice boomed. "Well, how the hell are you? I've been meaning to check up on you. How's that baby on board?"

"She's good. I'm good. But I need to go on maternity leave two weeks early."

There was a pause. Normally this would be handled by the scheduler, but going on leave even a few days early meant everyone would have to be updated stat: Labor and Delivery, the Prenatal Unit, the Mother-Baby Unit, the OR, the ER, and the post-op units. "Are you *sure* you're good?" he asked.

Absolutely not. But he didn't need to know that.

FOURTEEN

Only one officer showed up to take the stolen-vehicle report, an older man who looked even more tired than I felt. It took him less than ten minutes to do the paperwork, and as a bonus, he made me feel stupid about not activating the OnStar tech that had come with my car. "If you'd turned that on, ma'am, we'd have had it back for you in thirty minutes."

Rochelle had said we wouldn't need to subscribe to the service. She'd said it was impossible to steal. Apparently neither of us had considered the fact that someone might simply take the keys.

"And you're sure you didn't leave the fob in the car?"

Glaring, I said, "Positive."

"It's easy to forget these things."

"If I'd left my keys in the car, I wouldn't have been able to get into the house. So my house key is gone, too." A little flame of panic flickered in my chest.

"Didja go back out to the car? To get something you'd forgotten?"

"*No.*"

But after he said it, I started to doubt myself. Shit, I'd made three or four trips carrying in the sandwiches and the drinks. I'd left the front door of the house ajar each time. The car was definitely unlocked when Bree found me sitting in the backseat, and I couldn't remember locking it *or* hanging up the keys inside.

Me. It could be all my fault. What, honestly, was less frightening? That Rochelle was fucking with me to scare me into giving her full custody of V? That Bree was, to keep me quiet about her baby's father? Or that I was losing my mind and just two weeks away from needing to be able to care for a tiny new human? Turning into my mother would be the most frightening thing of all.

After the cop left, I baked a batch of brownies and sat on the couch to rest for a moment before calling a locksmith.

I woke two hours later to the doorbell ringing and my heart hammering. Fear spiked through my extremities. Of course, if I did have a Peeping Tom / stalker / rapist who was coming back to the house to go after me, they *probably* wouldn't ring the doorbell. Not when they could use their own goddamn stolen key. But still, a sick fear coursed through me as I stumbled toward the door.

Maggie stood on the other side. "Hi," she said, holding up a small silver laptop. "I texted but I didn't wait to hear back. I've got a bunch of stuff on Domi to show you if you think this is a good time."

"You *scared* me." I motioned her inside and then sank onto the couch, still warm from my napping form. Maggie peered into the kitchen, looking at the impressive array of baked goods. "Wow. I recognize this particular baking mania. Did you even sleep?"

I took a deep breath. "Look. I'm going to try some more of this stupid asking-for-help stuff. Why don't you grab whatever looks best to you in there. Or anything else—there's cheese sticks and yogurt and fruit. And will you bring me a brownie and a glass of milk?"

She gave a mock bow. "I would be *dee*-lighted. Good job. I'll see if I can find you a tiara in there. I know this isn't easy for you."

"It's getting easier." I snapped my fingers. "Brownie. Milk. Tiara. Stat!"

After she brought me my unhealthy—what was it, late lunch?—she plopped down next to me and patted her laptop. "Okay. What do you want to know first about Domi? Because I could basically get you her childhood medical records at this point."

I heaved a sigh. I should have asked Rochelle if Domi was there, actually in bed next to her, when I called. Rochelle could have nothing to do with any of this. It could all be Domi.

"Hey. You okay?"

"I think someone broke in while I was in the bedroom last night. They moved a plant and gave me back that knife I told you all about, and then stole my car."

Maggie thumped backward against the sofa's back. She stared. "Jillian. You didn't want to lead with that?"

"*Or*—and hear me out—maybe it's all me. Maybe it's pregnancy getting to my brain." She was already shaking her head, but I went on. "I could have moved the plant and don't remember it. I use the knife for everything, so I might have just dropped it. The cop told me I probably left the keys in the car and that anyone could have stolen it. I thought he was full of crap, but when I thought about it, I *was* going back and forth yesterday before you all came over. Bree found me resting in the car." *Because I didn't feel safe in my home.* I took too big a gulp of milk and almost choked, spluttering in discomfort. When I'd recovered, I said, "I probably left the keys out there. But I can't deal with getting a rental to get to work, so I took Bree's advice and started my maternity leave. And before you say it again, yes, I'm staying here. There's no possible way I could move out right now. I cried trying to get a butter package open earlier. *And* I've got to call a locksmith." How had I not done that before accidentally falling asleep?

Maggie pointed at me. "That. Do that now. Do you have one you like?"

I shook my head, overwhelmed.

"Wait, I'll get one from Yelp." She opened her laptop, got me a number, and listened as they gave me a two-hour ETA. Great—more waiting for someone to show up after the fact.

When I was off the phone, Maggie said, "This is *horrifying*. You can't stay here anymore, no matter what you say. Come stay with me."

I covered my face, pushing back fresh tears I wouldn't allow to fall. "No."

"Then stay with Bree like she offered. Or with Camille. Or let one of us stay with you. You can't do this by yourself."

I dropped my hands and looked at her. "The plan was that I wouldn't have to." I didn't think I was crying, but salt water dripped into the corner of my mouth.

She looked right into my eyes, and her kind expression made me want to cry even harder. "None of this is fair. None of it. You don't deserve this."

Maybe I did, though. Maybe I hadn't finished making my amends for all the stupid things I'd done before I stopped drinking. Maybe all of this was my fault. That's what Mom would tell me. Maybe *she* was my karmic problem. Perhaps I was supposed to forgive *her*. As if I could.

My stomach knotted. "Enough. I can't bear myself right now. Show me what you've got." I tapped her laptop.

Maggie took a deep breath and then settled back next to me. She pulled a pillow onto her lap and put the laptop on it. "Can you see okay?"

"Yeah." My shoulders tightened.

She brought up a window. "So she was born Dominique Nilsson in Phoenix, Arizona. She's thirty-seven. Here's her Instagram."

"Ugh." It was all I could come up with. The picture that Maggie had clicked on was of Domi in a sparkly red holiday dress, a Christmas tree behind her. She looked like a Scandinavian huntress returned from an elven feast, all white hair and hectically, impeccably flushed cheeks. There wasn't a product at Sephora that could artificially reproduce that look. That was genes. I immediately felt like a troll, repulsive and bulging and hideous. "She's a nightmare."

"Apparently she's the head of the accounting operations division. You don't know any of this?"

"Huh-uh. I ostriched out. I guess now I have to pull my head out of my sandy ass."

"She used to be married to someone in marketing."

"Who?"

Maggie swiped through a few windows and said, "Don Bright. I guess she kept his name." She brought up a picture.

He didn't look familiar. Rochelle's work parties were always lavish and huge—over the years, I'd only met a fraction of the people she worked with. "Huh."

"Moving on." She brought up an Excel spreadsheet full of information. "She skis, hikes, and swims regularly. She vacations in Aspen and Paris, because she's one of those people. She went to ASU and then got her MBA at Wharton."

"I hate Wharton people." To be fair, I'd only met one in my life, an angry guy named Bob who had been insufferable to his lovely wife at a cocktail party, but still. "That makes sense."

"She's a registered Green but always votes Democrat."

"How did you—"

"Honestly, I thought it would be harder, but she has a *truly* terrible Facebook page. She shares everything on it, usually in meme form. I recommend you avoid her page for the rest of your life. It's private, so you shouldn't have too much trouble doing that."

"How did you get in?"

"Don't be mad—I unfriended you temporarily so we're not connected. I've never been connected to Rochelle, so I just asked Domi, and she accepted me in like ten minutes. She's got over a thousand friends on there—she can't be close to them all."

"Ew." I pulled a hot breath into my trollish lungs as another photo of Nordic perfection scrolled past. "She's exactly that stunning in person, you know. It's completely disgusting."

Maggie bit her bottom lip. "I've specifically been looking for some crappy photos to make you feel better, but she's a freak of nature. This is the worst one I could come up with." She brought up a picture of a younger Domi in a boat, her face creased in a toothy grimace. You could see the sweat on her brow. "She did crew at Wharton." Yeah, her face was contorted, but her shoulders were bare, gleaming with muscle and sinew.

"I've never been that cut in my life," I said.

"No one has. She's one of those people that women hate."

"Really?" I said hopefully.

Maggie screwed up her mouth. "No. I'm sorry. Apparently everyone loves her. I couldn't find one bad comment about her on Facebook, or anywhere else. She's on the board of the Los Angeles Regional Food Bank, and last year she raised over three million for them."

I sighed. "She's another Bree? At least I love Bree, otherwise I wouldn't be able to stand her."

"Okay, so there you're totally right. I saw a picture of the two of them at the same fundraiser for some small theatre."

I frowned.

Maggie went on, "I texted Bree about it and sent her the picture. She said Domi looked familiar but that she didn't actually know her."

LA circles were too small. "Please tell me that's all you found."

She folded her lips tightly and then said, "Honestly, I wasn't even sure if I should come over. But I figured maybe it was better to find this next thing out with a friend."

"Ah, shit. Really?" Whatever Maggie was about to show me, I didn't want to know. But my brain went there anyway—had Rochelle bought Domi a ring? Would she be that cold, to do that so soon after we'd broken up? We hadn't even had time to see the mediator. Surely they weren't *that* involved. Would Maggie show me a photo of a perfectly manicured hand with a diamond bigger than the one I hadn't been able to pry off my fat ring finger yet?

Maggie looked at the screen and then at me. Her face told me it was worse than a ring.

There, on Domi's Facebook page, was a photo. Maggie tapped the trackpad to enlarge it, but I'd already seen everything I needed to see.

FIFTEEN

The shot had been taken someplace where the grass was so green it looked watered by emeralds. The sky was a ridiculous Los Angeles blue. You could almost smell the sunshine and jasmine and Bleu de Chanel wafting from open convertibles.

Domi's selfie smile was radiant. In her raised, triumphant hand, she held a white stick with a pink plus sign. It was a picture of pure joy.

Her comment was short and simple. *It worked.* She'd hashtagged it #realfamily. The photo was one day old.

I slapped the computer shut.

"Jillian—"

But I was already up and moving through the house. I went into the kitchen and through to the dining room and down the hall. I walked into our bedroom and out again. I banged the nursery's door open and allowed myself to feel assaulted by Rochelle's nautical theme I hadn't wanted at first, just like the baby inside me. Then I slammed the nursery door closed. I couldn't *breathe*. I found myself in the back-yard without the memory of moving through the house to get there. My feet were bare, and I sank my toes into the grass that Rochelle had been so proud of. It was nothing—*nothing*—like the grass in that photo of Domi. This grass was an anemic version of the verdant lawn of that perfect place where Rochelle's new family lived.

Maggie had followed me out and stood silently next to the hot tub. Waiting.

I finally found the words. At least they weren't a scream. "Rochelle's having *another* baby."

"Yeah."

"She always wanted two, did I tell you that? Two kids was her dream. She couldn't wait another few months to try for the next one? *I was already pregnant when they met.*" I did desperate math in my head. Rochelle had said they'd met at work when I was twelve weeks along. I was dumped and they were shacked up two months later. So, if this was a normal at-home pregnancy test for a woman who was hoping for pregnancy, she was probably about five weeks along. "When she got pregnant, they'd been together for *maybe four* months. Who does that? Who *does* that? With someone else's wife? We're still married! It's not like lesbians get accidentally pregnant. It's not something we can't control, like, *Whoops! Look what we did by accident!* This is *bullshit.* It has to be Domi's egg, right? It *has* to be. It can't be Rochelle's again. I mean, it only takes two weeks for the hormones to take effect before retrieval is viable, but that would be insane. Right?"

Maggie simply listened.

"Now what?" My voice cracked with fury. "*My* baby will have a sibling that I wasn't consulted on? So what—I have to just accept that? Her family being my family?"

Maggie's voice was firm. "I don't know. But I'll help you find out."

V hadn't arrived yet. She was still safe inside me. And quite suddenly, I knew my baby's name. It fell into my head, and I knew it was the right one. Rochelle didn't know it. Only I did. The roaring in my ears got quieter as my child's name drowned it out. At least I knew that. I knew nothing else. "What do I do now?"

"You don't have to know yet."

"But I do. Today. Tonight. Tomorrow. The rest of the week. The month. What's going to happen? I have to know what to do next!" Panic constricted my breathing. I sat on the edge of the deck, letting my full weight thump to the wood.

"You take the next right step; that's all."

Maggie wavered in my vision. "I don't know what that is."

She sat carefully next to me. "Have you eaten anything? Besides brownies?"

"Two eggs."

"When?"

"An hour ago? Maybe?" What was time anymore? "No, maybe three hours now. Right before I napped."

"Okay. Good." She looked up into the sycamore's branches. "Are you tired?"

I shook my head. "I should be exhausted, but I'm too adrenalized." Poor V could feel it too. Her foot kicked a rapid tattoo against my uterus. I frowned and pressed my hand against her.

Maggie nodded at my stomach. "Can I?"

"Of course." I pulled up my shirt. "She's going bonkers."

For a moment we sat quietly in the rapidly dropping light. Maggie kept her warm hand on my skin, and V played hard little rat-a-tat-tat games with her.

Anger rolled inside my chest, pushing up into my heated throat. My words were tight. "What if it really is them messing with me?"

Maggie withdrew her hand. "Look, I know we weren't the most supportive before, when you were scared about the screen and the footprints, and I apologize for that. We were all minimizing it. We shouldn't have."

I shrugged. "You were fine."

"But now . . . I mean, honestly, who else could it be?"

I couldn't say Bree's name out loud. I just couldn't. It was too ludicrous—sure, she had a big secret and I knew it, but that wasn't enough to make a person terrorize another. "So if it's my ex and that woman, *why*, though? That's what I don't understand. I mean, I keep wondering if they want me to realize that I can't be a single mom, to scare me into giving them custody, but Rochelle *knows* me. She knows I would never, ever give V up."

Her eyes got bigger. "You really haven't figured that out?"

"Wait, no. Why?"

"Two words: unfit mother."

I gasped and felt V dive.

That was it. It made sense. They wouldn't try to make me *decide* to give V to them. They'd make me look like I was incapable of being a good mother and then take her. I was already doubting whether I'd be good enough. What if they could talk a judge into believing them? Domi and Rochelle wanted both babies. For themselves. How could it not have occurred to me? "But I'm going to be a great mom." The hope was flimsy in my mouth.

"I know that, of course. But they could make you look bad. What if you kept 'imagining' things, things they could prove weren't happening? What if they were keeping track of your texts, recording your calls?"

"I'm not crazy."

"I know you're not."

It hit me then. "But she wants me to drink over it."

Maggie, apparently, was way ahead of me. She nodded slowly. "I was thinking . . . maybe."

"But that's the last thing Rochelle would want." She'd always been so proud of me, so supportive of my sobriety.

"What would Domi want?"

My hands were cold, almost clammy, and my breath came too quickly. I suddenly knew what to do. "I want to go talk to her. Domi."

"Now?"

"Now. Face-to-face. I assume you were able to find their address online, too?" Rochelle had never given it to me.

"Of course." Maggie's grin was slow and satisfied. "Want backup?"

My heart thumped with relief. "I *need* backup. I have time to get there and back before the locksmith comes, I think. Wait. Shit. Can you drive, since I don't have a car anymore? I know you didn't plan on an excursion . . ."

"Hang on." She pulled out her cell. "I was supposed to meet a friend, but she's boring as paste compared to this mess. Let me blow her off real quick." Maggie *whoosh*ed a text. Then she stood and held out a hand to help me up. "Because I am *not* missing this. Let's take them some of your million brownies and see what size shoe Domi wears."

SIXTEEN

The house was generic Echo Park—a low-slung twenties Craftsman surrounded by two-story apartment complexes. Their house was on a slight rise and had a view that looked toward Dodger Stadium. From this distance, they'd have an amazing view of the fireworks. Rochelle must love that. I wondered how their first Fourth of July together had been. I gritted my teeth.

I rang the doorbell, then I rubbed the back of my neck, right where the tension headache was growing. My anger threatened to burn right through my skin.

"You okay?"

I nodded and then said, "No."

Maggie held the plate of brownies confidently. "You've got this."

The door opened. "Oh!" Domi looked startled for a moment and then her expression melted into a smile. "Hello! I didn't know we were expecting you." Her voice rose on the last word like it was a question.

"You weren't," I said lightly.

Domi was wearing a low-cut green maxi dress that showed off her cleavage. Unfortunately, it hid her feet from sight completely.

She blinked. "Come in, I'll get Rochelle."

We stood in a small vestibule that smelled like fresh paint. Their color palette was warm browns and deep oranges, as if they'd airbrushed pumpkin spice all over their walls. I could see the living room from here, with the same brand and size TV I had at home. I was confident Rochelle had picked it out. My right foot wouldn't stop jiggling.

"Jillian?" Rochelle was dressed for working at home, white tank and jeans. "Hi, Molly."

"Her name is Maggie. You should know that by now. And Jesus Christ, *Domi is pregnant?*"

Rochelle took a step backward. "How did you know?"

She wasn't denying it. It hurt like being hit by a car. My spleen was smashed, my ribs surely broken. "Social media, you moron."

"Facebook," Maggie clarified politely.

Rochelle turned around to look at Domi, now standing behind her. "Babe, we weren't going public."

"I didn't know she'd see it. I didn't think we were friends." Her face went pink. "I mean, Jillian, I'd *love* to be friends. I just meant social-media-wise, you know . . ."

In a cloyingly sweet voice, Maggie said, "Everything is visible if you know how to find it. There's *so* much information out there. It's dizzying really. Like that time you were arrested for being drunk in public in Isla Vista."

Domi glanced at Rochelle. "I was twenty-one!"

I spoke to Rochelle. "You always wanted two."

Rochelle folded her lips tightly. She couldn't deny it.

My spine felt like a rope on fire. "You couldn't have *waited*? At least until after our baby was born?"

"Look—"

"They'll be six months apart. You're basically going to have twins on your hands while V is with you. Do you have any idea how hard that will be?"

Rochelle flashed her palms at me. "This was never my plan. It just happened this way."

"*How the fuck does it just happen?*"

Domi stepped forward. Her cheeks were still that neon pink, but the rest of her seemed as cool as her flowy dress. "I was already working on having a baby. I was doing it on my own when we met."

"Bullshit."

She raised her eyebrows. "I can show you my records. Rochelle simply came along at the right time to help."

I pulled a tight grimace. "Turkey-baster style? How tender. Did you do it at home?" It was low and mean and I didn't care. "Or did you do it in a cold office after two cycles of IVF, like I did?"

Maggie leaned forward. "So sorry to interrupt, but since three out of four of us are pregnant, I know you'll understand—can I use the bathroom?"

Absently, Domi pointed down the hall. I still couldn't catch a glimpse of her feet.

Rochelle seemed to have found her backbone again. "I'm sorry you had to find out this way, Jillian, but I truly hope you can be happy for me."

I gave an exaggerated nod. "Oh, yeah. Sure. That's easy."

"Are you okay?"

"No, I'm not okay, you *asshole*. Can I talk to you in private?" Even in our biggest fights, we never called each other names. It felt good to do it now.

Domi glided another regal step forward. "We're family now. I stay."

I threw my head back and groaned. "For fuck's *sake*." Then I faced Domi. "Have you been inside my house?"

Her perfectly shaped eyebrows drew together. "Of course not."

"You've *never* been in my house."

The slightest pause. "No."

"I know what you did in the cottage."

Domi shot a fast look at Rochelle.

"Rochelle told me." Now I was the liar—she hadn't told me. But she'd hung up on me when I'd accused her of it. That was all I'd needed to know I was right. "You had sex in our cottage. And now you've proved that you are, in fact, a goddamn liar. So I assume you've also fucked in our bed while I was at work."

Rochelle stared at her shoes, the red Docs I'd gotten her for her thirty-fifth birthday.

Fury was gasoline to my flames. "I told you at the ultrasound, but I want to make it really clear. You can't have her. You can't have *my* baby."

Rochelle raised her head. "We only asked because—"

"Shut *up*. I know what you're doing, what you're planning. *Unfit mother?* Do you really think that would stand up in court? Or that you would actually be able to make me drink?"

"What are you talking about?" Rochelle lifted her chin.

I stared. Was she serious? "Did you steal my car?"

"Your *car?*" Rochelle's voice was close to a full shout, the one I hated. She went from zero to sixty in three seconds when she got angry, and she was two seconds away from being that irate. "What are you really doing here?"

"My car is gone! You're telling me you know *nothing* about that? Just like you know nothing about the knife moving, the gas leak, the windows and doors being open, the baby book being lost and then found."

"You think I would steal your car? When was the last time you saw your therapist, Jillian?"

She knew as well as I did that I hadn't gone to therapy in years. "Fuck you. Stop *lying*."

"Greg called me, you know." Her jaw was tight. "He's worried about you. And about the sheer number of times cops have been called to my old house."

Screw my neighbor. He should have checked in with *me*, not Rochelle. "It's *my* house. And you don't get to set foot in it ever again."

Her hands up, Domi leaped forward as if she thought I was about to slug Rochelle.

"We need to calm down here," she said. "Can we go sit in the living room and talk about this? We're adults. We're going to be co-parenting a child. I know it'll take time for us to work through this."

I crossed my arms as best I could over my enlarged, painful breasts. "I'm not sitting anywhere."

Domi nodded. "Fine, totally fine. Okay, where's your friend? Is she part of this conversation?"

"She went to pee."

"But is she part of this?"

I stared at her. Did she think I couldn't handle this myself? That I needed backup?

Rochelle rolled her eyes so hard it looked painful. "She means, is she your girlfriend?"

"Jesus! No! I don't move like you do, you piece of crap. She's my friend. She's *been* my friend. You know that." And that friend was probably going through their closet right now, so maybe I should kill a little more time. "Anyway. I need you to stop. I'll beg if I have to, if that's what it takes. Please, just stop. I'm getting new locks and a new alarm code. I'll meet you whenever you want to exchange the baby book, and when V comes, I'll do what it takes to make whatever this is"—I flapped my hand between Rochelle and me—"work. You can't take her from me completely. I will never, *ever* let that happen. But I won't keep her from you, either." With the words, my heart tore like a ripped valentine. It would be impossible for me to hand V to them for a day or a weekend or a week or, God forbid, longer. She was *mine*. But I would have to cooperate, or risk them trying to take her from me for good.

With perfect timing, Maggie came around the corner, trailing her hand along the wainscoting. "Sweet house, really. So much nicer than I thought a tiny house in Echo Park would be."

I felt a stab of pure pleasure at Domi's crestfallen face.

Maggie crossed her arms next to me and looked at Rochelle and Domi. "Did you get what you came for, Jillian?"

I didn't know. They hadn't confessed. They hadn't said they wouldn't do it anymore. They'd denied being involved.

But they hadn't been as surprised as I thought innocent people would be. Wouldn't a normal person be horrified that the mother of her child was possibly being criminally targeted? Wouldn't they want to help ensure my safety? Have ideas about protection? At least ask a few more questions about my car or the open windows and doors I'd mentioned? Sure, maybe they'd be hurt that I assumed it was them, but if they were innocent, they'd understand that I'd have to question them first.

They hadn't admitted guilt, but they'd done nothing to make me rule them out.

"I got enough." I turned on my heel, and we left, ignoring Rochelle's belabored sigh and Domi's entreaties to stay and work it out.

Once in Maggie's car, I let the heated breath rise in my chest. I panted as she started the car and blasted the AC.

She glanced at me as she put the car in drive. "Is that Lamaze breathing? Please say you're not giving birth."

"Just go."

She peeled away from the curb fast, palming the wheel in a U-turn. I was grateful. The last thing I wanted was Rochelle and Domi to see me melt down in front of their house.

Maggie drove. She stayed quiet. I tried to collect myself. It took a few minutes. I did not cry.

When she hit the freeway, I turned slightly in my seat and took a cooler breath. "So tell me. Did you find the shoes?"

Maggie glanced quickly at me and then over her shoulder to merge. "Nothing with that tread, as far as I could tell. But Domi has creepily tiny-ass baby feet. I'm no detective, but they did look like the exact same size as the footprints outside your window."

SEVENTEEN

Knowing that Domi had tiny feet didn't really help, though. It wasn't proof of anything. When Maggie dropped me off on her way to meet her friend, she wanted me to call someone to come stay with me. I told her I would but honestly didn't want anyone. Maybe I should have. Maybe it was stupid to wish to cocoon myself away, to wish for sleep to hide inside. But it was all I wanted. After the locksmith came and changed every lock on every door, I got in my bed and barely got out except to eat and pee for three days. Every woman I'd ever put on bedrest hated me for it, but at the moment I didn't see why. I didn't *want* to get up. When I was asleep, I wasn't worrying, and every moment that my body was calm was good for V.

I slept fitfully, though. Every creak of the house made me jump, and each time Fred leaped off a piece of furniture, my heart rate tripled. But I found not one open window, not a single door ajar. The baby book was always where I left it. All my knives stayed in the butcher block. (Which I'd hidden under the sink because I had one grisly nightmare in which, using just my bare hands, I'd tried to stop a faceless attacker from stabbing me. In the dream, the knife had gone through my hands, leaving my palms in ribbons.)

During those three days, I didn't leave the house even once. I ordered groceries, and I got a TaskRabbit to shop for the bookshelf brackets I wanted at Home Depot. I sent sunset photos to my mother and got no response, as usual. I read a mystery novel, guessed the killer wrong, and, six hours after I'd finished it, couldn't remember the plot. I kept forgetting to take my prenatal vitamins. As I walked my circular loop from the bedroom to the kitchen and back, I touched walls and keepsakes lightly. Every bookshelf, every picture hung on the wall, had been chosen by both Rochelle and me. Each room held a hundred memories of uproarious laughter and silly squabbles and everyday kindnesses. It shouldn't be possible to miss someone I was scared of. The new locks helped—I was the only one in the whole world with a key, and I'd been sleeping with my key ring under my pillow.

Just to be sure.

On the third night of my voluntary confinement, I got up from bed to pee and found a candle burning in the bathroom. It was one of the ones Bree had given me, the Feu de Bois.

And I hadn't lit it.

My heart thumped irregularly as I started to shake. I slammed the door closed behind me and locked it, immediately regretting it. I'd just trapped myself in a room without my phone.

I tried to calm my breathing, taking in a lungful of air.

Bree. My mind wasn't making things up. She *had* been in my bedroom, rooting through my things. She'd given me this candle.

Could all of it be her? I could barely wrap my head around how that would work, but I did know a few things. She was excellent at lying when she needed to. She was terrified about having her baby. She was too curious about me, and about my house, and I was the only one who knew her secret.

But did that equal a motive for breaking in? And how would she, anyway? And more to the point: *Why* would she? Just to light a candle? How would scaring me keep me quiet? I'd already promised not to say anything, and even if she didn't think I was trustworthy, I was. And how much time could she buy, anyway? Her due date would come eventually, and the truth—which had nothing to do with me— would be revealed.

It was too insane to think it might be her. It made no sense. But I stood and faced the closed door that led to the hall and yelled, "Bree? *Are you in my house?*" The sides of my belly ached, as if V was pushing her weight farther down, and my heart thrashed inside my chest.

I heard no response but the drip of the tub's faucet. Closing my eyes, I tried to think. A familiar smell hung in the room, sweet and jasmine, and it wasn't the candle's tree scent. It reminded me of the bubble bath Rochelle had bought for me.

I spun to look into the tub. At the drain of the bathtub, I saw a small pile of bubbles, as if someone had earlier taken a bath and it was all that was left.

A partial memory flashed in my mind like sunlight on water. *My fingers, tugging at the chain of the stopper of the clawfoot tub.*

Me. It was me.

As I sat heavily on the toilet lid, it creaked under my increased weight.

I'd taken the bath. It came back to me but only fuzzily, like an old TV set with a screen full of static. Right—I'd had restless legs again in bed, so I'd gotten in a carefully lukewarm tub to see if it would help. I barely remembered being in it. I'd almost immediately fallen asleep and had woken up cold, my belly rising high and dry above the surface. I'd barely opened my eyes while stumbling to bed, and I'd totally forgotten to blow out the candle I only had the dimmest memory of lighting. It was so nebulous and watery a memory that it could have been a dream. If I hadn't seen the remaining bubbles popping quietly at the tub's drain, I didn't think the memory would have come back at all.

My next step would have been to call the police, saying someone had broken in to light a candle in my home. Holy hell, had I seriously thought it could be Bree?

Yes, I had.

What was *wrong* with me?

Oh, God. I *knew* what might be wrong with me.

Instead of slowing, my heartbeat ticked up a few more notches. My chest ached as another memory coursed through me, and instead of pushing it away as I had been doing for days, I let it arrive.

I'd been about eleven. When I'd left for school that morning, my mother had still been in bed, always a sign of a bad day. I got home and let myself in as quietly as I could. If I could just get to my room without running into her, I'd have a shot at finishing my homework before she wanted me to help her in the garden or with the laundry.

My mother was respected in the church. "Eve Marsh is a true *healer*," her friends proclaimed with much thanks to their gracious God. Even I could admit that when my mom was the one doing the laying on of hands at the front of the sanctuary, people felt better than they did after Deacon Eldridge touched them with his big, black-haired fingers.

I never got it, though. As in literally: I never got that healing. Whenever I was sick, my mother would ask me what sin I'd committed to earn it; then she'd make me read the Bible to her while she ironed, not appearing to care when my feverish throat wobbled. When my appendix had needed removing, she'd said that praying would fix it. She didn't comfort me. She didn't lay a hand on my forehead or give me a soothing hug. I didn't even get a smile or a single herbal tincture for my fever. Those things were for other people, people in the church who'd earned her love, something I'd never been able to do. Apparently, I'd almost died of peritonitis after my appendix burst, something I heard my father yelling at her for when I got out of the hospital a week later.

We just plain avoided each other most of the time. I liked being self-sufficient, which was good, because I had to be. My father loved me, but emotionally, he wasn't much more support than she was. I'd once tried to tell my father that I was upset about squabbling with a friend at school, and he'd just hugged me sideways before asking me how I liked my teacher.

So that day, I'd snuck into the house, holding my finger over the cold metal latch of the door so it wouldn't click as I released it. I'd already taken off my shoes, and I'd successfully avoided the second step on the porch, which always gave me away with its squeak.

I planned on going right up to my room as fast as I silently could. But I was thirsty. I wanted water and maybe a cookie. Mom would probably be in the garden at this time of day anyway. She grew most of our vegetables as well as all the medicinal herbs she used to help people—people who weren't me. I tiptoed to the door of the kitchen, gathering my bravery to peek around it.

If it turned out she was sitting at the table reading her Bible, she'd catch me and I'd get in trouble for spying (because of course, that's what I was doing). That would mean extra time pulling weeds or raking, with an added bonus of at least fifteen minutes of being yelled at.

But if she wasn't in the kitchen, I'd get a snack.

The snack urge won.

I peeked around the edge of the door.

She *was* in the kitchen, and that should have made me jerk back instantly and continue tiptoeing up to my room. But something felt wrong.

The gas flame of the stove was turned high, but she held no pot to set on top of it. There was no food on the counter, no scent in the air of anything being prepared.

I watched her in profile as she stared at the blue fire. Her nose was long, like mine, and her expression was empty. She looked the way I felt when I stared at my math book but actually saw other things—the prior night's sunset, or my best friend Judy's horse—behind the page.

As I watched, my mother raised her bare arm and held the underside of it to the flame.

Somehow, I managed to suck my breath in silently. I knew the absolute worst thing I could do in that moment was to rush in and try to help, to pull her arm back, to cry.

She winced but made no more sign of distress than that. It was over quickly. The air filled with the smell of burnt hair and, more distressingly, of charred hamburger. With her back to me, she pulled out an ice pack, wrapped it in a dish towel, and held it to her arm. She bowed her head, and I heard her praying in tongues. Before she could turn and spot me, I backed up and made my way noiselessly up the stairs.

That night, she pulled my covers up sharply, her face back to its normal vaguely annoyed setting. The bandage on her arm was neat and tidy.

It wasn't until she was almost at my door, her hand on the light switch, that I found the courage to whisper, "I saw you."

She turned. "Saw me what, Jillian?"

"I saw you burn yourself."

She looked honestly surprised. "Really? I didn't know you were there."

"*Why*, though? Why did you do it?"

"What do you mean? It was an accident. While I was making dinner."

"Mom!"

She blinked at me. "I've had worse burns from that stove. I was just careless, that's all."

How could she lie to me like this? Fear stung the bottoms of my feet. "Mom, I *saw* you. It wasn't an accident."

She snorted and sounded completely, terrifyingly normal. "Oh, knock it off. Did your dad put you up to this nonsense? It's past your bedtime. Lights out, eyes closed." She clicked the light off.

I *knew* my mother. I'd made it my mission to study her, to know when I could get attention (not often) and when I was likely to get none (the rest of the time). I could read her moods like I read books from the school's subpar library. And I knew that she absolutely thought what she was saying was true. Somehow, she'd blocked out burning herself on purpose.

It scared me so badly I wet my bed that night for the first time in years. I got up early and, in humiliation, fed my linens to the washing machine. My father stumbled through the predawn kitchen to make coffee. I tried to tell him what I'd seen, the words bumbling out of my mouth in the wrong order, with the wrong emphasis. *Mom. Her arm. The stove. She meant it. She didn't see me. Not cooking.*

Dad pulled his flannel robe tighter over his pajama top. His eyes were tired. "Your mom's got some demons."

I imagined the gates of Hell opening, releasing evil spirits to drag her under. It wasn't something members of our church said lightly.

He rubbed his night-stubbled jaw. "It's not her fault. She doesn't remember when she does some things. It's like her brain swallows the information and it's gone. We just have to give her space, that's all."

Space.

So I gave it to her. We gave it to each other until I finally granted her freedom by obeying her order to leave her house for good at seventeen. I knew she'd finally be happy, with only my father and the church to take care of.

Now, in my own home, I was still sitting on the lid of the toilet seat. The scent of Feu de Bois hung heavy in the air, mixing with the smell of the bubble bath I barely remembered taking.

Dissociation.

It could come from any number of things, trauma or schizophrenia or PTSD. I'd never known why my mother appeared to have it, never known what it was connected to. And while, yes, I was a doctor, and, yes, I'd diagnosed her many times in my mind with various mental illnesses, I could never be sure of anything based solely on my childhood memory.

But what if—what if whatever it was she had turned out to be hereditary? What did that mean for me? What would it mean for my ability to mother my daughter? Would I be like her? Distant and cold and forgetful and uncaring?

Worst of all, what if I passed whatever it was on to my daughter? What if we raised V to be happy but she ended up being a victim of her own brain's betrayal after we'd done everything as right as possible?

I gasped, covering my mouth with my hand.

For that one, unforgivable second, I'd completely forgotten my baby couldn't inherit anything from me at all.

EIGHTEEN

The next day, Thursday morning, Camille texted from her car. *I'm out front.*

Bree had hired an Instagram-famous prenatal yoga expert to come to her house to lead us through a gentle workout. He'd been Kim Kardashian's combined yogi and doula. I didn't really want to move the body I was now truly, terribly uncomfortable inhabiting, and I *really* didn't want to do it in front of someone whose eyes were used to resting on the supple thighs of curvy mega-influencers. But I—for some reason—wanted to lay eyes on Bree again. I'd lit that candle myself, yes, but if there was even a sliver of a chance that it wasn't all in my head. . . . Oh, God. I hated that I was pulled into thinking about Bree like that. I was ashamed that I was almost (but not quite) hoping there was someone after me. The truth was, if someone was threatening me while I carried V, then it meant I was okay. *I couldn't* be the danger to my unborn daughter if the danger was outside my body.

No matter what, there was *something* going on with Bree, and I was haunted by it. I'd Googled her as deeply as I could, but everything I found made her seem even bigger than life, better than a single human being could be. She'd broken a skiing record in Aspen. She'd funded a girls' school in Africa. In gossip pages, she was photographed with the glitterati and seemed to fit right in. If she'd ever said out loud all the amazing things she'd done in one extremely long sentence, Bree would sound like a pathological liar, but the truth was Bree was just that good.

More important, Bree was my friend. That made me the paranoid-as-fuck asshole.

But it was far easier to think about Bree than to worry about me turning into my mother.

So I'd accepted Camille's offer of a ride to yoga and lunch.

I waddled outside when she texted, my yoga bag slung over my shoulder. Camille drove a Jeep, and I had to use the side-mounted rails to heave myself up into the seat.

"You can't keep driving this. I don't even know how you get in and out all day."

"I love my car. You look like hell."

I felt like it, too, exhausted and jangled at the same time. Every time Camille hit a bump, I bounced hard, up and down. I clutched my belly, trying to protect V from the worst of it. "Does your car have shock absorbers at *all*? This can't be good for the babies." The babies, I knew, would be fine. I was the one who was annoyed.

"Those getting free rides to yoga don't get to complain." Her voice was tight.

"Doesn't Olivia drive a Beemer?"

Camille shook her head. "No go. It's easier for me to drive this than have her freak out about how I park her baby. I can't stand it."

I studied her profile. She looked exhausted. "Are you sleeping at all?"

"Dude. It's all I do. On Monday, one of my employees caught me sleeping in a conference room. The stupid thing is that I have a couch in my office, and my door locks. I'm an expert at the work nap. But I'd had a meeting in the conference room, and apparently, I fell asleep and forgot to leave. I'm just hoping I was alone when my head dropped to my chest."

"How's the baby?"

Her face softened, and she patted her stomach. "He's good. Cramped. Sending me Morse code about getting a bigger apartment."

We hit a particularly deep pothole and both of us gasped.

"Holy shit," Camille said. "You're right. I need a softer ride for a while. Olivia won't like it, but I don't care."

I'd only met her once, but Olivia had struck me as one of those women so tightly wound it probably took a migraine or a twenty-milligram Ambien to knock her out. "How are you and she doing, anyway?"

Camille shot me a sharp look. "She's not cheating on me, if that's what you're worried about. Not all lesbian couples are the same."

It stung. But I managed to say lightly, "True enough. How's work?"

"It's *fine*. I'm getting enough done!"

I wanted to pat her shoulder or hand, but her body radiated tension. "I know you are. You always do."

"And *don't* call me a workaholic. I'm sick to death of everyone telling me that."

Once, when both Bree and Maggie were out of town, Camille and I had gotten together for lunch. We'd chattered quickly around the salads, which disappeared in minutes. Both of our phones sat faceup next to our plates. I would never forget the relief I felt when she said, "You mind if I . . . ?" We'd spent the last half of lunch working companionably in silence.

So now, I decided to simply nod and not argue with the obvious.

We were alike in many ways, including not being quite as easy in our skin as women like Maggie and Bree. Camille and I had things to prove.

After an awkward pause, she said, "Have you talked to Bree today?"

"No. Why?"

"No reason. Just curious." But her mouth tightened as she kept her eyes on the road.

"Is there anything going on I should know about?" Did she know the same thing I knew about Bree's baby's paternity? I wished there was a way to broach it safely.

Camille looked over her left shoulder so I couldn't see her face. "Nope."

"Really?"

Another one of those weird, tense pauses. Finally, Camille said, "Really."

We were silent for the rest of the short drive and I started to wish I'd stayed home, where it was quiet but at least I didn't have to interact with other humans. Today, neither Camille nor I seemed to have the energy to navigate around this weird block of ice between us. Honestly, I couldn't tell if it was more me or her. Nothing felt normal to me right now, not even the way I sat on the Jeep's rock-hard passenger seat.

When we arrived, Maggie was already at Bree's, as was the yoga instructor, a lithe, olive-complexioned man who had the calves of a ballerina and the face of a Roman statue. No wonder the supermodels hired him. He held up a hand. "I'm Tomas."

"Hi," we said.

Maggie blew a kiss at each of us and went on with her conversation with him. It was something about a pranayama breath of fire, and even though Tomas turned his body so that he was speaking to all of us, I just could not make myself care.

The white sectional had been pushed against the wall to make room for our mats, and as Camille and I walked over to the space, I caught sight of Bree striding quickly across the kitchen toward Hal. He was fussing with a coffee machine, saying something to her that I couldn't hear. Bree turned toward him with a ferocity I didn't feel comfortable witnessing. She was pissed, and Hal didn't look too pleased, either. Nerves strained tightly behind my collarbone as I looked at them.

So I stopped looking.

Camille and I unrolled our mats. Immediately and with difficulty, Camille got down on the ground. She started stretching, but I collapsed into the sofa instead. I wasn't ready to fight with gravity yet. Maggie and Tomas talked about increasing abdominal strength for birthing, but I didn't engage.

Bree approached with a broad smile, no trace of tension on her face. "Do you all mind if I steal Jillian for a few minutes?"

My heart thudded. "Me?"

"Come upstairs with me? I need your advice on a furniture thing."

"Really?" That wasn't my thing. I had IKEA furniture in my house, for God's sakes.

She gave me a look. *Oh.* It wasn't about furnishings.

From the front, I heard a door slam. Hal leaving?

Bree and I both clung to the banister rail as we heaved ourselves upstairs. At the top, Bree grabbed my arm with tight fingers and pulled me into the master bedroom. I hadn't been up here before, and normally I would have liked time to ogle its expensive-looking rugs and its retractable ceiling. But this wasn't a let-me-show-you-around visit, and my jitters ramped higher.

Shutting the door behind us, Bree said, "Who have you told?"

I took a breath before answering. "Told about what, Bree?"

"You know what."

I played dumb. "Your genetic testing? What would I share? I know nothing about what you're testing for or concerned about. Even though I would be the natural person to ask about these kinds of concerns.

What are OB friends for, after all?" Along with playing dumb, apparently I was also playing asshole. But she deserved it, at the very least for lying to my face.

Bree arched an eyebrow. "You're going to make me feel bad about that? I was freaking out."

I let myself sit on the cushions on top of the wooden chest that sat at the end of the bed. "You lied to me."

"I didn't want to."

Was that supposed to fix it? "Yeah, but you did."

"I'm *sorry*. Jeez. Sorry." She almost spat the words, and I could smell the fury coming off her. "Somehow our housekeeper found out. I had to fire her."

I arched an eyebrow. "And you think I told her? I like Rosia, but it's not like her number's in my phone."

"Then how the hell did she find out? You were the only one I told."

"Hey, you didn't tell me, remember? I saw the envelope of the most-used paternity lab in the nation. Is it possible you brought that into the house and she saw it? Since tidying is her literal job?"

Bree blew out a breath and looked up at the ceiling. "Maybe. Anyway. She's gone now."

"Why?"

"She caught me crying. She was so *nice*. You know I loved Rosia."

I didn't know that. The only thing I'd ever heard Bree say about Rosia was that she was good at making posole. "And?"

"When she asked me if her hunch was right, I admitted it was."

"So?" My impatience rose.

"So I had to get rid of her." Bree's expression made it seem like I should understand why.

"Wait, you cried on the shoulder of an entrepreneurial immigrant you paid to care about you, and then you fired her for being good to talk to? Do you know how that sounds, Karen?"

She flicked a hand in the air. "Don't call me that."

"If you loved her, like you said, then you trusted her, right?"

"I *did* love her," she insisted. "But I *employed* her. You can't trust anyone you employ."

The things I didn't understand about really rich people. "So why are you so upset? Sounds like you handled the problem."

Bree gave a ragged sigh. "I fucked up. I took the money out of my own account, not the joint one. But I forgot I'd put Hal on the account years ago, and he got notification of the withdrawal because it was so large. I didn't think fifty would trigger an alert."

At first I thought she meant fifty bucks, which didn't make any sense. Then it hit me. "You paid Rosia off? Fifty *thousand*? Was she blackmailing you?"

"No!" Bree's eyes went wide. "I told you, we were close. That was just a good-faith payment for signing an NDA."

I leaned back, my hands on the cushion behind me, and I stared.

She gave a moan and covered her face briefly. "I told him Rosia was having a family emergency and needed the money to go home and help. He knew it had something to do with her because it all happened on the same day. I used a different lawyer than our normal one, and I really thought he'd never know. But he's not stupid. He knows something more is going on."

"What did your sponsor say?" Bree's sponsor was a woman named Chris, a quiet knitter who sat and listened more than she spoke. But when Chris did talk, she said wise things that made you squirm in your seat.

Bree closed her eyes.

"You're kidding me. You haven't told her?"

"You and Rosia are the only ones who know."

"You have to tell Chris."

"I have to tell Chris," Bree agreed.

Yeah, and we both knew what Chris would tell her to do. She'd bring up the whole *rigorous honesty* part of the program. "You can't tell her because you don't think you can tell Hal the truth."

"I love him too much." It rang true—Bree's face held so much pain it was hard to look at her.

"What other choice do you have?"

She shook out her hands as if she were drying them. "Buy a white baby?"

My breath hitched in my chest. "*Bree*. Don't even say that."

She dropped into the easy chair next to the window. "I'm going to hell. I actually looked into it."

"How do you look *into* that?"

"Okay, I didn't actually look into it. But I found out *how* to look into it on the dark web."

"How?"

She rolled her eyes. "I paid a guy to set it up for me."

Of course she did. "So that guy could probably also track everything you looked at."

"I'm trying so hard not to think about that."

"You should have him whacked, probably."

Glaring, she balled a fist and shook it at me. "I should have *you* whacked."

She was undoubtedly teasing (wasn't she?), but I felt chilled, as if the temperature had just dropped twenty degrees. Even though my tongue was heavy, I made myself speak. "Seriously, Bree. What are you going to do?"

Holding the palm of her hand toward me in the air, Boy Scout style, she said, "I will not buy a baby. You *know* I was really only kidding, right? Okay, ninety-nine point nine percent kidding. I'll figure something out." She grinned at me as if this were a normal conversation, not one about how she'd searched the dark web to find out how to buy a white baby. "I've got lunch coming in after yoga from my favorite caterer. You'll love it. Wanna go down some dogs?"

I blinked, wishing my car were here, wishing I could get away from this emotional whiplash. Then I simply followed her downstairs. What else could I do?

. . .

Lunch was beyond, and why was I surprised? Bree had said "catered" but hadn't mentioned she'd sicced an entire event-planning team onto it. They arrived while we were getting warmed up by Tomas, the staff trooping through the house with so much stuff I wondered if there was a real party happening later that day, something we hadn't been invited to.

But no. All of it was for the four of us.

We wiped off our sweat as Tomas disappeared silently, probably paid and tipped by Venmo. Then Bree led us outside, delight shining on her still-damp skin. "Heaven, right? A perfect seventy-four degrees, and just wait till they serve the food!"

The staff had set up a tented pavilion right on the sand. White voile blew prettily overhead, and pink roses were twined into the structure. The table was a large square, bigger than the four of us needed, and extravagant bouquets of pink and white flowers filled most of the flat space. The china was real, as was the silver.

I fed you sandwiches and Tostitos. I barely managed not to say it. The last time Bree had hosted us for lunch at her old place, she'd gotten a simple Mediterranean platter for us. This was different. Why? What was she trying to prove?

A smoked fig and brie salad came first, served by a deferent, high-cheekboned young woman who was probably trying to get her big break in Hollywood when she wasn't slinging gold-rimmed plates. The salad was followed by a warm Greek chicken with kalamata olives and plump golden raisins served on black rice noodles with a side of tiny, tender-skinned artichokes. Dessert was a chocolate dome filled with almond and pistachio nougatine.

Bree had placed herself as host with her back to the ocean, but the rest of us had a spectacular view of the surfers waiting for the right waves to roll over, then rising to ride them. Even on a Thursday, the beach was full of runners and mom groups and men ostentatiously working out right in the middle of everything. Tourists eyed us, some obviously judging, others just as obviously impressed.

I sat across from Bree, Camille on my left and Maggie on my right.

Maggie mimed throwing something. "What if he'd hit someone with it?" She and Camille were telling us about something that had happened at the nine A.M. meeting they'd both been to, where a member had lost it and thrown a full cup of coffee at a wall because it wasn't hot enough for him. But I couldn't catch my thoughts and didn't care.

Bree laughed and participated in the gossip. She seemed fine. As if the conversation upstairs hadn't even happened. Her ability to move so rapidly between emotions was giving me motion sickness.

The thing was, I wanted my friend Bree back. I wanted the Bree I understood, the one who laughed way too loudly and didn't care, the one who took risks and climbed mountains because they were there and who wore five-inch heels because *she* liked the way her legs looked in them, screw everyone else. This Bree was different. Something pulsed off her skin—I could almost smell it rising from her pores. Anger, yes. Worse?

I was losing it. My shoulders were tight, and I gulped at my water. Did the others see it? Were they also confused? They didn't seem to be.

The server brought us decaf, and I regretted saying yes to it. But Camille had said yes before me, and she was still my ride unless I grabbed an Uber. That would seem rude. I wanted to go—I wanted to run to the house and through it and out to the street on the other side. I wanted to be home, where I used to feel safe. I wanted to be in my bed with the covers over my head. Or even better, I wanted to be somewhere that was nowhere near here. An anonymous hotel in Vegas or a boat in Baja. Somewhere no one could follow me.

It hit me then—I was *scared* of Bree, of the thing I wasn't understanding about her. And I hated it.

The conversation had shifted to a show Camille had in production about a woman stalked and killed by a boyfriend she'd had in seventh grade, one she hadn't heard from or even thought of in forty years. "The real ending is that the guy went to prison for life, where he killed himself, but I think we're going to focus on her daughter, who's left with the most massive PTSD now after finding her mom sliced into pieces like that. We need a good, tragic hook to hang it on; otherwise, it's just another murder, you know?"

Bree laughed. "Only in LA could that sentence be uttered, right?"

Camille sighed. "Remember when I used to get stressed-out about how much the team was paying for painters at my last gig? Boy, those were the days. I approved camera crews to film in antique malls. Now I'm approving a budget that spends tens of thousands of dollars on *blood*. Maquillage blood, but still, it's blood that represents what came out of a real, live human body."

A sudden sharp gust of wind lifted off some of the voile above us, sending it sailing into the sky. A caterer ran after it as we watched. I felt useless, a shipwrecked hulk.

Pushing her sunglasses onto her head, Maggie said, "But why do people need that tragic hook? Isn't the fact that the woman's mother died bad enough? I mean, I kind of get it, I watched that last one you did, about the new mom killed by the carpet cleaner. But I don't get why."

Camille said, "Yeah, great ratings on that one. The why—and this is just my opinion, but it's what they pay me for—is that people want to be taken right into it. Like, into the darkest heart of the very worst of it. They want to feel terrified, and they want to look up and see that their doors are locked and their loved ones are all safe inside. The second-best feeling in the world is filling the home that makes you safe full of furnishings and appliances and colors that remind you of your childhood blanket or your grandma's Bundt cake. You watch your sixty-inch screen from the oak sleigh bed that I talked you into buying on *Big Home Little Budget* six years ago. Everything in your house is perfect."

Someone had to ask it, so I said, "What's the best feeling in the world, then?"

"There but for the grace of God go I. *That's* why people watch Murder TV. They're safe and having a good day, while someone else is having the worst day of their lives, over and over again, streaming twenty-four-seven."

Maggie shook her head. "No way. The best feeling in the world is an orgasm. Or the slightly crisp outer layer of the perfect macaron. Or finishing reading a book right when your eyes get heavy. I'll take fucking gardening, and I *hate* gardening, over being happy that something bad happened to someone else and not me."

"But you watch my shows. Why?"

Raising her eyebrows and dropping her sunglasses back into place, Maggie said, "I don't actually know."

"You don't want to admit it. But you're a rubbernecker. We all are. Survival is a basic instinct. If you're watching someone else's house burn down, you're not on fire. If you can see the stalker, you're not the prey. *God,* I miss tile. Have I mentioned how much I miss tile? Yeah, I have. I know." She caressed her cell phone but didn't flick it open.

I shifted my body, ignoring the tug at my lower back as my belly swung. I didn't dare look at Bree, and fear made me feel green, but I forced the words from my mouth. "So, what actually makes a stalker come after his prey?"

NINETEEN

Camille tilted her head. "Stalkers in general? Because there are like five types of them—do you want them all?" She looked right at me, and my breath caught. "Or your stalker in particular? Has something else happened that you're not telling us?"

"No," I said.

Maggie said, "Jillian. Hey, are you okay? What happened?"

Bree said, "Oh, she's fine. Right, darling? Last-minute birthing nerves, right? You'd tell us if something else frightening occurred, right?"

Would I? I wasn't sure. "General stalkers. All the kinds."

Camille added cream to her coffee and then spoke, raising her fingers one by one. "First, we have the rejected stalkers, the ones who knew the victim, usually romantically. Then we have the intimacy seekers, you know, like the woman they caught swimming naked in Keanu Reeves's pool. They think they're loved by the target, or that they will be if they can only get a chance to know each other. Third, we have the incompetent stalkers."

Bree said archly, "Now, that's just sad."

Camille didn't smile back. "Yeah, it is. They're often mentally ill or mentally disabled and can't really understand that they don't know their victim. They simply want to be close. They're not usually as dangerous as the others, though there have been exceptions. Fourth, the resentful stalker feels persecuted and stalks out of righteous anger. And fifth, the predatory stalkers, the paraphiliacs."

I shivered. It sounded bad, but I didn't know the word. "The whats?"

"The ones acting on some fucked-up sexual urges. The child molesters, the rapists. Good TV in those. The network likes those best."

"Gross." The lump in my throat made my voice hoarse. "What do you think mine is, if you were to make a guess?"

Camille carefully picked up her coffee. "Well, if we think it's Rochelle or her girlfriend, then it's the ex-lover kind, right?"

Would I dare?

I had to. "What if it's not them?"

Camille frowned. "Something else *has* happened."

Yes. "Not really." Nothing I could tell them about. Seeing Bree in my bedroom. Knowing her secret. A candle she'd given me—no, I'd lit that myself. I couldn't just say I had a *feeling.* "The car getting stolen, I guess."

Maggie said, "But you told me in the car the other day that you thought you might have left the keys in it, right?"

"I *might* have," I snapped. "But I probably didn't. I never leave my keys in the car."

Maggie's lips twitched, and I could almost read the *Really?* above her head. At least she didn't say it.

Camille folded her arm. "You also said it could all be you. Hormones."

Paranoia. Dissociation. "But I hate that. Let's assume it's a stalker."

"Is that really better?"

Maybe. "Of course not."

Thankfully, Camille went with it. "Okay, so then what other kind of stalker do you think you might have? Any more old exes hanging around? Bad blood from breakups?"

"You know women. I'm friends with most of them, at least on Facebook."

Maggie said, "We still might want to look at some of those, you think?" She already had her phone out and was poking at it. "Okay, I'm on your page. You'll have to reaccept my friend request, then give me some of those names."

Bree said, "Someone who hates you from the hospital?"

I shot a glare at her. "No one hates me." Except maybe myself at this moment, for having the thought I kept having.

Camille said, "Not that you know of, anyway. I think we can strike out incompetence—if someone's screwing with you, they're talented. Do you think it's the resentful kind? Or the serial killer paraphiliac kind?"

I put my hands on my belly as if I could cover V's ears. "You're the expert, Camille."

She leaned forward and met my eyes, really *looking* at me. Something inside me sank. "What are you scared to tell us?"

V swirled, slow and deep, as the fear rose and choked me again. I didn't understand this feeling—I'd *never* been good at feelings. Why else did a drunk drink? Maybe I was feeling fear; maybe it was confusion, or worry . . .

Bree clapped. "Ooh, this is fun. Camille, you're amazing!"

Lord, that was *it*. My fear caught fire and turned to anger as if it were flash paper. My last nerve snapped so hard I could almost hear it ping. "Bree."

Still smiling, she chirped, "Yes?"

"What *were* you doing in my bedroom going through my drawers?"

The smile stayed but froze. "Pardon?"

"In my house. When I caught you—"

"I told you." Bree's gaze darted to the other women and then back to me. "I was looking for Tylenol."

The table went crystalline in my vision. I could see every curve of each rose petal. The prisms reflected through the crystal water glasses made shards of color sharp enough to cut. Would I—could I say it? For a moment, I knew I couldn't.

And then I did. "Do you think it's kind of weird that only minutes after that, we found that screen removed from the bedroom window?"

Without actually moving, Bree got taller in her seat. Then her eyes narrowed. "What exactly are you accusing me of?"

I shrugged, swallowing the fear in the back of my throat. "I'm not accusing you of anything." I glanced at Maggie and Camille. Their eyes were wide, and Maggie's mouth had dropped open. "I'm just wondering if anyone else here thinks that was as strange as I did."

Bree blinked, the only hint that she hadn't turned completely to stone like a mythological monster. I felt sick and guilty and elated all at once, my skin prickling with cold sweat.

Maggie's mouth snapped shut. "Jillian. Stop it right now."

I held up my hands. "What? Stop what?"

"She's your *friend*. You can't say stuff like that."

Camille backed Maggie up, glaring at me. "Are you serious? You think *Bree* is your stalker? And you baited me for info? What the actual fuck, Jillian."

But Bree still hadn't said another word.

I put my hands back on my belly. I needed to do this, to say this. "You'll notice she's pretty quiet. Cat got your tongue, Bree?"

She took a deep breath in through her nose and somehow got even taller in her chair. "I've simply never been so egregiously insulted before. I'm trying to figure out the best way to let you know how much you've hurt me."

I blew a *pfft* in her direction, hoping it came off as confident. "You are one icy bitch." The heat was still building in my body, and I wanted, suddenly, to throw her off her game completely. Just to see what would happen.

But I was terrified.

Maggie reached sideways and jerked my arm. Hard. "Jillian. What's wrong with you?"

"Me?" I pressed a hand against my chest. "There's nothing wrong with *me*." Or everything. I wasn't actually sure, but I'd boarded this roller coaster and strapped myself in. I wasn't getting off until we looped the loop, even if it ended with all of us hurling. "But look at Bree's belly, ladies. Did you know that's not Hal's baby in there? The color of the baby's skin is going to let Hal know that as soon as she pushes it out. Bree told me upstairs that she wants to buy a white baby."

As I spoke of skin color, the pink drained from Bree's cheeks. "How dare you." It was a whisper.

But the ride wasn't over. I had one more thing to say, if I could make myself—

No, I just couldn't. How dare I, indeed.

Then I thought of the fifty thousand Bree had paid Rosia to buy her silence.

Good God, Bree couldn't be out to steal my child. What would that even look like? Hire a hit man on the dark web to kidnap me and take my baby? It was an impossible, ridiculous, and completely insane worry, but as I held it in my lap in my tightly clenched hands, it became more and more important to speak it aloud. I didn't want the person out to get me to end up being Rochelle, the mother of my child, and I sure as hell didn't want it to be *me*. I had to push the vague idea out into the salt air, where it would either turn out to be true or turn to dust.

The ride turned upside down, and I said the words. "My baby's white, Bree." I patted the top of my belly gently. "And I'm worried that you can't stop thinking about that."

TWENTY

Bree exploded, leaping to her feet, leaning over the flowers, and slapping me across the face before I even registered she was moving.

My neck snapped to the right. My hand cradled my blazing cheek—there was no pain yet, just shock.

"Go," was all Bree said. She sat back down and turned to stone again. She wasn't even breathing hard, like I was. Only her lips moved as she said it again. "Go."

Maggie reached toward me again, then dropped her arm. "You didn't—you did *not* just say that."

Camille only stared, remaining completely motionless.

"Look at me," said Maggie.

I didn't.

"*Look* at me, Jillian, or I swear to God."

I turned to meet her gaze.

"You apologize to Bree. Right now. You've lost your damn mind.

We're your *friends*. You need to apologize. Make this right." Maggie's cheeks were red with white spots, and she was blinking as fast as I was.

"She's the one who hit me."

"Because you accused her of wanting to *steal your baby*. Is that seriously what you just said?" She was almost shouting. "That's what it sounded like, but please tell me I heard it wrong!"

What *was* I doing? Did I really believe Bree was out to get me? To get V? Rochelle and Domi could be behind everything happening to me, trying to get me to drink, trying to make me an unfit mother.

Or it could all be me, going down the road my mother traveled.

But Bree . . .

They were all staring at me. I couldn't speak, couldn't respond to Maggie's question. My feet dug their way into the sand and then back out again. Bree spoke again.

"Maggie," said Bree. "Darling. I don't need you to back me up."

Shaking her head, Maggie said, "You do! We are a *team*. I need you three, all of you. Don't do this to the Ripleys. We don't act like this!" She turned back to me. "Jillian, we can all admit Bree's got a bitch-stick up her ass sometimes, but that doesn't make her a psychopath. You understand that, right?"

Bree's eyes closed slowly. When she opened them, my friend was gone, and in her place was a woman I didn't recognize. "Maggie, I told you once already, but I'll repeat myself because you obviously didn't hear me. I don't need the help of a woman who fucked her way across LA to steal enough jizz to make a baby."

Maggie coughed in surprise. "Huh. It was really just the Palisades and a little bit of Santa Monica, if you're worried about it. But okay, then." Her hurt was obvious.

Camille finally spoke, her voice ragged. "Jillian, screw you for saying that to Bree. For even thinking that."

Spinning in her seat to face Camille, Maggie said, "Jillian's hurting. Can't you see that?"

"Oh!" Bree smiled thinly. "Now you're sticking up for her? Not on my side anymore?"

"I'm not that cool with slut shaming." Maggie's shoulders rose and dropped as her smile thinned to match Bree's.

Bree's head dropped and she raised a hand, her elbow still on the table. "I can't. I simply cannot. Jillian, haven't you done enough damage? Would you like to give Hal a call and tell him my big secret yourself? Would you enjoy that? Shall I give you his number? Or maybe Maggie has it. Who knows how many men are in her phone?"

My head was spinning, and the pain in my cheek was kicking in. I'd have a jaw ache to match the mounting headache soon. I knew on a deep level that I'd deserved the slap, and the shame tasted like vinegar.

Unless I was right about her.

Unless she was so good that this was all an act, and she was playing her part perfectly.

Maggie gave a short, harsh laugh. "I don't have time for this bullshit. Y'all call me if you come down from crazy." She got up and moved quickly, disappearing into Bree's house as we stared after her.

I stood, my knees wobbling underneath me. I took my purse off the back of my chair, reaching automatically into it for my keys before remembering that Camille had been my ride.

"I'll get an Uber home." Obviously.

Camille's head was down. She didn't look up.

Bree, though, kept her eyes on my face. She stared evenly at me, sending her glacial chill into my bones. Was it pain I felt radiating off her skin? Or hatred?

I stumbled to the open glass door, knowing they were watching. The doomed roller coaster was pulling to a stop, and I might be about to throw up—I wasn't sure. My face burned.

I didn't bother to knock the sand off my shoes before going through Bree's house to the street. No Rosia meant maybe Bree would have to sweep it up herself.

TWENTY-ONE

I used my shiny new key to let myself in when I got home. The head-ache was intense, and I needed to lie down, but first, I scuffed off my flats and pawed through the mail I'd grabbed on the way in. I wanted to collapse into bed and close my eyes until V knocked to get out, but paying bills felt like something normal, something I used to do a really long time ago, back when I was married and knew what my life was.

I looked at the clock on the stove. It should have been midnight, but it was only three in the afternoon. Shit. Okay, I'd go to the five thirty meeting, and then maybe see if my sponsor was free for coffee. I'd been playing phone tag with Nicole for weeks now, and I needed to talk to someone who might be able to talk some sense into me.

I sorted the bills, most of them still on autopay in our joint account until the mediator told us what to do with our finances. A heavy blue envelope addressed to Rochelle had arrived—she really had to get her mailing address changed. I held it, fingering the flap, peeling it back, bit by bit, until I summoned up the guts to open it all the way. It was a wedding invitation from someone I didn't know. Feeling like a criminal, I examined the handwritten note on the RSVP card. *Can't wait to meet your new plus one!*

I leaned back my head and groaned.

I went into the kitchen, and after a pause during which I considered how much shame I'd feel if I threw it out, I dropped the envelope and its contents right into the trash. An ugly sense of satisfaction grew low in my gut.

What a shitty day.

Heading down the hall with the sole intention of taking a nap, I paused outside the nursery.

I didn't remember shutting the door to it.

And I heard . . . music? My blood chilled as I leaned closer to the door. There was *a song* playing on the other side of the door. I heard a woman's voice.

I fumbled to unlock my phone, my heart already at double time. I dialed 9 and 1. My thumb hovered over the second 1.

Run.

Get out.

Adrenaline stung its way through my veins. Opening the door would be stupid. I should hit that extra 1 and get the cops here.

But Greg would be nosy, and he'd let Rochelle know if I panicked again—and the song was so soft that it could be coming from outside. It *couldn't* be coming from inside the baby's room.

I pushed open the door.

There was no one in the room.

But a lullaby played softly over the Echo device. "Hush little baby, don't say a word . . ."

I froze, stuck to the spot in terror.

"Mama's gonna buy you a mockingbird." The singer's voice was thin and warbly, like a record player going the wrong speed.

I sucked in a tight breath and then another one before taking one step into the room. Screw running away. The alarm hadn't gone off, or I would have gotten a phone call. If it hadn't, and if *I* hadn't turned on the music . . .

Wait. What if I *had* turned on the music? I couldn't have, though. I'd just gotten home only minutes before. There hadn't been enough time to forget doing something—this was the first time I was heading down the hall since I got home.

Right?

That had to be right. It *had* to.

And regardless, I refused to be chased out of my house by a fucking lullaby.

I stepped forward, holding my trembling hands in front of me, as if I were feeling my way into a dark room, instead of entering it in broad daylight. Fred meowed behind me, and I gave a short, sharp scream that did nothing to calm my heart rate.

But Fred didn't seem upset. He padded into the room and wound around my ankles. His nonchalance was the only thing that gave me the courage to rip open the closet, the only other hiding spot in the room.

Nothing was inside except what was supposed to be there. Tiny dresses on mini-hangers. A new vacuum I hadn't gotten out of the box yet. Extra crib bumpers and four different types of slings.

I whirled around as the woman's underwater warble sang the last words of the song to me: "And if that horse and cart fall down, you'll still be the sweetest little baby in town."

Holding my breath, I waited.

"Hush little baby, don't say a word . . ."

"Alexa, stop!"

Stupid Alexa kept going. She never listened to me. Rochelle said it was because I spoke too fast. *"Alexa, goddamn it, shut the fuck up."*

That she understood. The music quit. The only sound in the room was Fred's loud purring at my feet and the faint tinkle of water from the toilet in the hall that had been running off and on for months. And my breathing. I could hear it—ragged and winded.

I walked slowly and carefully through the house. I checked every room. Every closet. Under every bed. Adrenaline continued to fill my veins with cold acid, and I felt queasy every time I jiggled a window and heard the reliable soft beep from the alarm. Messing around with the home security app on my phone, I found I could pull up a history if I went deep enough into its settings. Camille had arrived to pick me up at nine fifty A.M. The app's history showed that someone had left the house and set the alarm to Away at nine fifty-one. That same someone had then gone to do yoga and accuse one of her best friends of trying to steal her baby. Not a single other someone had entered the house via any known entry point until I got back home.

Was Alexa smart enough to spontaneously play a lullaby in a baby's room? I knew the Echo devices listened to everything, waiting for their wake word, but what—in the past, she'd heard us talking about diaper pails, and played this? When I wasn't even home? That seemed like an excessive breach of privacy.

There *had* to be a good explanation.

I sat at the kitchen table in the chair Rochelle had always said was too uncomfortable for her bony butt. My butt wasn't bony anymore, and the chair was just right.

But what if there really wasn't a good explanation? What if that initial ambivalence I'd had about being pregnant was coming back, but I couldn't feel it? How could I stop it? What if it had never gone away completely?

What if I really *was* setting myself up? I pictured the burn scar on my mother's arm and the way she'd never recovered from my birth. *Prenatal depressive paranoia and dissociation.* It could happen. It *did* happen. Like the false pregnancy in the woman I'd almost killed, it was rare, but sometimes the pregnant brain couldn't be relied upon.

Of course, my mother hadn't been pregnant when she'd burned herself.

So it was back to me. My mother and me. *Our* brains were unreliable.

I remembered my blackouts, times when I'd wake up with lightning in my veins and a slow, sick thudding in my head. I'd spend long, terrified minutes going through my phone trying to guess what harm I might have caused when my brain wasn't in charge of my actions. Sexts, dirty pictures from people I didn't recognize, rage texts . . . It felt like that again, like I was only occasionally in the driver's seat of my brain.

And what about V? Babies born to depressed women could be less active and less attentive. She *had* been moving more sluggishly, I'd thought, but she was also running out of real estate, so I'd chalked it up to that.

No, no, *no.*

My brain wasn't a safe place to be alone right now. I didn't want to drink, so I didn't try calling Nicole. I didn't want to explain everything to her; I didn't have the energy.

Instead, I dug up a teaspoon of courage and called Maggie. It rang a long time, and I imagined her looking at her cell, trying to decide whether to answer.

"Hello?"

I could hear the wariness in her voice. I spoke quickly. "Please don't hang up."

She sighed. "You really fucked up. You know that, right?"

"Yeah, you think?" I rolled my neck, trying to ease the tension that curled at the base of it.

"Bree's not after your baby, you lunatic." But I heard a softness under her exasperation.

"Something's happening, though."

"*Is the baby coming?*"

"No! Sorry. Not yet. I'll text you as soon as she starts knocking on the door."

"And by door you mean clawing your cervix open with her tiny, perfect fingernails."

"What an image."

Maggie's voice softened a little more. "What do you need, Jillian? How can I help?"

I breathed a little easier. "I was wondering—and I know this is a big ask especially after this afternoon—but I wanted to know if you'd spend the night with me tonight. I'm . . . I'm freaking myself out."

"What happened?"

"I honestly can't tell. Weird things."

"Like what?"

I took a breath. The oxygen was still trapped in the tops of my lungs, so I tried to push down my diaphragm to get more air. It would have been nice if I knew where my diaphragm had gone. V seemed to be swinging from it. "When I got home, there was music playing in the baby's room."

"And . . ."

"I didn't put it on. It was playing 'Hush Little Baby.' Wouldn't I remember if I'd played that on repeat?"

"Rochelle. Domi. One of them went in while you were with us."

"No, remember, I got new locks. They don't have the key." I ran my fingernail along the scratch in the table. It had been there as long as I could remember, and I didn't know where it had come from. "And the alarm says no one came in."

"They're screwing with you remotely, then. Do you have one of those smart-home thingies?"

"Yeah, in almost every room. That's what it was playing on. Rochelle liked to control the lights with them."

"Then she's got the app on her phone. It's a hundred percent her. Call her."

I groaned. "I can't. You saw how it went last time."

"You *have* to. And yes, of course, I'll stay tonight. I can't be there till about seven, though, is that okay?"

"Whenever is fine." But had Maggie fully forgiven me for earlier? Did I need a longer olive branch? "I have so many snail masks, you don't even know. I'll order pizza and get ice cream delivered. You like that raspberry truffle one, right?"

I could hear the smile in her voice when she spoke. "Good memory."

"Thank you. For coming." I meant it, the gratitude warm in my chest. It didn't even feel that weird, asking her for help. If Maggie had asked me, I would have been thrilled to assist her—why did I always think I didn't deserve to ask for help when I was struggling? Because maybe I was a jerk about it, thinking that I was the special one, the one who never needed help. Just like Mom.

"Yeah, yeah. See you later. Call your ex."

I poured myself a big glass of orange juice and sat back down with it. I took a deep, cleansing, meditative breath, which didn't help at all. "Screw it," I muttered, and hit dial.

"Is it time?" Rochelle's voice was even more excited than Maggie's had been.

"I've still got a week to go. You know that."

"What, then?"

"Music was playing in the nursery."

"And?"

"I didn't turn it on."

A short pause. "What does that mean?"

"That means the Echo in the baby's room was playing 'Hush Little Baby,' and if you're trying to creep me out, I'm begging you to stop." My voice broke as emotion I didn't predict filled my throat. "I just can't anymore. I'm too tired. Please. I don't care if it's you or if it's Domi, please stop."

Her voice was immediately angry. "If there was music playing in the nursery, *you* turned it on. We would never do anything to you. Jillian, you're carrying my baby."

My baby, my head whispered.

"All we want for you is the best. The best health, the best care, the best life. Any way we hurt you, we'd be hurting V. You *know* that."

I was silent. I wanted to believe her, but I couldn't.

"Jillian? I say this because I care about you. You need help."

I could actually feel my blood pressure rise, could feel my brain flood with heat. "Oh, *fuck*—"

She interrupted me before I could decide on *you* or *off.* "You've got a lot of feelings going on, and I know that's scary for you."

It turned out that a well-seasoned marital fight could flip to full-on just as fast when the marriage was over. Faster, maybe. "You always say that. This isn't a feeling I'm confused about."

"It's okay. You know that. Feelings are confusing, and it's okay that you're overwhelmed." She had that pedantic, smarmy tone I hated with all my being.

"It's not a *feeling.* A freaking lullaby being played without my consent is *abuse.*" I sounded ridiculous. I could hear it.

"Do you have someone to talk to? Someone you can let in?"

There it was. Her rallying battle cry. *You never let me in!* The last time she'd shot it at me was when I was at her car window, pleading for her not to leave me for the woman she'd just told me she was in love with. *You should have let me in, Jillian.* The unstated *Because someone else did* hung in the air as she drove away.

No. I wouldn't accept this. I was bad at sharing feelings, yes. I could admit that. But I hadn't imagined the lullaby—the sound of it hanging heavily in the air wasn't an emotion. It was a fact. "I'm pretty fucking clear on this, Ro—"

"Hang on a sec." I heard something on the end of the line. Rochelle said, "Domi, what?"

Domi's voice was pitched so high she sounded like a little girl, but I couldn't understand her words.

"*What?*" I heard muffled whispering, and then Rochelle muttered, "Jillian, I'll call you back."

"Wait. What?" I stood up from the table and walked onto the back deck. The afternoon was heating up, so I sat under the big red umbrella. It had been the last household thing we'd bought together that wasn't for the baby.

But she'd already hung up.

A helicopter roared angrily overhead as I watched three bees stabbing at the lemon tree's flowers. Our—*my* backyard had been an oasis. Now I felt like taking a blowtorch to the delphiniums Rochelle had put in and abandoned before they even bloomed.

What were they talking about?

What were they planning?

An agonizing five minutes later, she finally texted. *Domi was setting up the babies' room using my phone. She named it Nursery, not knowing I'd named the one at your place that.*

I tried not to get tripped up by "babies' room," plural. Her answer felt too convenient. Too easy. I typed, *You're saying she played one song on repeat, for fun? One really creepy lullaby?*

She thought it wasn't working on our end. And she was playing Billie Eilish, not lullabies.

Seriously?

But, in classic Rochelle fashion, the message went unread. She'd said what she wanted to say, and then she'd put her phone down.

Domi had done it on purpose. She must have.

But . . .

What if she really hadn't? What if it wasn't any of them, of us? *Rochelle. Domi. Bree.*

I gasped as something hit me—my brain making a connection I hadn't seen coming.

Tori Newbold. The woman I'd almost killed the last day I drank, the woman who thought she'd been pregnant. What if she'd come back to find me? I'd looked for her six years before, a year after I got sober, but hadn't been able to find her. Neither had the private investigator I'd hired.

I opened Google and put her name in again.

And there she was. A Facebook hit, the first time I'd ever seen anything come up for her. I clicked so fast my finger accidentally hit an ad and it took five long seconds to get back to the right page.

Tori Newbold was alive. She was in the world. In my head, she'd been lying in the operating room for the last seven years. In my imagination, she was still on the table, a mask covering her face, her skin as washed out as my soul had been.

But Tori Newbold had a life. A family. She still had that red hair and those freckles, but the smile was something I'd never seen, big and broad and truly beautiful. She lived in Portland, Oregon, with a man I assumed was her husband. They had three children, none of whom looked like them. Adopted? Her womb had been irreparable. I didn't remember details of her surgery, but that had been clear.

And she looked happy. All her posts had something to do with the kids—T-ball scores and good report cards and falling in various ponds and creeks. Hilarity seemed normal for her family of five, and I couldn't find a scrap of time when she could have flown to LA, messed with me, and flown home. I scrolled all the way back to Christmas and had to stop when the photo of her perfect tree surround by mountains of presents almost broke my heart. I was so *happy* for her.

At the same time, I hated feeling the possibility of a good explanation slip through my fingers.

It was back to Rochelle and Domi. Or Bree.

Or me.

What if I'd done it, somehow played the song on the Echo?

I *had* made a playlist of lullabies on Spotify already, including songs I thought I could stand to hear over and over again, and I knew "Hush Little Baby" wasn't one of them. But I opened my phone to double-check, just in case.

I clicked out of Facebook and hit the green Spotify button, opening the playlist called *V Love Songs*.

And there it was. My heart dropped into my stomach.

"Hush Little Baby" sat at the top of my lullaby list, the very first song. It also showed as the last played song. I touched it and heard the same awful, warbly voice.

I stabbed the song closed, wishing I could shove away the fear that filled me the same way. I dumped Spotify altogether, dragging it into the phone's trash can. *Do you wish to remove this app? Yes? No?*

I jabbed Yes as hard as I could.

TWENTY-TWO

Maggie was as good as her word, arriving right at seven.

"Look." I showed her. "I got the Popeye's pizza from Abbot's, your favorite. And four different kinds of ice cream, including the raspberry truffle."

She nodded, rubbing the top of her belly. "If this is an apology, I'm going to have to accept it, because me and the little one are starving. Do you mind? I don't even want to take the time to sit down before I eat this first piece." She reached for a slice, and I passed her three napkins.

We ate standing next to each other. I had to swallow carefully around the tense lump in my throat.

"Okay," Maggie said as she licked her fingers. "*Now* we can talk. What the hell, girl?"

I held up my hands. "I'm telling you. I don't think I can trust this brain right now."

"And *that's* exactly what Rochelle and Domi want you to believe. You know that!"

"But—"

"If you say Bree again, I swear to God. You know you're going to have to apologize to her, not to me, right? And I think she's going to need more than pizza. Me, we've already established what a slut I am." Her smile was wry, but her voice was back to its normal warmth. I felt relief bathe my heart.

"I know. I will." *Maybe.* "Want to watch TV and turn off our brains?"

"Hell, yeah, I do."

We watched *Letterkenny* as we painted our nails. She did my toenails, since she could reach them and I couldn't, which was above and beyond the call of duty since I hadn't gotten a pedicure in months. Then we watched *SNL* sketches on YouTube on the TV. I wanted to stay up all night with her. I was exhausted, but I felt scared to close my eyes.

But when I couldn't stop yawning, she said, "Bedtime, lady."

Groaning, I said, "I guess you're right."

As I struggled to my feet, the doorbell rang.

I looked at the clock on the wall. "It's almost midnight."

Maggie said, "Okay, I don't like that."

She followed on my heels to the door. I used the peephole but saw nothing except taillights heading west down the street. By the time I opened the door, the car was gone.

Sitting on the doormat was a white box wrapped with a big, fancy red bow, about the size of a shoebox. I didn't recognize the wrapping from any Venice store I knew, but I could tell it was expensive. Upscale stores trained people to make those kinds of bows by hand.

Something from Domi, maybe? To make up for the Echo scare she thought she'd done but had actually been me? My heartbeat throbbed behind my eyes, and I wanted to slam the door shut on it.

But at the same time, I needed to know what it was.

Maggie stopped my arm from reaching down for it. "Are you serious? You don't know who that's from."

"I know. But I should find out."

"Why? We should just leave it out here. What if it's a bomb? Maybe we should call the police."

"It's probably not a bomb." But I felt a jolt of doubt as I said the words.

"I guess—who drops off a gift in the middle of the night?"

"Someone like Domi, who wants to apologize?"

Maggie frowned and nudged the box with her toe. "I think it's too light to be explosive. But this is freaking me out. Seriously."

"Let's just take it inside."

She was right. The box was so light it almost felt empty. Maybe I should have been warier—and I was definitely nervous—but the truth was I was also so relieved to have someone to witness whatever *this* was that the naked fear faded to a vague unease.

"What if it's a poisonous spider? Or a snake?"

"Ack. Don't say that." I reached for the bow. "I'm opening it."

She got out her camera. "Hang on. Okay, I'm filming. If something blows up and we don't make it, the world can use this video to avenge us."

"I know you're kidding, but you're also stressing me out." I swallowed hard and then tugged on the bow. It opened, parting like a curtain.

"I'm not really kidding," she said unhelpfully, her phone still aimed at me.

I lifted the lid.

Inside was light pink tissue paper.

"Oh, good," said Maggie. "A baby gift delivered at midnight. What could be creepy about that?"

Carefully, my heart beating rapidly, I parted the paper folds.

I saw the head of the doll first. At first glance, it was darling.

Brown hair made of yarn. Blue eyes drawn on—cunningly so. Even though they were simply penned in with some kind of fabric marker, they looked as if they were smiling along with the red embroidered mouth. "It *is* a baby gift. Maybe the Postmates driver left it in his car earlier and just found it. Maybe he didn't want to get in trouble for not delivering it?"

But before Maggie could agree with me, I pushed back the rest of the paper.

"Fuck *me*." I jumped backward.

Maggie lowered her phone. "What? What is it?"

I pointed.

Maggie took one look inside the box and then backed up quickly, almost tripping on the rug. "Oh, no. No, thank you. *No*."

The doll, made from what looked like rough linen, was naked. Two nipples were drawn in like the eyes had been. The nudity wasn't the horrifying part. No, it was the doll's belly that had made bile rise in my throat. The stomach was big and round, sewed crudely onto the body of the doll with sloppy, handmade stitches.

And in the center of the doll's stomach was a miniature knife, like one that might be in a dollhouse, plunged in to the hilt.

TWENTY-THREE

"Oh, hell no," said Maggie. "There *is* something going on around here!"

I held my hand to my own belly. "I *told* you that!"

"Well. I guess I just thought—"

"You didn't believe me!"

"I'm sorry about that." She shook her head as if to clear it. "But I do now. What do we do next? You want to call 911 or should I? You're probably tired of calling."

I loved that *we*. "If we call 911, then the cops come."

She nodded slowly. "Yes. The cops coming is the whole point."

"Nuh-uh. If a police car pulls up, Greg notices."

Maggie spoke slowly, as if to keep from scaring me any further. "Who's Greg, honey?"

"Don't patronize me," I snapped and immediately felt bad about it.

"Sorry. My neighbor. He's best friends with Rochelle, and he's an insomniac. He tells her everything."

She pulled the box toward her and took out the doll, holding it up. It was wearing black felt clogs like my Danskos. "Look. Jillian, this doll is a *threat*. It's a pregnant, stabbed doll. It doesn't get clearer than this. You think it's Domi?"

I rubbed my temples. "I don't know," I said.

"Call Rochelle."

"Now?"

"Now. See if Domi's with her, or if she's driving like hell toward Echo Park."

"Damn it."

Maggie nodded encouragingly as I took out my phone.

Rochelle answered in one ring. "Is it happening?"

"Not now. I keep telling you, I'll text you when it does. I'll be a little too busy to call. Is Domi with you?"

"What? Yeah. Why? I told you, that lullaby thing was an accident."

Maggie could obviously hear both sides of the conversation. "Are they at home, though?" she stage-whispered.

It didn't sound like Rochelle was in a car, but what did I know? "Can you drop a pin for me? Show me where you are?"

"I'm at *home*, Jillian."

Her dismissiveness was enough to make me want to stomp my foot like a powerless five-year-old. "Please. I need to figure something out."

"Figure what out? What are you doing?"

Maggie held out her hand. "May I?"

Since I was striking out and getting angrier by the second, what did I have to lose? I handed it over.

She pasted on a smile to match her cheerful voice. "Oh, *hi*, Rochelle. This is Maggie. Look, something scary just happened here at Jillian's, and I was here to witness it. She's not making any of this stuff up—it's real. And she very much needs the support of you and Domi right now as she gets closer and closer to bringing your *precious* baby safely into the world."

I made the universal gag-me symbol.

She went on. "Just to put her mind at ease, would you drop a pin for her of your location?"

I heard Rochelle grumbling, but then my phone dinged.

"Fabulous," said Maggie. "Can I say hi to Domi, please? I want to make sure everyone feels reassured that we're working together."

Rochelle said something I couldn't understand because my speaker distorted from the volume, but Maggie didn't even flinch. "I know," she said. "This is so hard on all three of you. I get that. It would ease Jillian's mind so much, knowing Domi is okay in her pregnancy, too, and what's best for both of them is best for the babies. Let's keep that mama cortisol low, am I right?" She winked at me. There was a pause. "Oh, Domi. So good to hear your voice. Thanks for helping out with this. Jillian is telling me to thank you both and that she hopes you're feeling well in this first exciting trimester." Another pause. "Yes. She's safe. Oh, you bet I'll keep you posted. I'll get your numbers from Jillian and text you if anything changes."

Like I had Domi's number in my phone.

She hung up. We looked at the pin Rochelle had sent. They were both in Echo Park.

They hadn't been lying. They weren't out dropping scary dolls on pregnant exes' porches.

On the one hand, I was relieved that the woman who was the bio-mother to my child wasn't driving around trying to terrorize me. On the other, goose bumps broke over my skin as I realized all over again that I didn't know where that left me.

Maggie grabbed her laptop and waved me to the couch. "Starting over, then. Let's go to Facebook. Exes, people from work, anyone else in your life you don't trust. Who's on your list?"

I closed my lips firmly. I only had one other name on my list, and I knew she didn't want to hear it.

But it must have been written on my face.

"Jillian? *No*. I will seriously repack my overnight bag and take myself home if you even utter her name."

I called her bluff. "Bree."

TWENTY-FOUR

She raised her eyes to the ceiling. "I can't believe you said it out loud. Come on. Do you honestly think Bree would steal your child? Like, for *real?*"

I shrugged.

"Like, fetal abduction."

I blinked. She'd just said the words that I couldn't even bear to think. "Exactly." It was rare but it did happen. I'd never had it happen to a patient I was in charge of, but a colleague's patient had miraculously survived an attempt a couple of years back. The patient had almost died in the attack, and her baby hadn't made it.

Maggie said, "Camille produced a show on *exactly* this. I binged all four episodes last Sunday. Womb raiding, they called it."

My abdominal muscles tightened around V at the term. "Oh, my *God.*"

"Did you know, it's almost always a woman, never a man, who does the planning? Although on Camille's show there were a couple of men who did the removal of the babies either because they were involved with the crazy lady or were hired by her to do it."

Fred jumped off the couch and slunk out of the room while I replayed the shocking words in my head. *The removal.* The doll was fifteen feet away, but in my mind, I could clearly see the unsteady line of stitches attaching the doll's belly to its body. "Bree does have enough money to hire someone," I mumbled, but for the first time I heard how it sounded. Would Bree, a woman I'd been friends with for years, really *murder* me to take my baby? What would she do with her own, for God's sakes?

Maggie raised an eyebrow. "I can't argue with that. Okay. You don't want to call the cops, but *someone* is threatening you. So I'll humor you in order to prove it isn't Bree, and *then* we can call the cops. Agree?" She started tapping at her laptop again. "Let me do my magic. Maybe we can find the baby's father."

"Okay, but if you—"

"Shh." She held up one hand, typing with the other. "Wow. Did you know she has her own Wiki page?"

I moved closer to look over her shoulder. "Yeah."

"Why am I surprised? Here's the motorcycle ride she did from Nepal to Mongolia. Apparently they made a documentary about it."

"I know. She doesn't lie about this stuff. Did you know she also has a wing named for her and Hal in the Monterey Bay Aquarium? She's too perfect. Don't you think she's too perfect?"

"I'm not calling her a liar, and I think she's *interesting.* Not perfect." Maggie shot me a serious look. "But I can admit that now you've got me nosy about her."

Bree desperately wanted a baby her husband would accept as his own in order not to lose his love or his money. "Oh, God, this is batshit," I said.

"Please let me remind you that this batshit idea is yours. Did you check court files or restraining orders?"

"I have no idea how to do that."

"She's a public figure. Legal stuff like that always gets leaked if someone's semi-famous." More clicking and tapping. Then Maggie croaked, "Holy crap."

"What?" I watched, but she was clicking and opening pages too fast for me to follow. "What is it?"

More files flashed open. "Restraining orders. Two of them."

"Hers, against someone? Or against *her*?"

"Against her. Nine years ago. Hang on, let me blow this up for the details."

I leaned against Maggie's shoulder, and she turned the computer so it faced me more. Bree Sydenham, arrest record 17632, San Francisco. *Battery. Stalking. Harassing.*

"Oh, my God. I *told* you. I told you, Maggie!" I hated that I was excited to find this. I hated that I was exulting to my friend about finding out something terrible about another friend. But I'd felt it. I'd known it.

"I just—I can't believe it." Maggie punched her hand into the cushion next to her. "This is—hang on, I need more." She made the PDF bigger, so that we could read the specific complaints. *Trespassing. Breaking and entering. Disabling house alarm. Threatening gifts sent to reporting party. Petty theft. Reporting party thinks subject has something to do with her stolen boat but has no concrete evidence.*

"It's identical," I breathed. "It's exactly the same. Who?"

"Ayla Ramsey? Do you know who she is?"

I shook my head. The name rang no bells.

The excitement drained from Maggie's voice, as if she'd just realized what we were looking at. "No. I mean, Bree is something else, but . . . I guess I'm feeling overwhelmed."

At least she knew what her emotions were. All I knew was that my body was electric, as if I were being continually zapped by a low-level current. "Me, too."

"How do you even steal a car, anyway? How do you steal a *boat*? Are there, like, YouTube tutorials or something?"

"In my case, you simply steal the keys. In the boat's case—I don't know. Hire someone?" It sounded right as soon as I said it. Bree had hired someone to get her on the dark web. She kept paid security on standby. She'd paid fifty grand for an NDA to keep an employee from talking.

"Fuck." Maggie's voice was sober. "Jillian, I'm *really* sorry I didn't take you more seriously."

It was good to have someone actually listen to me, and believe me. "It's okay."

"No, it's not." She pushed the laptop away. "Honey, you know we have to call the police."

"No," I said.

"But if it's Bree behind all this stuff, who cares if Greg calls Rochelle?"

I shook my head. "I can't risk it. Nothing changes the fact that Rochelle wanted full custody. I can't look bad in front of the mediator."

"You're being *stalked*. This isn't about looking bad!"

Ice crept down my arms, and my fingers felt cold enough to snap in half. "It *is* about looking bad. Rochelle and Domi may not be the ones doing this, but what if they use this to argue I can't protect my own baby in order to get full custody? Bree has so much money that she could make all this go away, and then I'll just look crazier than I already do."

"So, what? You're just going to wait? Until the stakes go even higher?"

"I just . . . I need some time to think. I want to go to the police with enough proof for them to actually do something about it."

Out of the darkness in the back of the house, Fred flew into the living room, slammed his butt into the side table, and raced out again, his nails scrabbling for purchase on the hardwood. Maggie gave a short scream, and I jumped so hard I hurt something in my neck.

"What the hell was that?" Maggie leaped to standing, her hands at her lower back. "Is he reacting to something?"

"Jesus, I hope not. He just gets the zoomies sometimes in the middle of the night. The alarm didn't beep, but—" I took a deep breath. "I guess we should check anyway."

Maggie gave me an incredulous look. "You think? *Yes, we should check.*"

As we walked around the house, she kept up a steady muttered stream of words behind me. I heard things like, *this is too much, this is bullshit, this is not okay.* It should have made me more nervous, but instead, it was a relief to have someone saying out loud what my mind kept screaming.

We checked the baby's room, my bedroom, and the office. I touched every window's lock, making sure it was in place. Something creaked in the attic. It was a familiar creak—it happened at least a couple of times a night as the roof cooled. But for the first time, I pictured someone up there in the crawl space. Maggie, braver than I could ever be, propped up the ladder and poked her head into the low attic. She eased her way down the ladder, shaking her head.

Nothing was out of place.

Still, after we'd walked through every room and were back in the kitchen, Maggie said, "I hate all of this." Looking at the doll still resting in its box, she said, "I want to take that outside and throw it away—"

I finished her statement for her. "But it's evidence."

"Damn, Jillian." She leaned on the counter next to me. "I don't think I can stay here."

My face tightened as I tried not to react, but my vision narrowed. I wanted to clutch at Maggie. I wanted to wrap my arms around her legs and beg her to stay.

But instead, I said stiffly, "I totally get that. I'll be fine, I swear. I've got the alarm, and I've got Fred, the useless slob."

"No, you idiot. We're going to my house."

The wave of relief that washed over me made me shiver. After our fight at brunch there was no way Bree would suspect I was over at Maggie's. It was perfect—I'd be safe while I figured out what to do next before getting the police involved.

"Let me put out extra cat food and pack a bag." Suddenly, I couldn't move fast enough.

TWENTY-FIVE

With middle-of-the-night traffic, it only took fifteen minutes to get to the Palisades. I'd hit some kind of wall. As I'd packed a bag for several days, I felt the way I had that day, long ago, when I'd left my mother's house. I was sure I was bringing the wrong things to Maggie's. A swimsuit. Laser-cat T-shirt. Extra underwear. My birthing go-bag. A box of Mother's Cookies, for God's sakes.

Maggie didn't force the chitchat on the way. From time to time, I'd see her in my peripheral vision turning her head to check on me. Delayed-onset fear was whapping around in my chest, and I was too scared to really think hard about anything at all. I counted streetlights to try to calm my breathing—I couldn't get much beyond twenty or so before I lost count and had to start over again.

She made a right on Montana instead of continuing on the Pacific Coast Highway and slowed in front of the twenty-four-hour Whole Foods, appearing to contemplate. I could think of nothing worse in the whole world than grocery shopping. "Can we just go straight to your house? I really don't need anything."

Her eyes were on her rearview mirror as she stepped on the gas and kept driving north. "I think—no." She switched lanes, jerking the wheel abruptly.

I frowned. "Unless you really want to, that is."

"Someone's following us."

I sat up straight. "Seriously?"

"I wasn't sure until I got off PCH. No, don't turn around. Use your mirror. Help me figure out if I'm imagining it or not."

I flipped down the vanity mirror. "The car right behind us?"

"No, the one behind that. Its lights are kind of high, you see them? With the smaller outside lights? Like a truck or something. The street-lamp was out at the corner, so I couldn't get a good look at it when we turned. I swear to God it's been behind us since the turn onto Lincoln."

Lincoln was two blocks from my house. There was no way a car would follow us this far by chance. "Maggie, I don't want this." The words sounded stupid, but I'd never meant anything more.

"Hold tight." She hit the gas and blew the red light at Twentieth Street.

I held my breath and closed my eyes. My head pounded painfully.

Palming the wheel like Vin Diesel, she went right on Twenty-First Street and took an immediate left on Idaho. She pulled into the drive-way of a small apartment complex. Then she cut the engine and the lights.

"Did we lose it?" I whispered the words, as if we could be followed by sound.

"I don't know."

We both turned our heads, staying low, as a black truck roared past going at least twice the speed limit. It kept going north on Idaho.

"Ha!" Her voice was triumphant. "Okay, now we go before it comes back to look for us. How was *that*, baby?" She held up her hand for a high five.

I gave it to her, but I didn't feel the same sense of victory. Instead, the panic leached from my bones into my blood, fear icing the muscles that lined my veins as Maggie sped down Twenty-Second to Alta and then headed toward the beach on the side streets. "Would she hire someone like that to scare me?"

"Honestly? I don't know. But we're going to find out." Maggie gave me what was probably supposed to be a reassuring smile, but I wasn't sure I'd find reassurance anywhere tonight.

"But Bree knows where you live." What had seemed like a great idea—the security of staying at Maggie's house—now seemed stupid. I'd kept my eyes on the mirror, but I hadn't seen the same light pattern behind us. If we had been followed by Bree or someone in her employ, what did it matter that Maggie had lost them? They could still beat us to Maggie's if they wanted to.

"I have a really tall security gate that I usually never close because opening it takes so long and I'm impatient. But we'll use it as long as you're here. Both it and the house are on a closed circuit, monitored by a system that detects sound as well as motion. It picks up rats' footsteps on dirt, I shit you not."

I groaned and rubbed my temples. "I really appreciate this. You wouldn't believe this headache."

"I've got Advil at the house. And don't mention it, seriously. You'd do the same."

"Tylenol, right?" Ibuprofen was unsafe during pregnancy.

"That's what I meant. Tomorrow we'll figure all this out. Tonight, you don't have to worry about a thing."

Inside her house, Maggie's guest room smelled like clean sheets and mint, and the pillows were fluffy. She started to say something about extra towels, but I stopped listening.

Safe. I was safe.

My house—it would never be the same again. The truth had been filtering in during our drive, but it was suddenly big enough for me to hear it. I'd have to move. I'd *have* to leave. No matter what happened in the future, I'd never feel safe there again. While pregnant, I'd have to make a new home, where I'd live by myself. While I was at it, I'd make it a fortress. Could builders do moats nowadays? Could I afford to buy a bunker? Jodie Foster's panic room flashed through my mind.

"You good?" Maggie stood at the door, hand on the light switch. "You need anything else, call out. I'm just across the hall, and I sleep lightly. I'll come running."

"Thank you," I said. "Thanks for taking care of Violet and me."

Her eyes softened. "Violet?"

I smiled sleepily. "That's the first time I've said her name out loud." It felt good to share it with someone. With Maggie, in particular.

"It's gorgeous. A perfect name." She paused, putting her hand on her belly. "We're building our own families now, Jillian. This is it. This is *our* time."

"I'm happy we're friends," I said. *See, Rochelle? I let people in.*

"Me, too. Okay, sleep well."

As I drifted off to sleep, I promised Violet that I'd do whatever it took to keep her safe.

TWENTY-SIX

I awoke with something that felt like a hangover in a room that wasn't mine—it smelled sweet and rich, like an expensive candle. I gazed through blurry eyes at a room I didn't recognize. A rocking chair sat on an orange rug.

The oversize red tank top I had on wasn't mine, nor was the black skirt that rode around my hips. I didn't recognize the orange poppy-covered sheet I was lying on.

I didn't remember anything about going to bed. How did I get here? *Where* was here?

I tried to push myself up into a seated position so I could clear my head, but my leg seemed caught by a leather cuff attached to a ring of steel that was chained to the wooden bed frame.

I laughed out loud in shocked surprise, although if this was a game, I hated it. "Hello?" My voice caught in the dry terror that coated my larynx.

I swiveled my head to the right.

The doll.

The one I'd found in the box on the doorstep at home, the one that I'd opened while Maggie watched.

But instead of the doll having the round, pregnant belly, now the belly had been ripped off, leaving only red batting trailing to her linen knees.

I sucked in a choked breath. I couldn't—I didn't—

Maggie—I was at her house—I had a dim recollection of going to bed, pulling up the covers around me.

But I wasn't in the guest room I'd slept in the night before. This was a nursery. *I was bound to the bed.* The horror of it, the *feel* of it, made breathing almost impossible. I sat up awkwardly and hunched, wrapping my arms around my belly as much as I could.

"Maggie!" Bree must have found us, must have gotten in. Had she drugged us in our sleep? What had she done to Maggie?

I dragged a breath into my lungs and yelled as loudly as I could through my ragged throat. "*Maggie!* Are you okay? Shout if you can hear me!"

The door opened silently.

Maggie entered. She appeared unharmed, dressed as if she were going to a fundraiser in a long gray button-down tunic, gray pants, and high black boots.

"Hey, sweetie." She didn't look the slightest bit upset.

That single fact sent a chilled electrical pulse through my body.

I blinked my eyes hard and bit the inside of my mouth. It hurt, and I tasted blood. I wasn't dreaming. "Maggie. I don't—" Nothing made sense. There was a low buzz at the back of my sinuses, filling my head with noise.

"I turned the heat up so you wouldn't be cold, but let me know if it's up too high."

I was freezing, but feeling cold was the least of my worries. "Maggie—

you didn't do this to me. Right?" Her eyes looked normal—that was the thing that terrified me most. "Did you? What—why—?"

This was some crazy prank. Some really stupid shenanigan. Maybe she was filming me and she was going to send it to the Ripleys. Maybe they'd all come in in a moment and laugh, and as the one with the closest due date, I'd be done with the hazing part that I didn't know about.

But somehow my heart knew I was lying to my head. Fear, fresh and aggressive, zapped through me. My hands started to shake.

"Oh, you *are* cold. But I can't put a blanket on you. I'm so sorry about that."

"Why." It wasn't a question as much as it was a single panted syllable.

"I know you'll understand—I just can't have you hide Violet from me. But I'll turn up the heat."

I wanted to physically wrest my baby's name out of her mouth. "Maggie, this isn't funny. How did you change my clothes? Where are mine?" I didn't see them anywhere—were they in the closet? Had they actually been hidden from me? What about my purse? My keys? Jesus, my phone. If I didn't have it—"Where's my cell?"

She grinned as if we were in on a joke together. "You didn't seem to mind at all last night. You shucked off your clothes as soon as I asked you nicely. You also happily gave me your purse and your phone. It's all in a safe place, don't worry."

The Tylenol she'd given me the night before. Fuck. "Why—" I kicked with my left foot, and the chain actually rattled, as if I were suddenly the star of a horror movie. "Maggie, you're really scaring me. Why am I—" I couldn't even say the word *shackled*. I was too terrified to utter it, scared it might make it really true. My teeth started chattering, clacking painfully in my mouth.

"Honey, you have nothing to worry about. I'll bring you whatever you need. I just need to keep you safely in this room."

Maggie wasn't *crazy*. "But I don't get it. I'm here because I wanted to be. Remember? We came here to get me out of my house." Around the boulder of fear in my throat, I managed to say, "I don't understand. How can I help you with whatever this is?"

"Oh, Jillian. That drive to help is one of the things I adore most about you. I love that you help women have babies and that you help women *not* have babies when they shouldn't have them."

I couldn't respond. My brain was having a hard time keeping up, still fuzzy with whatever she'd knocked me out with. Was Maggie a secret pro-life zealot? How long ago was it that I'd told her I'd had an abortion? It was on the beach at Bree's house, and that was what, more than two weeks ago? Had she been planning this since then?

Should I lie to her? Tell her that I regretted my abortion even though I'd made it clear I didn't? Or maybe it was about my practice. My lips pressed against each other, trembling, as I tried to decide on the best course of action. "Maggie, I don't do abortions. Sometimes I do the D&C if a birth isn't viable." This wasn't true—I was making it up on the fly. Of course I provided abortion services when I needed to. I also provided compassionate prenatal care and caught as many babies as I could. "I'm so sorry if you thought that."

"Oh, I totally understand. It's just that you owe me something, and you haven't been aware of it. That's all. I'm here to collect." She smiled again. "Compassionately, of course."

I was an inch away from whimpering. "Please. *Please* tell me what you're talking about. I swear I'll help you in any way I possibly can. I'm here for you." I scrabbled at the bottom sheet I was sitting on. I didn't think a sheet could protect me much from anything, but I wanted any kind of protection I could get. I pulled a corner of the sheet off the bed and held it over my belly.

She stepped forward and slapped me hard across the face. The pain was instant, and my neck snapped sideways as I fell over.

I gasped before slowly pushing myself up again. I held my hands out in front of me, in case I could stop her from doing that again. It was the second time I'd been hit by a friend in two days, but while I'd been shocked by Bree's angry slap, this strike was so much worse. It didn't feel out of control or even angry. It felt like a warning.

Maggie's pleasant expression hadn't changed, not a single cloud passing over it. "Oh, I really don't like doing that. Please don't cover your belly. That part's important, okay?"

I struggled to catch my breath and then, using every bit of bravery I had, asked, "Maggie, you're my friend. I will do *anything* to help you."

"You mean that?" She looked at me gratefully, as if I'd bought her a chai latte.

I nodded as my tongue explored my mouth. I tasted blood as my head rang. "I don't know what this is—" Tears flowed down my cheeks—I hadn't even been aware I was crying. It angered me; I should be fighting, not crying, but she stood just out of my reach now. "I'm not even sure who you are right now."

"Jillian!" She looked troubled by my words, her eyebrows drawing together. "I hate that you feel that way. I'm the same old Maggie, can't you see that? I haven't changed at all. Maybe you didn't quite see all of me—maybe you weren't looking hard enough. But I've been right here for you, waiting, all this time. Come on," she chided me eagerly, as if we were playing a game. "You have to know what this is about. I'll give you one last chance."

One last chance or what? Was she looking for an apology? "I don't—I don't know what I did. But I'm sorry for it. Let me help. I know something's terribly wrong, and I'll do anything I can. I don't want you getting too stressed—think about *your* baby."

That smile crossed her face again. Pure, delighted sunshine. She cradled her belly. "My baby. You're right." Her voice was warm, and her eyes were bright. "Let's talk about my darling little girl."

She dragged the rocker in the corner over, still staying out of range of my reach. "You fell asleep so fast last night I didn't get a chance to ask you what you think of my nursery."

"Oh," I gasped. I was grasping at straws. "Yeah, it's great. So cute.

I love the yellow." Was that the right answer? Was that what she needed to come out of this? I cast my eyes quickly around the room. Should I comment on the block-letter *ABC* prints on the walls? The carved dark-wood changing table on the far wall that must have cost a fortune?

"I love it, too," she said, rocking slowly back and forth. "What does the paint remind you of?"

My thoughts wobbled. "Lemon."

She frowned slightly.

I changed tack. "No, that's wrong. It's too dark for lemon. It's kind of orange-yellow. School bus? Is that what it is?" I anxiously scanned her face to see if I was going to pass the test.

Maggie shook her head slowly, as if I'd disappointed her. "Close. But not quite right. School is definitely a clue."

School shoes. School clothes. School supplies. It came to me then, and relief lit my veins with hope. "Pencil. It's pencil yellow."

That same smile brightened her face again. "I knew you'd get it. I got them to mix the color specially for me. It's almost too bad no baby will ever sleep in this room."

Cold from my neck to my waist, my shivering got worse—a spasm of fear shook my torso. "Maggie, *please* tell me what I can do for you."

She just kept the rocker moving, slowly forward, slowly back. Her feet left the floor and then touched back down. "Check this out." She pulled a Papermate mechanical pencil from a pocket. "Remember this?"

A green feeling slicked the back of my throat. Something sparked in my memory but then shorted out before I could grab it.

Maggie held the pencil between her teeth as she unbuttoned her shirt slowly from the top button down, as if she were doing a strange, seated strip tease. Her bra was black, and her almost twenty-seven-week bulge was taut, her belly button already jutting out.

Whatever this was, I didn't want it. "Maggie, no."

But she didn't listen. She lifted her arm high, smiling kindly at me the whole time. Then plunged her fist toward her abdomen.

She stabbed herself in the stomach with the pencil, bending forward with an ear-splitting cry.

Then, keeping the pencil deeply inside her, she drew it through her skin and pulled so hard her whole belly opened wide.

As I screamed, she *laughed*.

TWENTY-SEVEN

Instead of the rapidly pooling blood I expected to see pour out, cotton stuffing exploded out of Maggie's belly. She kept rocking the chair as she tugged out more and more batting. It filled her hands—white clouds that expanded the more she pulled. She got hold of a red string and yanked. A rolled piece of paper was tied to the end, and she held it up in victory. "Look! The piñata contains a surprise! And it's for you!"

What the fuck what the fuck what the fuck—

She held up the paper and unrolled it, her fake belly pulled wide open, batting hanging to her knees. "It's got your name on it and everything."

JILLIAN. The lettering was in red, big block letters.

Underneath it, black letters read, *SURPRISE!* A pink rattle was under the words *IT'S A GIRL.*

"Isn't that fun? I thought you would like it," she said. "It's a girl! It's *your* girl. Your Violet."

Nothing made sense, but images slammed into my brain faster than I could stop them. Tori Newbold, driving a bloody mechanical pencil into her intestines. Blood running out from under the privacy curtain. Shards of the pencil's yellow clip carefully cut out of her upper intestine. My breath foul in my surgical mask. The knowledge my career was over. "But Tori's in Portland."

"Oh, good! You found her on Facebook! I've been maintaining that for a while now. Doesn't that woman look like I used to? We could practically be sisters."

"Her family."

Maggie nodded. "Is real, of course. Her real name is Shannon. Obviously, she doesn't know I borrow her pictures for the Tori page."

"You're her," I said with the tiny bit of oxygen I was able to drag into my lungs. "You're Tori."

"Finally!" She dipped her head cheerfully. "Margaret Victoria, in the flesh. You really never recognized me?" Her expression moved from happiness to proud delight, as if she were asking me if she'd managed to keep the surprise party under wraps. The rocker lurched faster.

"*No.*" I couldn't get enough air, like I was sucking on a tube. "I didn't." But I could see it now. She'd dyed her red hair to that dark brown, or maybe the red had been the fake color. "But you had . . . *freckles.*" So many orange freckles. I wasn't misremembering that, was I?

Maggie looked pleased. "I never liked those freckles. Laser treatment is amazing, right?"

She also must have been thirty pounds heavier seven years ago. When I met her at AA, if she'd looked familiar, I didn't remember it. Everyone kind of looked familiar in the recovery rooms after a while.

"But your sonogram." She'd shown the Ripleys her first sonogram, passing her phone around proudly. She'd loved that I'd said the baby had a nicely shaped head.

"Too easy. FakeaBaby.com. Less than twenty bucks."

"The things at my house? The footprints? The knife?"

Her eyes lit with what looked like real pleasure. "You never once looked at the size of my feet, did you? I was even wearing those same shoes *at* your house. I just unlocked the laundry room door as I left that day and let myself in that night."

It was the one door I never opened, so I never checked the deadbolt.

"I moved the plant and the knife, and I even sat across the street, watching the cops roll up. No one looks at a white lady sitting in a nice car."

I seemed unable to blink. "But I set the alarm that night."

She raised one eyebrow. "I tried 1234 and then 4321. I was either going to set off your alarm and freak you out, which would be okay, or I was going to get in and rattle you that way. After that night, I had your house key *and* your code."

Rochelle had wanted a code that was difficult to remember. She was the one who dealt with numbers all day. But I said I wouldn't have been able to remember something complex or unique after a marathon shift. I'd insisted on a stupid-simple code, never thinking anyone would actually try to guess it. And the night the plant had moved, when Maggie was in my house, I'd been in the bedroom, where I couldn't hear the soft beep the alarm made when a door was opened.

"Cracking doors and windows when you were gone was almost too easy, but sometimes the simple stuff is the most effective. I got into your laptop while you were at work—you should really have a lock code on that, by the way. Then I could log into your Spotify on my phone, since your password autofilled visibly, another thing you should eventually fix. Playing that song on repeat was a fun touch, right?"

My mind raced as I fought a sick sense of relief. *It wasn't me. It hadn't ever been me.* I wasn't my mother—I hadn't been losing my mind; I hadn't been dissociating. I hadn't been sabotaging my own pregnancy. I hadn't been out to get myself.

And under the relief and the terror, I somehow found I had room for another emotion: shame. Rochelle and Domi and Bree—none of them had been out to get me. How could I have ever thought they were?

It had been Maggie all along. But I still didn't understand how she'd done it all. "The baby journal. You didn't have a key then, or the code."

She raised an eyebrow. "I knew you rarely locked your back slider, and you never used to set the alarm."

"But then I changed the locks."

"Don't you remember who suggested that locksmith?" She looked satisfied. "A hundred-dollar tip goes a long way."

And I'd only changed the locks, not the alarm code. "The gas leak?"

"The what?" Her frown looked real.

"Not you?"

"I wasn't trying to *hurt* you, Jillian! Surely you don't think I would ever do that."

I didn't have any idea what I thought anymore, so I kept staring at her shredded plastic stomach. I couldn't take my eyes off it. If I'd ever looked straight at her belly even once for more than fifteen seconds, it would have been obvious. It looked like it was meant for the movies, but only at specific, head-on angles. When I'd hugged her, it had had the right resistance and firmness to feel real. "It's exactly the right size," I said stupidly.

"Silicone. Amazon."

"The doll?" I refused to look at it. "You were with me when it was dropped on the doorstep."

"TaskRabbit, my darling. Good question, though. I sewed it myself! Aren't you impressed?" She rocked forward to grab it off the bedside table. "You didn't even know I sewed, did you? I'm not just an excellent baker—I excel in all the domestic arts. I did this by hand, not even using the machine. I wanted to get her right, and I think I did." She smoothed the doll's yarn hair.

Did she expect me to congratulate her on her home ec skills? "Where's my car?"

"I parked it downtown, key in the ignition. Do you have comprehensive insurance?"

Dumbly, I nodded.

"Oh, good. Hopefully it's really stolen by now. You might even get a check worth more than what you owe on it." She carefully laid the horrible doll over one knee.

The pieces were clunking into place in my mind. "That truck was never chasing us, was it?"

"It was just driving too fast. I turned in front of it whenever I could see it signal. Not easy, since it was two cars behind us, but I thought I did well."

"And Bree. You made all that up about her." I'd only looked over Maggie's shoulder at her laptop when she'd been showing me what her "search" found. "The restraining order wasn't real."

"*That* I'm proud of. That shocker about the paternity of her kid let me know that I was doing everything right, that this was meant to be. After you asked me to spend the night, I only had a few hours to get all that together and make the forms look real." She shook her head. "Although, honestly, Jillian, why you would trust what one person said they found on the internet is kind of baffling. The coincidence that she'd have a restraining order against her with exactly what happened to you? I expected more from you."

I expected more from you. Was she parroting my mother's words back to me on purpose?

Maggie wasn't done chastising me. "Seriously, it's a good thing this baby will have Rochelle's brains and not yours." But she said it lightly, as if I'd giggle along with her.

"But you wanted me to call the cops about the doll!"

"I had to sell it, didn't I? Besides, so what if they'd come? It wasn't like they'd think about pinning it on me. My prints were already all over the doll and the box, just from touching it with you."

"What if I'd given birth early?"

"That would have been harder, but I had a plan B. Get it?" She smiled.

"How long . . ." I didn't really know what I even wanted to ask her. Or, no, there were too many questions—a million of them lined up like planes readying for takeoff in my mind: *How did you find me? How long have you been planning this? How did you know I was an alcoholic? How did you know to find me in the rooms? What if I'd never gotten pregnant? What are you going to do now?*

But I didn't have time. There was something worse coming, and it had to do with V and a frighteningly long-term plan.

I had to get away.

If I could break free of the leg chain, I could throw myself out the window, wrapping my arms around my belly to protect it from glass damage. I was barefoot, but I didn't care. With the level of fear that coursed through me like electricity, I would be faster than her. I'd have to be. And surely the crash of the glass would draw someone's attention somewhere, and if it didn't, I'd just scream until someone heard me.

"How long what?" She was staring at me.

I'd pulled on the chain when I'd woken up, but that had only been with the power of my arms. For this move, I'd use all of my body weight. I'd break it and get free because I *had* to.

I didn't waste time planning it any more than that.

Taking a deep breath, I launched myself off the left side of the bed, moving as fast and hard as I could toward my salvation, that window.

But the chain was stronger than I was. My right leg kicked toward the window, but when I felt myself caught by the chain, I spun halfway around in midair. I couldn't land on my belly—that was the most important thing. So I crashed onto my right hip, having torqued my belly under and around almost the whole way. My right foot was on the floor, but my left foot was still crossed over it in the air, the chain holding strong. My left knee screamed in agony.

I'd lost all my breath in the fall. God, I'd been so stupid to try. What if it made her angry? Coated with humiliation and sick with terror, I used my right leg to awkwardly push myself back up onto the bed, twisting it under the left one. The leather of the cuff burned my skin, and I wrestled the tank top over my bump. My swollen breasts ached. I was making so much noise, so much clattering and thumping, that I couldn't hear Maggie behind me at all. When I twisted to look at her, my arms raised automatically in case she was charging at me.

But Maggie hadn't moved except to continue swaying slowly back and forth in the rocker, the doll still lying over her knee. "Okay, sugar. I probably wouldn't do that again if I were you. You're bleeding." She pointed to where the leather had opened the thin skin at my ankle. "But then again, I can't force you to do anything you don't want to do. Besides staying in that bed, that is. You'll have more room if you get out of bed on this side, though."

I looked where she pointed and saw for the first time that the ankle chain was hooked around another, longer looped chain that had halfway slipped off the end of the bed. It meant if I got out of the bed on the right-hand side—toward Maggie in her rocker, toward the door behind her—I'd be able to stand up and perhaps move a few feet away from the bed.

"That should help. I'll set up your toilet in a minute."

The words themselves were so terrifying I nearly wet myself.

Maggie leaned forward and set the doll back on the nightstand, facing me. Then, reaching inside her open tunic, she tugged on a pair of white strings at her sides. The ripped prosthetic belly fell forward into her lap.

I said slowly, "I tried looking for you once. I actually hired a private detective to try to find you. I wanted to make amends. When I couldn't find you, Nicole said that it was my higher power's way of telling me not to reopen old wounds. She said I'd just have to make living amends."

Maggie nodded placidly as if all this made sense. "Oh, living amends is exactly what you're making now. I was married when I went to your hospital, and I went back to my maiden name after we divorced. He couldn't handle the infertility you left me with. Too bad your private eye wasn't very good, was he? *I'm* the one who found what I was looking for, and I didn't need a PI to do it. I've been watching you for a long time. Remember, you used to post to a doctors-in-recovery forum? Supposed to be anonymous, but you use MarshDr for everything."

"That's how you found me in A.A." It was a really smart idea, honestly. Meetings were filled with people who came and went—no one could know everyone.

She shot a finger gun at me. "*Bam.* What better way? You were *so* fucked-up when you were treating me."

My mouth tasted metallic. "You knew I was drunk."

"You were slurring so much I could barely understand you. When you got sober and then married, I knew you'd probably get knocked up at some point. You or Rochelle, although obviously I hoped it would be you."

I pictured Rochelle chained to the bed instead of me. That would be the only thing worse than it being me—to put her in a place she hadn't done anything to deserve. "You've been watching me since you got sober."

She rocked backward in the chair with laughter. "You are *adorable.* You're not getting it. I've never been an addict."

TWENTY-EIGHT

My heart thumped hard against my ribs. I knew *nothing* about this woman.

"Your parents?"

"Oh, that part was true. Plane crash in the Azores. You can't make that shit up. It's true, what I told you about losing my whole family that night. I've been trying to get one back since then. I blame you, of course, for my husband leaving me. I'd have been willing to adopt, if he'd stayed, like good old fake Tori Newbold on Facebook. You know she actually has friends on there? She's not even a real person, but she has friends."

I had friends, too.

I had friends I'd thought I could trust.

I could only guess at what she wanted to hear, but I was more than willing to say it. She didn't need to trap me to get an apology. I'd been wanting to apologize to the woman I'd hurt so badly for so many years. So I spoke through my terror. "Maggie, I am so terribly sorry about what I did to you. I'm sorry from the bottom of my soul. That was the worst night of my life."

Shit. They were the wrong words, such *stupid* words—I could feel that as soon as they left my mouth.

Her soft smile went rigid for the first time. "What a tragedy that night was so hard on you."

I needed to get the words exactly right. "That's not what I meant. What I did to you was unforgivable. I wasn't in my right mind, and you were the one that got hurt. I was callous and uncaring, and I would do anything to change what happened that night. I'm not sure how to make you believe this, but I've wanted to say this to you since then. I was worried about my job that night, but you lost a child. There's nothing harder than that."

Maggie's eyes filled with tears.

I went on, "Truly, from the bottom of my heart, I am eternally deeply sorry for what I did to you, Maggie. I beg for your forgiveness though I don't deserve it."

She put her hands together in front of her chest and then raised them to her face, as if praying. Her eyes closed, and her lips moved. Every muscle in her body looked like it had been tightened with a key, and a purple vein stood out in her forehead. The corners of her mouth were white with tension.

I held my breath. I waited.

Her lids fluttered open, and her body relaxed. The hint of her normal smile returned. "Anyway, like I was saying, I connected the two chains so that you can stand on this side of the bed for the toilet."

Damn it. I hadn't gotten through to her.

She stood. "I'll go get that, while I'm thinking about it."

The fact that I hadn't peed in the bed was a fucking miracle, but I desperately didn't want the mattress to be wet as well as cold.

Maggie opened a door to what appeared to be the en suite bathroom. She brought out a bright blue bucket. Setting it next to the bed, she snapped what looked like a toilet seat onto the top of it. "Look what REI had! They call it a luggable loo. The bags are supposed to trap odor, but who knows? So. Do you need to go?"

I thought I'd felt fear before that, but what flooded through my brain then was worse. I was instantly nauseous in a first-trimester way.

I gagged and swallowed. "Yes." I moved to the edge of the bed.

She looked vaguely surprised, as if she thought I might not have to. Well. She'd never actually been pregnant, after all.

I had no underwear on, only the skirt that wasn't mine, so it was easy to sit on the seat. The bucket wobbled a bit as I urinated. The relief I felt was overwhelmed by the shame of her watching me relieve myself.

Then the nausea came back. *Fuck, fuck, no . . .* But my body told me it was too late. I made a garbled noise and lifted myself just enough to fall to my knees in front of the bucket, which now smelled of my own uric acid.

"Oh, no. You feel that badly?"

I couldn't answer. I didn't have much to throw up, but I dry heaved for at least a minute, inhaling the plastic scent of the liner and urine, trying very, very hard not to think about what the scent might change to if I didn't get out of here soon. I lifted my head for fresh air.

I'd failed in my apology, but I'd try it again as soon as I could breathe. I'd use different, better words. I had to try; I had to make her see that I truly *was* sorry about what I'd done to her seven years ago.

Or . . .

Maggie was close to me. Really close. My arms were shaking too hard to be of much use, but if I breathed steadily and slowly, maybe I could be fast and strong enough to throw her to the ground. *Then what?*

I'd have to knock her out.

I pretended to dry heave a little more—which wasn't difficult—while I tried to breathe deeply enough to smooth my nerves. "Water," I said. Should I make it sound more like begging? I wasn't far from it, anyway. I kept my head close to the rim of the bucket. "Please? Please can I have some water?"

"You poor thing. Throwing up is the worst, isn't it? I'll be right back. Sparkling or still?"

As if I cared. "Anything."

"Still water, I think. The carbonation might make you gaseous, and that would make it worse. I'll be right back."

Maggie left the door of the room open, and I leaned back, away from the bucket. My mouth was an acidic nightmare, and for a sharp second I longed for a toothbrush and toothpaste. *Forget that.* I needed to calm my heart rate and be ready to *act.*

She would come in holding the glass of water. I'd still be hunched over the bucket, and I'd lift my hand wearily for the water. I wouldn't look at her. That way, even if she'd planned to put the glass of water on the floor so that I couldn't grab at her, she'd hopefully take pity and actually hand it to me.

Then I'd pull her to the ground somehow and knock her out.

Knock her out? This was *Maggie.* How was this real?

V gave a slow stretch followed by a rapid rat-a-tat, a visceral reminder I wasn't in this alone. The thought wasn't a comfort—it was a horror. *I* was the one who had to protect Violet at all costs. I took another long, slow breath, ignoring the way it hitched in my chest.

Okay, exactly how would I knock Maggie out? I had nothing to hit her with. The only things in reach were the plastic bucket and the nightstand, which looked lightweight, maybe bamboo. Was that on purpose? Did she think I'd have this idea? The rest of her furniture wasn't this cheap Cost Plus–looking stuff.

My empty stomach turned as V kicked me again, this time hard in the lungs. I'd just have to somehow knock Maggie's head onto the floor. Luckily, the room had a Spanish tile floor covered by three small orange rugs, easily pushed aside.

I had to get this right. I dropped my head and rested both hands on top of my belly. I usually prayed to something outside myself, a universal source I wasn't sure I even believed in. But right then, I prayed directly to Violet. "Please, little one. I'll get us out of this. I promise. I have to get us the fuck out of here." Then, desperately: "*Please.*"

I heard footsteps in the hallway, and I leaned forward over the bucket again. I took in another breath and pictured white light filling me, the white light my meditation teacher always told us to fill ourselves with. I usually thought it was silly, but right now, I was dragging that white light into me as hard as I could in case light equaled power.

Maggie entered. I didn't look up. I fake gagged again and weakly held up my hand already curved to take a glass. My arm shook.

"I'll set your water over here."

Instead of looking at her, I dry heaved again, this time for real. I let my hand fall to grip the side of the bucket and coughed. I spat and held my hand out again, resting my forehead against the flimsy toilet seat's rim.

"I'm sorry you feel so terrible, honey. It'll get better, I promise."

I didn't move but faked clearing my throat. Then I moaned just a little, for verisimilitude.

"Fine. Here it is."

I heard ice clink in the glass as it got closer to me.

One, two . . .

I sprang.

TWENTY-NINE

I whipped my body sideways and grasped Maggie's extended wrist with both of my hands. She leaped back, but I had her, and my grip was tight.

The glass smashed to the tile floor between us. I pushed up on my knees and yanked her arm as hard as I could. She took a step forward to counterbalance herself, but I was too fast, and the floor was too slippery. She crashed to the floor, and for one terrible second, a flash of worry about her baby sped through my mind.

But Maggie wasn't pregnant.

Right now, my friend Maggie, someone I loved, was the enemy.

She kicked sideways at me as I scrabbled to get closer to her. My bulge slowed me down, and my leg jolted as I reached the end of the chain, but her hair was loose. As she tried to twist away from me, I managed to get a large clump of it in my hands. I held it tighter, getting both hands around the hank. She punched at me, but I held fast, clawing her closer. Her boot connected with my knee. A shard of glass bit into my upper arm. I didn't care.

Maggie continued to strike out at me, but I pulled my hardest until I was finally in position. I forced myself to my knees, using her hair for purchase, and when her head was seven or eight inches above the tile, I whipped my hands up and then down, slamming her skull against the tile with a sickening thud. I recoiled automatically, letting go of her and scrabbling backward, smashing into the bed. If I'd had anything left to vomit, I would have.

She was still breathing. *Thank God.* What if I'd killed her? Adrenaline continued to flood into my blood, nauseating me even more.

Maggie appeared to be either stunned or passed out. I didn't care which, as long as it gave me this moment. I felt frozen in fear, a deer too scared to run from a lion.

No.

I had to be the lion. Blood dripped from my upper arm where I'd cut it on the broken glass. I was still shackled but at least I had time to work on how the hell to get the restraint off. The leather cuff was thick, and the metal locking it around my ankle was keyed.

Would Maggie have the key on her?

She still wasn't moving. Her breathing was shallow, but that might be because she was lying on her side folded at the waist. I had to take the chance that the key was in her pocket, and I had to look for it now. I scrambled toward Maggie as fear ripped through me. Her pants were thick stretch twill with long thigh pockets, the kind intended to hold a cell phone. I could reach the left one easily. It was flat and didn't appear to be holding anything. I touched it lightly—I'd feel a key if it were there.

Nothing. That meant I'd have to roll her to her other side. Shit.

Maggie groaned low in her throat, and her eyelids fluttered, not quite opening all the way.

Faster. I pushed at her hip, hard, rolling her onto her back. I was sweating from every pore. Her mouth dropped open but her eyes stayed closed.

Something crinkled in her pocket. Shoving my hand into the stretch fabric, I pulled out a crumpled receipt. A tiny metal key tumbled out with it, landing in the spilled water.

Maggie came up with a scream as I reached for it, hitting me hard in the shoulder with her torso. I flew, landing on my left hip, my hands still outstretched. I tried to regain my balance and lunged for the key.

It was a bad mistake, one I only realized as she shoved me against the bed frame. I should have gone for her again, not for the fucking key.

"If you *ever* try something like that again—" She'd struggled to her feet, so much lighter and faster than me.

She drew back her booted foot and kicked me hard in the high ribs. I cowered, sheltering my belly, as the pain ripped through me. I could feel something tear—an intercostal muscle? Or had a rib broken? I lost my breath again, this time from the lancing pain near my lungs.

"Up! On the bed!" She kicked me again, this time in my glutes. Less painful but equally terrifying.

"Okay. Hold on. Let me get my balance." My voice was a gasp, and my gaze fell on the key, still in the water surrounded by broken glass. I heaved myself and my stomach up but stayed in a crouch, moving as if I were about to fall onto the bed. At the last second, I dove for the key.

She shoved me so hard that I fell sideways, crashing into the nightstand.

Bashing her head into the ground had simply made her angry, as if I'd head-butted a hornet's nest. I had no weapons. I'd already known that she was strong, but I hadn't known just *how* strong she was.

Was killing me her goal? I crawled my way up onto the bed before she kicked or shoved me again. "Maggie—I don't know what you want, but hurting me won't—"

She gave a huge, exhausted sigh as she leaned to pick up the key. Sliding it back into her pocket, she said, "I'll store this in a safe place much farther away from you. You're not getting it, are you? I don't want to hurt you. I love you. I really do, hon." The short endearment made me shiver. "I'd *really* rather you survive this whole thing, but if you end up dying because you choose to be a dumbass, it'll be on you. Don't forget that. My baby girl will be fine if I get her out of you fast enough. So. Let's not fight anymore."

I stopped breathing, an icy wave of sheer dread freezing me into place. *Her* baby girl? She couldn't take Violet from me. "You can still let me go, you know. People will be looking for me, but I won't tell them anything if you let me go."

Maggie smirked at that. "No one's looking for you."

She said it with such confidence that my heart sank.

"I have your phone, remember."

I thought fast. Maggie didn't know my passcode—but I had fingerprint access on it, too. Of course she'd used my finger to open it when I was knocked out. "What did you do?"

"I sent a little e-mail to everyone saying that I'd talked you into going on a little road trip with me to San Diego. Close enough to be believable in your condition. You said, and I think this is almost a perfect quote, *What a lucky woman I am to have a friend like Maggie.* Sent to, let's see, Rochelle, Nicole, Camille, and Bree. Oh, and you asked Rochelle to ask Greg to feed the cat."

My heart rose from the murk it sat in. Greg would know something was wrong when his key didn't work, when I hadn't thought ahead to give him the new one. Rochelle would know I'd never leave without making positive Fred would be okay. They'd be suspicious enough to—

"Don't worry, you told Rochelle where you hid the new key, and I left my copy there. I won't need it again."

Then they knew I was with Maggie. That was something at least, wasn't it? When I didn't check in after a few days?

But it was like Maggie could read my mind, and maybe she could. I had no more energy to keep my face unreadable. She said, "And before you ask, I don't give a fuck if people know that I was with you. I won't be here when they come looking." She fanned herself with her hands. "Lord. I need a drink. I'll be back soon, okay? Try to get some rest. Don't be such a dick next time I'm in here."

She gave me a strained smile and left the room, kicking glass shards out of the way as she went.

Maggie wanted my baby.

THIRTY

But Violet was *mine*.

Terror pushed acid into my mouth as the door closed behind her, and I panted in pain. I was pretty sure at least one rib was broken, but my breath was still coming okay, so it hadn't punctured a lung. "It's okay," I said inanely to Violet, my hands tight against the skin of my belly. "It's okay, it's going to be okay. It's okay."

It was so far from okay that I wasn't sure I'd ever see okay again. But I had to *think*. I had one job now, and that was to protect my daughter, no matter what it took. I had to be ready when Maggie came back. She'd sounded serious about not wanting to hurt me. If she had intended to cut Violet out of me, killing me in the process, she would have done it while I was passed out from whatever she'd given me. Maybe she was planning to allow me to give birth naturally. I wasn't due for six more days. Could she possibly plan on keeping me here that long?

Shivers wracked my body and I tried to wrap the sheet around my legs.

No one was coming to rescue me. I let the knowledge slam into me. The people I was closest to thought I was on a road trip, and I'd alienated most of them anyway. Everyone from work knew I was on maternity leave. They were expecting to see me when I went into labor and not a minute before. No one would be looking for me. No one except Fred.

If I gave birth here, not a single person would know except Maggie.

What if things went sideways during the birth? Would Maggie actually call an ambulance if things went wrong? What if I needed a C-section? Maybe Maggie had done research on how to get a baby out of a woman. There had recently been a detailed video on a prepper website that showed how to do an emergency at-home C-section. It had led to two at-home caesarean births that had resulted in sepsis and death for both mothers, and only one of the babies survived. It was all we had talked about for days at work. The site had been taken down after the IP provider had been ordered to pull it, but that info was likely still available somewhere online, probably in multiple formats. And that was probably the kinder, gentler, educated fetal abduction. Mothers had been opened like a can of kidney beans, their attackers slicing a circular ring around the belly. The vast majority of women didn't live through it, and while the babies tended to fare better than the mothers, it wasn't good for them, either.

Was that something that Maggie would actually do? Was it something she'd thought of?

The pain in my ribs was easier to bear than the fear that threatened to engulf me. My teeth ached from clenching them so hard. I kept my left hand on my belly, and V gave a few slow kicks, ones that didn't have a lot of energy. I would choose to see that as her being tired, like me. Nothing more. V was fine. She would be fine—I would *make* her be fine. But I wouldn't—couldn't—think of her as Violet, not while Maggie was anywhere nearby. Maggie knowing my child's name already gave her too much power.

After maybe thirty minutes of staying still, I stopped shivering as the painful fire around my rib cage spread, pushing an almost pleasant warmth through my body. I was exhausted—unbelievably so. I tried to keep my eyes open, but my lids were just too heavy, and when the door opened again, I knew I'd drifted off for at least a few minutes.

"I brought you some water." Maggie tossed a plastic bottle of water onto the bed next to me.

She had changed, no longer wearing the long gray tunic. I wondered if she'd torn it as we fought. Now she was in a dark blue floral blouse and tight jeans. It was still jarring to see her natural waist—I hadn't expected to see it again for many months.

"No." When I spoke, my throat was rough, as if I'd been screaming for hours. I realized I had no idea what time of day it was. Maybe midday, by the light outside? "I'm not thirsty." What a lie. I was dying for water, but I couldn't trust her again.

"It's sealed," Maggie said.

If I drank the water, I would have to pee. If I had to pee, I'd have to stand and move and deal with the porta-potty bucket, and that would flare the agony in my chest. Right now, I felt like I was still slightly in shock, and while my teeth still chattered intermittently, that rush of warmth kept me still. I moved slightly and winced.

"I didn't mean to kick you as hard as I did," Maggie said. "How are you?"

I didn't look at her. "Cracked rib, I think."

"Well, shit. I'm sorry about that. But you did start it. Okay, might be hard for you to open that if your chest hurts." She grabbed the bottle quickly, only getting close to me for a second. She cracked the bottle's lid and left it sitting on the flat edge of the headboard. "It's right here when you want it. Do you want some Tylenol? Would that help?" She held up a hand. "I swear it would just be over the counter."

No. I didn't want one single thing from her, ever. The only things I wanted were to keep V safe and to get away. None of my other desires mattered. But I had to be polite. For now. "Maggie." I tried to remove the grit from my voice. "False pregnancy is so painful. I know that. I really do."

She folded her arms and leaned against the wall. "That's sweet. But it was never false."

I forced myself to go on. "It was just a thing your body did, and you have nothing to feel ashamed of." I pushed myself up to sitting, gulping at the pain. "You did nothing wrong. It's what the brain does sometimes, and it's terrible and awful and unfair, and I wish to God it hadn't happened to you."

She tilted her head, as if she were watching something curious, like a kitten trying to stop a car. "Don't forget you're an OB, not a therapist."

"You're right." I kept my voice as calm as I could, feeling as if I were swallowing screams with every word. I bowed my head for a moment. "You're totally right. I'm not a therapist. But let's go back to that moment, if you can. That day when I told you." I dared to look right into her eyes.

Yes, those were the same brown eyes I'd looked into seven years ago. I could see that now. I was ashamed for not recognizing her before this moment. My heart ached as if it had been sliced in two and sewed together backward. My voice shook, but I continued. "I sprang your diagnosis on you in a terrible way. I've never regretted something more than that day in all my life."

"That's not what this is about."

But there was a hesitation in Maggie's voice that told me that this mattered. "There's not a day that I don't think of it. When I was told you had a false pregnancy, I had one job to do, and I didn't do it. The only priority in a case like yours is to take care of the patient."

"The mother," she corrected.

"The mother. You should have been my only priority. I should have taken care of you, and I didn't. I was careless and stupid. That was my fault, not yours. Not one tiny bit of what happened to you was your fault."

She shook her head. "Don't you think I've read every single article on pseudocyesis that's ever been published? I know exactly how the brain works, and why it occurs to certain women and not others."

Did she, though? Pseudocyesis was still such a rare occurrence that no one in medicine really claimed to know what was happening in a woman's body when she grew a baby that wasn't there.

Maggie went on. "The problem is that you got it wrong. You diagnosed me wrong. I *did* have a baby inside me."

"I'm the one who screwed up, Maggie. I'm the only one. I did it so badly, so terribly. I'm sorry with every fiber of my being."

"You're chained to a bed. Of course you're sorry. I went in pregnant. I left without a child. That's a stillbirth." Maggie blinked and then rubbed at her eyes. "Stop trying to hurt me. Didn't you do enough of that, back then?"

I should have known better. Delusions didn't respond to common sense—that was part of what made them so problematic. If a person believed her brother had been murdered, then getting her brother to talk to her didn't fix the delusion. That was a fake brother, an actor, and everyone was in on it. The delusion just got bigger and more convoluted.

So common sense wasn't going to help. The fact that I'd truly been sorry every day for handling her case so badly wouldn't help, either. Lamely, I still said it. "I'm sorry."

Maggie didn't respond this time. She left the room briefly to get a towel and dustpan. She swept up the glass and mopped up the water on the floor. I saw a stripe of red blood on the towel and remembered the back of my arm. My ribs hurt so much I'd forgotten to even think about that cut.

I let my head fall back against the pillows, bone weary. Adrenaline still fired through me, but it wasn't enough to numb the rib pain, which was getting mixed up with lower back pain from trying to sit up in the bed. How would I even push? Oh, God.

Also, I had to pee again, which felt like the end of the world when I thought about how I would have to move to get to the bucket.

Maggie finished sweeping up the glass. She looked tired. Less pleased with this whole thing. "I'm going to leave you alone now. But look." She pulled out her phone and showed me the screen. On it, I saw the room I was in in miniature. There I was on the bed, my belly looking much smaller than it felt. The angle was weird, and Maggie appeared huge—the camera must be on top of the changing table. Yep, there it was. I could see it now. It wasn't even hidden, just sitting there in plain sight.

"This is for your safety. And for Violet's safety. Please don't try anything stupid. All I want is the best for both of you."

It turned out there *was* something that could make me feel worse than I did, and that was knowing she'd be watching me. "Whatever." I closed my eyes as if I didn't care.

But I cared. I cared so much I could die of it.

I waited until the door was closed behind her before I yanked the bottle of water off the headboard and guzzled it down. It tasted old, as if it had been in a case in the back of a car for months, but I needed it.

I hobbled off the bed, gasping from the pain in my ribs, and lifted the lid of the stupid loo bucket. I sat and peed. When I wiped myself, there was a spot of blood on the tissue.

Fuck. Oh, goddamn it. I put my hands over my mouth to prevent the cry that wanted to fly out. If my mucus plug was moving, if this was part of the bloody show, that would mean that labor was becoming more imminent. It didn't mean I'd give birth in the next hour, or even in the next day, but it was proof that my baby was starting to want out.

"Violet, please, no," I whispered, my hands still over my mouth.

Black spots flickered in my peripheral vision, and my cheeks started buzzing. Then my fingertips went numb. My breathing was harsh in my ears, and it was that—the sound of my panting—that clued me in to what was happening. I'd never had a panic attack before, but enough of my patients had that I recognized it when I heard it. It roared over me like a train, all heat and smoke and noise. My chest burned with pain that radiated from the center of my body. If I weren't a doctor, I would have sworn I was having a heart attack.

And knowing that it wasn't one didn't seem to help at all. My body *screamed* it was dying, cursing me that I was doing nothing to save myself—but I knew the only thing I could do was wait it out.

Sweat dripped down my forehead into my mouth, and shivers wracked me. I hauled in one tight breath after another, trying to slow them, trying to hold the air for a second before exhaling, slowing its release from my lungs, but nothing in my body was cooperating.

I just held on.

Long minutes later, I'd recovered enough that I could see again with no black flashes. My fingers and toes tingled painfully as the blood flowed back into them.

"It's all right, Violet," I breathed. "We're going to be all right."

I had no way of knowing if that was true. But, as my breathing eased, I did know one thing for sure. I knew labor. This blood could be normal discharge, not the bloody show. I would take this one tiny, terrifying step at a time.

And somehow, I would *not* go into labor here.

I finished wiping, throwing the second wad of paper into the bag under my ass, but I continued to sit there for another moment, grateful that the bucket had an actual toilet seat. I didn't think I could have held my off-centered weight over a bucket's rim. I didn't even have the energy to glare at the camera. I knew I'd have to stand in order to fall back on the bed. I'd have to guide the shackled leg up first, followed by the rest of my body, without jarring my ribs. I was simply too exhausted to move yet.

I leaned forward, putting my face in my hands. For one long moment, I pictured it—me giving birth on her bed, her having to deal with a retained placenta, or much worse, resuscitating a respiratory-compromised baby. I tried to be logical about it but couldn't.

My fingers trembled against my face. Then I dropped my hands, opened my eyes, and saw it on the floor. My weapon.

THIRTY-ONE

It was a long shard of glass attached to what must have been the base of the tumbler itself. Maggie had left it behind, three feet in front of me, right under the edge of the sheet that hung off the side of the bed. The piece of the rounded bottom was attached to a knifelike three-inch glass spike.

I took my time getting up from the toilet. I took the one step I could take forward and then let my free foot take the next step. My toes were mere inches from the glass. I raised my arms overhead in an attempt to look like I was just stretching, but I overdid what my ribs could handle, folding almost immediately. I bent at what used to be my waist, gasping.

So much the better. It must be obvious that I was in pain. As the agony subsided, I stretched again, slowly this time. Then I reached for the sheet and bent to tuck it in as best I could.

With my shackled left foot, I carefully moved the glass toward the head of the bed. I hoped it wouldn't cut me, but honestly, it was only an idle wish. It didn't matter if I bled from somewhere else.

But I didn't get cut, and I moved the shard to where I wanted it to be, right where I could dangle a hand off the bed to pull it up later. I sat on the edge of the bed and twisted, lifting my chained foot onto the bed first. Then I fell backward, my other foot following. I groaned with pain, then tried to breathe steadily through it. No need for Lamaze yet.

Then I felt it.

A strange, almost pleased feeling rolled through my body.

Joy, that was it. That's what was coursing through my veins. A pale, ethereal joy that made me suddenly want to laugh. Good grief, my ribs didn't even hurt anymore.

Only a rich, sleepy euphoria.

I smiled and closed my eyes. When I wasn't keeping my torso still, when I wasn't thinking about the bulk I held in my womb, there was no pain. I wanted to keep this yellow joy flowing. I wanted to fill myself with this heavy liquid gold that radiated its color from my body as I lay there. I thought if Maggie was watching, she must be able to see it. It would make her happy

—and—

No.

I dragged open my eyes.

Dizziness flooded me. But I wasn't nauseated. My eyes just wouldn't focus. The empty water bottle on the nightstand wavered into two bottles and then back into one.

Shock. Maybe it was shock.

But I knew it wasn't.

Maggie had drugged me again. She'd lied about the bottle being sealed. I was falling asleep, and I wasn't going to be able to stop it. I struggled to sit up, but it was too late. Whatever she'd given me in that water bottle was too strong. I was being pulled out like the tide—I was in the water, gliding, floating, and right as I was pulled under, I allowed myself to do the unforgivable.

I let myself enjoy it. As I was sucked beneath the dark waves, I took the giddy ride that I wanted more than anything. For less than a second—but it was a second that mattered so much—I was completely, perfectly happy.

THIRTY-TWO

I gasped my way awake, confused for a moment not to be in my bedroom. Then the memory clobbered me as hard as the pain in my ribs did. My throat was dry, and I had to use the bathroom again. Of course. There was another water bottle at the side of the bed. It had no cap. It was full and probably laced. I wasn't thirsty. Yet.

The light at the window made me think it was almost sunset—I'd slept the whole afternoon because of whatever she'd given me. GHB, maybe? I hadn't tasted it in the water, except to notice that it tasted particularly flat. I'd always assumed that date-rape drugs just made you pass out, but apparently there was a body-brain high to it. I'd felt it. I'd loved it. I'd *craved* it.

What the fuck had it done to my baby?

"I'm sorry," I whispered to Violet.

Then, of course, I had to stand and get to the toilet. So I did. It hurt like hell to move. The long shard of glass was still right where I'd left it—Maggie hadn't seen it, thank God.

I looked at the water bottle next to the bed, and then, with a whip of my left arm, I knocked it off so that it splashed everywhere. I wouldn't even let myself have a single second to consider drinking it.

I could still hear the water blurping. If Maggie was watching, maybe if I went for the shard of glass, it would look like I was trying to pick up the bottle. She probably wasn't watching me one hundred percent of the time, but it was risky to chance it. This might be my best time. I reached down quickly and grabbed the long shard of glass by its rounded base. I hid it behind my Violet bump on the non-camera side as I turned to get into bed, and then awkwardly shoved it under the pillow I wasn't using, and then I gasped my way onto my back like a dying trout.

Everything hurt.

Fucking Advil. That's what I took at home. Two years before, I'd broken my leg getting off a ski lift, and I'd only allowed myself Tylenol and Advil, back to back. The power of my prescription pad had never felt so strong before, but with the help of meetings, I'd made it through the physical recovery with nothing more than that. I'd almost hoped I would need surgery so I could get the five seconds of the high you got when you went under.

Now? I wanted Vicodin. Screw that, I wanted Demerol, even though it made me nauseated. I wanted morphine. One of the docs in the ER liked to say to his patients, "Morphine? More *fun*, am I right?" when the high hit them and the pain went away.

I hated myself for every hot tear that slipped down my face. I gasped for breath around the sobs, but they were coming too fast, and I was immediately light-headed. If I could stop breathing, at least the fear would cease. *But Violet.*

Violet. Just her name was a full sentence in my head.

She was everything. And I was going to lose her if I didn't fight harder. I'd always been good at fighting—I'd fought to get through residency, and I'd fought my way back from addiction, a war that at times felt like a daily battle.

But this . . .

Violet.

I closed my eyes and tried to think.

At some point while I'd slept, Maggie had come in and set a fresh sheet and a puffy blue duvet on the bed. She must have changed her mind about me covering myself, and I was sharply—cheaply—grateful. I pulled the duvet to my chest, then over my face. Some light still got through, but at least I was able to hide a little.

I couldn't seem to stop crying.

The door creaked open. I let the duvet drop, hoping she wouldn't hit me again. I didn't say anything, and the tears kept coming.

The side of the bed dipped as Maggie sat next to me. She rubbed my back in small circles. "You poor thing," she said. "You poor thing."

And in a moment I didn't plan on ever forgiving myself for if I lived through this, I allowed her to comfort me. Just for a moment. The drug must have still been in my system, making me accept the unacceptable: emotional support, given by Maggie.

Then I grasped fully what I was allowing, and I rolled farther away from her, hugging my belly as best I could. The bed was narrow enough that by moving, I was on the edge again, lying on the other pillow.

I felt the form of the glass underneath the feathers. That long knife-like shard, attached to the smooth part of the base of the broken glass.

A thin bit of stubborn hope rose.

Later, when it was dark, maybe I could slice off my shackle.

Or maybe—I could do worse.

My breath hitched in my chest, not related to the tears. The shock of the thought was enough to stop the crying. What kind of worse could I do?

One jab, up into Maggie's neck. If I hit the carotid hard enough (and it would take force), she would bleed out within minutes. I felt light-headed at the thought. Jesus Christ, how was I here? How had this happened?

I couldn't do *that*.

But what if I had to? What if it ended up being my only choice?

"It's going to be okay, sugar," said Maggie from behind me. "It's all going to be okay in the long run."

The long run in which I didn't have my daughter? That wasn't a long run I could live in.

Maggie said, "I know this is all really hard for you. What can I do that will help at this point? With the birth?"

Not steal my fucking baby. But I tried to think, though my brain felt cloudy and sluggish. "You know I'm not due today, right? Or even tomorrow."

"I'm not worried about that."

Was there anything she *was* worried about? Could I make her worry about something? "Do you have alcohol? For sterilization?"

She moved around the bed and then sat in front of me on the floor, crossing her legs underneath her. Her sympathetic smile was abhorrent to me, but on the traitorous side of my brain that knew her as a friend, her smile felt like a comfort. "I have absolutely everything we could possibly need. I have hemostats, curved Kelly clamps, ring forceps, a needle driver, and everything else, all boiled in water then wrapped in a clean sheet and baked in my oven to sterilize. Honestly, it's the only time I've ever used it in this house. I have an umbilical clamp and umbilical tape. I have bulb syringes and swaddling blankets. I've done my research."

Her level of planning made me exponentially more nervous. "Do you know how to stop my bleeding if I start to hemorrhage afterward?"

She nodded like a model pupil pleased to be asked something she knew the answer to. "Fundal massage. But I won't be doing that."

It felt like she'd punched me. "Because you want me to die."

"Oh, Lord, woman. You seriously need to get over that one." She raised her arms over her head and gave a long stretch. I spent two seconds thinking about kicking her full in the gut as hard as I could with my unfettered leg, and then let it go. I had to wait for my moment.

"I'm trying," I said.

"If you hemorrhage, you'll die without a transfusion, right? I can do a lot with what I have here, but I can't give you a transfusion. So there's no point in fundal massage. If you die, I'll be brokenhearted. It has to be obvious that if I'd *wanted* to kill you, I would have just cut Violet out of you that first night."

At some point, I'd figured out why she hadn't done exactly that. "You couldn't do it safely, and you knew it. If you hit one of my main arteries, she wouldn't live long enough to take her first breath."

She blinked. "No, I *studied*. I know how to do it right."

"If you take her, you'll get caught."

She did that head-tilt thing again, the one that made me feel like a particularly dim five-year-old. "Honey, I have a private plane on retainer. The pilot is ready and waiting to take off at twenty minutes' notice. He'll file a false flight plan and change his call sign when we land. New identities cost less than a Birkin bag."

"I'll find you." But my words wobbled.

She glanced at her cuticles. "Even if you did, we'll be in a country with no extradition to the US."

"I'll find you and take her *back*." I could barely breathe and my eyes felt hot. "Maggie, how is it possible that we're having this conversation? This is you. And it's me. It's just *me*."

"It's always been you." She put a gentle hand on my knee. "Maybe in seven years, I'll let you see a picture of her. That's how long I've been waiting, after all."

I shuddered. The hope I'd been trying so desperately to hold drained like liquid being flushed away. It swirled and was gone.

So was Maggie. She left the room saying she'd bring me something to eat later. She didn't appear to be worried about leaving me alone anymore. I didn't blame her—my two escape attempts had been utter failures.

I was covered in sweat, burning up and freezing at the same time. Maggie was stronger. She wasn't injured, she wasn't addled from being drugged, and she wasn't thirty-nine weeks pregnant. If I kept fighting, it might end up even worse for Violet. What if I fell? What if my heart stopped and Maggie couldn't get her out in time? I was failing at taking care of my daughter before she'd ever taken her first breath.

I was a worse mother than my own.

"I don't know what to do," I whispered. I wasn't talking to Violet. I wasn't even talking to myself. I was simply stating the truth, the thing that made me feel like I might stop breathing altogether.

Incredibly, my eyes were heavy, and not in a drugged way. I was just exhausted. I swore to myself I wouldn't sleep—that I'd stay awake and be with Violet. If these were my last hours with her, I couldn't sleep. I needed to be with her, to soothe her. This much fear, and adrenaline, and cortisol—Violet would absolutely have it in her veins, too. She was kicking less than she normally did. The fear clotted around my heart.

Stay awake. Stay with her.

Be her mother while you still can.

But my body betrayed me. On a wave of pain, my eyes drooped and then closed. My brain gave up the fight one more time.

THIRTY-THREE

I dreamed my mother was sitting on a beach in a low-backed chair, the sunset lighting the sky orange and purple around her. Scrolling through her phone, she deleted the pictures I'd sent her one by one. Then she turned to face me. "You would never have been a good mother anyway."

When I came to that time, there was no lag in knowing where I was. I knew I was in the Pacific Palisades, trapped in hell on the edge of a continent. It was still dark outside.

But something had changed. I had a new piece of knowledge I'd never had before.

My mother hadn't been talking to me when she'd said those words as I left her house forever. She'd been talking to herself. She knew she'd never been a good mother. She'd been uttering her deepest fear out loud.

And there, in Maggie's house, tied to a bed, without the slightest clue what I'd do next, I realized one new, huge truth. I wasn't a worse mother than my own. Violet, right now, was as safe as she could be in this situation. Continuing to make sure she was safe was the only thing that mattered. And even though nothing had changed, and even though I felt physically worse than I had when I went to sleep, the dream had shifted everything.

The fierceness had come.

It swamped me. I was almost drowning, caught in the undertow of its sheer power.

I'd always thought the fierceness arrived when a woman gave birth, when she went from being pregnant to being a mother. How facile an understanding that had been.

I was *already* a good mother. Unarmed and armorless, I would stop an entire army to keep her safe, striking every soldier down one by one.

Carefully, I reached beneath the pillow to make sure the glass was still there. I would only get one chance before Maggie knew what I had. She was physically stronger than I was. I had to be fast and sure.

I couldn't kill her, though. Even though the fierceness was in me, even though I *would* kill her if she actually attempted to murder me or Violet, I wouldn't kill her just because she wanted to take Violet from me.

I was a fucking doctor. I could do better than that.

One stab to the gut. Once I perforated her small intestine, the sewage leaking into her abdominal cavity would guarantee a rapid death without immediate surgery. If she had that surgery, she'd have a pretty good prognosis. I'd make that crystal clear to her.

Then I'd use the glass to cut off the ankle cuff, and I'd step over her still-bleeding body to get out of this house, find a phone, and call 911. Worst-case scenario, if I couldn't find a phone, I'd get myself down to the highway at the bottom of the street. I'd be covered in blood, so someone would call 911 even if they didn't stop (it was LA, after all), and we'd be saved. Violet would be safely inside me. She'd be okay.

When I'd passed out earlier, hunger had barely existed. But now, my empty stomach twisted. I grabbed at a protein bar Maggie had left on the nightstand and shoved it into my mouth, praying it wasn't laced with anything. If I was going to destroy her, I needed energy.

When I'd finished it, I pushed myself up to sit with my back against the headboard. The higher my head was, the clearer my thoughts seemed to become.

One shot.

I got only one shot at this. I could not fuck it up.

I heard Maggie's footsteps in the hall, and instead of my heart speeding up, I could feel it slow with my attention, like it did when I was scrubbed in to a surgery. I focused on nothing but her proximity. Where was she in space? How did she move inside that space? This would be surgery, too, perhaps the most important cut I'd ever make in my life.

"Hi, you." Maggie looked adorable. She wore a dark-green top with black yoga pants and green ballet flats. She'd done her hair in soft waves. Her lips were glossy. How many outfit changes had she planned for this part of her play? "How are we doing now?" And for God's sakes, she still had that cheerful affect. Like she was my friend, like she was just regular, everyday Maggie.

I realized that I would be the one to break that expression. Now I was a warrior. I *wanted* to break her.

I swallowed my strength and smiled back weakly. "Hi," I said in a whisper.

She blinked and gave me a double take. "You okay? You look like shit."

"I don't feel good." The plan came to me then, as fully fleshed out as if I'd had a month to plan it. "I want to write V a letter—you wouldn't mind, would you?" I broke off and coughed. It didn't sound faked—it came from my core, and it jarred my rib so much that I knew the pain on my face would look real because it was.

"A letter?"

"A short one. I'm scared that—" Tears rose, tears I couldn't stop. Perfect. "I'm scared that I might not make it through the birth."

Maggie blew out a breath. "This again?" But she took a step closer to me. It was working.

"No, I get it—you don't want to hurt me," I said. "This is different. I never told you that my mom almost died in childbirth with me." It had been the opposite, actually. She'd always bragged that she was at home and mopping her kitchen the day after my birth, with me napping on the table she'd just polished. "At the hospital, they already have my team set up. I know you're prepared, but with a family history like mine, you can never be sure. You don't ever have to give her the letter. But I want you to have it. Just in case, in case you ever decide to tell her about me—" Another full cough. I felt a twinge of concern that I was so easily coughing, that my lungs could produce this noise on command.

But my lungs were part of my body, and my body was preparing to win this battle. The sound of the cough was enough to make her furrow her brows in what looked like real concern.

"I'll need—" I let my voice trail off and put my hand to my head. "Whew. That was weird." I left a beat between my words. Then I started in a smaller voice. "Can I have a pad of paper, if you don't mind, and then you can . . ." I closed my eyes and let my head sway once forward and then back.

"What? What is it?" Maggie stood up quickly but put her hand on my knee. Good. I needed her touching me.

"I don't know—I don't know what's happening." I let myself slump from my upright position to lower in the bed. I turned sideways, so that my fingers could touch the edge of the pillow the glass was under. "A little dizzy . . ."

She was right next to me then, her hand on my left shoulder. "What should I do?"

"I'm good. It's fine. All good. Just the pen and pad of paper." I let my head fall suddenly toward the bed and caught it again, bringing it back up with a shake. "I feel like I'm going to . . . pass out or—I dunno . . ."

"Is this normal?" Her voice was tighter.

"No. This shouldn't be—shouldn't be happeni—" My head dropped heavily onto the pillow. "Peripartum cardiomyopathy. My rib, maybe infection—I'm so sorry, you'll have to . . ." I let myself fall to whispering, hoping she'd fall for my bullshit.

She knelt. "I have to what? What do you need?"

"If I pass out, then the birth might—"

"Might what?"

My hand gripped the broken base of the glass, slicing my thumb in the process. The pain was fuel, necessary and sweet.

I moved so fast that molecules didn't have time to get out of my way. I moved so fast that the sound of my swing had a two-second lag. I struck at her stomach, pushing the glass right through her top. I was used to a scalpel—shoving glass into someone was more difficult than I thought it would be, and I had to push hard through the resistance of her skin. But I suddenly understood what hunters felt like, when killing their prey was the only thing that would keep them alive. She was my sport, my sustenance.

Maggie crashed backward onto the floor, her mouth open in shock. She jerked the glass out of her stomach, throwing it away onto the tile, where it shattered further. Her hands scrabbled up, lifting her shirt, trying to close the wound, but if I'd done it right, there was no way she'd be able to. I waited for the blood to start. It wouldn't take more than thirty seconds if I'd struck it right. I was feral—I wanted to *feel* her blood on me. She would beg me to save her, to call 911, to do the surgery myself. Her mouth opened and closed twice. Her eyes blinked as if they were trying to send Morse code.

But the river of blood I craved didn't flow.

On her back, curled into a half sit-up, she pulled up her shirt and tugged down her yoga pant waistband. There was blood, yes, sliding over her fingers. But not enough. A long, raised scar twisted above the fresh blood—the evidence of when she'd stabbed herself in the stomach as I'd stood just outside her hospital curtain.

"You *bitch*," she breathed, looking down at the wound below her belly button.

I understood instantly—the resistance I'd felt in stabbing her was because I'd hit the waistband of her yoga pants. I'd probably only sliced an inch into her actual body.

She hauled herself to standing using the frame of the bed as support.

Terror lanced through me, and pain—real pain this time—shot up through my arm, blasting into my brain. I held up my right hand. The edge of the glass had sliced my palm deeply. I couldn't feel my pinky or ring fingers, which was probably good, because the pain from the rest of the hand was almost unbearable. Maggie was barely scratched, but blood flowed freely down my forearm to my elbow.

And then something popped deep inside me, the feeling low and internal. I could have sworn I heard it, but I knew I couldn't have, not over the fear that roared in my ears as loudly as if Maggie were screaming into them. Violet kicked once sharply and then went still. Warm fluid gushed between my legs in the rhythm that Maggie's blood was supposed to.

"My water just broke," I said stupidly.

Maggie turned on wobbly legs and disappeared into the hallway. I heard her go, and then, seconds later, she was back. She carried something in one hand I couldn't quite see through the tears that filled my eyes. Why would she have—was it a small baseball bat? A long white pen?

In the moment I realized it was a large marble rolling pin, it was too late. My brain couldn't get either of my arms to rise in time, and when she hit me full force in the head, I was already tumbling forward into blackness.

THIRTY-FOUR

I didn't wake slowly or easily the next time. The pain was all consuming. There was no space in it for me to breathe, and most of it was from a contraction I thought I'd die from. The pressure at my rib cage and at my temple where she'd struck me would have been unendurable had it not been for the pain around my entire uterus.

Outside, it looked like late afternoon again, but time made no sense. Had I been in labor for hours? Days?

Maggie was there, I knew that, but I couldn't look at her even if I'd wanted to, being too busy trying to figure out exactly what my body needed from me. Something told me to get up on my haunches, and I knew it was right—being reclined was one of the most uncomfortable positions for any woman in labor—but I couldn't move, and I didn't know why, and I couldn't take the time to figure it out. I just had to get through it.

I breathed the way I'd told a thousand women to breathe. It helped only because I was doing *something* that wasn't dying, which my brain insisted I was doing. Not that I could listen, not that there were words coming from my brain that made any sense at all.

I held on. I needed to live a couple more minutes. After that, I could figure out how to live a few more.

The contraction slackened, and slowly, *so* slowly, focus filtered back into my brain. This couldn't happen. Not this way. There had to be a way for me to keep my daughter inside my body until we were somehow out of this place, in safety.

Maggie was next to me, petting my arm. She murmured, "Good girl," over and over again. If she meant it to be soothing, it wasn't.

I wanted to fight her, to claw at her, but I couldn't lift either arm.

Flexible plastic handcuffs were strapped to either wrist, zip-tied to something I couldn't see under the bed or the mattress.

And there was an IV in my left arm. It looked like it was running a bag of normal saline, the line high and out of the way. That explained why I wasn't thirsty, and why I had to pee so goddamned badly. A motherfucking *IV*.

Panic doubled my heart rate, in direct contrast to the slow, methodical pace of the liquid flowing into the drip chamber. Of course I was strapped down. She probably thought I'd tried to kill her. She couldn't know I'd planned on having the medical establishment save her life in order to allow her to go to prison. I'd had good reason to stab her, and I didn't regret the attempt. But lying there panting, I realized—coldly and painfully and much too late—that maybe I should have gone for her carotid after all. There was a strong chance I wasn't getting out of here now, and I'd done that to myself.

"You can understand my caution," Maggie said.

She looked terrible. Her skin was pale, a gray-blue. She hadn't changed out of her bloody clothes, and a clumsy gauze bandage was visible under the hem of her shirt. At some point, she'd wrapped my right hand equally badly in the same gauze. I knew my hand hurt, but it couldn't quite reach my brain through the relief of being out of the contraction.

All things considered, though, Maggie looked like she was doing a hell of a lot better than I was.

A friend of mine had been in Mexico City in 1985, in full-blown labor when the 8.1 earthquake struck. Wanda always said, *My body shut down. The contractions just stopped. My cervix snapped closed, even though later the doctor said it couldn't have happened. All I know is that it did. We were out in the streets, trying to help people, trying to save ourselves. I closed my body so I could keep her safe. I didn't let her out for two more days.*

But *how?* How did I do that? How could I shove the hurricane back into the bottle?

I wasn't giving up, no matter what. "What's your genius plan now?"

Maggie narrowed her eyes, making a face I'd never seen before. "Get that baby out as soon as possible."

"It might take a while. Babies do that." Taking a long time birthing felt like my only option. She hadn't gagged me, thank God. Maybe someone would come to the door, and I'd be able to scream loudly enough that someone would call the cops.

Maggie shook her head. "My baby's on her way, and she's coming fast."

A rivulet of cold sweat from the last contraction snaked down my face. "What do—" But I felt it—my uterus was gearing up for the next one. Unless my time sense was completely off, it hadn't even been ninety seconds since the last one eased off. "What the fuck?" I snapped a look at the IV pole. This wasn't right. "What did you do?"

"Pitocin. A whole hell of a lot of it." She pushed her hair away from her face. "I told you I knew what I was doing."

Oh, no. That was bad. "Maggie, *how much?*"

She smiled and scrunched her nose. "Forty units."

Jesus fucking Christ. There'd be no way to slow this down. This was what older, less educated (and mostly male) doctors used to do to get their patients done quickly so they could go play golf by noon. The contractions, which were about to be constant, would cause dilation.

But then it dawned on me. It gave me something to hold over Maggie. I could scare her. I took a shaky breath and widened my eyes. "No! She won't be able to handle this!"

"You mean you don't *want* to handle it. You realize that you confessed that you never even wanted this baby, right? You said that. Out loud, to all of us. So don't try to bullshit me now."

I gasped as the contraction gathered me up in its hand and squeezed me like a sponge. I couldn't continue the conversation—there was nothing in my brain that could form language until it was done. All I could do was what I told my patients to do: I pictured myself climbing a mountain. I had to get to the top. I had to keep walking even though each and every step got harder. *Breathe in, step, step. Blow out, breathe in, step, step. Blow out. You're at the peak, breathe one, two, three, four . . . again . . . now it's easing up . . . easier and easier . . . and big breath, blow out . . . and let everything go limp like you're falling.*

"No," I whispered as I rolled down the mountain. I needed to rest so that I could climb it again. And again. I was drenched in sweat. "You probably just killed my baby." I didn't actually believe it. I couldn't believe it. *I would not let her die.*

But I wanted to hurt Maggie. I wanted to hurt her *so* much.

"You're lying." Her cheeks went red over her pallor. "You're *lying*. I researched it."

Forty units would probably be okay, honestly. But she didn't know that. "That's way too much. Fifteen units maybe. Even twenty units. But anything more than twenty-five units will cause tetanic contractions. That'll kill her. My uterus won't be able to relax to let blood flow through the placenta." I let myself believe it for a moment, long enough to fill my eyes with tears. "In utero. Out of utero. It doesn't matter. She won't make it through this. You're a monster."

Maggie pushed away from the bed. Without another word, she left the room.

I guessed that I had about sixty seconds before the next contraction kicked in. I had no idea how dilated I was. I tried to drag as much air into my lungs as I could, tried to focus on the outside of my body, what it felt like touching the air. Up the mountain again. *Step, step. Breathe in.*

Just as I was getting pulled under again, Maggie burst back into the room.

She was sobbing.

And she was clutching a scalpel, triangular and elongated.

THIRTY-FIVE

The scalpel looked like a BD number 11. Not the one I would have chosen myself. But the contraction was about to tear me in half, and I could only gasp: "*Not now.* Not during a contraction." That's all I got out before I turned into an animal again, but it was enough.

She stood next to the bed, staring, the scalpel held tightly in her hand. Every time my eyes flicked over her, she winced. Time stopped and then disappeared altogether. Minutes wound around themselves and turned into eons and back into seconds. I kept climbing the mountain, alone, carving footsteps out of pain and breath.

Apparently, though, some small, unknown part of my brain had been working on the solution while I hadn't thought I'd been capable of a single thought. When the contraction finally slacked off, I had the answer.

"If you try to cut her out of me, I'll move my hips at exactly the wrong time." My voice shook. "You'll slash either her or her cord. I'll make sure of it." I could never be that precise when I wasn't holding the blade, and I'd rather die than hurt V. But Maggie didn't know that.

On her face, I saw just the flash of the expression I needed to see. She was unsure. "You won't kill your own baby."

"Like hell I won't. I've done it before."

She gasped.

"If I die, she dies. I promise you that. Your only choice is to help me give birth to her." Because I was going to need help. I could feel it. The next contraction was coming too fast—it was almost on top of me already. I thought Violet wasn't in the right place, but without being able to reach down and touch, I couldn't be sure. "And I'll need my hands."

"Fuck you." She set the scalpel down on the small table next to me. "I won't cut unless I have to. But I'm not freeing your hands."

The contraction took over, and through it, I managed to grunt words at her. She lifted my shoulders and helped me scoot back a bit in the bed. I tried not to bear down, which was *impossible*. How had other women listened when I'd told them not to?

Maggie got behind me and stayed still as I used her as a bolster to push against.

She told me when I asked that it was three in the afternoon.

Then, an eternity later, she said it was four.

Then, another eternity during which I spent all those thousands of years wanting to die while at the same time wanting nothing more than to live through this, to take my daughter away to safety, she said it was four thirty.

Maggie had been moving around me, going where I told her to, but for the last hour, she'd been between my legs. She'd said she saw the baby's head once, but then it went away again as Violet turtled.

The contractions weren't separate by then—they were all one, and I simply didn't have the option to die. So we kept going. Me, and Violet, and Maggie.

Maggie was with me. I'd forgotten the intensity of my fear of her, because she'd been rendered almost invisible. I was dying anyway, my body and brain told me, just like every other woman to have had a baby in the history of the world. No human felt that amount of pain and lived, so the brain gave up and said, *Okay, we're dying.* And even *that* didn't get you out of it.

I was beyond control. My vagina burst into flames—we called it the ring of fire in Labor and Delivery, but it turned out that wasn't a fucking euphemism.

And then it was time.

"I'm pushing," I managed to grunt. I saw only the top of Maggie's head nodding over my belly as she crouched between my knees. The push was beyond longing or desire. It was the only mandate that had ever existed in the world.

"I see the top of her head again!"

I couldn't do this. I couldn't. The cracked rib felt like it was shredding my lungs. I was dying. I was dead but trapped in hell. I couldn't breathe—there wasn't time or space in the pain to breathe even for a second. But somehow I was still grasping at some air and there was enough and then—

Maggie said, "The head is out! She's facedown! Is that normal?"

I nodded. There was no relief. I'd expected an iota of ease as the hardest part was over. But it was even worse. "Cord? Place your index and middle fingers"—I broke off with a wheeze, sweat pouring down my face—"in the crease of her neck, and follow around to see if the cord is wrapped."

"I don't feel a cord."

Thank God. It would all be over soon. Two or three more pushes, and she'd be out.

But it didn't happen. Three pushes turned to five, and then ten. "Maggie, there's something wrong," I said, meaning it this time. She didn't seem to hear me.

Some of my pain had changed to numbness, and I knew the baby was blocking a nerve. At least that was something. "Maggie!"

She startled and raised her head to look at me. "Why isn't it happening?"

"She's stuck. Probably shoulder dystocia." I panted. "Anterior shoulder stuck behind my pubic bone."

"What do I do?"

"I need my hands, Maggie."

Her response was fast, the single syllable hard-edged. "No."

"We have less than five minutes before she suffers permanent brain damage. We need to move her. Or she and I both die." I wasn't bullshitting her now, and maybe that came through because Maggie left her post between my legs and scrambled to get the scalpel from where she'd left it on the side table. One flick, and my right hand was free.

She scurried around me to release the other one; then she threw the scalpel into the hallway.

My brain was a turbine roar of panic, but I knew what I had to do, and I knew what I had to get Maggie to do. I reached behind me and threw off the pillows.

"I have to be flat." Then I gasped, "Stand to the side of my legs."

"Not between them?"

"You have to be at my side. Move."

She did.

"Now," I panted. I had to be *fast*. There was no time. My words had to be precise. "I'll pull my knees toward my ears. Help me bend my legs. Ninety degrees at the knee. Yeah, like that. Exactly. Use your left arm to push against the bottoms of my feet." The chain on my left foot rattled as I held my feet up, bent as if I were sitting in a chair while lying on my back. Maggie's skin was cold against my feet.

"Good. Push my legs toward me as hard as you can, and at the same time, I need you to use your right hand to push down just above my pubic bone as hard as you can." I couldn't think—were these the right instructions? How many times had I used these maneuvers in my practice? A hundred? A thousand? And never, ever, from this vantage point.

Maggie looked confused. Terrified. I was sure I looked worse. With her left hand and arm pushing my bent legs toward me, she put her hand on my lower abdomen. "Here?"

If I could rise up, I realized, I could grab her by her bandage. I could strangle her. Or break her neck.

But I could hardly breathe, and besides, I only had one desire in the world, and that was to get my baby out of my body alive. "Use the palm of your hand and all your weight." Suprapubic pressure was no joke—when my nurses did this move, they got almost as sweaty as the mom did. Maggie would have to press from the baby's back straight downward to collapse the shoulder under my pubic bone.

And it meant there was no one there to catch the baby. I had to stay flat. I could barely breathe, but I gasped, "Once we get her top shoulder out—" I ran out of breath entirely, and for three seconds I panted, conscious of every heartbeat that Violet was in distress. "Then she's going to—come out so fast. Let her land on the bed. Get ready to move around my legs to her."

She met my eyes and nodded. Every piece of tension that had built between us fell away and I felt closer to her than I'd ever been in all the years of our friendship.

"You can do this," she said.

I believed her. And I believed in her, too. "*You* can do this. All your weight." I was dialed to 100 out of 10. I had to push, and I couldn't wait a second longer. "*Now!*"

It was as if I'd pulled my body apart with my bare hands. I could almost *see* Violet's anterior shoulder squeezing under my pubic bone. On a savage howl, I pushed my girl into the air. Maggie let go of my legs and released the suprapubic pressure and got in between my legs just in time.

"I've got her," Maggie said. "*I've got her.*"

THIRTY-SIX

I couldn't lie back and wait for everything else to happen like other women. I wanted to pass out, but unfortunately, I was still the doctor. "Give her to me. And your kit. We have to get her to breathe."

It was as if she hadn't even thought of that as a possibility. "Jesus. Yes. Here." She handed me Violet, who was the same color as her name.

"Hello, baby girl, hello." I breathed so fast and hard that I knew I was in danger of either passing out or hyperventilating. Most women, when handed their babies, had a real chance to greet them.

I didn't have that time.

Violet should have made a noise by now. It was taking too long.

I suctioned with the blue bulb syringe to get the mucus out of her nose, then her mouth. Her pulse was good and strong. I'd usually do the basic neonatal resuscitation program with at least an O_2 blowby, letting the oxygen flow freely across her face, but I didn't have that. I'd do manual infant CPR if I had to. I hated that my poorly wrapped, bloodily gauzed hand was touching Violet's skin at all, but I felt no pain from it anymore.

I felt no fear, though. I rarely did with a newborn in my hands. I just felt determination. She *would* breathe. I firmly rubbed her back and flicked her feet. It didn't work, so I kissed my little girl for the first time, giving her one quick puff, my lips on hers.

Then Violet gave a cry, that tiny kitten mewl, and my breath hiccupped in my chest as I swallowed the sob that threatened to strangle me. "Towel?"

Maggie reached toward her stack of supplies and shoved a towel at me. I dried Violet with it to stimulate her, and then I rubbed her back and the soles of her feet vigorously, my bandaged right hand only slightly slowing me down.

I finally had a second to look at her—to really see her. Her face was the typical angry old man's face—deep creases in her forehead as her downy eyebrows rose and fell. I caught the tiniest glimpse of her eyes, dark wet gloss. Her lips worked, parting and panting. She had a clump of dark, wet hair right on top of her head. Her skin was so red, with the cruddy white vernix caught in every beautiful crease and fold. I cursed the tank top that had bunched underneath my breasts, but I managed to pull it over my nipples so that it was a tight band around my chest, leaving most of my torso naked. I draped another towel over Violet, keeping her skin against mine, warming her.

"What time is it?" I asked.

"Exactly eight P.M."

"Time of birth, seven fifty-eight," I estimated. My voice shook. Outside the window, the sun was falling, red and orange flares shooting into the sky. A perfect time to be born.

Maggie was next to me, leaning over to look at my baby. "I'll cut the cord."

If she did that, she could take Violet and run. My left foot was still strapped to the bed. I'd never find them. "You don't want to do that until the placenta is delivered." I often gave a tiny bit more Pitocin after birth to get it to come faster, but God knew I didn't need more. I felt another contraction gathering. "I need you to guide that out, too."

"You're kidding me."

No one *ever* thought about the placenta. "It can be disastrous for her lungs if you cut the cord too soon." Another lie, delivered perfectly.

Violet opened her eyes all the way then, and I swear she was in on the lie with me. She snarfled a rattled noise that was just perfect. Her right eye closed and then opened again. A wink. I almost laughed out loud.

"Please, Maggie. Then I'll tell you how to cut the cord."

And then I'd have to—what? Once that was done, if I wasn't hemorrhaging, I still wouldn't have the strength to fight her. With a groan I tried to trap in my throat, making sure my hands were soft on Violet and didn't lock around her during the contraction, I pushed one last time.

"So disgusting," said Maggie.

She was wrong. I loved delivering the placenta and seeing it for what it was—pure magic. Its existence was how a child came into this world as a healthy human being. But most people didn't think like I did.

My legs trembled and my knees shook. I could probably straighten them now if I wanted to, but I never wanted to move again. Violet was the perfect weight on top of me.

I wanted to clamp the umbilical cord myself, but instead, Maggie went to work. She'd done her research, clamping and cutting at just the right place. "Is that better? Is her color okay? Is she supposed to be that purple? Is she getting enough oxygen?"

I wanted to lie to Maggie again, but the words slipped out, unbidden, their truth too pure to hide. "She's perfect."

Maggie reached forward to take her from me.

My arms wrapped around Violet on their own. I couldn't control them. They formed a cage around her.

As Maggie drew back, I saw fresh blood trickling out from the bandage at her stomach. She was as drenched in sweat as I was. She was shivering. I could feel that I was, too. "Don't forget," Maggie said. "I *saved* her. I'm in charge here."

She'd moved away, though. She wasn't willing to hurt Violet to get her out of my arms.

And she wasn't dumb—she would probably just wait. I was sure she knew that shortly after birth, most new mothers did one thing, and they did it well: They fell asleep. They fell into the kind of deep sleep that people pay millions to drug manufacturers to replicate. I was going to be fighting that soon. I could hold Violet tightly now, but I couldn't stay awake forever.

Normally now would be the time—after all the tests and measurements—that a nurse would be showing the new mother how to get her baby to latch onto the nipple. The way Violet was squirming against me was a great sign. She wanted something, and hopefully that something was food.

But I couldn't feed her now. Intuitively, I knew that would be the worst thing I could do in front of Maggie, but the need was so strong—I hadn't expected this urge to be so fierce. I knew without ever having done it exactly how I would curl my baby to my breast, but I could *not*, not yet. Pushing the urge away was almost impossible, but I realized I needed to keep Maggie's attention on me, not on the child she wanted. I sure as hell didn't want to distract her with getting Violet to suckle at the milk-engorged breasts Maggie didn't have.

I had to get my leg unshackled. That was the only remaining important thing. There was no chance for us if Maggie didn't cut my foot free.

What if I could flatter her into wanting something new? I'd already tried to fool her a couple of times, and she'd naturally be on guard. But she was tired; her defenses would be down. My own defenses were nonexistent, but I had to ignore that and keep climbing the mountain.

I would embroider a lie she had no option but to believe.

So I took a deep breath and said, "Maggie. You win."

She frowned. "What?"

"I'm too fucking tired. You win." The lie bloomed in my mouth like a blue hydrangea. "I can't fight anymore. If I keep fighting you, she'll get hurt. I've done everything I could, and now I just want Violet to be okay." I presented her name again to Maggie like a gift.

"You're not serious."

I looked right into her eyes, something I didn't remember doing yesterday. Yesterday I'd been made of nothing but anguish and fear and pain.

Today, though, I'd given birth. I felt the brilliance of it in my chest, the heat coursing through my limbs. Together, Violet and I were a goddess of light. Maggie would be extinguished by our radiance. "While I was giving birth, I really *got* what I did to you those years ago. I couldn't imagine it before. How could a woman go through what I just went through and be told it wasn't real? I don't know how you lived through it."

"Oh!" She looked shocked.

"I have an idea, and it means I let her go with you."

Her face was still guarded. "Wait. Do you actually mean that?"

Her desperate need to have Violet would work in my favor. I nodded. "With all my heart." I would give Maggie the moon, and she wouldn't know it was cardboard until I was gone. "I only want her to be safe."

She clasped her hands in front of her in prayer, as if she were in a choir. "She'll be *so* safe. So loved."

I kept my voice tentative. "So, what if . . . what if you changed your plans a little? What if . . ." Even though it might be my only hope, it was still almost impossible to say the words. "What if the three of us became a family?"

Maggie barked an incredulous laugh. But she didn't rush forward to rip Violet away from me.

I hurried on. "We've been such friends for years. I already love you like a sister." The words shredded my heart to say. "We were pushed together by fate. You can feel that, right?"

Maggie bit her bottom lip. Was she listening to me? Could it be that I'd hit an actual nerve? "You owe her to me."

But her voice wasn't sure. There was a chink in her armor, one that hadn't been there in a while. Whether or not it was the result of seeing Violet with me, I needed to work it.

"We could live together. You can be my—" My what? My nanny? She'd bridle at that. Besides, I'd need to let her think she had the power. "I mean, I'll be your co-mother. If one mother is good, two will be better. *Please* let me help you with her." It was so absurd, but I'd run out of things to try.

"Rochelle."

I hadn't even *thought* about Rochelle during all this. Her baby was in danger from this woman, too, but somehow, I'd wiped her out of my mind completely. Right now, Rochelle's potential pain meant nothing to me. I was numb in so many places of my heart, but the one where my baby lived, that wasn't numb. That was in agony.

"Fuck Rochelle," I said. "She betrayed me. She wants to take our baby from us. I don't give a shit what country you were planning on going to. I'll go, too. We won't let them find us."

Maggie didn't answer, but her fingers trilled at her bandage. Her gaze was firmly fixed on Violet, now cradled in the crook of my arm. I *hated* that this was the way my child had been brought into the world. In fear, to a mother whose blood coursed with adrenaline and cortisol and abject terror. I hated that this time wasn't about me bonding with her. Instead, I was protecting her from another woman who wanted to—

—who wanted to take her and give her the best life possible.

I knew that.

Maggie's intentions were to take perfect care of this little girl. She wanted to love her and give her everything. There was nothing Violet wouldn't have. Maggie would do her best to make her happy.

But it was still wrong. That was the bottom line. I couldn't snap her out of the belief that Violet was rightfully hers, but I might be able to change the trajectory of it. She was wobbling, mentally. In fact, she appeared to be teetering in person, too. Where she wasn't splashed with blood, hers and mine, she was bone white. She swayed in place.

I tucked Violet more firmly into my right arm, even though moving at all made my torn hand and my broken rib throb so intensely I wanted to cry. But having Violet pressed against me was a feeling I never wanted to end. She fit against me perfectly.

With my left hand I reached out to Maggie, trailing the IV tubing.

A long second elapsed. She stared at my hand as if she had no idea how the tube had got there, or why she was even in the room.

Then she took my hand. I squeezed. She squeezed my hand back.

"We could really do this," I said. "We *can* do this together. This baby is ours, we both know it." The back of my throat tightened, but I kept going. "Maybe that's why we got so entangled with each other over the years. You watching me. Me looking for you. The way we just fit as friends, instantly. We can raise her together."

"You're lying." But her voice was soft.

"I'm not." I held her hand tighter. "I'll sign anything you want."

"You'll say you were under duress."

Of course I would. "You can film me. I'll swear happily that I'm under no duress at all. That this is what I want. Because this *is* what I want. Can you imagine Violet's life? With both of us as mothers? She'd be the luckiest little girl in the world."

A corner of Maggie's mouth tilted. "Hmm."

Holy shit. Maybe it was exhaustion, or maybe it was something else. I could almost imagine it, for real. That felt dangerous, but I kept going. "Do you have a house already? Where we're going?" I was pushing it so hard—she would grab Violet and run if I screwed this up. But I had to continue to be brave.

Maggie shook her head.

"So we'll get a big house. Two master bedrooms, with a small one in between, for her nursery. She'll sleep between us." I swallowed my fear and leaned into the fantasy. "I'll paint my room light green, and I'll have a rocker. You might want something different, of course. Maybe a low sofa in your room, next to a cradle? When you're tired of cuddling her, I'll take her, and give her back the minute you wake up. Maybe I could volunteer at a women's clinic somewhere. If you felt comfortable taking care of her all day."

"What about nighttime?"

"We'd share the time. Together. We'd be a real family, just the three of us. We already love and support each other; this would make it bigger. We'd make it real. Two parents in love with their child." The kind of family that Maggie hadn't had.

The kind I hadn't had, either.

"We could take turns feeding her," Maggie said.

She was buying it.

Heck, *I* was almost buying it. "Of course."

Maggie looked down. At first, I thought she was looking at her blood-spattered shirt, but when she raised her head, there was simple happiness in her eyes. "I can feel my milk coming in."

THIRTY-SEVEN

No.

The word flew through my brain and my body so fast that I didn't have time to school my expression. I knew it was written all over my face, all over my body. She saw the *no* as clearly as if I had said it.

She jerked her hand out of mine. "You're full of shit."

"I swear I'm not—Maggie, I'm sorry. The milk thing just surprised me; that's all. Of course we'll both nurse her." But the spell was broken. I'd stab Maggie again—harder and deeper and *better*—before sharing my daughter with her.

Maggie took a wide step backward, out of my range. "Here's what's going to happen. I'm only going to say this once. I'm going to escort you out of this house and leave you to get help. Like I said, I don't want you to die."

Except that she'd been ready to cut my baby out of my stomach and kill me in the process. "How will you explain where you got her? To get a birth certificate, you'll have to do some fast-talking. I can help you with that."

"She'll get one where we're going. That's already sorted out. When we're ready, when she's old enough to know what kind of person you are, I'll get us new US passports. You can meet her when she's old enough to hate you. Now, *that's* a good reason for you not to die."

My blood throbbed violently. Violet someday hating me was almost more painful than the thought of Maggie taking her from me in the first place. "They'll know something happened here. You'll have to sell the house. Or someone will eventually break in. How are you going to explain all this?"

Maggie shook her head slowly. "You really are so blue-collar, aren't you? It's charming, really."

Shit. If you hired people who had a reason to stay quiet and gave them a shitload of money, there probably wasn't a lot you couldn't get done.

"I'll tell the authorities."

She laughed. It *had* sounded so fucking stupid coming out of my mouth. "You tell them a woman stole your baby, but you don't know what country she went to? They might believe you, but they won't know where to look, and they'll give up within a year. And that's with major media coverage, which as a white middle-class woman, I assume you'll get."

"Facial recognition. Eventually, we'll find you."

"Again, honey." She fanned her fingers next to her jawline. "Didn't you ever wonder why you didn't recognize me instantly at the meetings? It wasn't just the weight or the missing freckles. I need you to know this—I'm not worried about you. You can start an international manhunt for me. It won't matter."

I'd make a list of every single country without extradition to the US. I'd work triple shifts; I'd work hard enough to be able to afford to hire investigators in each one. Eventually, they'd track down a . . . a single mother with a daughter? It would be a needle in a million haystacks. It would never work. DNA might put her back together some-day with Rochelle, but I bet that wouldn't happen for a couple of dozen years. Anyway, why would Maggie's daughter—was I really thinking of Violet that way?—sign up on a DNA website if she thought she already knew where she was from?

There *had* to be something I was overlooking. There had to be a way for me to help Violet. For me to help myself.

Nicole's voice rose in my mind. *What's in your hula-hoop?*

Violet had been. She'd literally lived in the center of my hula-hoop. The second she left it, I'd lost control of her.

The only moment I had for sure was this one. The one that I was in. The moment in which I needed to open myself up to what was real. What was in front of me.

Maggie held all the cards.

I was powerless. Totally and completely powerless.

What if this was all the time I'd ever get with Violet? I couldn't let it be wasted in fear.

I couldn't help save my daughter. It had nothing to do with the size of my love for her. My lack of control and my love for her were two truths that had to coexist. I loved her, and I could not save her. The feeling of these two truths colliding in my heart hurt more than anything had in my whole life. And I would just have to feel them. Accept them. I tried to relax my limbs as I let the terrible truths circulate through my body.

My chest hurt like my heart was ripping in half, but I ignored the pain. I surrendered, this time for real.

I said, "May I have a few minutes with her? Alone?"

Maggie threw her hands into the air in disgust, but then she crumpled forward, her fingers flying to her bandage.

I said, "You need to go re-dress that anyway." I looked into Maggie's eyes again, like I had when Violet had made her entrance into the world. "I swear on my life I won't try anything."

"I can't believe a word you say. All you've done is lie."

"This is all the time I'm ever going to have." I hated that my voice broke on the last word. I wanted to show some semblance of strength, but the truth was, I had none left. Tears ran unchecked down my face. I only had this left—the chance of a few minutes with Violet. "Please, Maggie. I'm begging you for this."

"I don't know." She grimaced, glancing away and then back at me. "You'll hurt her to keep her from me."

Maggie wasn't going to believe anything from me except the unvarnished truth now. So I put my feelings—my real ones—into the air. "I swear on Violet's life that I won't hurt her. Her safety matters more than anything else to me. I have nothing left to lose." *Except her.* "I can't control the outcome here. And I love her too much to try."

I knew Violet was already almost gone. She was nuzzling at the skin of my inner arm, snuffling.

I wanted to feed her. Just once. "Please," I said. "Please let me have this time."

She pointed at the camera. "I have to get my stuff together anyway. But I'll be watching you every single second. If you try anything, I will kill you."

I didn't need her to say it again. I knew she was serious. "I know."

"Ten minutes. Fifteen tops." She left the room.

I felt something inside me drop away. The rest of my life, maybe.

Then I looked down at my daughter. For the first time, my eyes got to feast on her the way I'd wanted to since she'd made her way out past my pubic bone.

For these short minutes, Violet was mine.

I checked every part of her. She had fuzz on her cheeks and her jawline. I ran my fingers over the swell of her tiny belly. I peeked under her arms, at the perfect cheesy folds there. I touched the velvet of her skin, felt the minuscule eyelashes, watched the way her eyelid creased. I smelled her neck and kissed her shoulder.

I scooted backward so I could be more upright. The discomfort in my ribs and in my lower half should have been agony, but it wasn't. It would be later, if I lived through the coming separation, but it wasn't a worry. Being away from Violet was impossible to imagine, and I didn't have time to waste.

I settled my tiny daughter at my breast, holding her head at just the right angle. I touched her lower lip to my aching nipple. Her mouth gave the smallest, almost inaudible smacks, her eyes screwed tightly shut.

A sigh released, and I barely knew that it was mine. I was too busy trying to memorize her every moment. Her smell was animal-like and sweet and totally, totally *mine*. If it would keep her safe forever, I'd eat her like in a myth. I'd devour her, and she would cut herself out of my stomach when she was full-grown, bursting into her warriorhood.

But all I had was this minute. All I could do was be in this place, right now with the girl who was inside my hula-hoop for just a few more minutes.

She latched onto my nipple then, lightly at first and then so ferociously I was shocked. How many babies had I seen do this? How many mothers had looked up in awe? I knew from having to remove babies at awkward times how tightly they locked, but feeling her pull at a different part of my body was a visceral thunderbolt. It was so deep I could feel it in my womb, where she'd still been safe less than an hour ago.

I took a deep breath in as I memorized the curve of her head, the way her tiny fingers starfished against my skin. Her weight on my chest was as light as a hummingbird and as heavy as gold. I reveled in the warmth under her body and the coolness of my skin where she wasn't touching me.

A slight shiver pulsed through her, so I pushed away the towel that had been on us, reaching for the duvet that Maggie had left next to me. I pulled it across us, leaving enough of a gap that my eyes could continue to feast on the side of her face. I could have drawn her ear exactly, and I wasn't an artist. I just knew it—I *recognized* it. This perfectly whorled ear should have always existed, and the fact that it hadn't until now was an artistic tragedy. I breathed her in, taking delight in the fact that because I could smell her, I was literally inhaling cells that were *hers,* that came from her body. I was drunk on her, my head spinning with love that was so big it filled first the room and then ripped off the roof and filled the world. No one had ever loved like this, and at the same time, I knew that it was an everyday, ordinary occurrence, which made it even more magnificent.

She was a miracle.

The grief that I held behind my eyes threatened to come forward, and I pushed it back. I couldn't—I didn't have time to feel it. Not yet.

BANG.

The door of the room burst open, and Violet and I both jumped. I automatically pulled up the blanket a little higher, hiding Violet as much as I could.

"I'll kill you! I swear *I will kill you!*" Maggie ripped off the blanket and before I could start to react, she'd torn Violet away from me.

THIRTY-EIGHT

"No!" My voice was a shrill scream, and I threw myself toward her. But I was stopped short and painfully by the leg shackle. "Please! I swear I wasn't hurting her! She was cold! You didn't say not to use the duvet!" My arms, my nipples, my whole body, hurt with need. I *needed* Violet.

My baby started wailing, her first real baby cry, not the kitten mewls she'd made earlier. She was scared, and I could do nothing to help her.

Maggie took her to the changing table and laid her down. She opened a drawer. I couldn't see Violet anymore, only Maggie's back.

Please don't hurt her. Please, please don't hurt my baby.

"I swear to God I was just keeping her warm." My teeth chattered. "I didn't mean to take her off-camera. I wasn't thinking. Please, can I—"

"Shut up. Jesus, shut the fuck *up*." She took a tiny diaper out of the drawer, then withdrew a pink onesie from another one. Her voice wasn't back to normal—it was laced with something acidic and terri-fying. "Come on, sugar. Let's get you dressed. We're going for a ride later."

If I thought I'd felt fear before, it was nothing compared to this. "Please, Maggie. I'm sorry. I'll do anything."

There was a bassinet next to the changing table that I hadn't noticed—had it been there the whole time? The skin on the back of my neck tightened.

She lifted the bassinet and set it next to Violet on the changing table. "What a good girl you are, Meg." She glanced over her shoulder at me and then back at Violet. "I was going to keep Violet as your name—it *was* pretty—but I'm sorry to say that your birth mother ruined it for you. You're my little Margaret Junior now, my sweet Meg. Are you ready to go with Mommy into the living room?"

A faint hope swelled before being dashed immediately as I realized she wasn't referring to me.

Maggie lifted Violet—*not* Meg—propping up her head effectively if awkwardly. Maggie had practiced all this, a terrible thought. Then she slid her into the bassinet, and Violet lolled sideways, almost too small for it. Maggie took what looked like a crib blanket and rolled it, wedg-ing it around Violet's tiny slumped body. My baby's eyes were already closing, the crying stopped. She was as tired as I was. Probably more so.

I wanted to watch her sleep for the next five years. I probably only had seconds left. The grief tugged at me again—if it got me, I'd stop breathing.

"*Maggie.*" What next? I couldn't offer her anything she didn't have. If I offered her the entirety of my savings and retirement funds, they'd mean nothing to her. Our friendship, which I'd cherished, had never been real. I had nothing to trade.

"Can I at least say good-bye to her?" I could barely say the words.

Maggie didn't answer at first. Instead, she set Violet on the floor in the bassinet. I hadn't noticed until now, but she had changed yet again—a high-necked black tunic, a long gray cardigan, and thick black leggings. She wore high, flat boots. She'd done her makeup, understated as usual but managing to hide the pallor she'd had before. She would raise no flags. Not one. People would compliment her baby and be impressed with how she'd kept her trim figure.

Maggie took a deep breath. "I'm not a sadist, you know. You think that, but I'm not. Of course you can say good-bye." She moved toward me, holding up two zip ties. "I've got to secure your wrists again, though."

Every cell in my body tightened with fear. "But—"

"Just so I can let you say good-bye to her. No blanket, and no hands, just her on top of you. You understand—I can't let you hurt her. Then I'll cut you loose again so we can get on the road."

On the road—what did that even mean? Did it matter, though? I gave a brief nod. I had to kiss Violet's head one more time. I *had* to.

I whimpered as she replaced the zip ties around my wrists. Now she would get Violet, put her on my chest one more time.

But instead of going back to lift Violet from the bassinet, Maggie tugged the IV pole a little farther away from the bed. While pulling something out of her pocket, she gave me a strange look. "You know how I enjoy giving the perfectly chosen gift."

Her words sent another chill through my body. "I don't need anything—just her. Please."

"This'll be even better than my snickerdoodles. You'll like this. In fact, I can pretty much guarantee you'll *love* this."

She held a three-part syringe in one hand, and in her other, a small bottle of what looked like airplane vodka.

My mouth went dry. "Maggie."

"I've read up on it. Don't worry, it's only vodka. You'll get drunker, faster." She connected the Luer lock to the tubing.

A tidal wave of terror roared toward me, but I couldn't even beg her not to do it. I didn't have the words.

"Oh, did I say it was only vodka? Silly me. I added a little bump of something, too. Call it your push gift."

It was too late for me to find the words I was missing. A rush of cold flashed through my veins, and I smelled the vinegary tang of it in my nose. Then it raced into my chest cavity, and a warmth flooded me with something I didn't know I'd been dying for.

I should have screamed. I should have used all the strength I could gather to pull against my restraints. I should have gone down fighting.

Instead, I just let it happen. She was taking Violet—the only thing that mattered in the world. Why fight the only comfort I could imagine? She pushed a second syringe as tears ran down my face and into my ears.

Then I felt it—the extra thing she'd added. Heroin. I'd only ever done it once, but I remembered it like it was my longtime lover finding me in the dark. My skin flushed, prickling with heat that was almost orgasmic while at the same time goose bumps rose over my flesh. My mouth went so dry I couldn't move my tongue. Every single part of my body was heavy as iron, and I imagined myself falling through the bed, falling through the floorboards, right through to the center of the earth. All I could hear was the beat of my heart, which was also the only thing I could feel now. All pain was gone. If I'd been able to move my right hand, which I couldn't because it weighed a thousand pounds, I knew it wouldn't hurt. I couldn't feel my groin area or my rib or my aching breasts. I knew that I'd had a baby, but that time was gone.

The grief had fled, chased away. I didn't know what grief was. My body and brain and soul were centralized now on the fixed focal point of this euphoria that made everything go away.

Everything was gone. All my pain and loss—finished.

I could finally relax. I closed my eyes and fell.

THIRTY-NINE

A low whooshing rumble filled my ears. I thought perhaps I was lying in the backseat of a car, but I couldn't lift my eyelids to confirm. I was on my side, and I thought I should be uncomfortable, but mostly I felt numb.

I had to open my eyes.

There was another bump, and I knew this sound—tires hitting a pothole on the freeway.

What was happening? I couldn't remember where I'd been before this. Work? No, I was on early maternity leave from the hospital. . . . Where was Rochelle? She would—no, she had Domi now.

Open your eyes.

I was finally able to force my eyelids open a crack. When I did, I immediately regretted it as the swaying of the car upset my equilibrium. Nausea filled me. I wanted to sit up, I wanted to wrap my arms around my baby bulge, but my limbs still wouldn't respond.

Would my mouth work? "Hello? What's going on?"

There was a pause. "Honey, do you not remember?"

A downpour of relief flooded through me to hear Maggie's voice. It helped assuage the pain that was starting to light every part of my body on fire. Something was so terribly, awfully wrong, but at least Maggie was here. She'd be able to help me. "What happened to me?"

"Oh, my God, Jillian. Stay awake, honey. I'm going as fast as I can."

"Where . . ."

The car accelerated. "We're almost at the hospital. Can you stay awake for just another minute? We're almost there." I saw her reach to her right, toward the dark, out-of-focus bulk of a baby seat sitting on the passenger side. Didn't she know they went in the back? I wanted to tell her that she was doing it wrong, but the correct words wouldn't come out of my mouth.

My right arm finally woke up a little, tingling. I touched my belly.

Terror ripped through me. I was deflated. This wasn't the size I should have been. *"My baby."*

Abruptly, the car swerved and skidded to a bumpy stop. I was strapped in, or I would have rolled forward off the seat. As it was, pain bloomed inside me, a pain like I'd never felt, a demon gnawing on every organ I possessed.

Her car door opened, and a second later, mine did, too. She was scrabbling at my seat belt as she yelled behind her, "Help! We need help here! Can someone help?" To me she said urgently, "Come on, sweetheart, we're at the ER. We need to get you help." The seat belt was undone, and she helped me prop myself up.

The fear in her voice stirred something deep inside me. I had to move. I had to save my—"Baby," I said.

"The baby's fine. She's right here. But you need help, Jillian. You have to get out of the car."

It was dark outside. As my first foot hit the dirt, then the second, I was confused. This wasn't a hospital ER portico. No, this was—

We'd stopped at the dead end of an empty road. To the left, the ground curved steeply down to waves crashing below. No ambulance. No security running to see what the yelling was about.

I looked into her face, and in one flash, it all came back. "No." I meant to scream it, but it came out as a whisper.

"Mine now," was all Maggie said.

My legs crumpled and I hit the dirt, the pain so intense that I couldn't breathe.

Then she and the car were gone with a screech of tires, her rear lights illuminating the night with red that faded to black.

She took Violet with her into the dark.

The world wobbled back and forth in my vision before I could make it stop swaying. For a long while, the ocean to my left roared both below and overhead, in front of me and then behind me.

In the very periphery of conscious thought, I realized I might fall off the edge of the cliff. I tried very hard to care. But I couldn't. I wanted the feeling back—the one I'd had just before I'd passed out. I wanted that forever. I wanted heavy peace followed by total unconsciousness. Was that what death was? If so, why were people scared of death? I wanted that quiet followed by nothing.

But Violet.

I dragged myself to standing by pulling on a metal guard rail. Part of it was broken, holding to its post with a single rusted screw. It was all that kept me from tumbling over. Far below, the waves crashed white on the dark sand. I could hear a highway somewhere in the distance, but it sounded a long way behind me, probably at least a half mile away. It wasn't possible I could walk that far. I didn't know if I could walk ten feet. I needed help.

I was still in the tank top and skirt she'd put me in, both of them now covered in blood and worse. Inanely, I patted myself down, in case she'd stuck my phone in the skirt's pocket. Of course she hadn't.

Where the fuck was I? The road Maggie had sped away on went up and out toward that highway I could hear. No lights, no houses, only a row of trees on either side of the street. That was uncommon around here, unless she'd taken me someplace far away. Usually, roads to a lookout point also had multimillion-dollar houses to match the view.

Something about this place was familiar, though. Wheezing, I turned my head again to look at the guard rail and down at the water. It reminded me of a place Rochelle and I used to go to picnic sometimes.

I *knew* this place. To the right were three parking spaces, all empty. There was a set of stairs, almost hidden unless you knew they were there. Now that I looked, I could see the first step carved out of a rock. This *was* the same spot we used to go to. I held on to the rail for another second while I tried to clear my head and remember. Rochelle was the one with the good map memory. I always forgot what streets things were on. But I could do this.

There wasn't much out here; I knew that. One exit up the highway was a place with a diner and a surf shop, but I couldn't get that far. But wasn't there a . . . a deli? No, it was a convenience store. At the end of this road, which couldn't be more than a quarter mile long, there had been a store where we'd once bought very bad coffee to drink on the beach.

I would have to get there. I didn't have a choice.

I took two wobbly steps, and then I fell onto my knees, wracked with an intensity of pain I'd never felt before. I kept my head down and panted. If only a car would come out here, a couple parking, a felon, anyone.

But no one came. So I pushed myself up using both hands, hoping the pain in my ribs would distract me from the pain in the rest of my body, that it would relieve some of the agony in my heart, but it didn't. It just hurt like shit on top of everything else.

Keeping my body bowed and my head down, I started to shuffle through the darkness. If I could keep moving, I could get anywhere. Eventually, I could shuffle the length of the world and get Violet back—no, not that; if I started to cry now, I'd never stop. Crying would come later. Maybe. If I lived to see later. Who knew what was going on inside this broken body? At the next streetlight, I lifted the skirt to look at my inner thighs—they were streaked with blood, but all of it dry. I knew that could change quickly—if I had a cervical tear, a real danger with such a fast birth, I could suddenly hemorrhage, bleeding out right here along this road.

It took forever, but I finally reached the spot where the road met the main street that led up to the highway. And there was the convenience store, just as I'd remembered it. Built to look like a small red barn; the neon lights glowed. The word *Michelob* blinking into the night had never looked so beautiful to me before, and it had looked pretty good in the past.

I stumbled through the parking lot and pulled on the door.

It simply thunked, metal on metal.

Closed.

I couldn't swear, or cry, or lie down and not get up, or anything else I wanted to do. I pressed my forehead against the glass and banged. Was there someone in there? In the back? Maybe the kid who closed at night was crashing there illegally. Maybe the owner had been thrown out by his wife and had put a cot down in the back. Someone had to be there.

Help me.

But no one came. There were no cars in the front parking lot. And where the hell were the pay phones that used to be everywhere? I knew cities had gotten rid of a lot of them, but wouldn't a convenience store parking lot be one of the last holdouts? The thing that might have saved me was extinct.

Still bent over, my neck and spine trembling at a forty-five-degree angle to my legs, I moved to the edge of the building, where, in the darkness of the side lot, I spotted a truck with steam inside the windows. I didn't care if I interrupted active coitus—I'd offer them anything (as if I had anything) for the use of their cell phone.

I shuffled closer, calling out, "I'm sorry to bother you, hello?"

No one in the car responded, and I still couldn't see inside it.

I knocked softly at the driver's-side window. *Please don't shoot me.* "Hello?"

The door swung open, and I stumbled backward.

The smell of meth hit me full in the face, chemical and harsh. I hated it when people came into the hospital on it—they moved too fast and unpredictably.

"What do you want?" The guy was alone—pale and skinny and nervous-looking, with the hollow cheeks of full-blown use.

"I need help." The words felt foreign, but they were all I had left.

FORTY

"Holy *shit*. The fuck happened to you?"

"Can I use your phone?" I lurched forward accidentally and caught myself with my right hand on the truck's frame. I choked back the scream of pain.

"You need a ambulance or something?" The man's eyes shifted to the space behind me. "Is someone coming after you?"

"Please, your phone?"

"Here." He held it out to me by the edge, as if scared to touch me. "But make it fast. I don't need to be here if the cops come."

I turned my back, facing away from him. Nine-one-one answered in three rings.

"My baby was stolen," I said after I told her where I was.

"Ma'am?"

"A woman took her."

"When was this?"

"Maybe half an hour ago? I think she was headed to Burbank. The private airport there."

"How old is the baby?"

I turned to look at the man in the truck. "What time is it?"

He looked startled but said, "Almost five A.M."

I'd been out that long? What had Maggie been doing that whole time? I spoke into the phone. "She's about nine hours old, I think."

"Ma'am?" The dispatcher sounded incredulous and I didn't blame her. "Do you need an ambulance?"

"No—"

The phone must have been loud enough for the guy in the truck to hear the dispatcher, because he shouted, "She needs that ambulance! There is a *lot* of blood on this lady!"

I told him to shut up and then gave her Maggie's name and description and told her as much as I remembered about her car. "She's going to Burbank. You have to shut down the airport. She's got a private plane that's on standby. There's no traffic. She can be there fast. She's kidnapping my *baby*. Can you shut the airport down?" I struggled to remember the name of the private airline she said she always flew. "Billion Air! She's going to Billion Air."

The dispatcher said something I didn't understand in a muffled tone and then said, "Ma'am, I'm sending you an ambulance. How old are you?"

"I'm fine. I don't need—"

The guy yelped, "Yeah, she does!"

"—I just need you guys to go the airport and stop Maggie Barnswell from getting on a plane!"

The dispatcher made a noise in the back of her throat. "I'm sending an officer to you, too. He'll be able to help you."

"Can you shut down Burbank or not?"

"That's not on me, ma'am; that's on TSA. We don't have jurisdiction over airports. But my officer will be able to relay what needs to happen."

"They don't have TSA at the private airport!" Did they? I couldn't remember. "But it needs to happen *now*. I am a *doctor*." This woman didn't believe me. She thought I was crazy. But honestly, I knew I wouldn't believe me, either.

"The officer will be with you soon. Are you safe in that location?"

I gave a good hard look at the man in his truck. The door was still swung open, and he was now slumped down in the seat, his chin almost on his chest. He'd just yelled at the dispatcher over my shoulder, but now he appeared to be almost asleep.

I wanted whatever he was on.

But I didn't have a good answer for the dispatcher, so I hung up.

The man didn't move.

"Here's your phone."

Nothing but a soft snore.

I jabbed him in the shoulder with it. "Hey."

"Shit," he mumbled. He looked at me as if seeing me all over again. "Oh, shit. The cops are coming? I gotta get outta here."

"Please stay with me." The words were out of my mouth before I could stop them. I was begging a junkie to stay with me because I didn't want to be alone.

And then an urge prickled my skin, an old pain added to the new.

And the guy picked up on it as if he were psychic. "You want some? Got twenty bucks?"

There it was. The hit he'd give me would be small, a point, maybe. It would cost him five bucks out of what he had. But he'd have twenty to go get more.

I shook my head. My mouth was so dry I couldn't speak again.

He looked up the road and back to me. "Or forty? I'll really light your fire for forty."

One last time, I shook my head mutely. I didn't have another *no* in me. If he asked me one more time, I'd do it. Why not? My sobriety was already blasted away. Instead of having seven years, I didn't even have seven hours. I still felt a little loose limbed even under the body-crushing pain, so I probably didn't even have seven *minutes* yet of being clean.

I shuffled another inch toward him. He already had his kit out.

There was no way I was getting Violet back.

It would take at least an hour to talk any cop into even understanding what I was telling him, let alone believing me. By then, Maggie would be on whatever plane she'd hired. I knew she'd been telling the truth, and I knew she'd have it perfectly planned.

Whatever I did, I'd already lost Violet.

I lost the ability to hold myself up and dropped to my knees in the gravel. I heard the guy ask me if I was okay over my head.

I'd lost her. It was all my fault. If I hadn't been drunk that night so long ago, if I'd never met Maggie and hurt her—

I gave up. It was over. Violet was gone.

I barely had the strength to lift my head, but I said, "Yeah."

His thin face looked more like a skull than a head. Grimacing, he held out his palm. "Money."

"I'll have to pay you back. I swear I'm good for it." I stood, moving as slowly as I could. Everything burned now, as if nerve endings were slowly coming back to life. I needed relief.

"Fuck you, lady." He lurched forward in his seat and started the engine.

I closed the gap between us, my knees pressing against the running board. I could smell the chemical sweat of him. He couldn't close his door with me standing in it. "Wait! You can take me to the ATM after. You can have double. Triple." Sixty dollars to escape this pain for even a single second would be a bargain.

He bared what was left of his teeth at me. "ATM's in front of the store."

In the distance, I heard a siren approaching. The guy's eyes went wide, and he moved fast, his leg shooting out as he tried to kick me away so he could close his door.

He missed. The second time he kicked he got me in the thigh, but

I barely cared. I was fighting with a meth-head for drugs in a parking lot while my baby was being kidnapped.

Jesus. What had happened to my feral mothering instinct, the fierceness that had come over me earlier? What was stronger? My addiction or my love for Violet? What did I want more, being sucked into a black morass I'd never climb out of or facing the pain of losing her with a clear head?

It wasn't a maternal urge that made me move. It was a realization, a really simple one.

If I was high, I *couldn't* love Violet, even at a distance. Not clearly. Not the way a mother should.

My mother hadn't loved me the way a mother should. And I refused to be a mother like her, even if I had no child to raise. This had to end with me.

His third kick landed on my hip. I grabbed his foot, wrapping both hands around his ankle as my ribs howled. The siren was louder now. I pulled as hard as I could. The guy yelled and kicked with his other leg as he clutched the steering wheel, but honestly, he didn't stand a chance. Physical pain didn't matter to me like it did to him.

I kept pulling, twisting his foot as I did, so by the time I yanked him out of the car, he was almost belly down. As he fell out, the side of his head smacked the doorframe. When he landed in the dirt, he was unconscious but breathing. I launched myself into the driver's seat, slamming the door closed. I gasped in white-hot pain as my vagina hit the torn plastic, as I used my shredded abdominals to ratchet the bucket seat closer to the steering wheel. I panted, willing myself not to pass out or throw up.

An ambulance roared into the parking lot and cut its siren. I rolled down the window, still gasping, and pointed down at him. "He fell," I said.

As the paramedic started to speak, I punched the gas.

FORTY-ONE

On the highway, I fumbled with the guy's phone. He didn't have it password protected, thank God.

I couldn't call 911 again. They couldn't help with the airport, plus there was the tiny detail that I'd just carjacked someone, which I was pretty sure was a felony. I needed help. But who?

Rochelle. I had to tell her, but this wasn't the time. Not yet. My heart splintered as I thought about trying to explain to her the events of the previous day. I wouldn't be able to even *start* to make her understand what had happened. I needed immediate assistance, not a long, emotional confrontation in which I explained to my ex how I'd lost her child. Not right now.

No. I needed actual boots-on-the-ground *help.*

Nicole. Your sponsor was the one you were supposed to call first. But I'd only barely dodged getting high for the second time in one day—I understood the first time wasn't my fault, but the second time, when I'd wanted it almost more than my own child, that was going to take some debriefing. Besides, I realized with a jolt that I didn't know her number by heart.

Help.

Yeah. Prayer was good and all, but I needed more than that, too. Who did I call when I needed help? People called me; I didn't call them.

And then I suddenly saw Bree's license plate in my head. CALBREE.

Fuck, I'd been so wrong about Bree. Instead of trying to help her when she'd needed it, I'd actually believed she'd wanted to hurt me. Yeah, she'd been a horse's ass about a couple of things, but she was scared of losing Hal forever. Instead, Maggie had been the dangerous one. How had I gotten it so wrong with both of them?

And now I needed the woman I'd accused of the worst thing imaginable to help me save my daughter—the baby I thought she'd wanted to take from me. I wasn't even sure if she slept with her ringer on, let alone if she'd take my call.

But I had no other choice.

Traffic was light, a small mercy as I struggled to figure out what numbers were what letters. As her phone rang in my ear, I pleaded with whatever was listening that she would roll over in bed and answer.

"Yeah?"

"Bree. It's me."

A pause. "Jillian?"

"I need you to just listen. I need your help."

"Hang on a—"

"I'm sorry, I can't hang on. I'm on PCH, headed toward Burbank Airport. I just stole a truck."

I heard her snort.

"I'm not kidding." I hit ninety and overtook a slow-moving Miata. "Maggie kidnapped me. She's the one who's been stalking me. I'm sorry I thought it was you. I owe you a real apology later, but right now I need you. She tied me up and induced my labor. She took V from me, and she's headed for the private airport, where she has a plane waiting to take her to a country where I won't be able to find her. Help me. *Please*."

There was a heavy pause. My heart fell—I wouldn't be able to talk her into believing me. I'd have to do this on my own. I would fail, Maggie would get away, and I'd die because living would be impossible.

"This is real?" she finally said.

"Yes."

"I'm on it."

I saw a flash of white behind my eyes, my relief so acute I could almost taste it. "What are you going to do?"

"I'll shut down the airport. Just drive."

If anyone could do it, it was Bree. She probably had a private line to the head of the FAA. "I don't have my phone. I'll be at this number."

"Damn, girl. When I told you to get better at asking for help . . ." And she was gone.

Traffic stayed light, still too early for the gridlock to start. I wasn't the only one going a hundred. I'd push it harder, but I didn't think this hunk of bolts would rattle even a single mile an hour faster. The truck sounded like it was about to come to pieces, but as long as it didn't do that until I got to Burbank, I didn't care. Thank God the guy'd had a full tank of gas.

I'd managed to get the cell phone to direct me to Burbank's private jetport. Google Maps said taking the 405 up and then hooking down on the 5 would be faster than going east on the 101, which had a reported accident slowing traffic. But three miles outside the exit for the airport, traffic slowed, and then finally stopped in the predawn darkness.

I hit the brakes, cursing. Tears of frustration made the taillights ahead of me wobble and swim. I couldn't do this. I couldn't wait.

But Maggie would have hit this, too. That stall on the alternate route still showed as blocking traffic, so we were undoubtedly taking the same freeways.

And—unlike me—she had a good reason not to stand out in traffic. She couldn't risk getting pulled over. At the very least, she had an infant in the front seat and would get a ticket for that, which would slow her escape down by ten minutes at least, minutes she didn't have to spare.

Me? I didn't give a shit. I had not one goddamned thing to lose. If a cop tried to pull me over, I'd make him chase me all the way there, sirens wailing to let Maggie know I was coming for her.

I moved five lanes to the right through the sluggish traffic in less than thirty seconds, a maneuver that would normally have taken at least a couple of minutes. I didn't use my blinker, and I didn't ask. I pushed, not caring who hit the truck as long as it remained drivable. The other drivers leaned on their horns with long, angry blares, and I appreciated them for alerting the next lane that I was coming in. Hitting the right-hand shoulder, the tires kicked up rocks. I did forty in the non-lane, the fastest I dared go with the frequent on- and off-ramps. Twice, cars saw me coming in their rearview mirrors, pulling halfway out of their lanes to block me from passing on their right. The first one I almost hit. I hung an inch from her bumper and honked my horn for so long that she pulled back into her lane, flipping me off.

But the next car that pulled in front of me wasn't intimidated by my proximity or my horn. A Tesla 3, it took up the whole lane in front of me. Immediately, we were down to doing two miles an hour, the same as everyone else.

My baby was up ahead of me, about to be lost to me forever. Did this guy seriously think that going slowly would stop me?

I checked for airbags, but the truck was old. No warnings on the passenger side, none that I could see.

So I hit the motherfucker.

FORTY-TWO

I didn't hit him *that* hard, but I didn't hit him that gently, either. His car was rocketed forward. My neck snapped forward painfully, but honestly, what was more pain at this point? I was a ball of nerve endings, all of them shrieking. I was sure the bumper was dented, but thankfully, we hadn't locked together. (What would I do? Carjack him, too? Get in his driver's seat and drag both cars to Burbank?) The truck was still driving just fine. When his brake lights came on, I stayed behind him until he was out of his car and coming for me on foot. Then I yanked the steering wheel left and cut off the car coming up in the slow lane. I passed the guy, who was yelling so loudly I could hear his words clearly through the glass. "You fucking bitch! I'll sue you—"

I had to creep forward for the whole car length it took to get past the Tesla, with him tugging at my locked door handle and screaming the whole time, but as soon as I passed it, I got back onto the side shoulder and floored it, leaving him a flyspeck in my rearview.

There must not have been a single highway patrol officer on the freeway because I blazed free and clear, picking up speed and bravery as I went. A couple more cars appeared to consider pulling in front of me, but it must have been obvious even from a distance that I'd run clean out of fucks. They all thought better of it, ducking back into the slow lane at the last minute.

I reached the San Fernando exit, blasting off the freeway like a rattling rocket. I screamed down North Clybourne, plowing off the road where it dead-ended into the parking lot. I took Billion Air's oval driveway at fifty, slamming the truck's wheels into the red curb in front of the doors. Sliding out of the vehicle, I groaned with pain. As I'd driven, adrenaline had numbed some of my trauma response, but it all came back now. *Don't pass out, Jillian. Don't pass out.* Tensing all the muscles I could bear to squeeze, I walked toward the doors. What I should have been doing was lying down until the dizziness passed, but if I could raise my blood pressure a bit by clenching my extremities, I might avoid fainting. If I was lucky.

A young woman dressed in a red jacket strode toward me. "Oh, my God! You—"

I knew I must look like the walking dead. "It's an emergency!"

"You, uh, you can't park there!" She looked over her shoulder to the young man who stood at the doorway security table. His eyes widened, but he put himself in front of the glass doors, barring my way.

I wasn't prepared for this confrontation. Maggie had said there was no TSA, but I supposed if Hollywood people used the jetport they'd need some kind of private security. My brain stalled and went into freefall.

The woman said, "Ma'am, I can see there's clearly a problem. Can I—can I help?"

My brain snapped back into place. "You have a woman who just came through with a baby. I'm her ob-gyn." What the hell could I say that they would believe?

Then it struck me. I *was* the doctor. The question was what *wouldn't* they believe? I gave myself a second to breathe and think, holding up one hand and bending forward at the waist. Then I said, "Her husband was driving down from Santa Barbara and missed the birth. He also missed the message from her that she was doing well and wanted to fly home. He came to the hospital right after I released her. I was talking to him outside when a car lost control on its way into the ER driveway, and he was killed." I gestured down at myself, my words tumbling over themselves. "I was also—injured. I worked on him for fifteen minutes, but I couldn't save him. I have to be the one to tell her—I have to tell her his last words for their child. My team called ahead to try to ground the plane—did you get that order?"

The guy looked at the woman. "I heard something in dispatch about Malibu PD calling in an incident, but—"

"That's right," I cut him off. "That was us. You know who my patient is, right? You recognized her?"

They both shook their heads.

"Oh, God. I have to get to her before the media does." I looked over my shoulder as if a reporter might be right behind me.

The guy was nodding along with my story, but the woman wasn't buying it as hard as he was. She said, "We can absolutely help you with this. I'll simply need your driver's license and your hospital ID first."

I had nothing in my hands. I made a one-second show of patting the skirt's empty pockets. "I raced here from the hospital, and I left my purse in my office."

"I'll just need you to wait out here until we can ascertain your identity, I'm sorry."

"You *really* don't know who she is? You're not pretending?"

The man leaned forward. "Who is she?"

The woman shook her head. "Sorry, I'll need your ID first."

Whoever trained her needed a raise. I was a second away from bolting past them but I knew I needed her on my side, to get me through the airport and to wherever Maggie was. "Look. Call UCLA Medical Center, Santa Monica. Ask if I work there. Jillian Marsh."

"How do I know you're Jillian Marsh, though?"

I lowered my head and then raised it, letting her see my real face. "This is, truly, an emergency. I can't give you more than that."

She spoke to her phone, asking it to call the hospital. She kept it on speaker and asked to be transferred to Obstetrics, which was really fucking smart of her. It took seven rings for them to answer, and Lisa Weston's voice at the nurse's station had never sounded sweeter. Before the security officer could speak, I grabbed her phone out of her hand. She stared at me, shocked, as I said loudly, "Lisa, it's me." Nurses knew doctor's voices by just a word or two. "I need you to verify my identity by saying my name and that I work there."

"Jillian?"

"Please do this for me. I'll explain everything later."

"I'm worried. But okay. Whoever this is for, you're talking to Jillian Marsh. She's an ob-gyn in our department."

"Thanks." I disconnected and handed it back. "My patient's name is Maggie Barnswell. I need you to take me to her as fast as possible. She can*not* find out she's a widowed single mother from the media. If she does, the lawsuits will be civil, and they'll be on you personally."

The woman nodded as she stood straighter. She picked an iPad off the desk and flicked though it. "Ms. Barnswell just boarded. Follow me."

My right hand shook, sending spikes of pain through my body—we had to hurry. Maggie could leave—the plane could take off, and that would be it. "Can you stop the plane?" What if it took off?

"I sent a message through the system for it to stand by until we get there. Do you need—maybe a wheelchair?"

"No." I must have looked as broken as I felt. But we couldn't waste time on her going to get one. I limped as quickly as I could after her, ignoring my full-body pain as best I could. We wound through the terminal, if that was in fact what it was called. It looked more like a formal living room with plush chairs and enormous, thousand-dollar bouquets of flowers. There was a coffee bar and a regular bar, and servers were setting out a full breakfast. I smelled bacon, and my stomach roiled.

She led me to a set of double doors, waving a hand at the man who stood next to the actual red velvet rope that stood across them. So American. Regular people got whole-body scans. The über-rich got a velvet rope.

We went through and out onto the tarmac. She pointed at a limo sitting next to the long panes of terminal glass. "You can ride to the plane in comfort, or we can walk."

"Just—which plane is it?" Nine or ten small planes sat parked in front of us.

She pointed to a small white plane, the farthest one, at least a hundred yards away. The steps were still down, the door open.

I started to jog toward it but realized three steps in I couldn't do it. My knees buckled and my vision darkened as pain threatened to take me all the way down. "Limo," I gasped.

She flagged the car toward us. It was already moving our way—the driver must have seen me stumble. Her radio chattered at her, and she said, "All our planes just got grounded. You don't need to worry about her plane leaving yet."

Bree. Thank God.

The woman opened the door for me before saying something to the driver and pointing at the jet. She didn't get in.

Even though I knew the plane wasn't going anywhere, I begged the driver to hurry. Maggie still had Violet. I couldn't move fast enough, so he had to.

He hit the gas as if he'd been waiting for someone to tell him to, and I used the few seconds it took to get there to try to steady my breathing. I wasn't sure I was going to be able to stand up when we got there.

He parked near the plane's stairs. "Do you need anything else, ma'am?"

Inside me, a river of fear started to flow, so wide and deep that it drowned the pain. "Can you stay? Just . . . in case?" In case what? In case I needed someone to drag my body parts away after Maggie ripped me into pieces?

"Yes, ma'am. Of course. My name's Tony. Yell if you need me." He looked concerned, and I couldn't blame him. "Are you in danger?"

My heart thudded in my chest. "I think I am. Yeah."

"You need the cops?"

I thought about it. I doubted they could help at this point. "Maybe later. But right now, can I borrow your cell phone?"

He turned his head to look at me. "What for?"

"I want to record audio."

Tony had no reason to trust me. Not one. But he lifted his chin. "All right, then." He took out his phone and opened the recorder. I stepped out of the car and slipped it into my pocket. Whatever happened, at least there'd be a record of it.

Even so close to the plane, it was still hard to get to it. My entire body screamed that it was inches from dying and that I needed to stop everything, including breathing. I pushed my brain into overriding that demand. A man in an orange jacket was headed our way—to close up the steps? So the plane could take off? Had they ungrounded the flights already?

No way in hell. Not without me getting to my daughter first.

First step. Second step. Up the mountain. *Breathe.* I pulled on the handrail as if it were the hand of salvation itself.

Would there be a flight attendant? Would I have to fight a pilot? My heart beat as if it was trying to jackhammer itself out of my chest.

But at the top of the steps stood only Maggie.

FORTY-THREE

Hands on her hips, Maggie stared down at me as I heaved myself up the last three steps. "I've got to say, I am *really* impressed."

All she had to do was to kick her booted foot out and connect with my chest or my head. If I were her, I would. I'd kick me right down the steps, and I'd give the pilot an extra thousand (or ten thousand—I wasn't sure how much this kind of thing cost) to roll away, leaving my body on the tarmac.

But instead, she stepped forward and held out her hand. My head was swimming, and I was panting so much I choked on my own spit. I gripped the step rail more firmly. "I can do it." My teeth were gritted so hard I doubted she could hear me over the roar of the wind and another plane's engine as it idled. Her plane seemed to be turned off, not rumbling at all.

"Yeah, I can see that." She stepped back into the cabin. "I'm so impressed, actually, that I'll invite you in. Just until my pilots get back."

She wasn't doing it out of the kindness of her heart, I knew. She couldn't risk making a scene outside the plane, couldn't risk anyone stopping her now. When the pilots returned and were inside the plane, she'd have backup.

I ducked my head as I entered. The interior was shadowy, with only a few window shades open to the early morning light. Dimly, I saw white leather seats and, under the windows, a long table full of precut fruit and juices. I didn't see a flight attendant.

But there was only one important thing, and it wasn't my safety. *Violet.*

My gaze found her. Or at least, I saw the bassinet I assumed she was in. She made no noise—my heart hurt a thousand times more than my body did. "Is she—?"

"She's fine. You can look at her. But I swear to God, Jillian, don't touch her, or I *will* kill you."

I didn't doubt she could. I had about two more watts of energy with which to fight her, and I needed to save them for later.

And there she was, my beloved. Round cheeks and tightly shut eyes. Both hands fixed in tiny white-knuckled fists. Her upper lip sucked on her lower one. My breasts ached with need. Every bit of desire I'd had for anything—ever—died in comparison to the way I wanted to touch her. Every drink I'd ever tossed down my throat, every illegal substance I'd ever sniffed or snorted, the way I'd desired sex and food and even air—all of it added up to nothing compared to the way I needed to feel her skin under my fingertips.

Help.

I stepped backward. It was the most difficult thing I'd ever done in my life.

"Good choice." Her voice was light and sweet again. We were back to the fake-friendship thing. All right. I could do this.

Maggie leaned against a white seat, shaking her head slowly. "Damn, girl. Again. Respect. I didn't expect this."

She did, in fact, sound impressed, which made sense. With major bodily damage, no cell phone, and not a dime to my name, I'd managed to get all the way to the airport, through security, and onto her plane.

What came next? Would she kill me? What would a pilot do if he boarded his plane and it was full of my blood? Surely they wouldn't take off, or was that simply a question of price, too?

"What now?" I needed to accept that she had all the power. I had none.

"How did you get here?"

"Carjacked a junkie."

Her eyes widened. "You dazzle me. I simply did *not* see this coming. I'll ask you the same question. What now?"

Me? I had no fucking clue. I'd gotten here, but I didn't have a plan. I just shook my head.

"I expect you'll try to tell the pilots that you're the mother and that I've stolen her from you, but I've already paid them a year's salary each to ignore whatever my alcoholic sister Jillian says if she makes it this far. Which, to be fair, I didn't know you would, but I knew I'd regret it if I didn't have everything planned out. Are you the reason the planes aren't taking off, too? The reason my pilots are trying to bribe someone inside right now?"

"That would be Bree, actually."

Maggie actually laughed. "Of course it is. Would you like to have a seat?"

I hated myself for it, but I didn't think I could stand for even thirty more seconds. I sunk slowly, so carefully, into a chair that faced backward, toward the bassinet in which Violet lay sleeping. I ignored the pain and the black sparkles that danced at the edge of my vision. An empty formula bottle was on its side on the table next to it.

I caught my breath.

Maggie turned her head to follow my gaze. "Oh, she's so good at the bottle already. Such a good little eater. I'm only supplementing. Until, you know."

She'd faltered a tiny bit. I didn't allow myself the hope that wanted to push its way into my brain. "Until your milk finishes coming in."

"Do not fuck with me, Jillian."

"I'm not."

"Or humor me."

"I swear to God, I'm not." Her delusion was real in her mind, as real as the pain I felt from my engorged nipples, from my massacred groin, from my shredded right hand, from my entire broken-ribbed body. "I get it."

She melted gracefully into the chair opposite me. Our knees were a good two feet apart. I was grateful for the separation and the fact that I'd have at least a second or two of notice if she launched herself at me.

"Seriously, what did you expect to happen when you boarded?"

I closed my eyes for a second and took another deep breath before opening them again. "I have no idea. I guess you'll try to finish stealing my child."

"*My* child." She didn't trust me.

Nor should she.

I said, "In *Alien*, Ripley never backs down. We're Ripleys. So I guess we'll fight some more. One of us will win. The other one might die. That one'll probably be me."

Maggie frowned.

"I'm tired, Maggie. I'll do anything for her; you know I will. But I'm trying to also be realistic here. If I don't die, but you take her, I'll want to die, so I guess that's the same thing."

She looked down at her lap, then up at me again.

For a split, heart-stopping second, her face was the same face she'd worn in the hospital seven years before, right after she'd opened her belly, before she passed out. I finally truly recognized her. She had the same grief-stricken, disbelieving eyes.

Quietly, Maggie said, "Then you'll finally know how it feels to lose a baby."

But I already knew. "It's like the ocean."

She frowned. "What?"

When she'd driven away with my daughter, when I lost Violet, I finally knew what it felt like. "It's like you've been dropped out of the sky into the ocean. You have no life preserver. No boat. No one can help you. The ocean is thousands of miles wide, and you're in the middle of it, and every place where the salt water touches you, you burn. You can never get out. You can never drown, either. You have to stay there. Adrift. Alone in the ocean, nothing around you but the water and the freezing cold and the knowledge that you'll never feel joy again in any shape or form. Your heart becomes the water, and then your body does, too. You're still you, but you're also the ocean, and you know you're lost forever."

Her eyes were brimming with tears that refused to fall. I thought mine should be, too, but I couldn't find where tears lived. So I closed my eyes to say the rest of it. "And that's just a tiny bit of what it's felt like to lose Violet. You had it worse than I did because you never got to hold your child. I'm so sorry that happened to you, Maggie. You never deserved that."

When I opened my eyes, Maggie was staring at me. I hadn't heard her move, but now she held a knife in her right hand. It was long and vicious-looking, its serrated blade flashing bright as it caught a sliver of sunrise through the window. *Civil dawn*, I thought.

She leaned forward, remaining in her seat with every muscle tensed. The knife shook in her hand.

I kept my gaze on Maggie's face. One tear dropped from her left eye, then it was matched by her right eye. Her whole body was trembling. Funny. Mine seemed to have finally stopped shaking.

"I *will* kill you, Jillian. I didn't want to. I did *everything* not to have to. But I will. You know that. You're *making* me do it."

I pulled out the phone and showed it to her. "It's all recorded. It's already uploaded to the cloud, in case you grab the phone and try to delete it." I didn't know that it was backed up anywhere, but it was all I had.

Maggie panted a breath and leaned forward, propelling the knife forward through the air. It stopped, hovering in her hand in midair, twelve inches from my chest.

I remained completely still. "If you do take her from me, even if I'm not around, she'll someday find out what you did. I guarantee you that. And she'll learn that the person she thought loved her most was nothing but a common thief. She'll end up alone, without parents to love her." Our eyes locked. "Just like us."

"Go to *hell*." But I could feel Maggie realize I was right, could feel the knowledge move through her body as surely as if I were touching her skin. The knife shook more violently in the air in front of me. I knew if I tried to strike it away, the fight would be on.

Instead, I waited, my breath tight in my chest.

Finally, she said, "It's not fair, though. It's not *fair*!" She sounded like an angry, lost child. I imagined she'd sounded exactly the same on the day her parents' plane crashed.

"It isn't," I agreed. I had never meant anything more deeply in my life. Not my Hippocratic oath, not my wedding vows. This was the deepest truth I held.

Sirens wailed. We both ducked our heads to look out the plane's windows. A gate in the fence had been opened, and four police cars were racing toward our plane at top speed.

Maggie's eyes wavered in their tears as she raised the knife high.

I raised my hands to block her first blow.

The blade plunged toward me. I tensed, knowing I would simply fight until I couldn't fight anymore.

Then the knife stopped in midair for the second time. Maggie's mouth twisted and she finally managed to say, "I can't live without her, Jillian."

Maggie changed the blade's direction and, with a guttural cry, drove the knife into her own stomach until the blade was sunk to the hilt.

FORTY-FOUR

I launched myself forward. *"No!"*

Maggie's eyes were screwed tightly shut. Air puffed out of her lips in short exhalations as her arms dropped to her sides. With my damaged right hand, I tried to hold the handle of the knife steady, attempting to stabilize it against her skin to keep it from moving. If the knife was removed, it would probably kill her. With my left hand, I fumbled with her seat button. If I could get her chair to drop fully flat, I could do CPR if I needed to without dragging her to the ground, which would definitely dislodge the knife.

Grabbing the blanket on the chair next to hers, I wrapped it around the knife's hilt and applied pressure as best I could around the wound. *"Help!"*

The driver outside—Tony—would he hear me?

I heard the stairs rattle as I finally got Maggie's seat flat. She was still wheezing. If she'd hit her abdominal aorta, she'd bleed out in seconds, a minute, tops.

From behind me, "What should I do?"

I didn't turn my head. "Tell the cops to order an ambulance, stat. Stab wound. Tell them thirty-seven-year-old female, 27-Delta-3, self-inflicted stab wound, clear to enter." I gave the code for a stabbing victim with critical injuries, praying Tony would remember what I said. I'd passed a fire department right next to the entrance of the airport as I'd driven in—with luck, they'd be in quarters and not on another call. "Let two of the cops on board to help me with her, but try to keep the rest of them off."

Maggie's eyes fluttered. "Hurts."

My heart thundered, roaring in my ears. If she could whisper, the knife probably hadn't hit her aorta. "You're okay," I said, but my voice was hoarse. "I've got to keep applying pressure. It's going to hurt like hell."

She shook her head and closed her eyes again. The knife could have hit the hepatic artery or the portal vein near her liver. Just because an arterial hemorrhage wasn't pulsing the knife out of her body didn't mean she was going to make it. My fingers shook as they tightened, pushing down on the blanket, and I felt my right palm break open again.

Violet started whimpering in her bassinet, little whuffle-squeaks. But I had to stay with Maggie.

Tony banged down the stairs, and I heard shouts outside. Then a cop burst into the plane, his gun drawn. He was followed by two more. "Where's the knife, ma'am?" His shout made Violet start to cry.

I shook my head as I watched Maggie's face go whiter and whiter. "Jesus Christ, put your guns away. I'm a doctor, this is self-inflicted, and the knife in still *inside her body*. One of you come help with stabilizing this knife. Tell the paramedics that the patient is Delta, maybe going to Echo." Echo was the worst, meaning pretty much dead. I wanted the ambulance to come as fast as it could, and the word would speed them up. Maggie's breathing was getting worse—becoming slower and more ragged. "Don't you dare go anywhere," I threatened her. "Don't you dare."

In her bassinet, Violet's crying turned into a full-fledged scream as the youngest cop fell to his knees next to me, hastily drawing on rubber gloves.

Tony was behind the cops—he pointed at Violet, his eyebrows raised.

I nodded and tried to steady my hands on the blanket. My shaking could only hurt Maggie.

Obviously a father, Tony picked up the bundle of Violet one-handed while talking to one of the officers.

I heard more sirens approaching on the tarmac. "Maggie, come on. Stay with me. Please, Maggie." I was begging her again for something different than I had just hours before. "Please stay." I didn't know if I wanted her to be okay because she'd been my friend or because I wanted her punished. It didn't matter either way.

The paramedics were with us then, swarming the plane and roughly moving me and the cops out of the way. Two cut her out of her clothes while two others hooked up the twelve-lead ECG. I watched as they secured the knife in place, keeping the pressure firm around it, and I saw them look at the long, jagged scar that ran above and to the side of the knife.

She was packaged for the trip in what felt like seconds. "She's de-satting," one of the medics said. "We gotta load."

I stood with immense difficulty from the crouch I'd been in. "Where?" I couldn't picture which trauma center was closest.

"Providence Saint Joseph, ma'am." The paramedic seemed to really look at me then.

I swayed. "I'm going, too."

"There's another ambulance on the way for you. Sit tight, okay?"

I could feel my palm dripping blood. I turned and reached for Violet, but for some reason Tony took a step back.

"I'm taking my baby with me, and I'm going with Maggie in the ambulance."

"No can do." Then the paramedic's voice changed. "*Okay*, she's bleeding." He spoke into a mic clipped to his shoulder. "Expedite Alpha-27. Ma'am, I'm going to need you to lie down."

I glared at Tony first and then at the paramedic. "I'm *fine*. It's just my *hand*." I held it up to show him. "See? Now, give me my baby!"

But then I caught sight of the white carpet I stood on. It was turning dark red, and fast. Blood poured down my legs, hot and thick. "Aw, fuck."

Then the world went black.

FORTY-FIVE

I woke up in the hospital. That is, I'd *been* waking up—I could remember coming in and out, but I hadn't been able to stay awake until now.

I'd seen Violet's face once, I thought, and maybe I'd seen Rochelle's face, too? Nurses I didn't know peered down at me and then disappeared. It had all felt like a dizzying dream.

This time when my eyes opened, it felt real. As if I were perhaps partially alive instead of mostly not.

I heard whispers but couldn't make out the words. I studied the ceiling for a while, unsure if I'd be able to turn my head. Very slowly, I looked toward the window. So far, so good. My eyes were doing what I wanted them to, for the most part.

In silhouette against the brightness, I saw two women leaned together, whispering.

"Hi," I tried to say, but my throat was painful and swollen.

Rochelle was the first to reach me. Her smile was as bright as it had ever been, and she touched my arm gently. "Hi, you."

Bree stood at her side. "Hey, lazybones."

I wanted to cry but I didn't have the energy. Then fear lit the edges of my vision as more came back to me. "*Violet.*"

Rochelle choked, putting her hand over her mouth. I realized it was the first time she'd heard our daughter's name. "Violet," she whispered.

"She's perfect," Bree said. "We've just been calling her Little Ms. V. What a gorgeous name for her. You want me to go get her?"

I nodded. I wanted nothing else.

Rochelle looked at Bree and started to pull her hand from my arm.

"Stay," I said.

"Okay." She nodded at Bree.

Quickly, Bree said, "I'll get the nurse to come check on you, and then I'll bring you Violet."

What about Maggie? But I needed another moment to gather myself.

Ro took my left hand and squeezed it gently. I knew the look on her face, that pinched, desperate expression. When her mother had been dying, she'd looked like this. After she'd had her fourth miscarriage, this was the look she wore for months. Rochelle pulled her hand away from mine and covered her face with both hands for one long second as she tried to pull herself back together.

"It's okay," I said.

She dropped her hands. "If you felt like this—when we offered to take full custody—if you felt this scared of losing her, the way I've been feeling, realizing I could have lost her, and you . . ."

I coughed and then said, "Like I would have let you have her." I tried to smile to soften my words, but tears welled up instead. "I wasn't sure I was going to be able to save her for a while. Where's Domi?"

"Getting us some coffee."

"Good. Make sure she takes care of you."

Rochelle dashed at more tears with the back of her hand. "But—who will take care of you?"

Nicole. Bree, if she forgives me. Camille. Not Maggie. Never Maggie again. I tried to smile. "I have people." I pulled up the sheet to look at myself but I was in a pair of hospital pull-ups. Concerned, I glanced up at the IV.

"Yeah, you're on drugs. I mean, I told them that you're sober, so they're giving you the least amount of painkillers they can. But, Jilly, you had to have an emergency laparotomy to stop the bleeding. Something about compression sutures? I don't know. You're recovering, and you're going to be fine—"

I cut her off. "I figured it was something like that. It's not the drugs." Though the drugs would be something to deal with later, with Nicole's help. "You swear to me, Violet's really all right?"

Rochelle was letting the tears roll down her face unchecked. "She's perfect. You did amazing."

I finally let myself say, "And Maggie?"

Rochelle opened her mouth to respond, but a nurse came in.

"Look at you! So much better than you were a few hours ago. Have any questions for me?"

I would later, lots of them, but not right now.

Efficiently, she took my stats and hung another bag and made noises about how cute that baby was, and how she'd be here soon.

The second she was out of the room, Rochelle said, "It was a close call, but they think Maggie's going to make it." Her voice shook with something—when I looked into her face I could see it was rage, unfiltered in a way I'd never seen it before. Rochelle looked as if she wanted to destroy something. "I've never hated a person in my life like I hate her."

I felt it—that rage. For a second, I let myself feel it inside my skin, inside my very viscera. I let the wrath for the truly unforgivable thing Maggie had done roll through me. I opened my heart in a way my sponsor would have been proud of and let myself feel all of it—I let the poison ravage my system. I imagined what I could do to Maggie, what I should have done.

Now I could hate her for the rest of my life.

Then I took a breath.

There was no point. Hating Maggie would do me no good at all.

After all, I understood why Maggie had done all of it. She'd lost her baby. Maybe no one else would ever understand Maggie, but I did.

Joy warred with grief. All of it—*all* of this—was my doing. "It was my fault."

"You did nothing wrong, Jillian. She kidnapped you and stole our baby. When she recovers, she'll go to jail for a long fucking time. They have an armed guard sitting outside her room in the hallway."

"She had to do it."

"Okay," said Rochelle. "I know *someone's* gonna need a shit-ton of therapy. For sure. Until then, let me assure you, none of this is your fault."

"A long time ago, I took her baby."

"*Bullshit.* She talked to the cops a little already. You can't take a baby that never existed."

"I tried to stab her." I held up my bandaged right hand. I still couldn't feel three of my fingers. "Literally, Ro. I tried to stab her in the stomach." *Right where she'd stabbed herself. Twice.* "I only scratched her, but I could have killed her."

Rochelle looked shaken. Maybe Maggie hadn't told them about that part yet. "Self-defense." She took a breath. "You did everything you needed to, and *you're* the one who saved her life."

But—

Bree burst through the door then, a bundle held in her arms over her own round belly, a nurse with a clear Lucite bassinet trailing behind her. All thoughts of Maggie dropped out of my brain. I could only see the wrapped blanket and one tiny starfish hand.

Bree said, "Y'all can argue about stuff later, right? I'd like you to meet my goddaughter. Yes, I'm very proud."

"Gimme." I couldn't decide whether to look at Violet or kiss her or unwrap her, so I tried doing all of it at once. I fumbled at my robe. Rochelle helped me untie it. Bree unwound the baby blanket and helped me slip off Violet's hospital-issued onesie.

Then Violet was on top of me, skin to skin, and I think we were all ugly-crying by then, including the nurse standing behind Bree. All of us except Violet, who made quiet pops with her lips. I kissed her soft spot, feeling her gossamer hair against my mouth. I softly bit the tips of her minuscule fingers.

Bree sniffed and said, "Maybe we shouldn't have named ourselves the Ripleys."

I shook my head gently. It was a good name. I'd had to fight so hard. So had poor Maggie, the original host. Tears rose again in my eyes. Later, maybe, I'd be able to help Maggie fight for herself. If I could, I would.

"And you *do* remember naming me godmother, right?"

I smiled through the tears. "I do not."

"You did. A bunch of times. You basically begged me."

"Did anyone witness this blessed event?"

Bree's eyes were wide and innocent. "Just you and me in here. Also, you apologized upside down all the way to Sunday, begging my forgiveness for thinking I wanted to steal your baby like someone on Camille's television network. You seemed pretty adamant about the godmother thing. Said no one else would do, that it was the only way you could make it up to me."

Funny. In eternally different circumstances, in an alternate universe, I might have asked Maggie to be Violet's godmother.

But not in this universe. "You'll be a perfect godmother. No Disney princess shit."

"Deal. Except for the tiny Elsa dress I already bought her."

I smiled as a wave of exhaustion rocked me. The pain was okay, though—still at a dull roar. Violet snuffled against my skin. "What am I on?" I asked the nurse. "Can I feed her?"

She looked at my chart. "You haven't had anything for three hours. It'll be fine."

I led Violet to my nipple, which I hadn't noticed hurt like hell until she locked onto it. The intensity of the pain—sharp and shocking—felt the same as the relief it brought. I let my neck fall back against the pillow. Rochelle kept her hand on Violet's head. Bree kept her hand on my shoulder.

I kept both my hands on my daughter.

EPILOGUE

Three months later, I sat in my living room with Bree and Camille. I'd asked for their help, and they'd come. Because that's what friends did.

"I can't do it," I said.

Camille rolled her eyes. "You can."

We each had a baby in our arms. Camille's wee one was the smallest—this was actually their first trip out of the house that wasn't to the doctor's office for a follow-up. Baby Henry had come three weeks early and fast, but he was healthy and had one of the biggest shocks of dark baby hair I'd ever seen, a perfect tiny Elvis.

I said, "No. You're wrong."

"Let's just get it over with." Bree buttoned herself back up, her son Liam resting on her lap, waving his arms in the air. She sat in one of the three wooden rockers I'd installed in the living room after I'd gotten rid of one of the sofas. "You can do hard things, Jillian."

I raised an eyebrow. "Are you Glennon Doyle–ing me?"

"Would you rather me Brené you?"

"Not that. I can't take it." I stuck out my tongue at her over Violet's head. "But come on, have some sympathy. I'm freaking out. Like, I'm actually scared I can't do this."

Bree stared at me. "Okay, you want big-deal scared? *You* try telling your husband while you're in labor that it's not his baby pushing out of your vagina."

I'd been there to see it—Bree'd wanted me at her side during the labor—and I had to admit it was a baller way to go. She had waited until a contraction passed before panting at him, "This baby might look Korean."

I'd rolled a chair over for Hal as he went white, and he'd collapsed into it.

Then she'd said, "I relapsed."

I'd gasped at that even though she hadn't been talking to me.

She'd been covered in sweat, her face fierce. "It was one night only, when I was in New York in December. But you're this child's real father, and you always will be. I'm sorry that I cheated on you. I've never done it before, and I'll never do it again. Will you forgive me?"

I'd tried to fade into the background, which was easy since it was normally my birthing room.

Hal's mouth had just opened and closed like a carp. Bree looked at me. "How long do I have till this is over?"

I wasn't her doctor, so I'd checked with Kelli's expression before answering. "It's always hard to say, but I'd guess maybe an hour?"

Bree had nodded. "You have an hour to forgive me, Hal. If you leave, I get it, and I'll accept it. But if you stay and catch the baby, he's yours for life."

Hal had caught Liam, and he'd barely let him go since. It was a miracle he wasn't here now. His daddy blog had exploded, and he'd been offered a gig writing for *Parents* magazine.

I was so glad Bree had forgiven me. And I'd forgiven her, too, for lying to me when she was scared, and for snooping in my room (she'd admitted she wanted to see what kind of porn I had). The other things, telling the girls my secret ambivalence about motherhood, being a jerk at lunch—those were her cactus spines, and they made her strong.

Now I held Violet gently. She'd just melted into a sleepy weight in the crook of my left arm. "You are the warrior queen, Bree. I'm a normal human being."

Camille laughed. "You really want to tell us you're not a fighter, Jilly?" Both of them had started calling me that. I liked it.

Bree finished doing up her buttons. "Get out your phone."

A thunderclap of fear rolled in my chest. But I had to do this. That's why they were here.

I was on the couch on the middle cushion. Making sure I didn't joggle Violet, I gently moved Fred to the floor to make room. "Come sit next to me."

Camille, with tiny Henry still locked to her chest, moved gracefully, sinking into the cushion on my right. Bree thumped down on my left, bouncing Liam with a "Wheee!" as she did so.

"Okay, sweets," Bree said. "Let's do this."

I unlocked my phone.

I tapped on the text app, already opened to the chat history.

Mom.

I scrolled backward quickly, trying to hide the fact that instead of sunsets, I'd been sending her pictures of Violet, but of course they saw. Violet in her bath. Violet sleeping, her mouth open just the tiniest bit. Violet getting ready to howl.

"Really?" But Camille's voice was soft.

"It's time. You think?" Bree leaned her shoulder against mine.

I nodded. "Well. I mean, yes. It is."

I pushed and held the word *Mom.* Her contact card appeared.

"You can do it," said Bree.

So I did.

I hit Delete.

My phone asked me to confirm that I was sure.

"Deep breath," said Camille.

I nodded, taking one. My right hand was number than usual. PT was helping, and I hoped to be able to go back to work someday. I'd been scared the injury would end my career. It still might if I couldn't get the dexterity back that I needed for surgery.

And if that happened, it wouldn't make me a bad mother. Or a bad person. I was enough, right here on the couch, a recovering alcoholic with messed-up fingers doing the best she could. A wave of gratitude swept through me, but I hid it. Bree would tease me if I went soppy now.

I took a deep breath, swallowed the sorrow that rose in my throat, and told the phone that yes, I was sure I wanted to delete the information forever.

My mother's contact flickered away to nothing.

"Good job," said Camille.

"You're Mom now, not her," said Bree.

I kissed the top of Violet's head.

After we ate lunch, after we traded babies and marveled at their different hefts and moves, after they left, after I put Violet down, and during Violet's nap, when I should have been napping, too, I got out our baby book. Rochelle's last entry had been about spit-up and poop, and mine before that had been about the curve of the back of Violet's head. Okay, and about poop, too.

I picked up the pen. I could write about the way Violet had looked at me that morning, with wide eyes and an O of a mouth—a brand-new expression she'd never shown me before.

But I wanted to write something that wasn't only about her milestones.

I didn't know anything about motherhood yet. I was brand-new at it. I couldn't write smart, deep thoughts about it.

I wouldn't give advice to my daughter, either. She'd learn it all on her own with us as her safety net.

That only left one thing to write about.

I would just tell her how I loved her.

You were loved from the moment I felt you move for the first time.

You are perfect, exactly as you are. You will never have to change for me. You will always fit perfectly into my arms. I was born to be your mother.

If you win, I'll be your biggest cheerleader. If you fail, I will be the same, only maybe louder, so you hear me.

I will always let you know that it's okay to be only what you are, no more. You never have to pretend to be someone you're not.

There is literally nothing you can do that would ever make me love you less, although don't test me on this by becoming a serial killer. (I would pass the test.)

I don't care who you love or who you don't. I don't care what you grow up to be. You're already Violet, and you have always been Violet. Before you came, the world missed you, no one more than I did.

You are perfect.

I will not say you are my heart because you don't need that burden. Just know that I love you more than I thought it was possible for a human to love anyone.

I am the luckiest mother in the world.

AUTHOR'S NOTE

The nice thing about writing novels is that I get to try on alternate lives. I get to look through the main character's eyes during the writing, and sometimes I give her traits I have or want. I've always longed to live within walking distance of the beach, and in my twenties, I seriously considered becoming an ob-gyn or a nurse-midwife (oh, that road not taken). I think catching babies and living in Venice would be an ideal combination, so I gave Jillian those things.

But in this book, Jillian also got to be an alcoholic in recovery. That I *do* know something about. For a long, long time, I was fine. Then, for a couple of years, I wasn't fine at all.

Being what they call a "high bottom" drunk, I don't have an exciting story. I was lucky enough to step off the escalator before it took me all the way down to rock bottom, before I lost the dream job, the house, or my family. I was a boring Netflix-and-wine gal, toppling into bed at just the right time, telling myself that passing out equaled going to sleep. I'd stopped being able to both control *and* enjoy my drinking, and I was deeply, quietly miserable.

Once I finally wrote the words "I'm an alcoholic" in my journal for the first time, I felt a strange relief. It was the one thing I'd never wanted to be, but once I named it, I could work on finding the solution. I was in an Alcoholics Anonymous meeting three hours after I first wrote those three words, and I haven't had a drink since February 2018. Terrified, I walked into AA that first day expecting to find a roomful of shifty-eyed people taking furtive sips from bottles of moonshine. Instead, I found a roomful of normal people. They were lawyers and doctors and preschool teachers who seemed to be living regular lives so *joyfully*.

I wanted what they had, so I stuck around. AA is by no means the only way to sobriety, but it's the way that worked for this hardcore skeptic. Some will complain that I shouldn't have mentioned the name of our secret society in this novel, but I chose to take the route that Stephen King did with *Doctor Sleep*, sharing with the reader a purely fictional experience, based loosely on no one's experience but my own. I break my anonymity only, no one else's.

But this is not a book *about* addiction or recovery. Jillian's recovery is simply part of her backstory. In a way, I chose to present the gay story line similarly. This isn't a book about being gay.

I'm not just a gay alcoholic in recovery. Sure, I *am* those two things, and I'm not ashamed of either. But I'm also so many *more* things. I'm a singer in a yacht rock band. I'm a teacher. I'm forty-eight and I love my naturally silver hair. My bare feet are always callused. I have dual citizenship with America and New Zealand, and I'm currently planning our move to Wellington. I'm happy.

And because I don't numb myself to the difficult things in life anymore, I'm a person who can be really *present* inside this gorgeous life. I get to caress the velvety ears of our wobbly old dog, Clementine. I laugh at my wife's silly puns. At this very moment, I'm typing with my cat, Waylon, on my lap in a baby sling (yes, I'm that person) and his right ear is breathtakingly soft against my left wrist. I pay the bills and do the laundry and water the flowers in the backyard. I can find clear-eyed and clear-headed beauty in every motion and moment.

So I'm eternally grateful to have been able to write this story, and I'm so grateful to you for reading.

May you have great and simple present happiness, too.

ACKNOWLEDGMENTS

My deep thanks go to Stephanie Kelly and her incredible editorial eye—I've learned so much from you. Thank you for everything. And to the whole Dutton team—you knock me out, y'all. I couldn't be happier to work with each one of you. To Susanna Einstein, agent extraordinaire, thank you for believing in me for so long. I'm so grateful to you, always.

Thanks go to Wanda Klor for letting me use her earthquake-in-Mexico-City story, and to the daughter she locked safely inside herself, Eréndira Ibarra, a brilliant actress who is now a fierce mother all her own.

Speaking of fierce, Ripley-like mothers, I always describe my own mother as sweet, but Janette Frances Herron had a growl that could terrify attacking mountain lions, sending them skittering away like scared kittens. I miss you, Mom.

ACKNOWLEDGMENTS

It makes no sense why some mothers have to go through things that no mother should ever have to survive. While writing this, I thought often of Lola Herron, Juliet Blackwell, and Sophie Littlefield. All three are incredible examples of maternal ferocity that make me proud to know them and humbled to be loved by them.

For fierce mother, writer, and Alaskan nurse-midwife Lisa Weston, who catches babies for a living, thank you for your friendship and your expertise. Thanks also to another writer friend, Dr. Stacy Frazer, for sharing your knowledge, too. All medical mistakes in the book are my own. No one *ever* give me a scalpel.

For Holly Robinson—thank you for your unerring wisdom. And Toby Neal—thank you for the inspiration. To Catriona Turner, my thanks for your amazing attention to detail. (More fierce mothers. I'm grateful so many allow me to collect them.)

To Michael Bialys of the Gay Family Law Center, thanks for the legal advice. Again, any mistakes in family law are my own. Happy writing to you, Michael.

Thanks always and forever to Lala, my wife, who gives the best plot help a writer could ever ask for. I'm so glad we're on this ride together.

And to those of you in (and out of) the rooms, thank you. I'll surely meet some of you as we trudge the road of happy destiny.

ABOUT THE AUTHOR

R. H. Herron received her MFA in writing from Mills College, Oakland. She is the author of thrillers *Stolen Things* and *Hush Little Baby*, as well as the bestselling author of more than two dozen books under a different name. She lives and teaches writing in California.